Sarah Goodwin completed the BA and MA in Creative Writing at Bath Spa University. *The Private Jet* is her seventh novel to be published with Avon, following several years as a self-published author. She lives in Cornwall with her family and a very spoiled dog.

Also by Sarah Goodwin:

Stranded
The Thirteenth Girl
The Resort
The Blackout
The Yacht
The Island

THE PRIVATE JET

SARAH GOODWIN

avon.

Published by AVON
A Division of HarperCollins*Publishers* Ltd
1 London Bridge Street
London SE1 9GF

www.harpercollins.co.uk

HarperCollins*Publishers*
Macken House
39/40 Mayor Street Upper
Dublin 1
D01 C9W8
Ireland

A Paperback Original 2025
2
First published in Great Britain by HarperCollins*Publishers* 2025

A catalogue copy of this book is available from the British Library.

ISBN: 978-0-00-873279-0

Typeset in Sabon LT Pro by HarperCollins*Publishers* India

Printed and bound in the United States of America

There are estimated to be only 5,600 wild tigers left globally, according to figures published by the WWF.

Prologue

On screen the talk show host – Andrea Billingham, three-time BAFTA nominee for both daytime and factual entertainment – is dressed in a white flowing trouser suit and sits on a creamy sofa, under blinding studio lights.

'She's fresh from her miraculous escape from the Thai jungle; please join me in saying, "Welcome back, Lila Wilde!"'

Beaming, she raises an arm to beckon on her guest. Applause fills the studio, the whoops and cheers of an unseen audience. Lila emerges from the side of the screen, peering around at her new environment like a zoo animal being exposed to the public for the first time.

It's strange, watching myself on the overhead TV in the airport lounge. I remember being her – being that Lila, but looking at her now it's like looking at a stranger. Her skin muddy with a patchy tan and pink patches where wounds are still healing. She's been dressed in a khaki green jumpsuit and brown leather sandals. Even though I remember arriving in jeans and a T-shirt with a blazer. But, as with the lush monsteras in the corners of the studio, this get-up gives more of the impression the show

1

is going for – that she is somehow carrying the jungle with her wherever she goes.

Which is true, but not in terms of her fashion choices.

I rub my hands over my arms, goose-pimpled from the airport's overzealous air-conditioning. The marks have faded from pink to white now – the scratches and bites and scarring. But they're still there, if you look closely enough.

Lila takes a seat, scanning the audience warily. I can't remember what it was I was worried about. Who I thought might be there. Or what. But on screen, Lila looks afraid of . . . something. Twitchy and barely perching on the edge of her seat. The audience's initial burst of welcoming applause dies off very quickly, ending with a few awkward claps and some muttering, which Andrea quickly replaces with her own voice.

'Lila, how are you?' the host asks, her perfectly painted mouth pulling down at the corners. She practises this expression of sorrowful sympathy in the mirror – you can tell.

'I'm doing OK.' Lila's eyes are large and dark, reflecting a halo of studio lights. The eyebrows are drawn on and the eyelashes are fake but you can't tell on camera. 'Glad to be back home.'

'I bet!' Andrea flashes her veneers in a sympathetic grimace. She can probably smell the long-awaited award coming her way for this. 'Does it feel real yet? That you're really here, back in civilisation?'

I'm momentarily distracted from the interview by a man at the restaurant kiosk across the airport lounge throwing a bag of take-away onto the counter. He does it so hard that a coffee cup explodes in a shower of steaming liquid, which splashes all over his sandals. He starts to shout at the employee, about his order being wrong and, now, his feet being burned. I look back at the screen with a roll of my eyes.

A tiny crease appears on Lila's tanned forehead, between the drawn-on eyebrows. 'It's never felt anything but real. Probably more real than my entire life up until I got on that plane.'

There's a shift in the air. It's not exactly as clear in the final recorded product as it was on the day. When I could hear the studio audience moving, muttering. When Andrea's eyes narrowed sharply – which the cameras either didn't catch or it got edited around. There's no sharpness to her in the recorded version, no sign that she's annoyed that her guest isn't following the normal routine: agreeing and fawning, just happy to be there. To be alive.

'You did lead something of a charmed life – I should say you still do, right?'

A flash of claws there. A warning to the Lila on that spotless sofa to stay in her place. I watch as that other Lila, a year back in the past, absorbs the sharp tone without rising to it. Instead she nods her head slightly. I remember saying to myself: 'Don't let them see you sweat, babe' – one of my dad's more useful catchphrases.

'I do – obviously people like us, we have this kind of . . . insulation, from the world. We don't really experience it as it is,' Lila says, lightly, humbly. I'm still pleased with how it came out, actually.

Andrea laughs, doing a poor job of hiding her irritation that her bait hasn't caused Lila to snap at her. 'I'm not quite sure I'm in your league, Lila. My father wasn't ever on the cover of *Rolling Stone*!'

The audience titters politely. Andrea clearly takes comfort in this, and shakes off the momentary annoyance of Lila's disobedience.

'What everyone in the audience is wondering, I'm sure, is what happened the day you were rescued. The people at home haven't heard much about it, or to be honest, about anything that happened between the accident and the moment you came out of the jungle. You've been very tight-lipped, prior to today.'

On screen, Lila nods, still outwardly polite and peaceful. Inside I was a mess, trying to overcome the trauma I'd just experienced because I knew that if I slipped up in that interview, that would be it for me. A feeding frenzy would descend and Andrea would be the first of many to claim trophies from my hide. I didn't want to give her the satisfaction.

'It's been quite a busy week, as you can probably imagine . . . I've been in the hospital and there have been travel arrangements to make, not just for me but for the others, the people who survived.'

Andrea nods, soft expression back in place. 'And not everyone did, did they?'

'No,' Lila intones, flatly. 'There weren't many of us by the time we got out. But everyone already knows that part.'

Andrea ignores this last remark, a tiny jibe delivered in self-defence. 'I imagine it was really hard for you all, but for you, the ordeal didn't end with the rescue. We've seen there's been quite a surge in online harassment since you were found . . . most of it aimed at you. How does that make you feel?'

Lila's eyes wander to the ceiling, out of shot of the

cameras but crisscrossed with wires and lights. I remember being fascinated by it. So like the canopy of the jungle, dense and dark and blocking out everything outside. Creating a smaller world within the real one. A world with its own rules. Its own predators.

'Do you feel like it's nothing, compared to what you've been through?' Andrea presses, trying to get her attention back on the moment, on the hungry pack of cameras and the audience hidden in the undergrowth of chairs and shadows. 'Does it surprise you – that it doesn't hurt, after everything else that happened?'

'Oh, of course it hurts.' Lila shrugs, returning to the present, eyes flashing. This is where I should have held back, but I couldn't anymore. 'Is it not meant to just because I went through actual, physical pain? Mental torture? Nearly dying?' Her laugh is paper-thin and anything but humorous. 'It doesn't matter what I went through or if it was worse than some comments online. I do still have feelings and those feelings can be hurt. But that makes me lucky, doesn't it? Because if I was dead I wouldn't get to read about how much of a stupid bitch I am and how much people wished I'd died. How much funnier it would have been. I wouldn't have gotten to see all the hilarious memes people made about me burning to death or being torn apart by tigers.'

Silence reigns, like the coming of a storm. Is it shame, in that silence? Or anger that the joke has been spoiled? Lila pays no attention to the audience. Her eyes are fixed on Andrea. I remember how she looked at me then. I'd expected anger, or triumph, because she'd finally managed to make me lose control. But instead there was a flicker of something like understanding. Reluctant, but still there.

She knew what it was like to be visible, like me. And how cruel the online and offline worlds were to women who dared to be seen.

Of course that flicker was smothered almost at once, like a spark falling onto cold dirt. Her expression hardening, reaching for the next challenge.

'So, in answer to your question . . . it makes me feel lucky. That I lived long enough to be ridiculed for what happened. I mean . . . yeah. Part of it was my fault and part of it wasn't but I am lucky. Because I'm alive . . . and unfortunately not everyone else can say the same.'

'Do you feel guilty? That you escaped unscathed and so many other people didn't?' Andrea asks, eyes sharp and golden, unblinking.

I watch myself try and fail to contain the truth. 'I feel guilty, all the time . . . but I didn't escape unscathed. None of us did.'

The interview cuts to a break there and a ticker quickly takes over half the screen, flashing a reassurance that the 'Lila Wilde one-year-on interview' will be shown next, after a few words from their sponsor.

Chapter 1

'I am never coming here again,' I sighed, as the last one of our cases was deposited in the villa and I could finally relax. 'Look at my hair! It's so awful – I knew we should have gone somewhere with dry heat, like Egypt. Didn't I say that? Dry heat! Babes, are you listening?'

Turning from the pile of luggage, I found Bryce snapping selfies by the patio doors. Beyond them was the infinity pool, sun loungers laden with pillows and throws and of course the palm trees on either side, framing the view of the bright blue ocean where it stretched from the edge of the pool all the way to the blindingly bright sky. One tiny fishing boat was bobbing in the middle distance, smaller than a mayfly. The only thing spoiling the perfect view. I took a moment to soak it in.

I smiled slightly, watching Bryce snap his pictures. That was the fun part of dating a normal person: you got to watch them react to all the cool stuff for the first time. They didn't take stuff for granted and weren't so jaded they'd bypass the view like we were in some boring hotel in Hull. Even after a lifetime of trips like this, I still got a little thrill every time I saw the sea glittering on some foreign shore. I couldn't imagine being with anyone who didn't.

Once I'd basked enough in the gorgeous view, I turned back to the pile of matching suitcases. I had work to do.

'I need my straighteners.' I started to dig through the luggage for my vanity bags. 'I cannot function with my hair all fucked up, and I was going to record my yoga.'

'Well then you better get it done soon because we're going out later,' Bryce said, putting his phone away. 'The clubs on Bangla Road are meant to be insane. I don't want to miss anything.'

'Me neither – especially not after we flew all the way out here. But oh my God, this humidity! I literally just can't. I should have just had my hair cut short, then I wouldn't have to bother.'

'You would never,' Bryce snorts, and I run a hand through my long, blonde hair. He's right. My colourist alone would never forgive me if I let her get me all the way to platinum and then sheared off all her hard work. Besides, my hair was part of my brand.

I finally found my straighteners and carried them off to the bathroom. I was already regretting not having the concierge unpack for us. But Bryce was full of worry about the staff stealing from rich tourists in places like this and I didn't want him to be anxious, or have the hassle of replacing stuff. I mean, I could afford to but, God, setting up a new iPhone was exhausting without my assistant's help. I found Bryce's concern kind of endearing actually. He'd never been to anything more upmarket than a Hilton DoubleTree before we started dating. And even that was for his parents' wedding anniversary. But it showed that he valued stuff a lot, and wasn't about to go taking risks with it. Exactly the kind of guy I'd been looking for when we happened across one another.

In the bathroom I dropped my hair case on the white sofa and started hunting for outlets by the long champagne-coloured marble vanity. I plugged my straighteners in and left them to heat up on the side while I dug out my products, being careful of my nails – a fresh set I'd had done during the flight. Mariella, my nail tech, came out on my private jet to do them but she was on her way home now, so if I broke one I'd have to go to some random salon to get it fixed, and I didn't want to have to put myself through that. On top of all the other stress of travelling and trying to look my best for work.

With my product bottles safely uncapped using a little plastic tool to save my nails, I went through my routine – spraying and creaming my long hair and clamping the iron to straighten out the frizzy sections until they were silky smooth again. It was, I already knew, going to take so much hairspray to keep them that way but it couldn't be helped. Plus I thought it might help keep the bugs away.

While I double cleansed my face to remove my inflight skincare and then applied my post-flight routine, I could hear Bryce putting some loud music on and ordering a drink from room service. Still patting in my La Mer concentrate serum, I stuck my head out of the bathroom.

'Can you get me a mojito, if you're ordering?' I asked. 'Your girl is parched.'

'Already ordered you one.' Bryce shrugged. ''Cos I'm well-trained. I'll tell you when they bring them up.'

'Cool, thank you, baby.' I smiled. 'Can you get them to send more bottled water too? There's never enough at these places and I have to get at least two litres in or my skin's going to look dull.'

Bryce gave me a thumbs-up in the affirmative and picked up the remote for the concealed flat screen. The teak panels slid open at the touch of a button and he started jabbing at the control, switching channels and muttering about 'kick-off'. I rolled my eyes fondly. Great. Football – the time thief. Still if it kept him out of my way while I did a teeny bit of filming, so much the better.

I shut the door for some peace and started going through my other cases. I'd chucked some PR packages into them before we left so I could do some promo posts while we were in Phuket. There was a new foundation (twenty-eight shades, full sizes in a 'book' made of cardboard, each one named after a romantic novel – totally extra) and some new lip glosses called Honey Bunny. That package turned out to be so heavy because each one was floating in its own jar of honey. Such a stupid gimmick – it was going to be so messy to get at them. I checked the note in the box and rolled my eyes. It was a non-edible slime, with plastic honeycomb. Almost like they wanted to fuck up my villa and make me have to call housekeeping to take the rubbish away sooner than usual.

Unboxing could wait for tomorrow, I decided. In the meantime I just did my basic makeup routine with my tried and true faves – colour corrector and BB cream, then concealer to brighten, a bit of blush and contour, bit more bronzer for the holiday vibes, obviously some golden highlight to give me a glow. Then a good lipstick and gloss combo on the lips, eyeshadow, heated lash curler, mascara, liner and set. I finished spritzing my face with setting spray and wondered if I needed to add some falsies, just to give myself a bit more of a 'wow factor'. But no matter how natural they claimed to be I always feel like they showed on camera. So I left them for clubbing later. I'd just keep things natural for now.

'Heading out to film!' I called through to Bryce. 'Where's that drink?'

'It's coming!' he called back, sounding vague. Obviously absorbed in his football. I rolled my eyes. It'd just have to wait until I was done filming. That'd be a welcome refresher anyway.

The infinity pool had big 'stepping stones' poking up through it as a footpath to the relaxation arbour. Just in the shallow end, so there was still plenty of space to swim. I liked the image of them online because they weren't squared off or anything; they looked like real natural stepping stones. Even though they were obviously just pillars cast from some kind of concrete. But on film they'd look great.

I collected my tripod, camera, ring light and a bag of accessories and carried them over the stepping stones carefully. They were hot under my bare feet. The sun was really beating down and it had to be approaching thirty degrees already. The humid heat was worse than it was back in England, and somehow the air-conditioning keeping the villa crisp and frosty only made the outside world more unbearable.

The arbour, with its jade Buddha statue, water feature and frondy little plants, would make a great backdrop to a vlog and maybe the intro to a longer-form video. I was going to have my content editor, Alyssa, cut together all my footage later. Annoyingly she hadn't been able to come and film with us because of her sister's stupidly timed wedding, but I could handle it. Bryce was meant to be helping too but so far he'd been more interested in trying to get some stage time DJing at one of the clubs. I mean, fair enough, it wasn't like watching me film was very interesting for him. He didn't really get a lot of what I did for work and honestly I preferred that to being around someone in the business themselves. With all the infighting, criticism and competition that came with it.

With all the camera stuff set up I took the remote for it back with me and got changed out of my travel leggings and tank top into a camera-ready outfit. My stylist had gone running all over the place to find me a traditional silk *sinh* to bring with me. Obviously the best place to find a Thai skirt would be once I got to Thailand, but I needed it before so I could get my nails done the right colour or the whole thing would have been a waste of time. I wasn't sure why it had taken so long to find one, or why it cost so much. It was just a wrap skirt, albeit with a ton of embroidery. Worth a thousand pounds? I doubted it. But it wasn't like Dad was going to notice it on my credit card bill.

Dressed in my sinh and a cute cami, I found the singing bowl I bought at the airport to replace the one I'd forgotten to pack and took a lily from an arrangement in the bedroom to tuck behind my ear.

'Filming now!' I yelled, so Bryce wouldn't interrupt me when my drink finally arrived. Then I positioned myself on the stepping stones and hit 'record' on the remote before tucking it into my bralette. I crossed the stepping stones with my head up, trying not to trip because the last thing I needed was to end up in the pool and have to redo my hair and makeup. It was a little tricky to keep the singing

12

bowl up in front of me without my arms waving around as I tried to balance after each step. But I managed it.

At the other side I sat down with crossed legs, then got up again and repositioned the camera for ground-level recording. I took a few deep breaths and hummed, then picked up the sage bundle and my lighter. I got it specially customised for the trip, all done in silver, with an inset turquoise the size of a cocktail olive in a 'hand of Fatima' design. After wafting the sage around for a bit I lit a stick of incense and tried not to wrinkle my nose at the strong smell. I hoped it wouldn't get into my hair. I did a few passes with the stick and then some chimes with the singing bowl. Then I sat with my eyes shut for a few moments in quiet contemplation.

'Goal!!' Bryce bellowed from the villa.

'I. Am. Meditating!' I yelled, glaring back across the pool.

There was no response, other than a few birds flapping away from the villa, and I settled myself and hoped that my cheeks weren't too red now. Or else continuity would be a nightmare. A few more minutes of quiet reflection should give me the footage I needed. While I sat and waited it out, I mentally composed my voiceover: *Here, in a peaceful corner of Phuket, not far from the gorgeous Patong beach, I've taken a moment to recharge after our flight. Travel might be deeply rewarding, but it can also take a toll on the spirit. With some cleansing sage, I can remove the negative energies of other travellers and realign myself with a traditional singing bowl, handcrafted in Tibet. Here I am fortunate enough to have a private meditational garden, where I can reflect in gratitude for our safe journey and retune myself with Mother Nature.*

'Babe!'

I opened my eyes and twisted my head around to glare at Bryce, hopping across the stepping stones in his flip-flops and airport casual gym shorts.

'Bryce, I swear to God, if this is about football . . .'

'I got a gig! At *RAWR* – for tonight. One hour set, starting at one.' He beamed, the new veneers I'd paid for twinkling in the sunlight.

'Oh . . . cool,' I said, because it was his job after all and I did want to be supportive. Still, inside I was a little disappointed. I'd been hoping that he'd propose on this trip. Not be working. I'd dropped enough hints after all and caught him looking through my jewellery drawer – getting inspiration or finding out my ring size. I'd decided that I was done dating around and that Bryce was the best choice for me going forward. He was sweet, attentive and, best of all, he was just a normal guy. My dad had always said my mum was the love of his life, because she wasn't about the rock and roll lifestyle. She was 'just a girl from Highgate with a gorgeous smile, who loved him for him' and that's what made their marriage last. At least until she died, having me. Since then he'd married a couple of singers, a showgirl from Vegas, an heiress and most recently his new bassist. None of the marriages had held up. The bassist was currently dragging him through the courts for alimony. I sensed Dad would be putting out a new 'best of' album to try and recoup his costs on that one.

A wedding would also help to push my follower count up and give us so much stuff to post about. I'd been hovering at the 18.5 million mark for a while now, and a big wedding would push me over into the twenties. The sponsorships I could get for our honeymoon would be amazing. Plus Dad was starting to get keen on the idea of grandkids – his label must have mentioned something about it improving his image after he drove his car into that playground. It wasn't even like there were kids there at the time.

'I know, right?' Bryce flicked his dark hair out of his eyes and grinned at me. 'Guess this trip's gonna be one to remember. I was worried we were just wasting time being away from the London scene.'

He flip-flopped back to the villa and I watched him go before turning back and roughly stubbing out the stinky incense on the flagstones. A waste of time? This was my job. My follower counts were growing by the day and since announcing the Thailand trip I'd had sponsorship offers from everything from shaving brands to slimming supplements. The hotel and the jet and everything else was coming out of my allowance. But from this trip I'd be earning a lot more than it was costing. All my own money, none of it belonging to my father.

I sighed. Bryce just didn't get it. I didn't want to be 'Scott Wilde's daughter' forever. I wanted something of my own. Some kind of legacy to my name. Dad had his platinum records and his leather tour jackets framed in his office. His collection of mugshots from crashing his car or throwing a guitar off a roof while he was on a bender. He was infamous. Renowned. I wanted something like that. Something that said: 'Lila Wilde was here'. I wanted to be remembered, to be famous.

Otherwise what was even the point in being alive?

Chapter 2

After filming, my mojito finally turned up and I sipped it lying in the shade on a lounger, letting time roll by as the afternoon slipped into early evening. During the flight I'd received a ton of DMs and notifications to follow up on. I had a social media manager, Emily, to do most of the heavy lifting on my profiles, but I still liked to do a few replies by myself. To keep things interesting and make it feel authentic. I tapped away sending hearts and praying hands to my followers, directing them to my affiliate links and forwarding messages from brands to my agent to negotiate collaborations. I noticed a few hate comments. Just the usual stuff, but Emily was meant to remove them all. I frowned, wondering if she was slacking off while I was away.

> **Lila ur so cuuuuuuuuuuuuuute I would kill for your skin! – what moisturiser do you use????**
>> *Hey Hon, check my bio for the link on my affiliate page xx*

Are you going to see elephants in Tieland?????
I hope so! ☮

Ur mid and ur dads music sucks
Snore

Hope u get bit by a snake an die bitch
Yawn You need better material

Stfu and make me a sanwich!

I rolled my eyes and sent a kissy smiley face, then waited ten seconds so he'd see it, and blocked him. There were a few dozen more comments like that to go through, just on my most recent post. Emily really wasn't doing her job properly. Still, I'd only made the post before we got on the plane, so by the time I got back from the club later I expected there'd be more comments. I tried to always comment at least twice for haters before blocking them, and had Emily do the same. It was all good engagement and it gave my fans reason to pile on, leaving more comments to boost my videos up the algorithm. Genius.

At the bottom of my emails was a message from Dad's publicist, asking about my availability to appear with him at some premiere for one of his latest skanky girlfriend's straight-to-streaming films. Like I needed to see her running around in a bikini with an assault rifle for another two hours of my life. I deleted the email and toyed with the idea of blocking the publicist but hey, it wasn't her fault Dad was a dick. I hadn't liked any of

17

his wives or girlfriends – and I'd given up trying. They weren't interested in me either. I was just competition for his money and press attention. Which was exactly why I planned to marry Bryce – just a normal, real person. Who could give me real love that I could believe in, the way another influencer or some industry hanger-on couldn't.

'Babes, what do you think?'

I looked up and found Bryce standing in front of me, gesturing to his outfit. He'd changed out of his travel clothes and into an open-collar Hawaiian shirt from Kenzo in a tiger pattern that I'd just bought him for the trip. Paired with green chino shorts and the Dior boat shoes I got him for his birthday. Most of his jewellery was back home, but he'd brought a few heavy gold chains and medallions along. The tiger head pendant around his neck was an anniversary gift last year – yellow sapphires, black and white diamonds. The chain alone weighed five hundred grams. Solid, twenty-four-carat gold. Dad nearly confiscated my cards over that one.

'Great for RAWR, right?' Bryce asked, turning and popping the collar of his shirt, looking at his reflection in the patio doors. 'Or do we need to go shopping for something special?'

'Looks good.' I smiled at him, dropping my phone onto the lounger and shielding my eyes. 'You're going to knock 'em dead on stage.'

Bryce shot me a half-smile and looked me over. 'And what're you wearing?'

'Haven't decided yet.' I shrugged. 'I brought some really hot stuff though, so . . . shouldn't take long to pick something out.'

'Are you getting ready soon?' Bryce pushed, looking edgy.

'Is there a rush? I thought your set was at one? That's hours away. I could start getting ready an hour from now and we'd still have ages to party before you're due on,' I said, raising an eyebrow.

'Yeah but . . . you wanna enjoy the whole night, right? So we should go soon and make sure we find something to, you know . . . make sure we last 'til sunrise.' Bryce shot me a look and flashed some teeth suggestively.

I didn't usually have a problem with drugs. Like, hello, my dad was a rock star! I learned to roll a joint while he bounced me on his knee, and after his former drummer ODed at my tenth birthday party, he made sure I knew my limits. When I buy drugs it's no different to buying a Birkin bag – I pay a lot for the genuine article from a reputable supplier. None of your 'sold on the street', 'why is this is so cheap?' stepped-on crap. But we were hundreds of thousands of miles from home and I didn't have contacts here. We were just tourists and honestly I hadn't planned on doing more than drinking. I had an image to protect and brand deals with 'disrepute' clauses. Doing drugs in public when anyone could sell the pictures or post them online was a no-no. I had to keep that shit for private parties – invite only. With people who had as much to lose as I did, if not more.

'I don't know . . . can't we just get a couple of Red Bulls to stay clear-headed?' I tried, pulling my legs up on the lounger and sitting lotus style. Bryce didn't always get the whole 'image' thing so I opted for a different excuse. 'I don't want to be coming down for the rest of the trip, you know?'

'So we'll come down when we get home.' Bryce shrugged. 'Make the most of things while we're here. No point coming all this way just to sleep, is there? And it's Thailand, like . . . you don't come here to not get high.'

He wasn't going to drop it that easily then. Damn it. I was going to have to explain it, all over again.

'It just seems like . . . maybe more trouble than it's worth? I mean we don't really know anyone here or how to get hooked up with this stuff, or what's, like, available. I just don't want to risk it. And if anyone saw me on something it'd just blow up my sponsorships . . .' I trailed off when I saw Bryce roll his eyes. 'Which are my income. You know, that pays for everything?' I said, probably harsher than I intended to be. Especially as a lot of this trip was coming out of my dad's pocket.

'Fine.' Bryce slumped his shoulders and looked put out. 'Whatever. Red Bull it is then. But can you go get ready so we can get as much out of tonight as we can?'

I decided it was a fair compromise and shifted myself off the lounger. Bryce took my place, fiddling with his phone. I went inside to the villa's master bedroom and opened my suitcases and garment bags on the enormous bed. I'd bought a lot of new stuff for this trip, but now we were actually here a lot of it wasn't really what I wanted. A leather mini dress? In this heat? What had I been thinking? Maybe Bryce's idea for a shopping trip wasn't such a bad one. Though I doubted we'd find anything good in such a short amount of time.

I discarded dresses, shorts and skirts onto the pristine white bedlinens. Finally I settled reluctantly on an Oscar de la Renta crochet dress in rainbow ombré. It was at least made of cotton and only fell to mid-thigh so I'd be a bit cooler than if I wore a regular bodycon dress full of synthetics. I popped on some gold stiletto sandals and some bangles, each one sparkling with stones in all the colours of the rainbow, from Indian ruby to Tanzanian umbalite. Obviously I had to have chandelier earrings to match, dripping cold stones down to my shoulders. I put my hair up with a hair stick and left tendrils trailing down, then dusted myself with gold body shimmer and put on some slightly heavier, evening-appropriate makeup.

By the time I was done, Bryce was pacing about in the living area, on his second can of energy drink from the minibar. I was starting to wonder if he was nervous about the gig. He hadn't had one before, not one that wasn't just an open-mic spot. I cosied up to him and placed a kiss on his shoulder.

'You're going to do amazing, babe,' I assured him.

'Yeah, I know . . . let's go now, OK?' he said, and ushered me towards the door so quickly I barely managed to snag my gold clutch on the way out.

Outside of the villa the wall of heat was stifling. We got a taxi down to Bangla Road, because my shoes were very much not made for walking. But the car wasn't air-conditioned and the traffic was insane, practically gridlocked and with horns constantly going off and drivers yelling as pedestrians and mopeds moved between the cars. The leather seat was burning my legs in my short dress and I was absolutely fuming that I hadn't thought to get a private car and my driver sent over. I'd obviously spent too much time in New York and London, where getting a cab was easy and they all came with air-con.

I kept making eye contact with the driver by accident, via the rear-view mirror. I got the feeling he was looking at me funny and so I glared back at him, but he didn't seem to notice. Or care. Just bobbed his head to the music blaring on the radio and chewed tobacco, waiting for the traffic to move.

Bryce drummed his fingers on his thigh, sweat dripping down into the collar of his shirt. The skin there was already red. I'd told him to use SPF when we were on the plane getting ready to land, but he'd waved me off. I, at least, had a tan already and factor fifty on top, but Bryce was pale as milk and blond into the bargain. He had Scandinavian blood in his veins and sunburn all across his shoulders. I'd be covering him in aloe by tomorrow – I knew it. Just like when we went to Ibiza. He'd sulk and moan and then peel and moan some more. Bless him, he never learned. I'd have to take him to Bulgari to cheer him up with something sparkly.

I looked out the window and spotted a family of monkeys – a big one and two babies, scampering about in the mouth of an alley. I opened my mouth to say something to Bryce, but then closed it again. They weren't the sleek, exotic creatures of holiday TikToks – they were mangy and out of place, huddling together as the nightlife streamed past them on spiky heels and flash trainers. As the car moved on I saw more of them – rat-brown and fighting over rubbish, climbing on cars and being kicked at by pedestrians. It was horrible.

I thought of the perfect sea view from the villa, with its palm trees swaying in the breeze, and felt a stab of guilt. That view didn't just cost my dad thousands of pounds, it cost these monkeys their home.

'Just let us out here,' Bryce said, after we'd gone maybe a hundred yards in fifteen minutes. He was already getting out of the car and I had to scramble to get money out of my bag, nearly bending a nail back in the process. I chucked a few hundred baht more than the fare at the driver and clambered out into the sticky air. Bryce took my arm and started steering me through the stationary cars, onwards towards the Phuket equivalent of the Las Vegas strip – Bangla Road.

It was impossible to miss. Like a cross between downtown in a university city and Camden market. The street was heaving already with people going back and forth between the multiple night clubs, sex clubs and shops selling everything from fake Gucci to light-up rave necklaces and fried food. Most of the people around us were tourists. I heard German, Spanish, Polish and other languages I couldn't identify. All alongside a barrage of various UK, American, New Zealand and Australian accents. Most of the Thai people around were working: stallholders and hawkers, passing out club flyers or selling roses and cups of drink as they passed through the crowd.

'Look over there,' Bryce called over the crowd noise. I followed his gaze to the neon pink lights of a strip club, open to the street, where woman in bikinis were gyrating on poles, faces set in uninterested grimaces. I wrinkled my nose. If Bryce thought we were going in there, he had another thing coming. I was about to say as much when I was shunted from behind and felt something wet against my back. I turned in fury and found a cluster of lads, one of whom had just walked into me and spilled lager over my dress.

'Watch out,' he muttered, sullenly looking at his half-empty plastic cup.

'Watch yourself,' I hissed back.

'Ey! Mate – that's Lila Wilde,' one of his friends blared, waving his drink in my direction.

23

'You spilled your drink on Lila-fuckin'-Wilde!' another of them jeered, half singing it like it was a football chant.

'Can we get a picture?' the first friend asked, grappling his phone out of his pocket.

I was torn between annoyance and obligation. Bryce pulled at my arm impatiently but I ducked away and entered the group of lads to take a quick picture. Though one of them put his hand very low on my back and they all squeezed in closer than was necessary. I was used to it and didn't say anything. I didn't want them going online to moan about how much of a bitch I was, after all. Not that it would be the first time someone got me to smile for a picture and posted it with a story about what a cow I was.

Wriggling my shoulders in my sticky dress, I caught up with Bryce who was a few steps away, hovering. I winced as the wet cotton clung to my skin, reeking of lager.

'I'm going to have to go and change.'

'Are you kidding?' Bryce's eyebrows shot up towards the sweaty edge of his hairline. 'We only just got here and it took forever.'

'My dress is wet,' I hissed, wriggling in discomfort.

'Babe, it's like thirty-five degrees; you'll dry in no time.' He put his arm around me and kissed my cheek. 'Plus, you look hot as fuck in it and I don't want you to change because of that idiot.'

I sighed, but relented. He was right – I was going to dry out quickly in the heat.

'Look at that,' Bryce said, suddenly sounding excited.

I followed his gaze and at first was too stunned at the sight of a fresh fish stall in the midst of all the nightlife to realise he was looking past it to a little weed dispensary. It was really just a stall covered in jars containing pre-rolled joints, with a guy in front flagging people down and offering them 'sativa' and 'Thai sticks'.

Weed, I knew, was legal in Thailand and just as when we visited Amsterdam and Los Angeles, Bryce was going to want to partake. I didn't mind so long as he didn't stink up the hotel room with it. I'd never been a fan of smoking it for that reason.

I already had money out by the time he turned back to me to ask for some. He looked like a kid in a sweet shop as he shot off to haggle with the stallholder. I made my way over behind him, in no real rush.

As I crossed the road in Bryce's wake I staggered a little on my heels. The tarmac was cracked and uneven, and my stiletto lodged in a gap. I yanked my leg out and looked up in time to see a car headed right for me.

I expected it to slow but it didn't. A yelp escaped me as I tried to rush the rest of the way across the street, nearly twisting my ankle as I went. I barely got out of the way in time. The side of the bonnet actually caught my bag as I leapt out of the way. The driver didn't even seem to care. My heart was hammering and I was too shocked to yell after the party Land Rover driver who had so nearly run me down. No one around me seemed in the least bit surprised. It was as if it hadn't happened at all.

I'd been honked at for jaywalking in New York, had cars screech to a halt to avoid me as I ran after an Hermès scarf in Milan, but this was different. I'd nearly been hit. The driver hadn't seemed to care if I was still in the way or not. Like I was just a rat scuttling under his wheels.

Now really shaken, and even more pissed off than I was at having been splashed with beer, I joined Bryce and wrapped my arm tightly through his for comfort. He didn't seem to have noticed what had just nearly happened to me. Instead he had a fistful of joints, wrapped in brown rolling papers, and I could see the edge of a baggie poking out through his fingers. I considered mentioning what had just happened but with the adrenaline fading it just seemed like I'd be spoiling the night for no reason.

'What did you get?' I asked pointedly, eyeing the baggie.

'Just a few smokes for tomorrow, by the pool. Indica.' He shrugged.

'I meant the bag.'

He flashed innocent blue eyes at me. 'Bag?'

I just glared at him until he broke. 'Yaba. It's basically a caffeine pill – don't worry about it. I mean, it's like a hundred baht – that's, what, a couple of quid? Not sure what you think I'm getting for that.'

With no idea what that was, I couldn't really start an argument. And yes, it didn't seem like he'd be able to get hard drugs for less than the price of a small coffee. So I let Bryce steer me towards a club with a massive three-dimensional elephant on the outside. But while we waited in line I took out my phone and googled 'yaba'.

The searches popped up a lot of info and I tapped the top result. Yaba, known by many names, including the charming 'Nazi speed', was in fact not 'basically a caffeine pill'. It had caffeine in it, but also contained methamphetamine and God knows what else. I glanced at Bryce and saw him pop a pill as red as a Skittle between his lips. Tonight was going to be a long one. I just knew it.

Chapter 3

We hit three clubs in quick succession, getting drinks and dancing a little at each one. Bryce was edgy and eager to see everything. He didn't want to 'settle' on a place and miss somewhere better. It was a bit like being out with a hummingbird. We'd barely stopped at a bar before he was downing his drink and suggesting we move along. I wasn't entirely sure if it was just the excitement and overstimulation of Bangla Road or the pills he'd taken. I told myself that stuff probably wasn't even real – just some sugar pill for selling to idiot tourists.

I wasn't managing to convince myself, and to be honest I was getting a bit worried that Bryce was going to crash hard later.

The clubs were good, but nothing out of this world. Basically the same as the places I'd been partying in since puberty. Lights, thumping music and crowds of people looking to dance, grope and drink their way into tomorrow. At least the drinks were cheap and the music was good. But it was hot on the dance floor, with all the people packed in.

As we waited to get into RAWR ahead of Bryce's set – a

flashy club that was all gold filigree outside and pulsing purple lights – Bryce ducked off to get us some drinks from a street vendor. He returned with plastic cups of Coca-Cola jingling with ice.

'There, can't get dehydrated can we?' he said, toasting me and gulping it down.

'Can we have the ice here?' I asked. I hadn't bothered to look that stuff up. It was never usually an issue because in the places we stayed it was just expected that all the water was bottled and imported – even the stuff used to make ice. That's what I was paying for – the best.

Bryce shrugged. 'Looks fine to me. Don't be racist.'

'I'm not! I just don't want to spend the next few days camped out in the bathroom,' I snapped. But Bryce shot me a look that said he didn't believe me. Was I being prejudiced for doubting the water quality? I mean, we were in the city, not out in the boonies. It was probably fine, right?

I took a sip and made a face. It tasted like Coke but it was too sweet and there was something vaguely medicinal about it – it reminded me of cough sweets. Probably some knockoff version. Though I'd always thought Coke tasted really weird in America because they used corn syrup in it there. Maybe this was the same deal?

'What is it?' I asked. 'Coke?'

Bryce shrugged. 'Kratom.'

'Which is . . . ?'

'I don't know, babe – it's probably just watered-down Coke, or like . . . local Pepsi or something.'

I drank it because I was sweaty and hot from dancing and just, you know, existing in the sweltering climate. Bryce finished his first and dumped our cups in a bin when

I was done. We finally reached the head of the line and I paid for us to get in, because apparently DJing didn't get Bryce free entry, or a plus-one.

Although the outside of RAWR was designed like a golden temple, inside things were much more modern. The steps, walls, booths and the bar, along with every other available surface, were outlined in brightly coloured neon strips. Most of the furniture was clear Perspex and what wasn't was mirrored. It gave the illusion that the club went on forever, a funhouse of swirling lights, reflections and screens pulsing with repeating patterns, as if trying to hypnotise everyone dancing below.

The bar, bathed in a deep purple glow, was rammed with people buying drinks and waitresses collecting bottles for the booths and the VIP section. I got myself a cocktail and Bryce a beer, but as I turned to hand it to him, I realised he wasn't behind me. Exasperated, I scanned the crowd and eventually spotted him. He was between two guys in beige uniforms, and it looked like they were trying to herd him out through a set of doors marked with 'no entry' symbols.

I discarded my drinks on the bar and dived through the crowd towards him. By the time I got close to them, Bryce was struggling against the two men and one of them was holding up the baggie of yaba pills, waving it at him. My heart sank. They were security, or police. They had to be, and Bryce had been caught taking drugs. We'd only been out a few hours.

I reached Bryce just in time to hear one of the uniformed guys saying something about 'you pay' and 'drug test'. Oh hell no. All my warning bells were going off.

'Hey, what's going on?' I raised my voice over the

music and took hold of Bryce's arm so they couldn't drag him away without taking me with him.

The two of them exchanged a look and the taller of the pair glared down at me. 'Drug test – he doesn't want to take it, he pays 20,000 baht. He takes and fails – we take him to jail.'

Police then. Fucking hell. I looked between them, and noted the way they looked at my jewellery. Ah. So they were looking for cash – like the shady doormen back home who'd let me and my friends into clubs at fourteen because I bunged them a few hundred. They'd probably picked Bryce not because he had drugs on him – as most people in here probably did – but because of the small fortune hanging around his neck. I knew I should have listened to Dad and brought fake jewellery with me, but it just seemed so stupid to have copies made. Why even bother having the real thing if you never wore it?

They were asking for about six hundred pounds. It was whatever. I dug around in my bag and held up the money, basically all the cash I had on me. 'Leave him alone then – there, happy now?'

The taller man nodded to the cash in my hand and his short buddy took it from me, stuffing it away into a pouch on his belt. They nodded to me like they'd just stopped to check in and not to extort money from us, then headed back into the crowd. Probably to find more people to search and scam.

'You should have let me handle it!' Bryce yelled, over the music. 'I was fine!'

'Well, now it's over with – you're welcome. Come on, let's get a drink.'

I steered him back towards the bar and had to queue

again to get another beer and a cocktail for myself. Someone else had probably snagged the abandoned drinks as freebies in my absence. I wasn't surprised.

I was, however, starting to feel a bit weird. I'd thought it was the adrenaline of Bryce going missing for a moment and me having to confront the cops, but even after five minutes my mouth was still dry and I felt dizzy and vaguely sick. I downed my cocktail to try and make my tongue feel less like cotton, but it didn't really help. I felt alert but unpleasantly so, almost twitchy.

'Bryce?' I pulled at his shirt sleeve and he looked away from the DJ currently on the neon-outlined stage, frowning at me.

'What, babe?'

'I feel weird . . . I think I might be sick.' My stomach lurched and I thought of the ice cubes and what bacteria might have been swimming around in them. Oh God, I could not be seen throwing up.

Bryce's frown turned to surprised concern. 'Shit uh . . . OK, toilets, toilets . . . over there.' He gestured to two black holes, outlined in LED strips – doorless passages that led into the mirrored walls.

'Wait here for me,' I said, and stumbled off towards the loos.

The dim corridor was a respite from the dancing lights and reflections. Even if the floor was sticky under my sandals. I made it to the bathroom at the end, where stainless steel sinks were already wet and plastered with lost eyelashes and long hairs, the counters smudged with foundation and the dregs of white powder.

I looked into the mirror screwed to the wall over the sink and winced. My pupils were tiny and I was gleaming

31

with cold sweat. I cupped my hands and rubbed water over my face, heedless of my makeup. Either the heat was getting to me, or I was on something. I shut my eyes to try and stop the dizziness from taking over. Had Bryce slipped me one of his pills to try and get me to 'go all night' with him? It definitely felt like I was high on something – the brittle, twitchy feeling making my eyes dart around and my heart thump hard in my chest. It felt like my body was running away with me. I'd never liked stimulants for this exact reason. Anything harder than caffeine made me feel like my bones were about to jump out of my skin.

I found my way out of the bathroom and back to where I'd left Bryce, but he was gone again. I checked my watch – thinking as I did so that if Dad knew I'd worn an 80k Chopard Alpine Eagle out to the clubs, he'd ban me from using the jet for a year – and saw that it was nearly time for Bryce's set. Which explained why he'd ditched me. He was probably nervously pacing about behind the stage area. I was torn between wanting to wish him good luck, and being pissed because I was sixty per cent sure he'd put something in my drink. If he hadn't, someone else sure had. I swallowed a wave of nausea and tried to look normal. The last thing I wanted was for someone to snap dodgy pictures of me looking like hammered shit on a night out.

'Oh my God, Lila! Babes!'

I turned and found myself face to face with Bethan Mills, dressed in a white body suit with an ostrich feather skirt over the top and a lot of Lucite jewellery. She had pearls glued to her face and a cascade of blonde hair running over her shoulders. She looked like a cross between Miss Alaska and a Martian princess. She swept me into an air kiss, her white acrylic claws just barely whispering over my arms.

'So good to see you – come join us?' Bethan trilled, indicating the VIP section with a tilt of her head. It was on a circular platform raised a metre or so above the dance floor, surrounded by gold leaping tiger statues connected by red rope. The steps up to it were outlined in flashing LEDs and I blinked away the sharp darts of light that lingered in my eyes. All I really wanted was to lie down somewhere quiet.

'Sure,' I said, and smiled as naturally as I could. At least from the VIP platform I'd have a good view of the stage across the dance floor.

Now, I had never met Bethan Mills before, but I definitely knew of her. She was, like me, an influencer and her dad was something big in tyres or fisheries – something boring and kind of gross. But her whole thing was makeup and she'd blown up online posting all her looks and reviewing products. I'd seen her collab with a high-end lipstick brand last summer and she'd obviously done well out of it. Despite the animal rights furore about those leaked testing clips.

For people in our sphere, there's no such thing as a stranger, though. We're members of the same club as far as the public are concerned. A club where membership means always being ready with an air kiss and an invite, whenever and wherever the opportunity presents itself. Even if you're trying to mask that you're sweating bullets and feel like throwing up all over them. Especially then.

'Lila Wilde, everyone,' Bethan said, waving around the glass table at the centre of the platform, where three people were reclined with drinks. Two men and another woman. She was late twenties, like me and Bethan, and the guys were probably on the wrong side of thirty-five to be in here. Though one of them had a lot of Botox going on.

I recognised the woman but blanked on her name in the moment, my head spinning. I knew she wasn't in makeup like Bethan, but she was a lifestyle guru – just not the same type as me. Her whole thing was dressing up like a cute Disney princess idea of a housewife and baking pies or making lip balm from her own organic beeswax. Tradwife stuff like that, though I didn't think she was actually married. All very wholesome and safe, until she fired her assistant for coming out as bisexual. That was the last thing I'd seen of her that went viral.

'This is Kaitlyn,' Bethan filled in, gesturing to the redhead in a cut-off strawberry-patterned sundress and cream Mary Janes with lacy bows on them. Not very club-friendly but a brand's a brand. She smiled at me, face glowing with both sweat and a large amount of princess pink blush. What was she even doing in Thailand? I wasn't sure – it didn't seem to fit with her overall brand identity.

'And her boyfriend, Fletcher Michaels, who you'll know from TV,' Bethan continued.

Ah OK, now the Botox made sense. Fletcher used to be an actor in one of those ensemble kids shows about a giant family getting into hijinks. Not one I'd watched but I guessed it made him kind of a household name with people who hadn't spent their late teen years waiting backstage at the Grammys for their dad to finish boinking a pop star one year older than them. Normal people, who did normal things like watch TV. It also made him at least forty. Though he was doing a good job of shaving off five years with a little filler and possibly a cheeky little facelift.

These days Fletcher looked less like a TV has-been and more like he should be knocking at my door to 'spread the good word'. Not that your average doorstep Bible basher wore Ralph Lauren and 'American tan' foundation. Last I saw he was interviewing sixteen-year-old vegans on live TV and 'destroying them' with the power he got from being decades older than them, with media training. Bryce was a big fan, though thankfully he hadn't started eating raw steaks and testicles for every meal, which last I heard was Fletcher's thing.

Remembering that particular clip made my stomach turn over. Yeah, not helping with the dizzying nausea. I quickly tried to distract myself. The other guy looked familiar but I wasn't sure who he was until he introduced himself. 'Dash Filmore, from *Dudes in a Canoe*?' he said, as if fully expecting me to have never heard of him. But I had.

Dudes in a Canoe was a travelogue online series about travelling the world 'off the beaten path'. Another content creator Bryce followed. But not as religiously. Based on what I knew I wasn't surprised Dash was in Thailand, but in a club was another story. I'd seen clips of his videos and normally he was in forests and jungles, dressed in khaki and puka shells (not a great look on someone closer to thirty-five than twenty-five), on the hunt for a wild animal or climbing a dangerous trail, off to see something that 'no other tourist gets to see!'.

'Right, my boyfriend really likes you – both of your stuff actually,' I said, to loop Fletcher in. 'He's DJing tonight,' I added airily, trying to ignore the cold sweat trickling down my back.

'Cool,' Fletcher drawled, not looking up from his phone.

Dash nodded, more engaged. 'Great! Are you here for work? Enjoying Phuket? This is my third time here,' he said.

'My first,' Bethan put in, perching on the edge of his chair like a Persian cat.

'Same. Fletch has been a few times though, haven't you, baby?' Kaitlyn said, moving closer to Fletcher, who put an arm around her.

'Five times,' Fletcher said, still not looking up from his phone. I wondered what he was doing and guessed he was probably on his socials, arguing with randomers. That was very much his brand.

'This is my first visit to Phuket,' I admitted, and then, because my brain was mostly focused on not throwing up, I ended up adding, 'Did you guys see all the monkeys outside? Really sad that their home is now like . . . a nightclub. They've got nowhere to go.'

Bethan raised an eyebrow and glanced at Kaitlyn. Even Fletcher looked up from his phone for a second to sneer at me. I felt myself flush all over. I'd committed the worst kind of faux pas in a situation like this – giving a shit about something real. I was really off my game.

I cleared my throat. 'But my family has a house here – well not here-here but in Songkhla. We're not heading up there 'til after we get our fill of the nightlife though. It's kind of remote. Private.'

'Cool.' Dash grinned, my screw-up forgiven. 'So, who's your boyfriend?'

'Bryce Erlandsson – he's a DJ,' I said, knowing that none of them would have any idea who he was. Bryce basically didn't exist to anyone in my world until we started dating. I'd met him at a music festival Dad was playing and fallen for his half-Scottish, half-Swedish chiselled good looks and sharp blue eyes. Dad called him my 'arm candy' and yeah, I guess he sort of was. But it was nice to not be in competition with my own boyfriend, which had been the case before. I'd dated sports stars, musicians, actors and reality TV personalities and it had always been about their career and their goals. Bryce was an addition to my life, not the other way around.

'That him?' Bethan gestured to the stage, where the lights were spinning, welcoming a new DJ to the stage. I saw the light catch on Bryce's tiger pendant, sparkling like a disco ball. He'd unbuttoned his shirt completely, showing off his abs and the tattooed Chinese characters on his chest. He looked so hot, for a moment I forgot to be annoyed with him about the drink that had made me so ill.

'Yup, that's my boyfriend,' I said, flashing a smile at her, proud of him despite the weird dizziness still lazily stirring my brain like a spoon. Had he actually drugged me, or was I just overheated and a bit drunk? All I knew for certain was that I wasn't about to ruin the night and show myself up in front of Bethan and the others by bringing it up.

If Bryce had slipped me something, well, that was for discussing behind closed doors. Out here, for tonight, we had to be perfect. Like always. Especially now that people who mattered were watching, waiting for me to screw up so they could pull me down and claim my spot in the food chain. Whatever happened, I had to keep smiling.

Chapter 4

Bryce's set was only an hour but it felt longer. Time had started to feel really weird and I found myself struggling to focus as it sort of ran away from me, causing me to blank in conversation. I'd switched to sparkling water but it didn't seem to make a difference. I was no longer able to kid myself that it was just the heat and exhaustion from travelling. I was on something.

After a while the others seemed to notice that something was up. As hard as I tried to appear normal and unfazed, I couldn't control my expression or movements for long before getting distracted. I caught Kaitlyn and Bethan exchanging amused and slightly catty looks as I once again jerked back to alertness.

'Sorry, jet lag,' I muttered, sipping my water.

'You sure you're not holding out on us?' Fletcher laughed. Since my mouth had run away with me about the monkeys I'd had his attention. He was obviously waiting to see how I'd embarrass myself next. 'I could use something to liven up the evening.'

I shook my head, which was a mistake as I immediately

felt even worse. 'Just a few cocktails, and nothing for a while now. Just water and some kratom.'

'Kratom?' Dash repeated in surprise, leaning in with a frown as if he might have misheard.

'Yeah, it's like some watered-down cola . . .' I trailed off as his eyebrows shot upwards, making my heart sink.

'Kratom's a leaf. People use it to get high here, especially out in rural towns,' Dash said, looking both slightly amused and a little concerned. 'They mix it with soda and sometimes cough syrup with codeine in it.'

I thought of the weirdly sweet, medicinal-tasting Coke and felt panic flood through me. Shit. I *knew* it was that bloody drink! Bryce probably hadn't even known what it was. Just bought a couple of ice-cold drinks and not understood what was in them. I felt awful that I'd even suspected him of doing something underhanded. He'd just been sort of dumb and trusting.

'Oh my God, that's so funny,' Bethan giggled. 'What's it like? Where did you get it?'

'Bryce bought it from someone outside, a stall I think. Am I going to be OK? I feel a bit sick and dizzy,' I asked Dash.

He shrugged. 'Not sure. Never done it – just heard stuff. It's meant to be a bit like speed for some people, but it can work like an opiate for others.'

'Like heroin?' I hissed, unable to keep the horror off my face. Not only had I accidentally let slip that I was on drugs to this lot, I was on something that sounded much less harmless than a bit of weed. The word 'opiate' made me wince. If they mentioned this online and it got out to their followers and then went viral, I'd be in serious shit with my sponsors. I glanced at Fletcher but he was just smirking, not doing anything on his phone. Hopefully he'd keep his amusement at my expense private.

'I mean, you only had one, so you'll be fine,' Dash assured me, though he didn't look particularly certain. 'Your boyfriend seems OK too.'

I looked towards the stage and saw Bryce doing his thing, hyping up the crowd and playing from one of his digital playlists. He kept them on a USB necklace I'd had made for him, a sterling silver pendant from Parts of Four, engraved with his name. He did in fact look like he was perfectly fine – energetic and sweaty, but that was everyone in the crowd too.

'OK . . .' I said, making myself calm down and trying to downplay it for the benefit of the others. 'So I suppose I'll file this one away as a cultural experience. Like when I went on that peyote retreat.'

Dash snorted and I sipped my water, trying to remain calm even though my pulse was racing. I'd always been a bit of a baby about feeling out of sorts. A cold had me retreating to my bed for the day, humidifier and sleep mask in hand.

The end of Bryce's set came around and I was pleased he'd be back by my side soon. At least I'd have some backup, and a distraction. The thing about hanging around with other celebs is that you're always conscious of being tomorrow's 'tea spill' video. Or an industry rumour. I mean, one word out of place and suddenly Bethan was telling her hair stylist, he was telling another client, and then internet sleuths would work out that she was talking about me and it would be a whole thing. I needed Bryce as a buffer. It wouldn't matter if he did something out of pocket – boys would be boys and all that. Especially when they were just normal dudes. He'd get far less hassle than me.

I was thinking this when I heard my name coming through the speakers. I wrenched my attention to the stage and saw Bryce standing there, gold mic in hand.

'. . . my princess and my muse – will you marry me?'

I was abruptly blinded by spotlights, and the crowd exploded with cheers and whistling. My skin felt tight with horror. Suddenly Bryce's eagerness to get to the clubs and have me dressed up on time made sense. He must have been beside himself trying to get me to where he'd planned to propose, knowing I'd want to look my best for the pictures. What he should have known, was that I'd never – EVER – want to be proposed to in some sweaty club while buzzing on a cocktail of random drugs. My horror quickly turned to anger and humiliation as all faces in the crowd turned towards me. I had to smile through gritted teeth. Fuck.

'Oh my God, that is so lovely,' Kaitlyn cried, grasping Fletcher's hand. Her tone was overjoyed but her eyes simmered with jealousy and she was holding on to Fletcher very tightly. Almost pointedly so. He was looking over at Bryce, smiling slightly like he was amused by this whole turn of events, ignoring Kaitlyn's grip on his hand.

Ugh, if she wanted this tacky proposal so badly she could have it. Bryce and I had talked about this. It had been a lovely moment actually. We'd been floating in the pool at Dad's Vegas mansion and I'd told him about how I'd imagined being proposed to on the beach in Crete where my parents got engaged. Because Mum couldn't be there for any of my milestones, obviously, but it would feel like she was. But now he'd done this instead and I'd never have that moment back.

'Come on up here, babes!' Bryce called, and I got to my feet, only stumbling slightly in my heels, which were punishing my feet already. Everyone was looking at me and their faces were blurred, their eyes dark pits. My pulse was deafening and I could feel the sweat on my skin, sticking the cotton crochet of my dress to me. The attention, the kratom, the light bouncing off the ring in Bryce's hands, it all combined to make me feel like I was floating out of my body as I climbed up the neon steps to the stage. For a second I thought I was going to pass out and crack my head on the stairs.

Bryce took my hand and slid the ring onto my finger and even through a haze of stress I had to admit it was to die for – a huge, princess-cut diamond that had to be at least fourteen carats, maybe more. Easily the size of a pound coin. I'd only ever seen one bigger and that was Paris Hilton's infamously misplaced 2018 ring from Chris Zylka. It would have had any one of the Kardashians screaming, crying, throwing up with envy. Whereas I just wanted to scream, cry and throw up, even if the ring was perfect. Because this was all wrong. But we were on a stage, in public and the only option I had was to go with it.

I threw my arms around Bryce's neck – the image of young love – and he spun me around on the stage, kissing me with a smile on his face. The crowd were going insane and the house DJ had stepped in to restart the music. I told myself it was OK. I was pulling it off, and my anxiety dipped slightly. Even if the spinning had me holding back a retch.

'Is that a yes?' Bryce had to practically shout into my ear.

'Yes!' I screamed back. What else could I say?

Bryce led me down the stage steps and it seemed like everyone in the club wanted to shake his hand or pat him on the back. People were looking at the ring, touching my arms, calling out 'good luck' and 'congratulations, Lila!'. I was touched out before we were halfway back to the table, but I couldn't exactly shove people away from me. I had to keep smiling and thanking everyone.

By the time we reached the VIP section I was glad of the velvet ropes holding the crowd at bay. The new weight on my hand was making me acutely aware of my sweating palms. God, what if the ring slipped off and got lost? How had Bryce even afforded it? Had my dad known about this and ponied up the cash?

'Guys, this is Bryce – my fiancé!' I added, gushing as convincingly as I could. 'Bryce, you've seen Dash and Fletcher, but this is Kaitlyn – Fletcher's girlfriend – and Bethan – the makeup guru.'

'Hey, what's up?' Bryce said, and I hoped it was only obvious to me how desperate he was to impress with his 'too cool' demeanour. I just wanted him to pull focus from me for a bit so I could have a break.

Just then a waitress in a skimpy skirt teetered over on tall heels, carrying a tray loaded with glasses and an ice bucket of champagne.

'For the happy couple.' Bethan beamed. 'I remember when Anthony and I got engaged – it was the best night.'

Anthony who? I was drawing a blank, then I remembered some random skateboarding vlogger with like half a million followers. She'd snapped him up and he'd been on her channel a few times but I hadn't seen him in ages.

'How is Anthony?' I asked, to try and divert her attention from the proposal.

'Oh, he's fine,' Bethan said airily. 'Let's toast!'

She waved for the waitress to pour glasses and then raised hers, yelling her toast over the thumping music and the whooping of the crowd.

'To Lila and Bryce!'

'To you, babe,' Bryce said into my ear, tapping our glasses together.

'To us,' I said back, and sipped my drink. It was wonderfully crisp and cold, almost like liquid diamond itself. But it did nothing to still the churning in my stomach, or stop me thinking of the fantasy proposal I'd now never have. Still, the show had to go on, as they say. I thought of Dad and what he'd do in this situation.

I managed to get hold of the waitress as she was leaving, and thrust one of my cards at her. 'Drinks are on me for the rest of the night!'

'For the whole table?' she asked.

'For the bar!' There, that'd get them away from me.

Several people near the velvet ropes cordoning off the VIP section must have heard, because a general whooping went up and there was a surge towards the bar. Bryce squeezed me tightly. So tightly that I could feel how damp his shirt was, and the way his pulse was racing as his chest met mine.

'Babe, are you OK?' I asked, checking his eyes and finding that his pupils were pinholes. 'That drink you got us before – turns out it was some local drug cocktail – and you already had those pills . . .'

'I feel great!' Bryce grinned. 'I just got engaged to the love of my life!'

I made myself smile back, but I was still a little worried. I decided to stop him if he tried to take any more of the pills. Hopefully a few drinks would help bring him down and mellow him out.

The free drinks went over well, predictably. More and more people came by the VIP section to congratulate us and to slur their thanks for the cocktails and beers they were holding. But at least they were in manageable groups. A few people wanted pictures taken with us. I could practically feel the others quietly seething with jealousy that we were getting all the attention. It was kind of funny, given that they were the ones who'd been in the VIP area to start with. Normally I'd be thriving on it but I just wanted to get back to the villa and talk to Bryce in private.

Fletcher took Kaitlyn off to dance – I guessed to stop her pouting – and Bethan excused herself to the ladies'. Dash and Bryce got talking about Phuket and what there was to do and see around here. I found myself at a bit of a loose end, watching the crowd. Screw it, I just wanted to forget about this mess and try to have a good time. I felt oddly fizzy with pent-up energy and the dance floor suddenly looked like just the place I wanted to be.

'I'm going to dance,' I said, nudging Bryce.

'Cool,' he said back, holding out a hand for my bag so he could watch it.

Out on the floor I couldn't resist throwing my hands up to watch the spotlights glitter off my new diamond. I felt like a disco ball. The music pulsed through me, and my feet no longer bothered me. I felt like I could dance all night. Who cared about anything else? This place was fantastic, and everyone was so nice!

I had a cocktail and then some shots with a few lovely Australian girls. I danced with a few men – nothing sexy, just having a good time. One massive German guy put me up on his shoulders and spun me around until the lights blurred and I felt like I might fly off into the pulsing darkness over the dance floor. I laughed until I could hardly breathe.

It seemed like only minutes but it must have been longer, because I turned around and Bryce was there. It looked like he'd been trying to find me for a while, a crease of irritation and worry between his eyebrows.

'Babes, they're closing soon – it's almost four in the morning,' he called over the music.

Several people dancing near me voiced their annoyance at this. We were all dancing together and honestly I didn't feel like stopping. I had hours of partying left in me. Weren't we here to have fun? To party the night away? This was our engagement party basically – we couldn't just let it fizzle out because the club was closing.

'Let's all go back to my villa!' I yelled, and several people whooped, pumping their arms in the air.

Bryce looked around us, a lazy grin forming on his face. 'Babe, you'll never get this lot past the security gate – no visitors remember?'

Ugh, that did ring a bell. The villa we were renting was in a gated area meant to be both exclusive and safe. No extra visitors were allowed past the manned gate and we had photo passes to get in and out.

I sensed the flagging excitement of the crowd around me and pouted. If we couldn't take them back to the villa,

I didn't want to go back there. If it was just me and Bryce we'd have to talk about stuff. But everything else was probably closing as well so what options did that leave us? With my head fogged with cocktails and kratom, my veins buzzing with excitement, there seemed like only one reasonable choice.

'Who wants to come to my house in Songkhla!?'

Whoops and cheers went up around us, and Bryce grinned at me before sweeping me off my feet and spinning me round. In that instant I thought it was the single most perfect moment, on the best night of my life. One I'd remember forever.

To be fair, I was right.

Chapter 5

The car bumped over a pothole and I grabbed hold of Bryce's thigh to steady myself. My phone was sliding against my ear and I could hardly hear myself think over the traffic noise. The sooner we reached the airstrip the better.

'Work it out,' I insisted, for the third time, to the pilot on Dad's jet. 'It's like a seven-hour drive, John, and I'm not doing that. We'd be too tired to enjoy ourselves and there'd be no point being there. Also, think of all the animals we might hit on the road in the dark.'

John sighed heavily and I heard a rustle as he covered the receiver with one hand. There was murmuring and a few sharp, distorted noises, then he was back.

'We'll prepare the plane for a one-hour domestic flight to Songkhla – how many passengers will there be?'

'Um . . . I don't know,' I said, honestly. 'Let's call it around thirty.'

John sighed again. 'OK . . . thank you, Miss Wilde.'

I hung up and rolled my eyes. Obviously being a pilot was a big deal but he didn't need to have an attitude. Especially with what my dad was paying him to literally be on call. It was only an hour's work after all. It took longer for Mariella to do a fresh set on my nails for God's sake, and she never complained.

'Everything sorted?' Bryce asked. 'Sounded like kind of a struggle. The fuck was that guy's problem?'

'No idea. I guess maybe because it's kind of last minute and he kept whining about the "plan" but, that's what he gets paid for so, it's all good – they're getting ready for the flight now.'

I leaned back in my seat and let the night air buffeting in through the car window push my hair off my face, drying the sweat on my forehead. Outside the club I'd quickly raided an ATM and been able to hire a bunch of the party Land Rovers, painted bubble-gum pink and fire engine red, decked in LEDs with open backs like milk floats. My new friends from the club piled in and in a full-on motorcade we flashed and honked our way out of the Bangla Road traffic and into the far more aggressive Phuket general traffic.

Bryce put his arm around me as our car manoeuvred around mopeds and parked vans selling weed, vegetables and 'designer' clothes. Street hawkers came up to the open windows when we paused near them, selling clingfilm-wrapped sticky rice cakes, fried food and jewellery.

The humidity only seemed to be going up, even though the air was getting cooler. The pressure felt like it was dropping and I could feel the air thickening with the promise of rain. This would be the real test of my hair products. If there was frizz I would not be happy. At least the cooler air was making me feel less sick. Hopefully the weather would be dry when we reached Songkhla, though there was more than enough to keep us occupied indoors if it wasn't. The mansion had its own cinema, bowling alley and hookah bar. Dad may not have known the first thing about raising kids, but he knew how to party.

In the car with us were our fellow VIP guests. Kaitlyn was cosied up to Fletcher and he'd just bought her a rose from a vendor, waving banknotes out the window to get his attention. She was holding the wilted flower to her chest, obviously smitten with him. To me it felt like he just wanted to distract her for a while, and a cheap flower was a good way to do it. Fletcher was looking out the window as we passed a strip club.

Across from me, Bethan was using pale pink blotting paper to take the shine off her nose, eyeing herself critically via her phone's front camera. Dash, on the other side of Bryce, was looking out the window and soaking up the sights.

'You two sure you've had enough of Phuket?' he asked after a while.

I shrugged. 'We can come back – it's only an hour away.'

'And we'll have to get our stuff from the villa,' Bryce pointed out. 'But you've got to see this house, man – I've only seen pictures but holy shit, it's like the Playboy Mansion.'

I laughed. 'It is not!'

'It is though,' Bryce chuckled, nudging Dash's leg. 'It has three pools.'

'It has two, and a hot tub,' I said modestly. 'My dad bought it for his honeymoon with wife number . . . three? They lived there for six months and then got divorced – I had my eighteenth birthday there and he's let a few friends stay there since but we'll have the place to ourselves.'

'Why weren't you staying there then?' Bethan asked, looking up over her phone, her other hand now holding a miniature powder brush.

'Like I said, it's remote.' I shrugged. 'No clubs or anything, and the idea was to party but . . . that was before I got engaged.' I beamed at Bryce, stamping down on my brewing resentment, easy to ignore under the rush of expectation for the party. 'Now we have a reason to throw our own party.'

I could already see it in my head: our guests in the infinity pool and hot tub, music blaring from the outdoor speakers with no one around but the wildlife to complain. Out back was a platform with loungers and seats on it, a swim-up rest area with a fire pit under the stars. The indoor bar area had glass walls so you could see out into the jungle, and Dad swore he'd once seen a tiger prowl past the reinforced windows. Though I wasn't sure I believed him. But the whole outdoor area was surrounded by an electric fence to keep the wildlife out, so I supposed there was stuff out there.

I was fairly sure I knew how the gas grills out there worked and the deep freezers at the house would be fully stocked – as they were at all Dad's properties – with burgers, steaks and kebabs all ready to go. Plus the pantry and the hermetically sealed wine cellar would be bursting with champagne and all kinds of cocktail ingredients.

We reached the private airfield after a short drive and I saw Dad's plane ready and waiting – a sleek black jet with the 'Wilde' label logo down the side in blood-red claw font. The cars pulled up in a wonky semicircle and I paid everyone well while my club friends spilled out of them and looked up at the plane in awe.

John the pilot, as well as the two flight attendants – Janet and Stefan in their red uniforms – were waiting by the boarding stairs. Still riding a wave of excitement, I led the group over and beamed at all three of them as I ushered everyone on board. Even as foggy as I was with cocktails I could tell John wasn't happy to be there, and I had to fight not to roll my eyes at him. For what he got paid he should have been kissing my feet and carrying me up the stairs personally.

On board, my guests exclaimed over the spacious passenger area with its cream leather swivel seats and the bar at the back. I noticed that the usual food selection (caviar, charcuterie and fresh fruit) was missing, but then again it had been a bit short notice. I could survive without melon balls and croustades. At least the bar had the usual snacks if anyone was hungry – pretzels, peanuts and other pre-packaged stuff.

'Miss Wilde, will you be requiring tea and coffee service during the flight?' Janet asked, appearing at my elbow like a shadow, her red lipstick perfectly applied despite the hour.

John could stand to learn something from Janet, I decided. She wasn't glaring and bitching because she'd had to wake up and get ready for work, and she had a full face of makeup on and her hair was curled.

'I'm sure we're fine with just bar service. Thank you.' I threw myself into a chair and beckoned Bryce to join me.

'Nice plane,' Fletcher said, eyes moving over everything as if he was inventorying it for auction. 'Bet it costs your dad a fortune to run.'

'Cheaper than paying for all the extra seats he'd need for security on a commercial flight,' I said, a response I'd heard Dad give on more than one occasion. Lately the climate protestors had really been coming for him, and yeah, the plane wasn't exactly good for the environment but what was the alternative? Just not travel to do his job? When he'd last done a big live performance for TV, a group of nutters had thrown red paint over him. As if it was a shocking surprise that a rock star was wearing leather.

Then again, maybe it was the live snakes they took issue with. Or the naked women wearing them. People got upset over everything. It was exhausting just to watch them honestly. Sometimes, reading comments I received about stuff my dad had done, I wanted to yell back that I was just his daughter; he didn't actually listen to me. If I told him it upset me that he had naked women on stage, he'd just laugh and tell me that was where my money came from. Then pack me off to Chanel with his credit card to keep me quiet.

Janet came round with glasses of Cristal while John droned out his announcement that we were about to take off – seatbelts on, no smoking, no phones blah blah blah. As if we'd never been on a plane before like some tween little tourists. I swear he was only doing it to be annoying.

I sat back and relaxed with my drink in hand as the plane rushed down the runway and launched into the air. The swooping sensation of take-off in my belly only added to my excitement. Soon we'd be setting down at the private airstrip by the house. It was a bit of a trek up to the actual compound but there was a fenced-in road and a garage full of ATVs and SUVs. We'd probably be able to drive up there, providing we were reasonably sober when we landed. Not that it mattered on a straight road anyway.

As soon as we reached altitude everyone was up again, and I put music on and shimmied through the crowd. A Thai guy in his early twenties had taken his shirt off and was dancing up close and personal with a skinny redhead, waving the fabric over his head. Half his chest was taken up by a tattoo of some kind of cartoon character – one of those sword-wielding anime dudes. I passed by a tall, broad American guy trying to talk over the music to a shy Thai girl hiding behind her hair. I nearly walked right into the back of a laughing Australian woman in a beaded dress, the overpowering smell of cheap body spray rising from her in a vanilla-and-alcohol cloud.

'Sorry!' I said, sidestepping her with a wrinkled nose before straddling Bryce's lap and taking a selfie to show off my ring. I'd have to post them later once we arrived at the house. Dad was going to be happy too, once I told him. It'd be good press for him. The only person who wasn't ecstatic was me. I still felt like I was going through the motions as far as excitement over the engagement was concerned. The momentum of the dance floor had carried me this far but now we were stuck on the plane I felt myself starting to flag a little. Maybe Bryce was right and I did need to pop a pill or two to make sure I stayed on top form.

The plane jerked then, just once, like we'd hit a speed bump. I laughed automatically. It was just startled out of me, like we were on a ride at Disney World or something. Then we bumped again and my stomach contracted. I looked at Bryce and saw my own fear reflected back at me. What the hell was that?

Everyone had gone suddenly quiet, tense. The whooping and laughter turning to mutters and hushed voices. Another lurch had people gasping and one girl yelped in fright.

The chime of the announcement system made me jump.

'Just skirting a storm here. If everyone could take their seats and buckle up for a few minutes, that would be much appreciated.' John's voice was flat and professional. My muscles unclenched. Just a little bit of turbulence. It was nothing he hadn't seen before, even if it was the worst I'd ever experienced.

'Sorry, everyone!' I called out. 'Grab a seat for a few, OK?'

There was some awkward laughter and I saw everyone sag slightly in relief. They found their way to seats and I saw the Australian woman nudge the shy girl and say something that made her smile slightly.

There was another small bump and a few people giggled, like we were back on that rollercoaster and everything was fine. Everything *was* fine, we'd be landing soon and I could have a drink and relax and try to get past the complete let-down of the proposal.

'A storm?' Bryce said. 'Is that a problem?'

I forgot sometimes that he wasn't really used to travelling. He'd never even flown before we met. I kissed him and felt him relax under me. I liked that he looked to me to reassure him. It made me feel secure, like I actually knew what I was talking about.

'It's probably just . . .'

But I never got to finish that empty reassurance.

The plane pitched downwards, suddenly nosediving. The force and speed of it felt like it would propel my stomach up through my chest. I screamed, clinging to Bryce, and his fingers bit into my thighs. Around us bottles and glasses flew upwards and smashed against the ceiling. Shards rained down and the lights strobed. I heard the chime of the announcement system again but couldn't make out the words John was shouting.

Then suddenly I wasn't on Bryce's lap anymore. I was torn away by the force of our descent. I fell sideways and tried to catch myself on seats and squirming, panicking people. Everyone was screaming, being thrown from their seats and hitting the floor, walls and ceiling.

A shriek tore out of me. I thought I heard Bryce yelling my name in the chaos. Then my head collided with something hard, wrenching consciousness from my grasp.

Chapter 6

Andrea clears her throat and glances briefly down at the printed cards in her taloned hand. Lila, perched on the sofa, watches her unblinkingly. Still and vacant as a lizard frozen under the gaze of a passer-by. It's a slightly eerie calm, the stillness of something being hunted, or of a hunter. I can't actually remember what I was thinking in that moment. Perhaps I was just like that lizard, soaking up the heat from the studio lights and trying to survive. Andrea on the other hand, is definitely on the prowl, judging from the way she eyes Lila before firing off a question.

'According to statements from the taxi drivers you hired that night, you took thirty-three guests out on your plane. Not including yourself, your fiancé and a staff of three. So, thirty-eight people were on the plane when it crashed. Is that correct?'

'Yes.' Lila doesn't blink, just answers smoothly. It's a fact, after all, that has been in the news ever since the crash. This is not new information to her, to either of them.

'Do you think overloading the plane contributed to the crash?' Andrea presses.

'As far as I know, it didn't. But there hasn't been a full investigation yet.' Lila crosses one leg over the other and fiddles with a thin leather bracelet on her wrist. I can't remember what happened to that. My memories of the time after we left the jungle are full of holes, like a maggoty apple. 'I lost consciousness very early on. When we first hit the storm and turbulence started to push us off course.'

'You were only supposed to be in the air for an hour, heading to your father's thirteen-million-pound mansion in Songkhla?' Andrea says, causing several audience members to gasp, as she no doubt intended them to.

I get it, it's a lot of money. More than most people can really imagine.

Lila acknowledges that with a tilt of her head. 'Instead we ended up off course and heading south, over the Tenasserim Hills.'

Andrea turns to her audience and therefore, the camera. 'Known locally as the Thio Khao Tanaosi. A mountain range between Thailand and Myanmar, covered in dense jungle.'

Lila says nothing. That I do remember, looking at her and thinking, 'no shit'.

'Thirty-eight people, crashed into the jungle,' Andrea continues, undaunted. 'On a private jet worth over fifty million pounds – which split in two during the storm . . . apparently money can't buy safety.'

'It depends,' Lila says, apparently surprising Andrea, who glares.

'On?' she asks, archly.

'On whether there is any to buy,' Lila says. 'Here, or even in Phuket, money could buy you a nice big house, security system, perimeter walls, guards . . . anything you could possibly want. But out there . . . where were we going to buy things from? As soon as we hit that storm it wasn't about money. It was about luck, and our pilot's skill.'

I think of him with a twist in my belly. On screen, the ghost of me from a year ago seems to squirm with the same regret.

'Your pilot – that would be John Mercer. A former RAF flyer with fifteen years of experience.'

'Yes. John was an excellent pilot.' Lila sounds faint, even with the microphone clipped to her clothes.

'Yet he wasn't one of the survivors?' Andrea says, though she already knows the answer. It has to be on her cards, like everything else. She just wants her audience to hear it in Lila's voice. In her words. My words.

'. . . no, he didn't survive the jungle.'

'But he survived the crash?'

'Yes, though he was injured, like several other people.'

'Other people who didn't make it out with you?'

'. . . some of them didn't,' Lila says, and lets go of the leather wristlet, clenching a fist on her thigh. 'Some of the ones who weren't injured didn't either.'

'So, after the crash . . . how many of those thirty-eight people were still alive? Before everything else that happened?' Andrea prods.

Lila's chapped lips part as she pulls in a long breath.

Sitting in the airport I feel the answer like a punch to the chest before she says it aloud.

'Twelve.'

59

Chapter 7

I woke up to flickering orange lights, the glow seeping through my eyelids. For a moment I couldn't work out where I was. The club? My villa? It felt like I'd been hit by the mother of all hangovers. Sickness boiled in my guts, my head felt like it was clamped in a vice.

My head throbbed harder when I tried to lift it so much as an inch. When I tried to move my limbs I found them pinned in place, coming up against hard surfaces no matter which way I shifted. As if I'd been packed into a box. I let out a confused groan and tried to lift my head, only to have it hit something above me. A fresh rocket of pain sent bright lights flaring behind my eyes.

Was I in a box or a crate? It felt like it. Hemmed in on all sides and forced into a cramped little ball. My cheek shifted on the floor and I felt the fuzz of carpet. The boot of a car? My heart jolted – had I been kidnapped? Dad had warned me about it whenever I left Europe. He didn't even trust the Americans. 'There are a lot of desperate people out there,' he used to say, pointing his finger at me, skull ring winking. 'Never forget how much you're worth.'

But if I was in a car, it wasn't moving. There was that

at least. The floor under my face was still and lifeless. No thrum of an engine or the movement of wheels.

With my eyelids screwed shut as I tried to control the pulses of pain in my skull, I felt around and eventually realised I wasn't in a car. It was too small, too irregular. The plush carpet against my fingertips was too thick and soft to be in a car boot – even a luxury one. I dug my fingers in and breathed in the familiar scent of Dad's plane – the cleaning products and leather seats. That grounded me but it didn't reassure me. Yes, I knew where I was, but how had I ended up on the floor of the plane and why was no one helping me?

Reaching out, I found a metal support and followed it up to where it met smooth leather. I was squashed under a seat, in a footwell. Slowly, I managed to get my confused limbs out from around the metal supports and the shifting bits of rubbish that had gathered around me – glasses, handbags, bottles. I crawled into an open space and dragged myself upright with a chair.

My head was pounding and I could barely open my eyes without the emergency lights searing into my brain – a throbbing, awful orange that made my head ache. I struggled to make my legs take my weight. What happened? I couldn't work out what was going on. There were no voices, and it was so warm. Like the air-conditioning was off.

One of my knees buckled and I lurched, grabbing at a seat back. I remembered the bouncing, suddenly, how I'd stumbled then. There had been turbulence. What had John said? Some kind of storm or something. He'd obviously had to land. But why was the power out – the lights and air-conditioning? Why was I just left on the floor?

I tried to take a step and stumbled over a bottle on the floor. Prying my eyes open as best I could, I looked around for Bryce. The orange emergency lighting was flickering, making it harder to see. The heat intensifying moment by moment. I tried to take a deep breath and ended up coughing. The air was hot and foul and tasted like . . . like . . .

My heart leapt in panic as I looked down the plane and saw the flames flickering hungrily for the first time. As the confusion lifted from my brain I identified the smells of burning plastic and of fuel. Sounds started to filter into my awareness – sobbing, low cries and the squealing of metal as it groaned and strained. Beyond that and the crackling of the fire, came the unnerving shrieks and yelps, of animals in the dark.

I automatically staggered away from the fire, towards the cockpit. Towards the exit door. One hand crept up to my head, as if trying to hold it on. I'd hit it really hard, I remembered – possibly on the marble edge of the bar area – and there was blood, sticky against my fingers. No wonder my thoughts felt like syrup, oozing around in my skull. How long had I been unconscious and what had happened in the meantime? An emergency landing? But the fire . . . I couldn't make myself think straight. Trying to hold on to a thought was like trying to catch smoke in my fists.

'Bryce?' I rasped, clinging to seats with my other hand as I dragged myself towards the cockpit. Why was it so hard to walk? I kept stumbling and slipping. 'Bryce!'

There were dark shapes between some of the seats, but I couldn't focus for long enough to see if they were people, or discarded jackets and bags. I couldn't bring myself to reach out and touch any of them, afraid of what I'd find.

A spluttering cough made me jump, and I turned towards it in time to spot the bathroom door opening, practically snapping off its hinges as the person inside fought the debris on the floor to get it open. A figure fell out, catching itself on the nearest chair. I squinted. It was Dash – as bloodied and bruised as I was, but looking more alert than I felt.

'What happened?' I said, hearing my voice slur. 'Are we OK? Did we land? Where're we?'

He looked at me like I was insane. 'Land? Of course we didn't bloody land! Look at the fucking plane!'

I winced at the volume. My head felt like something was trying to dig its way through the soft flesh of my temple. What did he mean? I turned. The fire. I'd forgotten the fire. My brain cringed in pain. Looking around the plane it took me far longer than it should have to realise that we were also at an angle. That was why I was having trouble walking – the floor was slanting downwards towards the cockpit.

'We . . . crashed?' I managed. 'Where . . . Bryce!'

'You're bleeding – a lot,' Dash said, concern wiping the incredulity from his face. 'Come here, let me put something on your head . . .'

But I was already struggling away from him, looking for Bryce in the dark hollows between seats. Dash was moving around behind me, talking about the fire, but I didn't care about anything other than finding my boyfriend – fiancé, I remembered as my ring snagged on a seat. He had to be OK. He had to be.

'Bryce?' I called again, choking on a mouthful of caustic smoke.

'Li . . . la?' a voice croaked, and I spotted one of Bryce's feet, sticking out into the wide aisle. Like me, he'd ended up under a seat, but possibly on purpose. He was wedged in and trying to wriggle out.

'It's me, oh thank God you're all right.' I helped Bryce pull himself out and threw my arms around him. He hugged me back tightly and dizziness made my vision swim.

'I need you to help me here!' Dash yelled, and Bryce's attention snapped to him. I turned my head slowly, still feeling muddled, and saw Dash trying to pull a woman out of a seat. Her nose was bloody but she was moving weakly in his grip. I recognised her as the Australian with the loud laugh.

'Planes are full of fuel, dammit!' Dash shouted at us. 'This thing could explode – we have to get everyone off!'

It was as if my head had been wrapped in cotton wool, deadening everything, and he'd just stripped it away. Panic, true and total, swept through me. My skin went cold despite the fire and heat of the air. I started to shake so hard that my teeth clashed together.

'Move!' Dash yelled, and I flinched into action.

With Bryce scrambling along behind me, we reached Dash and he handed off the woman with the bloody nose.

'Get her out, and help me with the rest. We can't leave anyone behind,' he said, his hand shaking as he pushed his hair off his face.

Dash immediately moved on to the next person he could see but after checking them he left them in their seat. I turned away, stomach swooping with nausea. It was just starting to hit me. We'd crashed. I had been in a plane crash.

How many people were alive? How many were . . . and

where even were we? Was help coming? Why couldn't I hear sirens?

My thoughts were racing, making up for lost time as between us Bryce and I carried the Australian woman to the side door, the beads on her dress catching on my crocheted one. The door was already open, hanging at a drunken angle and below an inflatable yellow slide was half lost in dark bushes. Rain pattered over its surface. Had someone already gotten out? Where were they? I couldn't see anyone below and no one called out to us.

'Take her.' Bryce shoved the woman at me. 'I'm going back.'

'But . . .'

'Get her down there,' he called over his shoulder, already climbing back into the plane.

I looked down the slide. If I went down there I didn't know if I'd be able to get back up into the plane to help. But I couldn't just throw the woman down on her own. I struggled to manoeuvre with her weight in my arms, but managed to sort of collapse onto the slide arse first, with her on top of me. We slid down the plastic, which was already slick from the rain. At the bottom I tucked her off to the side so the next person down wouldn't hit her.

As I did so I spotted a leg sticking out of the bushes nearby. I reached out and touched it, trying to get the person's attention, but there was no response. I crawled over to take a proper look and found the body of a man – the buff American who'd been talking to that shy girl – lying in the bushes, face down. If he'd been the one to open the door and set the emergency slide off, he hadn't gotten far. Feeling bile burn in my throat, I crawled back to the woman.

65

She groaned as I tried to take her pulse. But she seemed OK otherwise. Nothing obviously broken and her nose was the only thing bleeding. As I stood up my vision swam and the earth seemed to lurch under me. My left eye burned and I wiped at it, only to have blood smear on my fingers. It was running from my head, down my face. I had nothing to mop myself up with, so I just dashed the blood away with my hand and wiped it on my dress.

There was no hope of climbing back up the slippery slide. I looked down the length of the plane and nearly sagged to the ground in shock. The rest of the plane wasn't there. It had sheared off and I couldn't see any sign of it in the darkness. Either it wasn't on fire or it was too far away to see.

The front section ended in a ragged edge, tilted up from the ground where the nose had ploughed into the earth. Flames ringed the torn metal, hissing and fighting the rain, and there were pieces of flaming debris on the ground. The air was full of cinders and sparks, between which giant moths and insects flitted about, drawn to the heat and light, avoiding the rain. Above me there was only darkness and the pinpricks of stars. Around me the jungle was like a wall of blackness, dense and impenetrable. The ground was uneven and covered in leaves, roots and plants. Not a single suggestion of a path anywhere. Aside from the alien whoops and shrieks of animals, and the patter of water, I could hear nothing. No sirens or traffic, not one solitary car horn in the distance.

Wherever we were, it wasn't near Phuket. It wasn't near anything at all.

'Help! Help me!'

I jumped as a voice rang out from the darkness nearby.

It was a man, though his voice was shrill with strain. I left the woman where she was and went stumbling towards the voice, which was coming from the front of the plane. I staggered over roots and fallen logs. Something scuttled over my bare toes and I kicked out, whimpering. I teetered as fast as I could, unable to see anything in the darkness. As I got closer to the voice – which was still grunting and crying out – I heard falling glass and the whine of metal under pressure.

I came to a stop at the front of the plane, where the nose was crumpled into the ground. The cockpit windows were smashed in, and a fresh shower of glass rained down on me as the thick trunk that jutted through the window swayed under the weight of the plane. It had passed through the window and, judging from the angle, it was being torn out of the ground as gravity tried to force the plane into the earth.

I saw a flash of white and as my eyes adjusted to the darkness I realised that it was an arm. The pilot – John – was reaching up, clutching at the air. I heard him sob, and my chest went tight. He was hurt. Badly. I could hear it in his voice.

'Oh my God . . .' My own voice startled me, and before I knew it I was scrambling over the crumpled nose of the plane, climbing towards the window. Something had taken over me and whether it was shock or desperation I didn't know. I just knew I had to reach him. I couldn't do nothing.

'Lila!' Bryce called, from the doorway, a man's arm slung about his shoulders. 'What are you doing?'

'The pilot!' I shouted back. 'He's alive! We have to get him out!'

Dash appeared beside Bryce and looked over at me. 'Can't get the door open from outside without a code – security precautions! He has to tell us what it is, or open it himself. Otherwise you'll have to break the window and climb in the front to use the internal handle!'

I was already doing it. I reached the shattered windshield and found a jagged hole, climbing up and sliding through, feet first. My high heels scrabbled on the console, catching on buttons, switches and broken glass. I slithered in, dress rucking up and my legs scraping over the debris. When my feet hit the floor, I flopped onto my back on the console and had to roll off to the side.

As I stood up, staggering, I caught sight of John's white shirt in the darkness. He was in his seat, and the tree was jutting through the window in the dead centre of the cockpit. It had only missed him by inches. He turned his head and groaned as I passed him.

'OK . . . it's OK, I'm getting help,' I stuttered, as I stumbled to the door and unlatched it. John would know what to do, once we'd helped him out of the cockpit. He'd been in the air force or something and they trained for this, right? He'd be able to tell us what to do, how to get out of here.

I turned back. As the light from the fire threw the cockpit into relief, I saw John clearly, and screamed.

Chapter 8

The tree hadn't missed him.

The trunk had, but not the branches, one of which was stuck straight through his chest, pinning him to the seat. I was still gaping at him when Dash and Bryce shouldered through the door and stopped short.

'Jesus,' Bryce hissed. 'Oh holy fuck.'

Dash just stared, speechless. Trapped in his seat, John sucked in a wet breath and more blood welled out of his chest wound. His formerly white uniform was soaked with it and his face was grey. He gulped at the air and looked at us with wide, staring eyes. Desperate.

'We need . . .' I faltered, feeling the urge to act but not knowing how. It felt like there were needles stabbing the backs of my eyes and I couldn't make my vision stop swaying. I met John's terrified eyes and felt tears prickling in mine. 'Pressure, right? To slow down the . . . the bleeding?'

'There's a tree through his chest,' Bryce said, like he was in shock. 'There's . . . he's done right? He's cooked.'

Dash didn't move. I cast about and spotted John's jacket on the other seat. I snatched it up and shook the broken glass off it, then hesitantly wrapped it around the branch. When I pressed down on it, John's breath hissed out of him in a long sigh. His eyes closed and for a horrible moment I thought he was dead. A tiny sliver of relief worked its way through my chest, that it was over, that he wasn't in pain, but then he blinked his eyes open and looked at me.

'How . . . bad is it? The plane?' he wheezed.

'It's um . . . it broke in half. I couldn't see the back when I was outside. It might have dropped before we hit the ground,' I said hesitantly, looking back at Dash and Bryce. 'He can't stay like this; we need to get him out of here!'

'He'll bleed to death.' Dash, apparently having found his voice, shook his head slowly, eyes fixed on John's bloody chest. 'We pull that out, he's dead for sure.'

John coughed and I whipped my head back around in time to see blood leaking out of his mouth. 'Need . . . to find the tail.'

'What?' I realised blood was soaking into the jacket, getting on my hands. He was bleeding so heavily. Dash was right – he was going to die. My thoughts shuddered to a halt at that. He was going to die right in front of me. Oh God. He wasn't even old, his hair barely turning grey at the temples.

'Listen,' John wheezed, one hand grabbing at my arm weakly. Like he knew he didn't have much longer. 'The . . . there's no black box, in the nose. It's . . . in the tail. Find, the tail.'

'Black box . . .' I repeated, but I wasn't sure what he meant. Wasn't that just to record stuff that happened during the flight?

70

'He's saying there's no tracker in this part of the plane,' Dash said. When I looked at him, his face was ashen under its tan. 'If anyone's looking to trace the plane, they'll find the tail, not us.'

John nodded slightly and his tongue writhed as he fought to speak again.

'Shhhh, don't, it's OK,' I said, because just watching him struggle was making me tear up, desperation bubbling up inside me. But John shook his head violently and grabbed for me again.

'No . . . plan,' he wheezed, so quiet now that I struggled to hear him. 'The tail . . .'

What did he mean 'no plan'? He didn't know what we were meant to do now? He didn't have a plan to get us out of this? I was kind of blindsided by how selfless he was being. John was dying and he was only thinking about us.

He choked, and I tried to tip his head forward, to empty his mouth of blood. But as I was cupping his face, I felt him . . . go.

I'd probably been in shock since I woke up, but that just threw me further down the black hole. My hand fell bonelessly back to my side and I just looked at him. He was dead. That word throbbed in my head in time to the pain in my skull. Dead, dead, dead, dead . . .

'Stop it!'

I was jolted back to myself as Bryce shook my shoulder. I'd been saying it, I realised. Repeating the word 'dead' over and over as my brain misfired, attempting to get itself back into gear.

'Sorry,' I said, the word sort of startled out of me. 'He's . . .'

'Dead, yeah.' Dash reached out and took the jacket from John's chest, laying it over his face. 'We need to look for anyone else who's still alive.'

'You said we might blow up,' Bryce said, a challenge in his voice.

'So find a fire extinguisher and try to stop the plane burning . . . or hurry up and get everyone off who's not fucking dead,' Dash snapped, shouldering past him.

I automatically moved to follow him and Bryce caught my arm, holding me back. 'He's not in charge, you know. It's your plane.'

The idea of being in charge right now, in the middle of all this mess, made me want to scream. If Dash wanted to take control of the situation I would gladly let him. At least he seemed to know what he was doing. I still felt like I was half in a nightmare, blundering about from one horror to the next.

'Just . . . do what he says,' I said. 'We need to help anyone who . . . anyone who's left.' I wished I had my phone, but it was lost with my bag, somewhere in the plane. I knew it wasn't likely to have signal but I knew I wouldn't fully believe that until I was holding it. Everything in me was screaming that I needed to call for help.

I followed after Dash and went from seat to seat, keeping my eyes open for my bag, a phone, or a fire extinguisher. Not that one would do much good against the blaze. I could only hope that the fuel was mostly in the other section. Though if that blew up, would it take the black box with it? If that happened we'd be screwed.

'Take her.' Dash handed a woman off to me and nudged me towards the door.

'And come back through the cockpit?' I asked, recognising Janet, the flight attendant as she was dumped in my arms.

'There's no point. No one else,' Dash said, voice like the broken glass raining down, sharp and cold. 'Get out of here and get back, just in case.'

My heart was in my stomach as I dragged Janet towards the door and the slide. Dash was behind me, picking up handbags and anything else that was lying around. I guessed to check for anything we could use. Bryce wasn't on the plane. I saw him as we came down the slide, standing at the bottom and waiting. Every movement made my headache worse. It felt like something was eating its way out of my skull.

The other woman I'd brought out was right where I left her. And I laid Janet out beside her. As I did so I noticed for the first time that there was a belt around her thigh and her red uniform skirt was soaked with blood. I'd always thought of her as being a real adult compared to me, but she was probably barely thirty. At some point she must have been crying; her mascara was all over her cheeks.

'She must have been cut on something: glass, metal,' Dash said, appearing beside me. 'My belt should hold it for a bit.'

'There's just the five of us?' I asked, glancing down at the man I'd seen before, dead in the bushes.

'Not sure. I heard people, maybe they got themselves out. It was a bit blurry for a while before I managed to get out of the toilet. The door jammed when we started to fall.' Dash was looking around us at the dense jungle, brow furrowed. 'Stay here and take care of them. I'll take what's-his-name and check.'

'Bryce,' Bryce enunciated clearly, but went with Dash even though he was clearly ignoring him.

I wasn't sure what to do on my own. But it didn't seem like a good idea to keep Janet and the other woman in the undergrowth near the . . . body. So I dragged them one by one to a clearer area a little way back, where the ground was mostly dry and shielded from the light rain. All that was left of the storm that had done this to us.

Janet was unconscious, but the other woman's eyes were open. She was shivering, the beads on her dress clicking together, and she didn't respond to me when I asked her name or if she was hurt anywhere else. I guessed she was in shock and hoped I was right. That or she was injured internally and I had no way of helping her.

I found a patch of burning debris and pulled a smouldering branch from the flames. There were plenty of dry leaves around, and I kicked them together with my sandaled feet before dumping the branch on top and waving vaguely to try and get the leaves to catch. At least that was something I could do. Even I could make fire from fire. I brought my hands up to my head and held it, trying to fight off a wave of nausea.

The other woman stirred as I was whimpering in pain and, when I glanced her way, I saw the white was glistening all the way around her eye – like the meat of a lychee. In the light of the fire I could see a crusted trail of blood and snot under her nose, and tear tracks through her foundation, smearing glitter down her face.

'Hey,' I said softly, frightened myself by the sheer animal terror on her face. 'You're OK. You're out of the plane . . . what's your name?'

It was just a throwaway question, the first one I could

think of. She'd ignored it before but now it seemed to focus her slightly and she started to breathe at a more normal rate.

'Summer?' she said, like it was a question. Her strong accent at work.

'OK, Summer. I'm Lila. You're not hurt anywhere, are you? I don't think you are but, if you're in any pain . . .'

I wasn't really sure what I could do if that was the case. I was honestly just talking rubbish, trying to feel my way through the situation. I didn't even know if the plane had a first-aid kit, let alone where it might be. Or how to use what was in it. I didn't even like watching medical dramas on TV and I'd certainly never learned anything as useful as CPR. Unless someone was overdosing on pills and needed to be forced to throw up, I didn't have any tips or tricks for situations like this. I wanted my phone more than ever – there was so much stuff I needed to google.

Summer shook her head, thankfully. 'Not hurt, just hit my face . . . We crashed?'

'We did,' I confirmed stupidly and reached up to cradle my aching head. I must have really smacked it good. I swore I could actually feel a dent under the blood.

I heard a rustling and jerked around to find Dash and Bryce returning, followed by a rag-tag group of people. Shockingly few people.

I recognised Bethan and Fletcher, who were carrying Kaitlyn between them. It looked like she'd hit her head, just like me. She also had a swollen eye and cuts on her face. Bryce was supporting the young Thai man (whose shirt was back on but unbuttoned) with the help of a broad, blond guy I didn't recognise. The shy woman struggled along beside them, limping on an injured leg. There was no one else.

'Fire, that's a good call,' Dash muttered, as everyone clustered round. Kaitlyn and the injured man were set down by Summer and Janet. 'We've got a sprained, possibly broken ankle on Araya here—' he indicated the young Thai woman – God she looked barely nineteen – and then the shirtless man Bryce had been carrying '— San'ya fell as the plane was coming down, might have a cracked rib or two from the fall. And this one's taken a blow to the head.'

This last was directed at Kaitlyn, who seemed barely conscious. My skull throbbed in sympathy.

'We should be careful of concussion,' the blond guy – German or Austrian, from the sound of it – pointed out. 'Is there a medical kit on the plane?'

'I don't know,' I said. 'John would . . . we'll have to ask Janet, when she wakes up.'

If she woke up, I didn't say. But I think we all heard it.

'That's it?' I asked, looking at the few anxious and bloodied faces gathered around the fire.

'Unless there were people in the other section . . . yeah. This is it,' Dash confirmed. 'And I doubt they made it if there were.'

Silence hung over us for a few seconds. Then the blond man spoke again.

'I'll go look for the kit. We should stitch that.' He gestured to Janet's leg.

'You a doctor?' Bryce asked, sceptically. The guy didn't seem old enough to be out of training, and Bryce always got a bit funny about smart people with degrees and good jobs.

'A nurse.'

Bryce sniffed, derisively. 'Go on then – there must be something on the plane.'

The guy just nodded and left, walking carefully but quickly over the uneven ground, towards the rear of the nose section. I looked between his retreating back and Dash's grim expression. At least we had Dash and someone who knew about injuries and stuff. My head was killing me and Janet needed serious help.

'So there's a rescue coming, right?' Fletcher said, looking up from Kaitlyn, who was bundled into his lap. 'Your pilot, he sent out a distress signal or whatever.'

I wet my lips, but it was Dash who answered. 'The pilot's dead. He told us the beacon's in the tail section – and we don't know where that is.'

'So no one can find us?' Summer asked, shrill with panic. A general muttering of unease passed over us.

Dash held up his hands for calm. 'They might not know exactly where we are, but the route we were taking will be on the flight plan the pilot filed. They'll know where to start searching, roughly.'

I thought of what John had said – about the 'plan' and shivered.

'There's . . .' the words 'no plan' stuck in my throat. Looking around at the group, their wide, frightened eyes reflecting the fire, I felt the back of my neck prickle. Did I really want to be the one to give them bad news right now?

'Lila?' Dash was looking at me. They were all looking at me, because I'd started talking and then just stopped. 'What is it?'

I swallowed, hard. 'There's . . . no plan. John said so before he . . . he just said there wasn't one.'

A quick flash of panic passed over Dash's face, smoothed away in a second. But I'd seen it. We were fucked.

'What kind of idiot pilot doesn't do a flight plan?' Fletcher demanded. 'How the hell else are we meant to get rescued?'

'There wasn't time,' I said, automatically, and that was met with dead silence. Shit.

'So it's your fault,' a strained voice said. I flinched. It was Summer, but she wasn't the only one thinking it. I could feel everyone's eyes on me. Feel the blame searing into my skin. I saw that her eyes were brimming over with tears. 'You did this.'

'I didn't know this was going to happen!' I said, the unfairness of it prickling over my skin along with the accusing gazes of the other passengers. 'Do you know how many times I've flown in that thing and it's always been fine? It's safer than driving!'

'Tell that to everyone else.' That was San'ya – the man who'd fallen from the plane.

'A flight plan wouldn't have stopped us crashing,' Bryce snapped, wrapping a protective arm around my shoulders.

'But it might have stopped us dying in the jungle.' San'ya folded his arms over his chest and glared.

'No one made you get on the plane,' Fletcher said, coldly furious. 'You're the one who decided it sounded like fun to grab a free ride to a stranger's party. That's hardly anyone else's fault.'

'Because we thought you knew what you were doing,' Araya cried. 'You never said you were going to put us in danger!'

The bickering rolled over me, all the voices blurring

together as my skull ached. The pain was getting worse and I could hardly breathe for the nausea. I felt like I was about to pass out again. They were right – it was my fault. I'd told John the flight plan didn't matter. I might not have caused the storm, and John might not have seen any reason to be concerned by it. But without a flight plan we were screwed and that was all on me.

Bryce bristled at San'ya. 'Why don't you take your ungrateful attitude and . . .'

A colossal boom tore through the rest of whatever Bryce was about to say. The jungle lit up for a fraction of a second, bright as day. A wave of hot air blew over us like a breath from a giant's foul mouth and the leaves and debris flew past.

Then, the screaming started.

Chapter 9

Bethan, Summer and I screamed, setting off a chain reaction of howls and whoops in the jungle. Bryce yelled loud enough to half deafen me, and Dash was already moving, skirting the plane but rounding it to have a look at where the explosion had happened. After the one flash it didn't seem like the fire was spreading. But it had been so loud and so sudden that I was still reeling from it. I didn't even think about what it might mean before Dash was running back.

'He's . . . dead,' he panted. 'Don't go over there.'

I imagined what he must have seen, and shuddered. That poor man had just gone over there, trying to help and now . . . Whatever it was, leftover fuel or a bottle or container that overheated, it had killed him in a second.

'Does anyone know his name?' Summer asked.

All eyes were suddenly on me. Like I should know. But I'd just invited whoever wanted to come. I'd never even spoken to half the people on the plane. I hadn't even recognised the guy when he turned up with Bryce and the rest of them.

'I don't know. Are you sure he's . . .'

Dash nodded, face set into grim lines. 'I couldn't get near enough to check his pulse, but . . . I didn't need to.'

I didn't ask for more details and neither did anyone else. I think we were all certain that we'd be happier not knowing. If any state out there could be described as 'happy'. I mean, we'd all just survived a plane crash and yet I don't think anyone around that fire felt particularly lucky.

'We should be OK back here,' Dash said, after long moments of fearful silence. 'Just . . . no one else go near the plane until the fire's gone out.'

I didn't think anyone was going to be in a hurry to go over there. But there was still the question of how we were going to help the injured without a first-aid kit. When nobody said anything, just kept looking to Dash for answers, I cleared my throat.

'Maybe there's stuff in the bags we can use?' I said, gesturing to the pile of handbags that Dash had been scooping up as we left the plane. There were quite a few – many of the passengers must have been women. I hadn't really paid much attention to who was coming along. I'd just been so excited and hyped up. Not to mention drunk and a little high.

Dash picked up a bag and started going through it without a word. I reached for one near Summer and she angrily swatted at my hands.

'I'll do it!'

'That's my bag,' Bethan snapped and snatched it away from her. 'And don't keep getting at Lila – we're all scared, we're all bruised and battered but it's not her fault we crashed, OK? It just happened. She's stuck here too.'

I felt a little flutter of gratitude for Bethan's defence of me, even if she didn't look at me while she said it. I got it, honestly. She was probably just as scared and angry as Summer was, but she wasn't about to let her attack me for it. It wasn't really about protecting me so much as keeping the normals in their place. Staying in control.

Slowly we all picked up bags, except for the unconscious Kaitlyn and Janet. The men went through their pockets too and we piled anything we could use into the largest bag, a very touristy nylon backpack. I searched bags and tried not to let on that my head was hurting so much that I could hardly stand having my eyes open. I didn't want to set Summer off again by looking for sympathy.

Slowly, the bag filled up with water bottles, painkillers, blister plasters, lighters and other essentials. We tried each mobile phone we came across and not one of them had signal, most of them had been smashed up in the crash or had run out of battery thanks to the long night spent clubbing. We also had a whole lot of cash and lots of plastic – credit and debit cards, IDs and membership cards.

'We should keep one of each,' Araya said, holding out a manicured hand for the IDs as we uncovered them. 'So we can show the police and their families will know what happened.'

We all nodded and started handing them over, but I glanced at the still-burning plane and wondered how many wallets and bags were still on there. Potentially being lost even as we spoke.

'Don't you have anything useful?' Fletcher asked Dash, pointedly. 'You're "Mr Outdoors" after all. Where's your Swiss Army knife and your GPS unit?'

'I have stuff; I just don't tend to bring it to night clubs,' Dash said flatly. 'But there's this.'

He unclasped a braided bracelet from his wrist. It looked like it was made out of plaited nylon rope and there was a little plastic compass on it.

'Very useful. I feel safer already,' Fletcher said, rolling his eyes.

Dash ignored him and started to pull the rope apart, unbraiding the bracelet and coiling the resultant rope up. There was quite a long length once it was all unknotted, which I supposed was the point. As he undid the bracelet, though, a long silver filament separated out, with loops on either end. The clasp, free of the rope, had a silvery bit of metal on it. Dash finished with the rope and held up the items one by one.

'Compass, rope, steel striker for making fire and a survival saw.'

Fletcher's lip curled, but he didn't say anything. I was impressed actually. The most my bangles did was fold down into a ring. Even if all the lighters we'd found ran out of fuel, we'd still be able to make fire. That was a relief. It was scary how quickly I'd reverted to that cavemanish fear of the dark. But out here it wasn't exactly like wandering through my New York penthouse at midnight to grab some water from the fridge.

'Can you use this to stitch wounds?' Summer was holding up some waxed dental floss.

'That would work, but we haven't got anything like a needle.' Dash frowned. 'Not even a fish hook, which'd do in a pinch.'

'Sorry, I don't tend to bring my fishing gear to the club,' Fletcher muttered.

Dash ignored him. 'Do we have anything like dressings, closure strips, plasters?'

'Blister plasters . . . but they're not big enough to close that.' Bethan gestured at Janet and the six-inch wound on her leg.

'What about glue? They use superglue in war films.' San'ya suddenly gasped, holding his side. His ribs were obviously causing him a lot of pain.

'Anyone happen to have some spare superglue in their pockets?' Bryce muttered, earning himself a smirk from Fletcher.

'Here.' I held out a tube of nail glue I'd found in one of the handbags. 'It's basically superglue, right?'

Dash nodded and took it from me. It didn't take long for him to rinse Janet's leg with bottled water and apply the glue, pinching the wound shut until it stuck that way. It wasn't pretty but it did stop bleeding.

'At least nothing'll get into it.' Dash sighed. 'Right . . . let's get those ribs wrapped up. I need fabric or . . .'

'Tit tape!' Bethan held it up triumphantly. 'Probably wouldn't hold a wound closed but, you can wrap it around his chest.'

Dash manoeuvred San'ya's shirt off and we all collectively winced at the sight of the bruises already blooming across his skin. It looked like he'd lost a fight with a gorilla. Dash wrapped his ribs as best he could and then moved on to check Araya's ankle and wrap that too. When he tried to look at Kaitlyn, still lying motionless in Fletcher's lap, Fletcher batted him away.

'I'm taking care of her – I'm her boyfriend.'

'She has a head wound,' Dash pointed out.

'So give me the glue and I'll stick it shut. It's hardly rocket science.'

Dash looked like he wanted to argue, but Bryce

handed the glue over to Fletcher and that was the end of that. Summer at least, like Bethan, only had scrapes and bruises. So Dash finally turned to me.

'How're you doing? You're not bleeding as much.'

'I think it's stopping on its own,' I said, wincing as I probed near the area and felt the newly forming scab pull tight. 'My head hurts like hell though. I think I smacked it on the bar.'

'Could be a concussion. You feel sick?' Dash asked.

'She's drunk, of course she feels sick,' Bryce said, before I could say anything. 'Just leave it. I'll take care of you, OK, babe?' He moved in closer and put his arm around me protectively, but I noticed he was looking Fletcher's way, not at me. Apparently he was taking his lead from his online hero. Obviously Dash wasn't one of his favourites anymore, given how dismissive he'd been of him earlier.

'Fine,' Dash sighed. 'But . . . try not to go to sleep, OK?'

I nodded, then winced as my scalp pulled. All I wanted to do was lie down and shut my eyes, but under the circumstances I doubted sleep would come easily.

'I suppose we wait for morning and try and find the tail,' Dash said, looking around at the group. 'It's probably obvious where it is and we can work out where it landed by the orientation of the nose here . . . Once we have the black box we'll be rescued. Eventually.'

'How eventually?' Bethan asked. 'I have a product launch in two weeks. I'm going to need that long just to get over what the stress of all this is going to do to my skin.'

Summer scoffed, not particularly quietly, and Bethan shot daggers in her direction. Summer just glared back, unflinching. Fletcher jumped on to the end of Bethan's question.

'I'm booked solid next week for a podcast and a news panel.'

'My mother needs me,' Araya said softly. 'She can barely walk.'

Dash held up his hands. 'I don't know, OK!? I have no fucking idea how long it's going to take, or even if someone out there knows we crashed. We're just going to have to wait and see.'

Silence greeted his outburst and Dash rubbed a hand over his face in obvious frustration. 'Look . . . I know I'm known for this stuff, for hiking my way across countries and all that, but there's a big difference between preparing to go on a long jungle hike, and being dropped into the wilderness with basically no warning. This is the worst-case scenario and we are not prepared, we are not trained and we all need to be working together . . . or we're screwed. OK?'

Several people nodded, myself included. I noticed Bryce and Fletcher sharing a look and tried to ignore it. If they wanted to act like they knew better that was fine. As long as they 'let' Dash make most of the decisions. Him I trusted. The rest of us? We were all just as clueless as each other.

Chapter 10

I tried not to sleep. You'd think it would be hard to drop off anyway, what with the adrenaline from the crash and the dangers of the jungle at the forefront of my mind. But my head wound had other ideas. Leaning against Bryce near the fire, I couldn't fight the throbbing in my skull that dragged me down into sleep. Despite our surroundings and the discomfort and danger, I didn't wake up until Bryce got up to go to the toilet in the trees. By then, it was morning.

I felt dreadful still. Hungover, definitely and possibly coming down off whatever was in that kratom. A massive bruise had come up on my head, and every move I made seemed to pull at the scabby lump and the hair matted down into the dried blood. I winced at every turn, feeling like my hair was coming out at the root. My thoughts were all shaken up still and my headache only got worse when I tried to focus.

The sunlight filtering in through the dense canopy overhead was muted and green. The dappled shadows made it hard to tell what was the shifting of leaves and what was something more, moving about in the jungle.

I saw birds flitting about overhead and not too far from where we were sleeping, a huge spider was moving slowly across the ground. I shuddered and kept my eyes on it until it was far away and out of sight. The idea of it crawling on me while I slept made me feel physically ill. My skin itched all over as if thousands of scuttling legs were touching me.

God only knew how many snakes and bugs and dangerous wild animals were lurking out there. I didn't know much about the wildlife in Thailand – it wasn't like I'd planned on schlepping through the jungle – but I had seen elephant sanctuaries online and wasn't in a hurry to get trampled to death by an angry herd of them. The other thing I knew about, was tigers. They featured on the websites, in the hashtags for Thailand online and on adverts at the villa entrance. I knew they were endangered but how endangered? Just how many of them were prowling around out there, with empty bellies and sharp teeth?

'Where's Dash?' Bryce asked, coming back from the treeline, still doing up his flies.

I looked around at the sleeping shapes near the embers and realised Dash wasn't among them. Panic hit my heart like a spider had just walked over my bare leg. Where was he? He was our one resource out here and he'd just wandered off? My temples throbbed with stress and pain. Damn it.

I got to my feet and staggered slightly, still a little wobbly. But at least the sickness had faded, to be replaced by the more manageable hangover. As I turned around to look into the trees, I heard a rattling noise and saw a bundle roll down the emergency slide on the side of the plane. At the top of the slide, Dash nodded to us, and then vanished back into the plane.

'Guess the fire's out,' Bryce muttered. 'Wonder if that guy's . . . still there.'

I shivered. 'Don't look, please. I don't want to know what happened.'

Bryce didn't contradict me, just shrugged and went over to the slide and picked up the bundle Dash had thrown down. It was a jacket, wrapped around some boxes of snack packets. He must have gone through the stuff stored under the bar. Another bundle rolled down the slide, this one containing some bottles of water and tonic collected into a red blazer that I recognised as flight crew uniform.

I bent to pick up the waters and carry them over to the unofficial campsite we'd set up. As I went, I winced at how damp my dress and hair felt – clammy with dew and sweat. I was also dotted in red welts from insect bites, which had started to itch infuriatingly. I guessed we'd all be in the same boat in that regard.

Fletcher woke up as we came over and I was relieved to see Kaitlyn blinking her eyes open, despite the massive bruise on her face. She was at least awake and seemed to know where she was. Judging purely from how afraid she looked. Summer woke too, and sat up, her face morphing in despair as she took in her surroundings.

'Breakfast?' Bryce offered the snack packs of pretzels and peanuts around. Summer took a packet without speaking to him, and practically turned her back to eat. The others were all stirring, woken by the light and the activity around them. I heard Dash come down the slide and tramp up behind us.

'Everyone needs to eat and drink plenty of water,' he instructed. 'Dehydration is a real risk in this climate and it will kill you before you even know what's happening.'

We passed bottles around and I watched Araya gently shake Janet awake. She at least looked less deathly pale this morning. Hopefully the nail glue was keeping her wound from reopening and bleeding again.

'Bethan, get up,' Fletcher snapped, nudging her with his foot. His overly gelled hair was stuck up in crispy clumps and he swiped at them in irritation as they flopped against his face. Bethan was curled up quite far from the fire, and her all white outfit was now yellow and black all over from the dirt and soot smuts, the feather trim ratty and bedraggled. She was going to be pissed.

'Beth, you need to drink something.' Kaitlyn reached out and shook her arm, recoiling with a gasp of horror. 'Beth!'

Dash was up and over to that side of the fire in an instant. No one else dared move. But I think we all knew. We all felt it. Something was very wrong.

Dash rolled Bethan over and we all saw immediately, that she was not only dead, but had been for a while. She was pale, greyish and her eyes were open and unreactive. But there wasn't a mark on her other than the scratches from the crash.

Somewhere deep inside my chest, I felt something snap. The last threads holding my hopes together perhaps. Maybe just my fragile calm. Either way I couldn't help it. A sob burst out of me and after that there was no stopping it. I clasped a hand over my mouth and cried. There was no one thing that triggered it. It was just everything.

Everything we'd been through falling on top of me like a shower of bricks.

'She wasn't even hurt,' Araya whispered as they all sat there in total stillness, waiting for signs of life that weren't coming. 'What happened?'

'I heard her get up – to go pee,' Summer said finally. 'It was dark and it sounded like she hurt herself on something, or tripped, but she came back.' Her voice rose defensively. 'She was fine! I figured she'd just stepped on a stone or something.'

'What the hell happened to her?' Fletcher rounded on Dash for an explanation.

'I don't know.' Dash held his hands up. 'There's a lot of dangerous stuff out here, could have been anything.'

'And she didn't notice or make a sound?' Fletcher was pale around the edges of his too-orange makeup, which he'd half sweated off. 'What if it happens to us? We can't just sit around waiting to start dropping like . . .'

Kaitlyn shrieked. A piercing, hysterical noise. We all drew back from her on instinct and I watched her scramble away on all fours, huge eyes fixed on Bethan's body. She struggled to her feet and hid behind Fletcher, who tried to push her away.

We were all looking around, between Kaitlyn and Bethan. Confusion and fear turned acidic in my mouth. My heart was skipping in my chest, the blood pounding under my bruised skull. Then Summer saw it.

'Oh my God!' She tripped backwards, flinging up a hand to point.

I looked and saw only leaf litter and Bethan's body – her angelic white outfit covered in smuts and dirt. Then it moved. A black shape that had been sticking out of her skirt, in the shadow of her thigh. It's tongue flickered and then the shape was sliding out from under Bethan's clothes – slithering across the ground.

Bryce grabbed my hand and pulled me backwards. Dash swore and I watched as San'ya's mouth fell open in shock.

I wasn't a snake expert, but I'd seen cobras in films before. The shape of their heads, fanned out and curved. Kaitlyn was sobbing and clinging to Fletcher as he tried to back away from her or from the snake I had no idea. We all shrank back, watching as the snake looped its way out of the clearing, apparently sick of us and our noise.

My shoulders sagged with relief once it was out of sight. Bryce didn't let go of my hand and I was grateful. The cold tide of shock was still rising through me. We'd been right next to her body, all night. That snake had been right fucking there with us.

Dash was the first to break the silence. 'She . . . must've stood on it or something. Rolled over in her sleep maybe. Could have bitten her and she wouldn't have felt it; those bites numb up almost immediately.'

There was a stunned silence as we all absorbed that. Bethan had been fatally bitten and hadn't even woken up.

'Why was it . . . doing that?' Kaitlyn whimpered. 'Hiding in her clothes?'

'Probably the warmth,' Dash said, reluctantly. 'Might have been drawn to the heat from the fires and then, when they went out . . .'

'It could have been any of us then.' Fletcher looked around, eyes darting in panic as if more snakes might appear from nowhere. 'We should have kept watch for . . . You didn't say there were snakes!' he accused Dash.

'Yeah, there are snakes in the jungle,' San'ya said, in a 'well duh' tone, apparently getting over his shocked silence. 'Scorpions and giant centipedes too.'

'Giant . . . ? How giant?' Fletcher asked, panicking.

San'ya shrugged. 'I don't know, like as long as this.' He held up his forearm. 'When it rains too hard they come into houses and get in your shoes. Bite hurts like hell. But to kill like that?' He looked at Bethan and shuddered. 'Cobras are the worst for sure.'

'Happens in Aus too,' Summer murmured, like she was trapped in a nightmare.

'Either it was too fast or she was too drunk but . . .' Dash sat back and regarded us all, grimly. 'At least she didn't know it was happening. That was probably a kindness.'

It didn't feel particularly kind at that moment.

Bryce stroked his thumb over my knuckles but it was a small comfort. I felt wrung out, scraped raw by the drugs and the hangover, beaten and bruised by what we'd been through since taking off. And it still wasn't over. We were in the middle of nowhere and as far as we knew, no one was coming to save us.

Dash remained stooped over Bethan for a while. I couldn't see if he was crying or maybe just checking for any further signs of a snakebite. But as my tears subsided I saw him set his shoulders and nod as if to himself, before he turned back to us.

'I think the plane's going to offer the best shelter,' Dash continued. 'So, we clear that out, make sure it's as secure as possible and then . . . we need to work out who's going to look for the tail. Because we need to get that black box as soon as possible.'

'Why can't we all go?' Bryce asked. 'If people are already looking for it we're better off going to wherever it landed, right?'

'I can't walk on this ankle,' Araya sniffled.

'And my leg is not up to standing at the moment, let alone walking,' Janet pointed out, having just downed most of a bottle of water. She was sweating a lot, I noticed, and hoped it was due to the heat and not down to infection.

Bryce rolled his eyes. 'OK so we carry you. Why do any of us have to stay here?'

Fletcher was nodding. 'It's stupid to split up. We should . . .'

'It's because we don't know where the tail is,' Dash interrupted, earning himself a black look from Fletcher. 'I was conscious for most of the crash, but I can't say for sure how long it took between the tail breaking off and us landing here. It could be miles back, through dense jungle, with no paths. That's hard going and we have limited food and water. It makes sense for the bulk of the group to stay here and conserve their energy, while one or two of us go and retrieve the box.'

'So you're going then?' Fletcher delivered the challenge with a pointed sneer.

'I am.' Dash nodded. 'I have experience hiking in places like this.'

'All right, who else?' Fletcher turned to look around the group. 'Because I'm not hiking off to God knows where just to turn around and come all the way back for you lot.'

'You should stay and look after Kaitlyn anyway,' I said, annoyed by his whole attitude. Bethan was lying dead, only a few feet away, and he was acting like he didn't care. I could hardly tear my eyes off her.

'What about you?' Fletcher ignored me and turned on San'ya. 'You can go. You'll be fine out there.'

'Because I'm Thai?' San'ya challenged, looking amused and exasperated in equal measure. 'Like I know the jungle any better than you – I'm from Bangkok, fucker. Not the country.'

'You knew about the centipedes!' Kaitlyn jumped in to defend her boyfriend.

'Because they get into houses,' San'ya stressed. 'If a rat gets in your house, does that mean you know all about wildlife, or can climb a mountain in England?' he scoffed.

'I'm not leaving Lila,' Bryce said, and took my hand in his. I gave him a grateful look and he squeezed my fingers. 'I'd die if anything happened to you.'

'I'll go.'

We all turned to look at Summer, but she was still looking at Bethan.

'I'm fit, used to the heat. I'll go. Besides, I'm not staying here to die with her . . .' She stabbed an accusing finger at me and I flinched.

'She didn't crash the plane,' Kaitlyn said, in the silence that followed. 'If the pilot had been any good he'd have . . .'

'Can we just get on with it?' I said, not wanting to hash it all out, not with Bethan's cold unblinking eyes on me. 'The people who are staying, we'll clear the plane out; you should get going as soon as possible.'

'That's a good idea,' Dash admitted. 'Just be sure to put any uh . . . remains, as far as you can from the plane.'

Oh God. I winced. I didn't even want to think about

that. Dash nodded to San'ya, Bryce and Fletcher. 'I'll show you how to use my saw, then we'll leave. You'll need it to cut bamboo and wood for fires, or to build anything you might need.'

'What if something else happens while you're gone – something . . . worse?' Janet asked hesitantly. 'What do we do then?'

Bryce rolled his eyes and spoke over whatever Dash was about to say. 'We're already stuck here, babysitting you all. How much worse could it get?'

Fletcher snorted a laugh and Dash looked ready to argue, but I couldn't take any more delays.

'We'll be fine,' I said, trying to sound certain. 'I think what Bryce means is . . . we've had the worst of it now. Right?'

Chapter 11

Dash and Summer loaded up the backpack with some water and food while we all stood and watched. It had started to hit us, I think, that they were heading off into the jungle. Into the unknown tangle of plants and shadows outside of the clearing the plane had carved out. To travel God only knew how far through all the snakes and insects and potentially tigers and other stuff. Hiking for however long it took to find the rest of the plane. I was glad it wasn't me. Even the idea of staying at the plane was scary enough but going out there felt like a death sentence.

We could only pray that they would make it and then make it back. Because they were our only hope. A thought that solidified into a ball of heavy wet clay in my belly. Without that black box we'd never be found. Even the plane probably wouldn't be seen from the air, what with how the branches had sprung back into place after we crashed through. Only a small gap remained where the tree we'd hit had been torn up.

'We'll go as far as we can and mark the trail with this.' Dash held up a tube of bright red lipstick from one of the bags. 'I'll put a cross every fifty steps. That way you'll know where we went if you have to follow us.'

In case they didn't come back is what he didn't say.

'What if you don't find the rest of the plane?' Janet asked, the only one of us still seated, nursing her leg wound. Araya's injured ankle was at least holding enough weight for her to move around a bit.

'Then when we're mostly out of food, we'll head back – then try again in a different direction,' Dash said. 'It's really all we can do, right? Keep trying until we find a way out.'

'But we will find it,' Summer said, face set and determined. 'Whatever it takes. We'll find it and come back soon.'

'Good luck,' I said, and meant it. But Summer just gave me a look and turned away. She obviously still blamed me for everything that had happened. I blamed myself too, for my part in it. I hadn't caused the crash but I had made it worse, and I'd been the one to invite everyone along for the ride. This was all my idea.

They headed off from the broken end of the plane. Dash figured if they walked straight from it, using his compass to stay on track, they'd eventually find the tail. It was only as I watched them go that I really processed that it wasn't a sure thing that they would find it at all. What if it had carried on after the front end nosedived? What if it had ended up in a crevasse or smashed into a mountain where they couldn't reach it? What if the black box had blown up in another fuel explosion? How much punishment could that box take before it stopped working? What if it had fallen into a river and been swept away?

But what choice did we have but to try? There was no other chance.

Once they set off the rest of us just stood there, each of us unwilling or unable to be the first to suggest anything or make a move. With Dash gone there was no leader anymore, no voice of authority. I didn't think any of us felt like leaping to fill that void just then. Instead, we paired off and went about clearing the plane out. Until crash debris and . . . everything else, was removed, leaving the plane looking weirdly normal. If you stood with your back to where the tail should have been, you could almost believe nothing had happened at all.

The inside of the plane was hot, almost unbearable without the light breeze from outside. One by one we drifted back outside to the camp. Looking around I saw the haunted feeling inside me reflected back in everyone else's eyes. We were all numb and horrified after the morning's work. Even Araya and Janet, who hadn't been able to help us.

Bryce wrapped his arms around me from behind, his forehead against my shoulder as if he was seeking comfort. I put my hands over his and held tightly. Glad he was there with me. Across from us, Kaitlyn and Fletcher were similarly huddled. San'ya had his knees up to his bandaged chest, arms wrapped around them, and both he and Janet were hunched and miserable.

The silence might have gone on forever, had we not heard a noise from the jungle. Above all the chittering and squawking of the wildlife that had become almost familiar. The deep, hair-raising snort, of a snarl. We all froze, looking at each other with wide eyes. All of my muscles were seized up, and my head ached with the pressure.

Then came a full-throated roar. As my heart clenched

up inside my chest, I remembered some inane man on a film set once telling me that a tiger's roar paralyses its prey with terror. So they dubbed that in for lions on screen. Nothing else came close to that sound.

Fletcher practically yanked Kaitlyn to her feet, his voice wobbling when he spoke. 'The hell was that? A fucking jaguar? A tiger? We should be in the plane. It's not safe out here!'

Bryce jumped up too, and attempted to lift me off the ground but I was frozen in fear. My mind was still trying to drag me back to the film set, where one of Dad's wives was starring in a stupid TV movie. Trying to bury me in a memory where I was safe. Where I was anywhere but here.

'Inside, now,' Fletcher yelped, urging us all to move, as he steered Kaitlyn towards the nose of the plane.

'What about us?' Janet asked shrilly, indicating her injured leg and Araya, who was getting to her feet but limping badly on her injured ankle. 'We can't climb up there!'

I paused and Bryce grabbed my wrist, pulling me onwards.

'Should we not . . .' I stammered.

'They'll figure it out.' He didn't look back. 'We need to look after ourselves first. Or we'll all be screwed. Let them take care of themselves.'

'Wait!' Araya called out.

I looked back and saw San'ya helping Janet to her feet, supporting her as he bent to help Araya up. He had this, they'd be fine. The three normals helping each other along.

We climbed up into the cockpit via the crumpled nose

and I saw that most of the glass had been knocked out of it and now littered the floor. Back inside the plane itself the fire and the explosion had left very little of the front section. It was about ten metres long, ending in the ragged burned edges and sharp twisted metal of the ruined section. Seeing the creamy leather seats and chrome tables ending in a scorched nightmare was surreal.

Fletcher had left Kaitlyn sitting down and was peering out of the burned end of the plane.

'You need to go to the other side!' he yelled down. 'Why can't you people do anything for yourselves!?'

'They can't get up there; it's too slippery. We need a ladder or a rope or something!' San'ya called up. 'Find something and come help me!'

'You find something,' Fletcher shot back. 'I'm not going back out there with that thing, whatever it is! I'm Fletcher-fucking-Michaels – I am not getting eaten for the likes of you!'

'It's gone!' Janet called up. 'We can't even hear it anymore.'

'It's probably stalking them right now,' Fletcher commented to Bryce, who'd gone to look down at the three people still outside. 'If we go down there, we'll just be sacrificing ourselves for nothing.'

'We could make a ladder,' I said, now that the initial adrenaline of fear was receding, allowing guilt to filter in. 'Dash left us the saw and there's bamboo – out there.'

'In the jungle,' Fletcher stressed. 'Do you want to go cut it and get savaged by an animal?'

I faltered and he sneered at me. 'Typical – women always expect men to do the dangerous jobs and then wonder why they don't get treated equally. Easy to risk someone else's life for your "principles" isn't it?'

I saw Bryce nodding slightly out of the corner of my eye and anger flared to life inside me, eating through my fear. Who the hell was he to tell me what I was and wasn't willing to do? I'd spent my formative years backstage at rock concerts, around my dad's sleazy managers and handsy bandmates, shepherding underage fans out of their reach. I got into a full-on fight with a bassist who wouldn't take my friend's 'no' for an answer, and ran across four lanes of traffic to stop a high-AF groupie from getting hit by a car. I knew all about dangerous conditions.

'Where's the saw?' I demanded.

'What?' Fletcher frowned at me, wrong-footed.

'Where is the saw? I'll go out and help,' I said.

'Don't be stupid,' Fletcher snapped.

'Yeah, it's not safe,' Bryce agreed. 'Why take the risk?'

'Throw it down!' San'ya called, apparently listening to us bicker. 'I'll cut it.' He said something in Thai that sounded like a curse and I heard Araya respond. They were both obviously pissed at us. I couldn't blame them. It was obvious Fletcher thought they were expendable because he was 'somebody' and they weren't.

I looked around and spotted the saw with some other bits Kaitlyn had put in order – sorted into piles that probably made sense to her but which only confused me. I snatched up the saw and made to throw it around Fletcher. He tried to stop me but it was too late. I threw it down and San'ya snatched it up off the ground and stalked into the jungle without a backwards glance. Araya and Janet, leaning on each other, glared up at us accusingly. I felt shame prickle over my skin and shrank back from their eyes.

'Nice one,' Fletcher spat. 'Now they've got our only saw.'

'They? We're all stuck here,' I pointed out.

'You know what I mean.' Fletcher shouldered past me and over to Kaitlyn, who was balled up in a soft leather seat, obviously still terrified of the noise we'd heard outside. What had made it and where it was now was also weighing on my mind.

'He's right you know,' Bryce sighed and I looked at him, surprised.

'It's your plane, and Dash's saw. They haven't contributed anything and just keep blaming everyone else. That's why they're them, and we're us.' He shrugged like it was just a fact, and went over to join the others.

'Us?'

'People the world is going to care about. Who cares if the rest of them get home or not? Like five people? You have that many employees for your hair,' Bryce said, scoffing.

I watched him go and wondered why I hadn't seen this coming. Less than twenty-four hours since the crash and the social order had already righted itself. Even lost in the jungle there were haves and have-nots. But for how long I had no idea. After all, what we had wouldn't last forever.

Chapter 12

'I understand that many of Bethan Mills' aka "BeMi's" fans have taken to the internet to mourn her and to blame you for her shocking death?' Andrea says, undeterred by Lila's flat, emotionless expression. Somehow both meditative and hostile in equal measure. 'Along with her husband, Anthony Bale.'

Anthony Bale whose follower count trebled overnight once news of the crash got out. Since Bethan was confirmed dead he's accrued another two million followers and the number is still rising even a year later. He's been milking the anniversary of the crash for all it's worth. Between that, the life insurance and the rumour that she had been about to divorce him for shacking up with her colourist, Anthony is doing very well out of his wife's 'shocking death'. Bethan's prenup would have left him with nothing but his skateboards. These days he's the owner of a penthouse in London and a villa in Tuscany. Still, he's had me in his sights for a while now – the potential of a lucrative lawsuit just waiting there for him to claim it when the well started to run dry.

'They have . . . I don't blame them for feeling that way.

It was my plane and I invited her on it. Even if Bethan died before the flight plan and the black box might have been of any use, it's still on me that she had the opportunity to be on the plane.'

I did not add that of all of us, Bethan was one of the lucky ones. She never saw her death coming. There was a certain amount of mercy in that.

'And many family members and friends of the, shall we say . . . less high-profile passengers have also expressed their anger over what happened. Recently the two older brothers of Francesca Maçon – a twenty-year-old French student who died in the crash – attempted to gain access to your hotel, to see you personally. Is that true?'

'It is. They did,' Lila confirms, her expression softening a touch. I remember that night, and how much I wished I had anything to say to them that would make their grief easier to bear.

'You declined to speak to them?' Andrea presses.

Lila nods slightly. 'I wasn't sure it would help, at this stage. They want answers and I don't have many. I didn't press charges over the break-in, and I understand that they're angry. I would be too.'

'There have also been allegations from surviving passengers that you, in particular, put yourself above them at certain points during the ordeal. That you said it was "your plane" and therefore "your rules" applied. Is that also true?' Andrea says, seemingly alert to every gasp and muttered admonition of her audience. All of them watching Lila, desperate to believe the very worst.

'There were . . . a lot of tensions and fractures in the group as time went on. Some of them were about me. Some I probably made worse. But for me it wasn't about "owning the plane" so much as . . . owning the responsibility.'

'For the crash?'

Lila's face turns thoughtful. 'Not just for that . . . mostly because I didn't step up after the crash and I should have. I should never have let things go as far as they did.'

Andrea tips her head to the side in feigned confusion. 'You mean when these fractures started, you chose the wrong side?'

'I didn't choose a side, so much as I just allowed one to form around me,' Lila corrects. 'I should have spoken up and tried to stop it but, I was just trying to make sure everyone liked me. That was my job at the time, after all – to be liked. To be important. To be "Lila Wilde". But it was stupid not to try and take a stand earlier.'

'Because later on you had to shift your allegiances?' Andrea challenges. 'Go crawling to the people you'd sidelined because they weren't in your league, before?'

Lila sniffs mirthlessly. 'Because if I'd done it sooner, I can't help thinking that more of us would have survived. Maybe that's just wishful thinking. Maybe there really was nothing I could have done.'

Chapter 13

As San'ya propped his slightly wonky ladder up against the plane wreckage, I wondered at how he'd managed to make it so quickly. Though it was clear he'd never made anything like it before and certainly not under pressure. After a few false starts and loose rungs, he managed to climb to the top. The glare he gave us forced me to look away, ashamed. He helped Janet and Araya up, and they pulled themselves over the edge and onto the floor.

Once all three of them were in the plane, San'ya turned on us and gave each one of us a hard stare. 'Thanks for all your help. Assholes.'

Kaitlyn, like me, looked ashamed, but Fletcher and Bryce met San'ya's annoyance with their own. It was very clear neither of them wanted the others in the plane with us. Even I had to admit that with three extra people, the nose section felt cramped and there weren't enough seats for everyone. The added body heat was already noticeable – like being on a packed tube train in the height of summer.

Araya sat down on the floor and reached up to help Janet down beside her. I noticed a thin ribbon of blood running down Janet's leg and realised her glued wound must have opened up again.

'Do you need more glue?' I asked, indicating her leg.

Janet looked at me with such open disdain that I flinched. She'd always been so nice to me but obviously that was just because it was her job. She looked like she loathed me.

'Is there any alcohol to disinfect it?' Araya asked, when Janet refused to say anything. 'Gin, vodka . . .'

I looked at Kaitlyn, who glanced Fletcher's way before shrugging. 'I didn't find any.'

'Bullshit!' Janet snapped. 'I stocked up after we landed in Phuket. There was plenty – you've taken it all for yourselves.'

'Well it belongs to Lila anyway,' Fletcher drawled. 'Her plane. Her liquor.'

All eyes turned to me and I could see that Fletcher wanted me to turn them down. To keep the alcohol for ourselves. Janet was glaring at me, her eyes filled with frustrated tears and both Araya and San'ya had expectant looks. Waiting for me to give in. My head was throbbing and I just wanted everyone to leave me alone and stop making it worse. I was starting to feel nauseous again.

I looked to Bryce for support but he was clearly on Fletcher's side. He saw me looking and shrugged. 'We don't know how long we'll be waiting to be rescued. And it's not like there's anything to do but wait.'

'So we should all just get drunk?' Araya said, voice harsh and disbelieving. 'Typical tourist – only here for drugs and drinking and dirty strip shows.'

Bryce glared at her. 'As if this country doesn't run on money from tourists.'

'Look, just, give them some vodka or something,' I interrupted. 'This is stupid and I don't want to fight about it.' I reached up and gingerly probed my head wound. It was oozing blood again, probably because of all the rushing around. My hair must have pulled free of the scab. I wrinkled my nose and wiped my fingers on the carpet.

Bryce looked to Fletcher, who reluctantly nodded to Kaitlyn. She got up and went over to one of the floor hatches and pulled it open. She returned with a single vodka miniature and handed it over to Janet before retreating back to her chair. Janet huffed a scornful laugh and started to roll up her skirt to get at the wound.

'You're welcome . . .' Bryce muttered, pointedly. But Janet ignored him.

'We should cover the end of the plane,' I said, trying to avoid any further outbursts. 'In case it rains or stuff flies in.'

'Like what?' Kaitlyn asked, in a tiny voice.

'I don't know like . . . insects and bats or, stuff like that,' I said, looking to San'ya and Araya for their input. Although they were city dwellers they had to know a bit about the wildlife. As San'ya had said, it didn't always stay outside.

He sighed, but nodded reluctantly. 'Bats could be a problem, and if it rains it might drive snakes and stuff up here.'

'Up your thoughtfully constructed ladder,' Fletcher said pointedly.

San'ya didn't even look at him, just addressed the air between our two groups. 'We could use the slide – it's already deflating anyway and we have the ladder now so . . . we could cut it free and drape it over the back of the plane. Weigh it down with metal or something at the top?'

'Sounds like a good idea,' Araya agreed.

Bryce nodded slowly, though I could tell he wanted to argue. Fletcher, as if sensing that he was on his own, just shrugged in a dismissive way and nodded to the end of the plane.

'Off you go then – not sure what you're going to cut it with though.'

He had a point, having slid down it I knew how thick and resilient the material was. A sort of dense rubberised fabric that the saw would take days to cut through. If it didn't break or go blunt first.

'Kaitlyn, did you find anything like scissors or . . .' I trailed off as she shook her head.

'Only like, nail scissors. An eyebrow razor . . .' She thought for a second. 'I think that was about it for sharp stuff . . . unless you count the corkscrew from the bar.'

'Because that's useful.' Fletcher sighed and Kaitlyn retreated back into herself, hugging the skirt of her rumpled strawberry dress around her legs. She looked like a kid who'd been scolded by a teacher.

'We could melt it – it's plastic right?' Araya said.

'Flame-retardant plastic,' Janet corrected. 'It's tear-resistant nylon with a special coating so if it deploys into fire, it can resist burning long enough for everyone to get out. I don't know that we can cut it but there might be a way to detach it from the box it deploys from . . . I don't know. I've never been trained to do anything but set it off.'

'Right so, I'll try and detach it,' San'ya said, apparently

trying to take charge. 'Maybe someone else can try and find sharp metal we can use to try and cut it if that doesn't work? There's tons of wreckage; some of it's got to be useful as a knife or a tool.'

'We'll look,' I said, when no one else jumped in. My eyes were drawn to Janet's leg, which she had rinsed with some of the vodka, but it was still bleeding. 'Kaitlyn, have you got any dressings or . . .'

'It's fine,' Janet hissed, moving to cover the wound up and accidentally nudging it with her hand.

'It'll get dirt and stuff in it,' I pointed out.

'I found a few pads – they might do,' Kaitlyn said reluctantly. 'Oh, and I've got some spot treatment – it's got tea tree, witch hazel. It's meant to be antiseptic . . . Bethan recommended it to me.' She caught herself and blinked hard, struggling to hold back tears. They must have been friends before last night, I realised. To me everyone but Bryce was a stranger. I wondered if anyone else had friends amongst the other passengers. If so they were keeping it to themselves.

'Let's go then.' Bryce broke through the tension and marched towards the ladder. 'Come on, Lila.'

He sounded kind of annoyed with me and I wasn't sure why, but I went anyway. As we climbed down I heard San'ya and Janet discussing the slide and how to get at the place it popped out of on the plane. I was surprised how sturdy the ladder was, for being made of bamboo and bits of vine. A few rungs on it shifted a bit but it got us down to the ground safely.

'So . . . sharp metal,' I said, looking around at the charred and warped chunks of fuselage. 'Plenty to choose from.'

'Lila, you need to wise up,' Bryce hissed, tugging me away from the plane.

'What?' I stumbled over the ashy debris and struggled to keep up with him as he towed me across the clearing.

'You can't just keep giving in to them – letting them have whatever they want. They're going to start feeling entitled to everything on the plane. To our food and water and what little medicine we have. It's not their plane and it's not their place to tell us what to do or make demands.'

'It was just one little thing of vodka—' I started, but Bryce waved me off impatiently. He was covered in sweat, and looked really agitated.

'It starts with one handout, and then they expect it – they start taking stuff for themselves and before you know it you'll be asking their permission to eat your own food and drink your own damn booze. You need to remember who you are – Lila Wilde doesn't go rushing around because some nobody says "go look for metal".'

I blinked at him. 'I think you're being just a little paranoid.'

Actually, in looking at him properly he did look kind of tense and twitchy. I'd thought he was sweating so much because it was hot and humid in the jungle, but now I saw how tiny his pupils were.

'Are you feeling OK?' I asked. 'Did you get hit on the head or . . .' I let the sentence trail, wondering if like Janet he had a wound somewhere that was getting infected.

'I'm fine!' Bryce said, too quickly. His eyes were all over the place, flying around and never landing on anything for a second. 'You're the one acting like you're just some pleb.'

He was acting really off; there was no denying it. Much

as he'd like to, apparently. If he wasn't hurt or running a fever, that left only one thing that I could think of. I just couldn't believe he'd be so fucking stupid.

'Babe, have you taken something?' I asked, trying to sound more worried than annoyed, even though it was unbelievably infuriating that he'd gone and gotten high at a time like this.

He rolled his eyes. 'Got to stay sharp – that's why they give uppers to soldiers. Ever hear of "Bolivian marching powder"?'

'I don't think it's called that because of like, the Bolivian army,' I said, but Bryce waved me off.

'We have to be alert. You know what happened to Bethan – she didn't pay attention for a second and now she's fucking dead. We could all be dead, like that.' He snapped his fingers. 'I'm not messing around here and I'm not waiting for those parasites to take everything for themselves.'

He was getting more wound up and I didn't want to feed into it anymore. At least not until the pills wore off and I could have a normal conversation with him. So I just nodded to appease him and started hunting around for any sharp metal in convenient knife-size pieces.

We got lucky after twenty minutes of searching. The explosion from last night had shredded a metal panel, and the long shards were practically perfect to use as machetes. Making handles was pretty easy – we just took some of the leather and pleather straps off the bags we'd found and wrapped them around the ends to protect our hands. The blades were all a bit wonky and only sharp in some spots, but it was better than nothing.

When we returned to the slide side of the plane, we

found it mostly detached anyway. San'ya and Araya were hitting the mechanism with a large rock and the slide fell, deflating in one long rush.

'Help us get it over there!' San'ya called to us. 'It's heavy!'

It took all four of us to drag it around to the back of the plane. San'ya and Bryce scrambled up and pulled the heavy slide material to the roof of the shelter, so the bulk of it was on the plane, with a section hanging down over the hole as a curtain.

'We need stuff to weigh it down!' Bryce called to us.

Kaitlyn and I gathered rocks and bits of metal. Fletcher watched with folded arms, as if supervising the work.

The covering made it quite dark inside the plane, but that couldn't really be helped. For light and air, we could leave the side door and the door to the cockpit open. But at least they could be closed at night.

'What do we do now?' San'ya said, once we'd all recovered from our exertions. 'Should we be . . . I don't know, foraging around for stuff to eat? Digging a toilet?'

'A toilet?' Fletcher scoffed. 'And then what, a three-bedroom house? We'll be rescued in the next few days. No point scrounging around out there with the snakes and the rest of the filthy wildlife.' He stretched out in a creamy leather seat and Kaitlyn passed him a beer she'd recovered from her stash. 'Here's to making do until the helicopters come.'

Bryce laughed. 'I'll drink to that. Babe?'

'Sure,' I said, and forced a smile. But inside I was wondering how far Dash and Summer had gotten since setting off, and how far they had left to go.

114

Chapter 14

That first full day in the jungle crawled past like a line of ants. Seemingly without end. By the time night fell I was exhausted just from existing in that place. Sitting there, listening to the jungle in fear, made everyone tense with the expectation of danger.

We were all hungover and hungry, thirsty and exhausted. Things were already starting to get to me – like the toilet arrangements. I'd had to pee in a champagne bucket in the cockpit, and wiped with cocktail napkins. My sticky skin cried out for a shower and my throat burned for a time when I could gulp water without worrying about running out. My dress was soaked with sweat. I was tired, sore and hungry. My nerves a jangle of frayed ends. My headache was fading though, thank goodness, and the bleeding on my scalp had stopped.

I think we were all simultaneously glad and frightened when it became dark outside. At least the day was over and there was less time to wait. Time was passing; we were going to be saved soon.

I was grateful for the plane – I couldn't imagine not having it as shelter away from the creepy-crawling creatures and the eyes of the jungle animals. Inside, with the doors closed and the slide blocking off the end, it was easier to pretend that we were just sweltering on the tarmac in Phuket. Passengers on a regular plane waiting for take-off.

We ate some bags of snacks and settled down to sleep as best we could. It became cold after night fell and we didn't really have anything to use as covers, most of the storage on the plane having been in the tail end. I thought bitterly of the faux fur blankets, soft as butter, or the quilted covers that we used on longer flights, along with the down-stuffed pillows. The slippers too, were lost in the crash and my high heels were killing my feet.

Bryce muttered bitterly about the clothes we'd just thrown away, and it took me a second to realise he meant the other passengers' clothes. I thought about sleeping under a dead person's jacket, and shivered.

In the end we just huddled for warmth. Bryce and I curled up on one bench seat. Kaitlyn and Fletcher took the other. On the floor, Araya and Janet slept on two cushions taken from the only remaining single seat, and San'ya lay over the bare seat itself, legs thrown over the arm, his hands tucked into his pits to keep warm.

I slept in fits and starts, never quite able to drift off completely. Every little noise and movement around me had me twitching awake, afraid a snake was about to bite me. But each time there was nothing but the breathing of the other passengers and the sudden stillness of the jungle as its inhabitants slept, with only the silent prowlers out and about below.

A few times when I woke up I saw the glint of wakeful eyes in the darkness. The others were obviously struggling to sleep too. All of us so on edge, so desperate to hear

Dash and Summer returning, carrying the black box with them. How long would it take? A day or more?

In the morning, stiff-limbed and itchy with mosquito bites, we gathered around to eat a breakfast of mini-pretzels and peanuts, washed down with tonic water. Hopefully the quinine in it would make us less attractive to the blood-sucking bugs, I thought. I was fairly certain I'd seen a TikTok about it.

'I think we need to start collecting water,' San'ya said, once we were done eating. Fletcher and Kaitlyn were lying back on their seat and Bryce was perched on ours, flipping his useless mobile phone over and over in his hands.

'We have plenty of water,' Fletcher pointed out, gesturing to the bottles of tonic and mineral water that Kaitlyn had lined up beside their seat. Eight two-litre bottles of mineral water and a few handfuls of single-serve tonic bottles. Dash and Summer had taken the individual mineral waters for themselves on the hike.

'And I suppose you wait for your bloody fridge to be completely empty before you order more food too?' San'ya said, rolling his eyes. 'We need to think ahead – start collecting now, worry less later.'

Fletcher just yawned theatrically. 'If you want to waste your time and go thrashing about in the jungle, go ahead. I won't stop you.'

'You're not worried?' Araya asked, sceptically. 'We could be stuck here for weeks.'

Bryce scoffed. 'Oh come on. Lila Fricking Wilde is missing. They're going to find us. Her dad's probably already hired a bunch of mercenaries and PMCs to comb the jungle. I bet when Dash and Summer make it back, we'll have had to wait for them with half a dozen commandos.'

117

Kaitlyn, who'd looked slightly sick at Araya's words, appeared to calm down. 'Yeah, we'll be out of here soon – no need to run around pointlessly wasting our strength and getting bitten by bugs out in the heat.'

Fletcher nodded, obviously pleased that she was agreeing with him. I had to admit, they had a point. Dad might not have shown up to any of my school events and probably wouldn't have been able to tell me apart from any other blonde celebutante, but he wouldn't rest until I was safe. No matter how much cash he had to fling at the problem. He was as generous with his cash as he was stingy with his time.

I'd once gone on a private yacht trip with a guy I met at the Grammys and although it had been fine at first, he'd quickly become demanding and aggressive. To the point where he refused to head back into port, because he wasn't 'done' with me yet. I'd managed to get an email off to my dad's assistant, and the coastguard of two different countries had come to intercept us. Along with a few hired guns in another boat, who Dad had sent to 'teach the tosser a lesson'.

Dad wasn't winning father of the year any time soon, but when the chips were down he was all in. Especially if it added to his hard-man image.

'Well, I'm doing it,' San'ya insisted. 'And you can watch out for yourselves.'

Bryce shrugged and lay back on our 'bed'. 'Knock yourself out.'

'I'll help,' Araya said, and looked down at Janet. 'You OK without me?'

Janet nodded, but I noticed she looked even paler than yesterday and she was sweating a lot. I hoped she wasn't sick or something. It hadn't occurred to me before but the mosquitos were probably dangerous. Didn't they give you malaria and stuff? We didn't have any nets to sleep under and I'd not remembered to put on any insect repellent before we came out, so we didn't have that either. I hadn't bothered to get any jabs or tablets because it was all so last minute. I was just brainstorming content ideas and realised Thailand would be such a goldmine.

I shivered and wished I had something to distract myself with. Worrying wouldn't fix anything now.

Araya and San'ya climbed out of the plane and I glanced over Janet's way, only to catch her looking at me. She quickly looked away, lips pressed into a tight line. Either because she was in pain or she couldn't stand me. It was hard to tell.

Bryce took out his bag of pills and Fletcher immediately noticed. 'What's that?'

'Yaba – you want?' Bryce said, offering him the baggie. 'I got plenty.'

'Uppers or downers?' Fletcher asked.

'Ups.'

Fletcher pulled a face. 'I don't fancy being more awake for this. Kaitlyn – didn't you have some benzos squirrelled away for later?'

Figured, I thought. She acted like a Fifties housewife, but she was a party girl under all those ruffles. I watched as Kaitlyn picked up her bag from its closely guarded position on the seat and rifled through it. She pulled out a kawaii little coin purse in the shape of a strawberry and tipped out a plastic pill sorter absolutely rammed with goodies. Even from a distance I recognised Xanax, OxyContin and Adderall.

Fair, if I was dating Fletcher I'd want to be off my tits all the time too.

She handed the pill sorter (shaped like a slice of pink grapefruit – cute) to Fletcher and he popped out a few pills, knocking them back with a gulp of the tonic he'd liberally mixed with vodka. Kaitlyn popped one or two and they both lay down, apparently intending to catnap the day away.

'Babe?' Bryce offered me his bag of yaba and I shook my head. He shrugged and took two. Then settled back and started playing with the ring grip on his phone, fidgeting with it.

With no one else to talk to I made my way over to Janet, who was as far away from our end of the plane as possible. Like there was an invisible wall between us and her, and she liked it that way.

'How's your leg? D'you need painkillers?' I asked, gesturing to Kaitlyn and her stash.

'I'm fine,' Janet said, and then winced as she shifted positions.

'OK, but tell us if you need anything – no point in sitting there letting things get worse,' I muttered, stung by her hostility.

'Yes, Miss Wilde,' Janet hissed, and then rolled over, leaving me staring at her back, my face flaming with embarrassment at the snub. I was just trying to be nice.

I retreated to Bryce's side and perched on the seat, trying to ignore how grubby and sticky I felt. I shut my eyes and imagined myself back in our villa, under the rainfall shower. I was standing on perfectly smooth, egg-shaped pebbles that had been specially chosen to fill the shower tray, massaging my feet. The water was body temperature and refreshing in the overheated climate.

I went through my vanity in my mind's eye and selected my Baccarat Rouge cleansing gel from Maison Francis Kurkdjian. I was washing the sweat and fear away with jasmine and saffron, creamy lather sliding over me and lapping over the stones. Bliss.

My attempt at meditating myself into a shower was ruined when San'ya returned. He puffed up the ladder, followed by Araya. The pair of them started talking almost at the same time.

'. . . trying to get up here last night.'

'. . . or tried to . . .'

'. . . but they'll only get bolder unless . . .'

'Shut it!' Fletcher sat up and glared at them. 'Trying to sleep here.'

My own annoyance was fading as I processed what the two of them were saying. Something was trying to get into the plane? In the night, while we were sleeping?

'What do you mean, trying to get up here?' I asked, shuffling over to them as Fletcher flopped back down, muttering mutinously and pawing at Kaitlyn.

Either they were too excited to care that I wasn't 'one of them' or it didn't matter. Araya turned her big eyes on me and spoke with worry and awe in equal measure.

'Monkeys – macaques – as we came back we saw them up on the roof and one was getting closer to the entrance when we scared him off. But he didn't run far. I've never seen that many before – with babies too.'

'Monkeys suck,' San'ya said, clearly unimpressed. 'I work in a hotel and the tourists bring them around by giving them food.' He broke into an exaggerated American accent. 'They're so cute and small. Howard, take my picture. No! They are small but they are not cute.

121

They bite and scratch you and if you get too close to their babies they'll try to take your face clean off like that!' He mimed swiping at his cheek with claws. 'Fuck. Monkeys.'

Araya rolled her eyes. 'We have one or two near our house sometimes. They don't bother us.'

'Because you are not an idiot who would try and pick one up. And you probably didn't have food. If you did they'd claw and bite you and try to take it,' San'ya said – obviously speaking from bitter experience. 'That's probably why they were sniffing around the ladder. They know there's food in here. They'll probably come in and go through everything while we sleep.'

'If they try that we'll just kick 'em out. They're not like gorillas,' Bryce scoffed, without opening his eyes. 'We saw them in town, like stray cats sniffing around.'

The idea of any animal climbing all over me whilst I slept made me shudder. I could imagine the monkeys with their tiny, too human hands and their grinning, sharp teeth. A whole group of them stealing our food and trying to take a bite out of us into the bargain.

'We should put the food somewhere else then. Somewhere they can't get it, where it won't bring them in here,' I said, sounding panicked even to my own ears.

'Like where?' Janet said, having listened to Araya and San'ya's report with interest. She now turned her scorn on me.

'I don't know . . . maybe we could drag one of those bar units outside and tie it shut? Or put it on its back and weigh it down with rocks. But there's no way to keep monkeys out if they decide to come in here after our food. And what if they have diseases and they bite us?'

That seemed to shut her up. I could tell that as much

as Janet didn't like me she didn't relish the idea of being bitten and scratched by a hungry, diseased monkey. It made Bryce sit up and take notice as well.

'OK so let's move a cabinet out – get moving or it'll get dark and we'll have wasted our chance,' Bryce interjected, scrambling off the seat and firing out words sharp and quick. The pills had apparently started to kick in.

San'ya looked Bryce over doubtfully, but slowly nodded. 'Does seem like a good idea. Keep anything from coming in looking. I mean, it feels like we're high up but there's holes underneath the plane. Boar could come up looking for food and they're worse than the bloody monkeys.'

'Aren't boars . . . pigs?' I asked, thinking of the cute pink farm animals and not really getting what San'ya was on about. 'They're not like . . . dangerous?'

San'ya gave me a withering look. 'Yes, cute little pigs – that'll bite through your bones.'

'But we could eat 'em,' Bryce said, patting his stomach. 'Some actual food! Not this nuts and crisps shit.'

'They can kill tigers,' Janet said, surprising me. She caught my look and shrugged. 'I saw it in a documentary. They have these tusks and they're really sharp. Can rip open a tiger's belly like it's an Amazon package. And they eat meat. They eat anything.'

I shuddered. Great. Venomous snakes, wild tigers, mosquitos, monkeys and now man-eating pigs. I was so beyond ready to get out of the jungle and back to civilisation. For now though, we just had to wait and keep our little slice of safety secure from outside threats.

That rescue couldn't come quick enough.

Chapter 15

In the end it was San'ya and Bryce who moved the cabinet outside. It was pretty thick and hefty, made of some kind of metal with wood veneer over the top. It had come loose in the crash but they still had to finish unscrewing it from the floor of the plane using coins and a lot of force. Once it was free they dropped it out of the side door and it didn't break when it hit the ground. A good sign.

Araya and I helped to drag it across the clearing the crash had created. Once it was over there we tipped it onto its back, so we could pile stuff on top and let gravity protect it. It also gave it a wide base and narrower sides. Which according to San'ya meant it would be harder to smash into. What he was basing that off I had no idea. But it sounded convincing.

We kept out enough food for the remainder of the day and locked the rest up. First locking the cabinet, then using San'ya and Bryce's belts to hold the handles shut and finally lifting some large bits of metal and bracing them on top. If anything tried to get in, we'd hear and be able to scare the pigs and monkeys away. Hopefully.

I definitely felt a little more secure in the plane, knowing we didn't have food piled up next to us, drawing animals in. We even took the empty packets out into the jungle and buried them as best we could.

That night it was cold again and we all huddled around in the plane. Despite the small space there was a good clear foot of unoccupied floor between us and the normals. They were clustered closer to the entrance, where the cold air came in. I wasn't sure which of us was imposing this distance. Maybe both groups wanted to maintain a buffer zone. To emphasise this, San'ya was lying crosswise, putting himself between Janet and Araya and the rest of us.

Fletcher and Bryce were drinking beers and whisky miniatures to pass the time and even Kaitlyn had a bottle of white wine she'd found miraculously unbroken. I had a few swigs from the wine to take the edge off my nerves and tried not to notice that no one had offered anything to the others, and they hadn't asked.

'Wish we could have a fire,' Janet said, after a while, shivering so hard that her teeth rattled like Tic Tacs.

'We'd have to camp outside for that,' I said. 'Smoke and fumes and all that.'

'I know . . . I was just saying,' Janet muttered.

'Could camp outside – take some sheeting off the slide and do something with it,' San'ya said. 'I'm not really sure how safe we are in here to be honest. Not like a sheet's going to stop a tiger getting in.'

I shivered and hugged my knees up to my chest. Bryce, sitting behind me with his legs on either side of mine, wrapped his arms around me. It did a little to keep me warm – though I was really starting to wish I'd worn literally anything alongside my crochet mini dress. Even sheer tights would have been something. Bare-legged and bare-armed, I wasn't only being eaten alive by mosquitos, but spending a second night shivering on the clammy leather banquette.

'There'd be more room, if you did,' Fletcher drawled, after knocking back the last of one warm beer and opening another. 'For the rest of us.'

A tense silence hummed between our little group and theirs. I looked down at my goose-pimpled knees and wished they'd all just shut up. It was hard enough being there; arguing and making shitty comments only made it worse. I just wanted to sit quietly and wait for the fucking rescue choppers to arrive.

But apparently everyone else had other ideas.

'You want us off the plane now?' Janet said, waspish despite her pale face and chattering teeth. 'Making us sleep on the floor not enough to make you feel special – you've got to make yourself a jungle VIP section?'

'If you're not happy in here, why don't you go make yourself a little camp with a fire? Go really native until help comes,' Kaitlyn muttered.

'You can't kick us out,' Janet snapped.

At the same time, Araya glared at Kaitlyn and said, 'Native, really?'

'Oh here it comes,' Fletcher sighed. 'Go on, play the race card.'

'You're a child,' San'ya bristled. 'All you've done is sit and complain and be a dick, when you're lucky to be alive. We all are.'

Fletcher was unmoved. 'Look, can you three get lost? It's depressing just looking at you to be honest.'

Bryce snorted and I felt the hair on the back of my neck prickle unpleasantly.

'Guys, can we all just . . .' I started, but Janet spoke over me.

'I've worked on this plane for years. I know it back to front. So why don't you leave?'

'You worked on it?' Fletcher repeated, in a patronising tone. 'Oh wow! Really? It's her plane, idiot.' He jabbed a finger in my direction. 'Not yours. So get out. Tell them.'

This last was directed at me. I felt my face go hot as everyone looked at me expectantly. Bryce held me tighter, but it no longer felt comforting. It felt like he was laying claim – the way Kaitlyn had grabbed up the bottles of booze.

'Everyone can do what they want,' I said, trying not to set anyone off. 'Sleep wherever, I don't care.'

Despite my best efforts, everyone looked kind of annoyed by that. I let out a long breath and nudged Bryce. It was dark and cold and I just wanted to go to sleep. With any luck we'd be found tomorrow and this entire argument would be even more pointless than it already was. We'd all go back to our lives and that would be that.

That night, sleep was even slower in coming. The cold was all-consuming and I couldn't get it out of my head long enough to drift off. Had we been inside a building, I'd have probably been fine. But as night fell there was nothing much to keep the sticky heat close to the earth. It evaporated into the air.

Bryce curled around me like a vine, tucking his hands under my boobs and his face against my neck. His beery snores were irritating me as I lay awake and miserably cold, and eventually I wiggled free and rolled to face him. At least like that I could sandwich my bare arms and legs between us. With a little warmth I managed to get to sleep.

I was woken in the morning by raised voices. Blurry and disorientated, my mouth dry and my eyes itching with dehydration, I rolled over to see what the fuss was about. It was Janet. She was shuddering on the floor while Araya and Kaitlyn argued over her and Fletcher watched, vaguely amused. There was no sign of San'ya but I thought I could hear the distant drone of the saw being drawn back and forth.

'What's going on?' I said, getting my feet on the floor, the touch of carpet a weird connection to the real world while we were surrounded by so much strangeness.

'Janet's sick,' Araya snapped. 'And this . . . *hŭa kuai*, won't hand over any more alcohol – look at her leg!'

Araya pulled at Janet's red skirt and showed the wound in her thigh. I covered my mouth with my hand. Yesterday it had looked a little red and swollen around the deep cut. Today the whole leg was noticeably larger than the other and the wound was a flaming red mess with a crusty, jagged scab down the centre, weeping fluid.

I hissed behind my hand, trying not to be sick. 'What is that?'

'Infection. Bacteria,' Araya said.

'And the vodka didn't work – so there's no point in using more,' Kaitlyn said. 'We might need it if we get hurt.'

'She is hurt!' Araya exclaimed, her expression one of angry disbelief. 'We need to clean the wound for her to try and slow the bacteria.'

'Holy shit.' Bryce had appeared behind me. 'What kind of bacteria? Can we get it?'

'If you get cut, yes. It's everywhere. The dirt, the water, especially out here. It's very strong and hard to kill with antibiotics,' Araya said. 'It causes these . . . ulcers. Deep, infections.'

Janet, locked in the throes of feverish unconsciousness, whimpered and spasmed on the floor. I looked at her gleaming, sickly pale skin and rounded on Kaitlyn. 'Give her the vodka.'

Kaitlyn, pink-cheeked and red-eyed, looked like she wanted to argue. There was a tense moment where I was sure she wasn't going to listen to me. Then she backed off and swept a hand over her rat's nest of hair, as if she couldn't be bothered to deal with this anymore. She opened her stash and handed me a miniature of vodka.

'That's the last one,' she huffed, and threw herself down beside Fletcher, who was just watching the goings-on with glassy eyes. Clearly already high again.

'Where's San'ya?' I asked, handing the vodka off to Araya, though I wasn't sure it was going to help much. Janet's leg was plump and mottled as a raw sausage.

'Outside. He's making a tent,' Bryce said, rolling his eyes.

'A tent?' I repeated, stupidly. 'Why?'

'The peasants are revolting.' Fletcher laughed, slightly too loudly. I wasn't sure what he'd taken but it was clearly strong. Kaitlyn tittered along with him, and knocked back a gin miniature, neat.

Araya shot both of them a look. 'We don't want to be stuck in here where we have to listen to this.' She gestured at all of us, aside from Janet and I felt wounded, even though I knew I hadn't exactly done anything to help matters.

Behind me, Bryce sucked his teeth, unimpressed. I tensed, annoyed. He wasn't helping things much, just

129

laughing along with Fletcher and lying around waiting for other people to have ideas and do stuff for him. Just like me, really. I winced, knowing I should have tried harder and done more since the crash. Done anything to try and keep the peace.

'I'll see if we have anything better than vodka,' I muttered, and went to the pile of stuff Kaitlyn had found and separated out from the food, drugs and alcohol category. There wasn't much to be honest. But I picked up every miniature bottle and packet of makeup to read the ingredients on the back. I wasn't a survivalist and knew dick-all about first aid but skincare? That I had done my research on.

'Here.' I passed over a spray bottle. 'This face spray has hypochlorous acid – which kills bacteria. And this toner is alcohol based, with witch hazel . . . so that might help.'

'I tried that spot treatment and it didn't do much. The infection is too strong.' Araya sighed, but she took both items from me and I watched as she cleaned the wound with vodka, then the toner and finally the hypochlorous acid. I hoped one or all of those things would help bring down the infection.

With that done, Araya sat back and felt Janet's forehead, then pulled a face.

'San'ya is going to build a fire outside so we can keep her warm at night. During the day she's getting too hot though. Feverish.'

'We'll be out of here soon. As soon as help comes I'll make sure she gets the best care in a hospital,' I promised. 'No expense spared, you have my word.'

Araya's expression was complicated and I couldn't

quite tell what she was thinking. She didn't look as hostile anymore but she wasn't entirely happy with me either.

'It's ready!' San'ya called up. 'Araya! Come help me cut some plastic – it's going to take a while!'

'I'll watch her,' I promised, as Araya looked torn.

She nodded and left me with Janet, who continued to shiver and mutter in her sleep. Twitching and whimpering like a dog having fitful dreams.

'With any luck they'll be out of here by nightfall,' Bryce said, apparently trying to console me.

'I hope we all are,' I murmured, but he didn't reply and after a moment I realised he wasn't listening. He was fishing a red pill out of his precious baggie, and popping it into his mouth.

Chapter 16

We really could have done with the slide at that point. Between them, Araya and San'ya carried Janet to the ladder and slowly lowered her down. San'ya clung to the ladder and took most of her weight while Araya held her under the arms from above. Despite their best efforts, they jostled her leg and she wailed in pain. It was awful.

San'ya, after a hard morning of work, was covered in sweat and sawdust from cutting bamboo and sticks to make a frame for their tent. It was covered with a jagged-edged scrap of the slide material and the edges were weighed down with debris and sticks stuck into the dirt. I watched from the open end of the plane as they laid Janet down and set about lighting a fire. They had some champagne buckets out, ready for rain too.

I watched them, my joints loose and syrupy with the heat as the temperature inside the plane climbed. It was stuffy and starting to smell like our ripe bodies. I wrinkled my nose, wishing we had something to clean with.

'Good riddance,' was all Fletcher said, and Bryce obviously agreed. He looked smug about the whole thing, though what he thought we needed the extra floor space for was beyond me. The seat cushions that Araya and Janet had slept on were already on the bench seats as extra pillows. Was that all they'd wanted? A cushion to lean on?

I was pretty sick of my 'friends' to be honest. So I sat at the other end of the plane, watching Araya as she went around the border of the jungle. She dipped in and out between the trees, not going too far. A few times she returned to sort through a few handfuls of fruit she'd collected – she'd bite one and either nod and set it and the rest of the same type aside, or spit it out and throw them back into the jungle. Sorting the edible from the bad, I guessed. I wasn't really sure how much knowledge she had about the stuff she was picking. If we were back home I'd probably be able to recognise apples and blackberries but nothing else.

The longer I sat there, idly scratching at my mosquito bites, the more restless I felt. Doing nothing and just trying to ride out the heat and discomfort until help came was only giving me more time to think. Glancing towards the others, I realised that was probably why they were so keen on staying high or drunk. Normally when I was frustrated and restless I'd go for a run on my treadmill, trying to exhaust myself with pointless exercise. But right now I wanted to put my energy into something that would help us. Only I had no idea what to do.

Araya returned for the final time, to sort her haul. Most of what she'd found from what I could see looked like a cross between a star fruit and a gherkin. Sort of light green and pickle-shaped but smooth and waxy. After three full days of just eating the odd handful of salty

133

snacks, my stomach was empty and I was desperate for something fresh. The pretzels and peanuts were relatively high in calories but they weren't filling and they made me thirsty. I looked away as she and San'ya sat down to eat what she'd found, my stomach complaining.

'We should bring the food back in here,' Bryce said, coming to sit with me. 'They'll only take it all.'

'They haven't so far.'

'Mmm, they're probably waiting until it's dark. So we don't try to stop them,' he said, like it was obvious.

I nearly laughed, it was so petty. 'We could just take it back off them. They must know that. There's no point stealing from us.'

Bryce looked a little irritated and rolled his eyes at me. 'You're too trusting, that's your problem. Too quick to give stuff away.'

'Since when?' I challenged, annoyed because after all it was my stuff. But he was already sloping off back towards the cockpit end, where Fletcher and Kaitlyn were sprawled on a banquette. I heard muttering and Kaitlyn's giggle. The back of my neck prickled, hot with more than just mosquito bites.

I tried to make myself feel better by going over the toiletry supplies, familiarising myself with what we had on hand and sorting them by type. Back home, at my permanent address in London, I had a skincare cabinet and sorting it always relaxed me. Lining up the jars and bottles, smelling their contents. I tried to imagine myself back into the relaxing shower I'd pictured before by sniffing a tiny bottle of eucalyptus cologne, but it didn't work.

Trapped in the sultry heat and out of bottles to

catalogue, I finally gave in and lay down like the others. I shut my eyes and tried to doze my way through the interminable hours of waiting for rescue. But without chemical assistance I was just worrying on my back with my eyes shut.

Neither Araya or San'ya asked for a share of the airplane food when Bryce stirred himself from his nap and went down to fetch us some lunch from the cabinet. He reported this when he returned, as if he was disappointed. Like he wanted there to be a fight just for something to do. He seemed to be getting restless but that was probably the yaba he'd popped on waking up. I was starting to worry that it was making him paranoid. I caught him looking at me funny as he took the pill from the bag – like he was prepared for me to run at him and try to take it. From the set of his brow I had no doubt that he'd shove me to the floor to protect his stash. This was a side of him I'd never seen before. One I couldn't predict as easily.

After eating, Fletcher and Kaitlyn slept again, soothed into a Xanax slumber. Bryce was amped up on yaba and I was going a little stir-crazy in the plane, desperate to do something but not knowing what or how to spend what little strength I could muster in that heat. I kept pointlessly calculating how long we'd been here and what could have happened in the world outside this place in that time. This was technically our fourth day in the jungle, our third if I discounted the night of the crash. But how could I, when it had been so pivotal? Surely we'd been missed almost immediately. Maybe before the sun came up over the crash site.

I heard a ripping sound and looked up to see Bryce pulling a small leather bag apart. One of the little clubbing

135

bags that we'd found in the wreckage. He was digging his nails into the stitching, pulling and ripping at it, single-minded as a dog at a chew.

I opened my mouth to ask what he was doing, then closed it again. What would he do if I interrupted him? Snap at me? Start an argument? Throw the bag at my head? He was clearly tweaking, just keeping his hands busy while the yaba flooded his body with energy. At least he wasn't starting anything with San'ya or the others. I just left him to it.

It seemed like the only thing I could do that was of any use was try to remove my broken, filthy acrylic nails. Without acetone I was limited to picking at the edges and trying to file them down with one of the cardboard nail files from the dispenser in the bathroom. A bathroom that was decidedly ripe from someone using it without realising there was no water and no way to flush. Gross.

When it came time to fetch some dinner up I was the only one awake, Bryce's yaba having worn off. So I took my turn to go down and raid the cabinet. I climbed down the ladder and went over to start shifting the debris. It was actually nice to have an excuse to stretch my legs. Logically I knew I could have left the plane any time, but it had started to feel like I was part of a tribe. Like I wasn't allowed to leave on my own, without a good reason.

It was impossible to get into the cabinet quietly and the idea of anyone 'sneaking' into the store only seemed more ridiculous once I was done moving the metal. I took out a few packets and bit my lip when I saw how low the supplies were getting. There had been a lot of packets but we were all eating multiple small packs for each meal. We only had enough for another day or two. If we rationed it to two packets per meal, per person. A serving of about two tablespoons of nuts or snacks apiece. Barely a bar snack for every meal.

I glanced over at the makeshift tent and then got off my haunches to go talk to the others, still trying to shake off the feeling that I was 'out of bounds' as one particularly stupid headmistress used to say. Araya was sitting on a heap of cut-down leaves, watching over Janet. San'ya was outside the tent, on the other side, sharpening sticks with one of the 'machetes' we'd made from scrap.

'What're you making?' I asked, to start conversation.

San'ya barely looked at me. 'Spears. Gonna see if I can kill a monkey.'

Araya caught my eye and pulled a face – the universal one that means 'men, amiright?' I half-smiled back.

'Do you guys want anything from the cabinet while it's open? Trade you for some fruit?' I asked, trying to sound casual.

'Probably not a lot left in there, right?' San'ya said, with the tone of someone saying 'I told you so' without wanting to use the actual words. 'Hope your friend comes back soon with Summer, and some help.'

'Me too,' I said, ignoring the jibe. I was thinking of Dash and Summer, and wondering if they'd already eaten their rations and how they'd get back with nothing to eat or drink.

'Here, take some bilimbis – four for one pack of peanuts. One each for you,' Araya said, holding up some of the weird pickle things. A peace offering, I thought. She seemed less aggrieved than San'ya. Or rather, she seemed used to being trodden on by others. I felt bad for her and

137

tried to look and sound as friendly as possible as I took the fruits.

'Are they good?' I asked.

Araya shrugged. 'Sour, but edible. I usually cook them in curry, which is nicer.'

'OK, thanks . . . hey, let me know if you're going out again tomorrow. I can't just sit around and wait anymore; it's driving me crazy,' I said.

'In there, with them? No wonder,' she said, and mimed slamming a drink back. I laughed, surprising both of us. 'I'll call up to you as I'm going, tomorrow.'

Excited to have some fresh food for the first time in days, and something planned for tomorrow, I hurried back to the plane. Inside I dished out the snack packets and the bilimbis. I decided to take the hit of the traded nuts from my ration. It wouldn't make much difference anyway. I was always hungry.

'What's this?' Bryce asked, as I was waking Fletcher and Kaitlyn.

'Araya found them – it's a fruit . . . or a vegetable. I didn't actually ask, but it's edible.'

'She gave them to you?'

'I traded her a packet of my nuts for them.'

Bryce snorted. 'She saw you coming. Probably poisonous, or tastes like shit.'

'Well, she was eating them,' I said, annoyed.

'Yeah, well.' He let it drop there but I got what he meant. He didn't think Araya was as discerning as us, clearly. Which annoyed me because before we'd started dating he was just a normal guy with a cupboard full of instant noodles and empty energy drink cans lined up on his windowsill like trophies. The first time I'd taken him

138

to an upscale restaurant he'd ordered chicken fingers, off the children's menu. I'd nearly died of embarrassment, would have if he hadn't been so adorably self-conscious. Where had that guy gone?

Fletcher and Kaitlyn were similarly unimpressed by the bilimbis. Kaitlyn held hers between thumb and forefinger and Fletcher didn't even pick his up, just looked at it on the seat where I'd left it and curled his lip up. Both of them acting like it wasn't even food.

I ate mine. It was indeed, very sour. To me it was sort of like a cross between a lemon and an unripe tomato. Sour and juicy and sharp. It wasn't bad and I could imagine it being nicer with other stuff – I rubbed the bitten edge of it in the salty peanut packet for some seasoning and it started to put me in mind of tequila shots – minus the actual tequila, unfortunately.

'Yuck,' Kaitlyn pronounced, after one tiny bite of hers. She laid it aside in her empty snack packet and pulled a face. 'That's vile.'

'I'll finish it,' I offered, because I was still very hungry. My stomach felt like it was shrivelling up inside me. Normally I had to fight not to eat, to keep myself in a sample size. This new situation wasn't any better in my opinion. Not eating when there was food everywhere made me feel in control, virtuous. Downright saintly. Not eating when there was no food around anyway was pointless and annoying.

Kaitlyn handed over her bilimbi and I snagged her empty peanut packet along with it, as a garnish. It was quite moreish with the salt but maybe that was just because I was so desperately hungry. The way that you can convince yourself that a mushroom 'burger' in a lettuce bun with carrot sticks is 'just as good' as a McDonald's once you haven't had bread or cheese for a month.

'Steady,' Bryce said, shooting me a disgusted look. 'Try chewing.'

Kaitlyn laughed and I slowed down, but didn't let them put me off finishing her food. I was annoyed with Bryce. Where did he get off being disgusted by me, when I'd seen him popping pills and tearing into a leather bag like he was a dumb animal?

Both Bryce and Fletcher ate their bilimbis, though they practically choked them down with a lot of theatrical retching and then opened more drinks to 'wash the taste away'. I couldn't help but think if they'd been sliced up by a Michelin star chef, Fletcher would have savoured every bite.

I was aware that I should perhaps knock a few drinks back just for the calories, but I didn't like the idea of getting tipsy out here. I kept thinking about Bethan and how easily she'd stumbled into death. I didn't want that to be me.

The other three knocked back drinks and I watched them until it got dark and cool enough to sleep. As the temperature dropped I curled up in Bryce's beery embrace and offered up a plea for whatever might be out there, listening – God, Buddha, the universe whatever – to please let us get picked up tomorrow. I promised anything and everything – I'd clean up my act, stop partying, I'd become a homemaker like Kaitlyn and have five kids. I'd talk to Dad more and forgive him for never being around. I'd never lie on social media again. I went to sleep making promises and I prayed that it would be enough.

When I woke up, suddenly, it was still dark. I shivered

and couldn't work out for a second if it was early or late. How long had I been asleep for? Then I heard Araya and San'ya yelling and realised that the cold hadn't woken me. Their screaming had.

I fought my way out of Bryce's arms. He and the other two were still stirring, fighting their way to consciousness through a fug of alcohol and pills. I stumbled barefoot to the end of the plane and pulled the edge of the canopy over so I could peer into the darkness. And it was dark. Capital 'D' darkness that plastered itself to my eyes like ink. The embers of the outer camp's fire were the only things I could see aside from a few stars and the yellow reflection of eyes.

There were animals down there, snorting and scuffling and ripping at something. For a horrible moment I was sure I was hearing Janet or Araya or San'ya being torn apart. Then someone stirred the embers up, grabbing a smouldering stick and waving it like a club. The stick flared to life, flames billowing from its end and I saw the brown bodies of the jungle pigs, fighting over the contents of the food cabinet.

The cabinet I'd left open.

I cursed and turned around, not really sure what I was going to do but knowing I had to do something. I blundered straight into Bryce and he grabbed my elbows. I flinched.

'W's goin' on?' he slurred, and I struggled free, looking for my shoes in the dark.

'The boars are after the food!'

Fletcher swore and I could hear him and Kaitlyn shuffling off their banquette. I didn't wait for them and gave up the search for my stupid stilettos, instead rushing back, past Bryce and climbing down the ladder. I missed a rung and fell, the shock of it making me shriek. But then I was on the ground and before I could even worry about snakes or sharp tusks or anything else I was running towards the cabinet. I had my arms up, screaming and yelling to scare the boars away.

In the near total darkness I heard them grunting and squealing, the scrape of their hard feet against the earth. A hot, bristly hide shot past my leg and then they were gone. Running off into the trees. Either because they were scared of these new two-legged creatures they'd stumbled upon, or because they'd eaten everything that was available. I could feel the empty packets scrunching under my feet, torn to shreds.

My heart was beating wildly with shock but guilt and fear were hot on the heels of that. This was all my fault. I'd left the cabinet weights off when I went over to talk to Araya and I'd been so eager to show off the bilimbis that I hadn't secured it.

'Are you OK?' I panted, peering at the burning stick and recognising San'ya as the person holding it. 'Did anyone get hurt?'

'No, we're fine. They mostly went for the packet food – I guess because there's fruit everywhere out there. It doesn't interest them as much.' He flashed the flaming stick in the direction of the tent and I saw Araya looking out at us, squinting into the dark. The shape beside her on the ground was probably Janet and she wasn't showing any signs of being awake.

'You should go back – no shoes isn't exactly a great idea,' San'ya said, gesturing to my bare feet. 'I'll light the way in case there're snakes.'

'Thanks,' I said, feeling small and stupid.

San'ya didn't respond to that but led me back towards the plane without comment. Like he was a surly cab driver carting luggage to the front door of a hotel. As we got there I saw Bryce and Fletcher at the bottom of the ladder. My stomach flipped in anxiety. Kaitlyn was peeking out from the side of the canopy as if too scared to come down to ground level. Come to think of it, she hadn't left the plane for a while now. We'd just been emptying the toilet bucket out of the broken cockpit window.

'I'm so sorry,' I said, as I saw them looking at the cabinet, visible in the light of San'ya's flaming torch. 'I didn't—'

I was cut off when Bryce grabbed me by the upper arms and shook me, hard. A high-pitched yelp was all I could get out.

'What the hell have you done? You stupid bitch!'

Jostled and too shocked to shake him off, I was trapped. Bryce's fingers digging into my upper arms so hard I could feel them bruising the bone beneath. He gave me a final jolt and then pushed me so hard that I stumbled over my own feet and hit the ground arse first. My tailbone flared with pain and tears leapt into my eyes.

No one said anything in my defence. Not even Kaitlyn. Looking up I could see the flames reflected in Bryce's eyes, all four of them looking down at me as if I was some strange animal that had wandered into the clearing to steal from them and make a mess.

'Bryce . . .' I stuttered, and reached up towards him. His tiger pendant flashed in the firelight, the diamonds glowing.

'You just lost all our fucking food,' Bryce said, cutting

me off. 'You got us into this mess and now we're going to go hungry, because of you.'

I wanted to yell that it wasn't fair to blame me for all this. I hadn't made the plane crash and I wasn't the only person who could have secured the food stash. The others had been right outside after all. But my throat was dry and for the first time I was afraid, not just of the jungle, but of them. Of Bryce.

'You can stay out here,' Fletcher said, turning away and climbing the ladder. 'Don't even think about trying to get up here – I'll push the ladder over myself.'

I looked at Bryce, but he was moving towards the ladder, leaving me behind. Beside me, I sensed San'ya drawing away. They were all abandoning me to the darkness. I shivered in the cold night air, very aware of my bare feet and naked arms and legs. Of how vulnerable I was.

'It's my plane,' I bleated, pathetic even to my own ears.

Bryce looked down at me from the top of the ladder. 'So go ask Daddy to kick us out.' He vanished under the canopy. 'We'll wait for him to show up, shall we?'

Chapter 17

Shut out of the plane, it was obvious to me that I wasn't wanted in the tent either. San'ya melted away into the night without a word, leaving me alone. Not even Araya reached out to me to give me somewhere to shelter. Even though I'd thought her the kindest of the passengers. The most likely to try and make peace. Apparently even she was pissed off with me.

So, with nowhere else to go and the fear of stepping on a snake in the dark, I sat down with my back to the ladder and wrapped my arms around my knees. My engagement ring nudged against my skin, colder than ice. I held up my hand and looked at it. There was dirt crusted into the setting from where I'd been digging and the sticky juices of the bilimbis had attracted other grime to it. Bryce had given it to me only a few days ago, and now he was acting like I was nothing. Like he'd never loved me at all.

My thoughts were as dark as the air around me during those hours. I was imagining the next day, the next night. What would I do now? Without food, without my shoes, shut out of the only shelter available. Were Dash and Summer on their way back with the black box? Had they already been found and was help coming? Or was I going to have to struggle on, alone now, as Bryce and the others watched me suffer?

Every time I thought about Bryce, about the way he'd looked at me, my chest ached. As tightly as I wrapped my arms around myself I couldn't stop my insides squirming in fear. Part of me was sure he'd relent and let me back into the plane. I was his fiancée for God's sake. He loved me. He'd given me a diamond ring the size of a gobstopper. He wasn't going to let me lie in the dirt waiting for a snake or a tiger to come along and kill me. He'd been angry about the food and I understood that, but he didn't want me dead. But I couldn't stop the twisting in my guts, like my body knew what my head wouldn't let me believe – Bryce didn't care about me anymore.

Things changed out here, fast. One moment we were drinking champagne in the air, the next we were crawling from the wreckage in a crash site. Bethan was alive when we went to sleep, dead when we woke up. What if Bryce had fallen out of love with me just as quickly? What if my mistake had pushed him over the edge and he hated me now?

I worried and agonised and cried into my hands until the sun rose. Once it did, I was sure things would be better. The anger would have blown itself out like a tropical storm and we could find a way forward. My mistakes, the destroyed food, it wouldn't matter anymore. We'd be on to the next thing. The next problem to solve.

I was right. But God, how I wish I hadn't been.

The sun rose and I roused myself from an exhausted half-sleep, the kind of sleep you get crashed out in other people's hotel suites after parties. I watched Araya get up and feed the fire. She didn't look at me and it felt very

146

purposeful. The not looking. Like she was pretending I wasn't there. Given the mess I'd made I couldn't even blame her. I felt terrible.

Then I heard laughter from the plane, and my grubby hands clenched into fists. They were laughing at me. On my plane. Bryce was up there, laughing.

I shut my eyes and let the guilt and anger swirl inside me sickeningly. I felt terrible about my part in our situation, but I was also pissed off that I'd been kicked off my own plane. Not just by a bastard like Fletcher, but by Bryce. By my fiancé, who was wearing thousands of pounds of gear I'd bought him. My skin crawled to think that I'd been afraid of him last night. Afraid of some wannabe DJ. In the light of day I could hardly believe that I'd backed down from him. In the real world I wouldn't have. Mind you, in the real world Bryce wouldn't have shoved me.

My brooding was interrupted by Araya yelling Janet's name. Her voice shrill and panicky.

I knew. Knew before I opened my eyes, that Janet was in trouble. I struggled to my feet and went over, staggering a little with exhaustion and muscle cramp. The pair of them were in the opening of the makeshift tent. Probably trying to stay near the fire.

Janet wasn't just pale anymore, she was greyish. Her skin unpleasantly sticky and slimy to look at, like she was sweating mucus instead of liquid. Araya had lifted the hem of her skirt and I gagged before I even saw the wound. I could smell it. The wound was oozing pus and the skin around it was shrinking away, as if trying to escape the poison. The swelling was worse and the surface of the wound was wet and pale yellow, like candle wax, shrunken in and rimed with black crusted blood.

'Oh my God,' I hissed, trying to breathe through my mouth.

'It's not getting better,' Araya said, stating the obvious. Of course it wasn't getting any better – Janet's leg was infected and we were probably hundreds of miles from the nearest hospital with only vodka and face wash to treat her.

'What do we do? What can we do . . . ?' I reached for Araya's shoulder and tried to steady myself whilst comforting her, but she pulled away from me. Even in that awful moment she didn't want me near her. My eyes stung.

I couldn't tear my eyes away from the suppurating wound on Janet's leg. It seemed to get worse as I looked at it, each new detail another cause for disgust and worry. There were reddish lines branching away from it, following the routes of capillaries and veins. The infection was spreading through her blood – even I could see that.

San'ya crawled out of the gloom behind them and looked Janet over. I'd started to think of him as capable and strong, like Dash. But he looked just as lost as I felt. Who was he really? Just some city boy who'd made a camp and a ladder that a kid could have knocked up in the woods behind his house. He wasn't a survivalist and I wasn't judging him for that – but it only made things seem worse. Knowing we didn't have anyone who knew what to do.

'Do we . . . try and cut it off?' I asked, when neither of them offered any ideas. It sounded ridiculous and God knows I didn't want to have to help hold Janet down while San'ya went at her leg with a saw but what other options were there? Even if we did somehow manage to get the leg

148

off, she'd probably only get another infection. Araya had as good as told us – the dirt and the water were swimming with aggressive bacteria. Even in a hospital, Janet might still die. You heard all the time about those super bugs and stuff, that antibiotics couldn't even touch.

I was grateful when San'ya shook his head. 'We'd just be torturing her . . . There's nothing we can do.'

'What's going on?' Kaitlyn called from the plane, looking out at us in her grubby strawberry dress. She sounded annoyed, and I guessed we'd woken her with our talking.

I glanced at Janet, who looked like she was out cold. 'Janet's leg's worse!' I shouted back. 'She . . . she might be dying.'

Kaitlyn and I locked eyes for a moment and then she was gone, back into the plane. The canopy dropped back into place, cutting them off from us and the horror outside. I turned back to the others.

'Could we . . . does cauterising do anything?'

'I think that's for wounds that aren't . . . that are just bleeding,' Araya said softly. 'They do it all the time on TV – in doctor shows. But . . . I don't know that it would do anything to stop the infection. We've tried everything we have – the alcohol, acid spray . . . even bleach wouldn't help now.'

I didn't want to give up. We couldn't lose anyone else, not after Bethan and the German nurse and John. The other passengers. So many people had died already and I couldn't stand the thought of having another body on my conscience. Janet was only here because of me, because she worked for me. This was all my fault.

Araya cleared her throat, but her voice remained small

and meek. 'I think the only thing we can do is try and make sure she doesn't . . . that she doesn't suffer any more than she already has. So, we need to give her something if she wakes up. To help with the pain.'

I understood the expectations on me at once. They were my people on that plane and they had all the drugs. I was the one who would have to act to end Janet's suffering and we all knew it. It felt like a test. A trial. Araya and San'ya watched me as I got up and went over to the ladder. Their eyes burning into my back.

At the top of the ladder I crawled into the plane and found three pairs of eyes on me, gleaming in the darkness. Kaitlyn was back at Fletcher's side, cosied in to him as if she was trying to disappear into his body entirely. But in front of them both was Bryce, blocking my way and looking at me like I was nothing more than a bug in the dirt. For a second I was certain he was going to push me backwards, let me fall. My chest squeezed with fear, even as I hardened my face against his glare. I wouldn't let him see even a flicker of worry in me. I wouldn't give him that power.

But my legs shook a little as I stood in front of him.

'Janet's dying,' I said, before I could chicken out and leave. 'She needs painkillers in case she wakes up before . . . it's over.'

'Do you have anything to trade?' Bryce asked, while the others looked on, lapping up the tension between us. 'And not more of that disgusting fruit or whatever it is – something worthwhile.'

'Like what? Another plane?' I said pointedly. I wasn't even really surprised by what he was asking. But I was hurt, because I thought he was better than the type of people I'd been around my entire life. I couldn't believe I'd been so wrong. *Everything is available and nothing is free* – drugs, contracts, gigs, merch, swag, women, it all had a price tag and the more someone needed it, the more you could jack it up. That was my dad's motto and apparently Bryce's too. I felt ill.

'Well, if you don't have anything to give us . . . how about you keep this place clean, find food for us since you ruined our stash, and you can take care of the shit bucket,' Bryce reeled off. He'd obviously been thinking about this, maybe since last night. Eager to flex his new power over me. 'And for that we'll give you, what d'you think, guys . . . four oxy?'

When I didn't answer immediately Fletcher rolled his eyes and deigned to speak. 'You could always just smack her in the head with a rock.'

I flinched, shocked by how brutal he was being. Bryce laughed. I just looked at him, appalled. How could he stay in here with Fletcher after that? How could he laugh while Janet was dying?

It was like looking at a stranger and I felt chilled to look in his eyes and see nothing. No guilt or uncertainty. Bryce wasn't in two minds about his behaviour. He thought it was fine. He thought it was funny. I had to get out of there.

'I'll do it, all of it, OK? Just give me the tablets.'

'Kaitlyn,' Fletcher said, and she twitched to attention, digging out the pill sorter and counting out the pills. Close up, she really did look dreadful. We were all unkempt and unwashed but she looked exhausted and strung out. I wondered how many pills she'd been taking, I hadn't really been keeping track. I didn't envy her being in here with the pair of them – Bryce and Fletcher. Though of course now they had a new 'housewife' to fetch for them. Me.

I took the oxy and turned to go.

'Babe?' Bryce said, and I turned back to him, hoping for a second that he'd relent. That this would just be a stupid joke he was trying to pull. I hated myself for thinking it, even for a second, after what he'd just said and done.

'Make sure you bring back plenty of food – yeah?' he said, a hint of warning in his voice. 'We want our money's worth.'

I wanted to yell at him, to call him every name I could think of and threaten him with Dad's lawyers, with his own mundane existence. Without me he was just a guy. Just a man with some half-decent playlists and a dream. But I couldn't make myself shout at him. I was too worried he might rush me, or snatch the pills back, or push me off the ladder.

I stalked to the ladder and climbed down with the pills in my palm, listening to them laugh together like a trio of monkeys in a tree. How fucking dare they? This was my plane. Even if the accident, our being stranded here was partly (mostly) my fault, that didn't give them the right to push me out. I wasn't too surprised at Fletcher and Kaitlyn – they were entitled arseholes anyway – but Bryce . . . I'd given him everything and he couldn't even stand by me for a few days? Instead he'd put himself above me, and now it was like I barely existed to him.

As I crossed the clearing though I had to admit to myself that I knew nothing gave them the right, they'd just taken it for themselves anyway. Just like everything else. Out here there was a whole new pecking order and I was falling, rapidly, down it, while Bryce flew to the top.

Chapter 18

The interview, or rather the first interview of the double bill, seems to be winding down. A ticker runs across the bottom of the screen announcing that the 'one year later' catch-up with Lila Wilde will screen shortly. Premiere, is the word they use. Like this is a film or a documentary and not a real account of a tragedy, spliced up with slots to advertise wax strips and travel insurance.

Around me no one else in the airport lounge seems to be paying attention. It's just background noise and colour in the lives of people about to get onto planes and fly across the world. Completely unaware of the horror they will most likely be spared by a safe journey.

'So, Lila, we actually have a surprise bonus guest for today's show,' Andrea says, as the ticker flutters off the side of the screen. Her voice is cheerful but her eyes hold a flicker of hunger. She's keen to drop the bait and watch the reaction it provokes.

'Oh?' Lila says, carefully blank. Not giving her the satisfaction. Lila's thumb is bleeding, ever so slightly. She must have chewed it during the advert break. A bad habit I fell into after rescue, gnawing on myself. A bead of dark

153

blood wells up and runs along the nail bed, sinking into the crease of it and spreading. Until that one droplet looks like a wound, raw and deep.

'It was all very last minute – very lucky we found a gap in his schedule.' Andrea glances down for a tenth of a second, clocks the bloody nail and her nose wrinkles slightly in distaste. If this wasn't live, or if it hadn't been at the time it was recorded, she'd probably have assistants rush in to dab the offending bodily fluid away. They're there to talk about survival and death and pain – but putting blood on the screen is a no-no. Far too disgusting. Not advertiser-friendly.

'Please join me in welcoming, Scott Wilde!' Andrea exclaims, gesturing to the screen behind the sofa with a flourish. Lila doesn't really react but I remember the jolt that went through me then, as for a second I thought Dad might actually be there, live in the studio.

He appears on the screen, sitting on a leather seat that must be in his tour bus. He's wearing sunglasses and his hair is pushed back in a bandana. There's a hint of smoke in the air around him, probably from one of his pre-interview joints. He raises a hand and waves casually, like he's appearing to fans and not a journalist intent on smearing his only child.

It hurts, even from this distance, that he agreed to that interview without telling me. Without talking to me at all. The last time we spoke before that TV appearance I was still in the hospital in Thailand and he'd phoned to say how glad he was that I was safe. That he really wanted to hug me, only he was on tour, so it would have to wait.

'Hey, Li,' Dad says, easily. 'Andrea – it's good to be here.'

'It's good to have you on, Mr Wilde,' Andrea says. 'I

thought it would be interesting to talk about what you went through, while Lila was missing, and how you're doing now, since her rescue. I understand you funded much of the search effort?'

'I did – and it's Scott, please,' he says, giving her a half-smile and all the Texas charm that won over my mother and every woman since. His accent always gets stronger when he's back home and today it's thick and lazy as honey.

Lila looks between them as if calculating the likelihood of Andrea being her next stepmother. Thankfully that hasn't happened. Yet.

'Right from the moment I heard that the plane had gone down, I was calling everybody – like "get my baby back, money's no object". I used every connection, every favour I was owed. Hell, I agreed to come do a tour in Thailand if they found her. She's my world,' he says, giving Lila a smile via the screen.

She smiles back, but her eyes are flat. I feel that flatness now, as an ache in my chest. The kind you get when you really want to believe someone, but you just can't.

'I was getting updates hourly,' Dad continues, scratching at his dark beard meditatively. 'Had my PA waiting for me at the side of the stage at every set, just in case we heard something. All the time I was up there, on stage, I was thinkin' *how's she handling it, my baby girl, out there in the jungle, helpless and scared?* Broke my fucking heart.'

Andrea looks at him with exaggerated understanding and the Lila on screen, and myself, are united in our disdain for her. I've never felt closer to the me I was back then, than in this moment.

'I understand your tour is sold out across the US and South America,' Andrea says. 'Congratulations. Are you planning to visit Lila in London afterwards or, is she flying out to see you?' Her eyes move to Lila. 'I imagine you'll want to keep air travel to a minimum, under the circumstances?'

Her faux sympathy is obvious, but that's not why Dad laughs.

'I bet she does!' he says, still smiling easily. 'No, I'll be coming back to the UK after my tour to prepare for Thailand. We'll see each other then, won't we?'

Lila nods.

'I was really conflicted about whether to carry on with my tour,' Dad says, confidentially, to Andrea and her hundreds of thousands of viewers. 'But hard-working people paid good money for tickets to see me play. I owe it to them to honour my commitments. And Lila's home now. You've got people looking after you, haven't you?'

'I do,' Lila says, and I think back to the flat in London, full of assistants, a chef, a driver, housekeeping staff. Someone for every job, except being there when I woke up from my nightmares, screaming.

'The thing about us Wildes,' Dad says, flashing his whitened teeth for Andrea, 'is we bounce back quick. I'm just glad everything's back to normal, and my girl's home, where she belongs. With all that nasty business behind her.'

Chapter 19

All that day and into the night, I sat with Araya and San'ya, waiting for Janet to die.

She only woke up once, and was in such awful pain that it took all the remaining OxyContin that I'd bartered for to put her under again. I began to wonder if Fletcher had been right in his cruel assessment. Perhaps Janet would have been better off if one of us had the courage to pick up a rock and end her life for her.

As it was, she passed in the darkness and we heard her go. The long rattle of her final breath like a moth trapped in the tent, fluttering wildly against the canopy, desperate for freedom. I felt numb and empty, sitting in the dark beside Janet's body and knowing she was gone. That we had failed. Someone else was dead because of me.

Araya bent over her knees and was clearly trying to sob as quietly as possible. I wanted to reach for her hand, to give some comfort and to receive some in turn. But the thought of her pulling away from me, angry and full of blame, kept me from doing so. San'ya lay still and quiet, looking up at the canopy overhead. All three of us alone with our thoughts.

157

In the morning, just after the sun had risen, I awoke to San'ya moving Janet out of the tent. I must have gasped, because he noticed I was awake, and indicated Araya's sleeping form with a tilt of his head. 'Don't wake her.'

I got up to help, but then realised we'd be going into the jungle and I had no shoes.

San'ya saw me hesitate and just pointed at Janet's feet. Like he was the good witch in Oz. Wordlessly I took the red leather pumps off her feet and slipped them onto my own. The heels were sensible one inches, blocks too. It felt very wrong for me to be finding any sort of comfort thanks to her death, but that was the world we were living in now. Maybe Bryce had a point when he said we ought to have taken the other passengers' clothes. Maybe he was just ahead of the curve on what surviving out here really meant – that everything was up for grabs and there were no rules.

We carried Janet out into the jungle, towards where we'd left the others. I could hear the humming of the insects as we drew near and it made me feel ill. San'ya, pale and drawn-looking, didn't seem to be doing any better than me.

As we got closer I heard a sound that wasn't insects. A low snorting and rustling. Something moving in the undergrowth.

San'ya stopped moving and I nearly dropped Janet at the suddenness of it. My naked feet slid about in the slightly too big shoes and I nearly stumbled.

'What is it?' I snapped, probably too harshly given the situation, but my body was alight with panic.

'Drop her,' San'ya said, voice tight. 'We can't get close enough to . . . we have to drop her here.'

My stomach flipped over. 'What do you mean "drop her"? We can't just . . .'

'There's pigs,' San'ya said, cutting me off, his voice strained with panic and the pressure of staying still. 'There's no way past and they're not going to let us go. If we don't drop her and go, they'll kill us.'

I didn't want to let go of Janet. To leave her there like that. But my hands went limp and I dropped her ankles, backing away as San'ya did his best to lower her shoulders to the ground, dropping her the last few inches as the pigs advanced. Their snouts sucked air greedily as they saw us off with squeals and snorts.

I turned and fled, heard San'ya behind me and didn't stop running until I burst into the clearing and collapsed onto my hands and knees. The sudden exertion and the horror had left me dizzy, and I retched weakly into the dust. San'ya staggered to a halt and put his hands on his knees. I heard him gasping for breath.

Araya must have heard us. She came out of the tent, pale as a ghost and came flying to our sides. She seized my shoulder and San'ya's arm in a strong grip.

'Where is she?' Her voice was uneven with tears and it quavered up and down like that of an old woman, frail and afraid.

'With the others,' San'ya said. 'Don't go back there. It's done.'

'But . . .'

'It's done,' San'ya repeated sharply, and he pulled away from her, stalking towards the tent. Araya watched him go and then dipped to her knees in the dirt, clinging to me.

'What does he mean, "don't go back there"? What's happened?'

I wanted to be kind, truly I did. But I was in shock and the smell of them was still in my nostrils, oily and clinging to me. In that moment I didn't just want to prevent her from seeing what I had just seen, I also wanted her to shut up. To leave me alone. To not make me think about it.

'It's been six days, Araya . . . what do you think's happened?'

She recoiled as if I'd slapped her. Araya practically fell over in her haste to get her hands off me and to scuttle away. She went after San'ya but stopped outside the tent as if realising it was pointless. He was just as fucked up as I was over it all. She turned back to me and watched as I lifted myself off the ground. Her eyes travelled down my legs to Janet's shoes on my feet and her eyes filled with tears.

I couldn't find anything to say to comfort her. I had no comfort for myself either, not at that moment. Every single one of my nerves was shredded to bits. We'd stayed up tending to a dying woman and now I was wearing her shoes, had just come back from throwing her body to the wild pigs. How on earth do you come back from that? I wasn't sure I could. That any one of the three of us could.

Instead I crossed the clearing and checked the ground for snakes before sitting down by the ladder. Since the night that I'd spent there it felt like the only part of the camp that was mine. That was safe. It was all an illusion but it was the only one I had.

A rustle overhead made me look up just in time to catch Kaitlyn peering out from behind the canopy. Her eye bags were big enough to qualify as hold luggage and she looked pale and sickly. Despite that, she'd put red lipstick on, as she did every day. Though the crooked smear of it made her look ever so slightly unhinged.

'Janet's dead,' I said, mostly because it was the only thought swimming around in my head. Janet was dead and she was being eaten. I wanted to throw up but my stomach was too empty.

'Thought she would be,' Kaitlyn said flatly. 'Fletch and Bryce want to know when you're going to bring some food. They're hungry.'

I blinked at her. The thought of eating anything right now made me want to heave. I thought of going into the plane and found my mind straying to the hungry, aggressive pigs. I shuddered, already desperate to avoid going in there with Bryce.

'Deal's a deal,' Kaitlyn pushed. 'You've got to keep up your end or else . . .'

Or else what? Were they going to ask for the pills back? They were already gone, stuffed down Janet's throat to try and keep her from feeling the agony of her approaching death.

But just then I didn't have the strength in me to fight. Or to face Bryce's anger if I tried to go back on our deal. It was just easier to fall in line and to carry my grief and horror with me. So I picked myself up off the ground and dusted my filthy dress down with my hands.

'Fine. I'll go and find something, if I can.'

'And the bucket wants emptying,' Kaitlyn said. 'That's your job too, now. That'll be a fun story to put in my story time vlog, won't it? That time Lila Wilde cleared up my shit.'

She dropped the canopy back after jabbing me with that barb, and I felt nothing really. No outrage or hate or hurt. I was too emotionally overextended for that. She was just trying to make herself feel better, in control, in charge. Frankly I wished she was. That someone, anyone, would take charge.

Six days I'd said to Araya. Four since Dash and Summer had left and no word from them yet. Had they found the tail and were they on their way back to us? Or had something happened to them? How long should we give it, before we followed the trail of lipstick crosses through the jungle? What would we find at the other end?

I thought of the boars, and shivered.

Chapter 20

I dealt with the bucket first, since I was already in camp. Once I climbed the ladder into the plane I found Bryce and Fletcher still lazing around. The close, humid atmosphere of the plane and their limp bodies reminded me of after-parties. Dark, oppressively hot rooms where models and actors crashed out on couches, smacked off their tits and so drunk they could barely stay awake.

I was actually glad that Bryce seemed to be out of it. I didn't want to run the risk of him confronting me about something – probably something he'd imagined. The thought of being around him didn't just make me uncomfortable, it frightened me. I had no idea what he might do anymore or what his limits were out here.

No one acknowledged me as I went through to the cockpit and picked up the disgusting ice bucket that we'd been using as a toilet. Since being kicked out of my plane I'd had to make do with the woods like San'ya and Araya – their buckets were set out to collect water. If it ever rained. I hoped it would soon. We had bottled water and had divided it up fairly evenly, but it wasn't going to last much longer. The weather was so hot and we were all sweating a lot, even while we slept. Water just leaching out of us all the time.

I tossed the bucket's contents out of the broken window and heard it spatter down the nose of the plane. Leaving the stinking bucket on the floor, I used the mini bottle of hand sanitiser wedged on the console and left the cockpit. I didn't say anything and I didn't look at anyone. The way you're not meant to look in the eyes of an angry dog. I just wanted to be done with it and get out of there.

Part of me was tensed for the ladder to be shoved over. I didn't fully let out a breath until I was on the ground. Relieved that I'd managed to get in and out of the plane without any trouble, I returned to Araya and found her hunched over on the ground outside the tent. She was looking down at the trampled dirt like she could see something there that I couldn't. I didn't want to disturb her but we had to carry on. We couldn't just let ourselves go to pieces or there'd be no one left when help came. That's what you did – you saw something horrible, you moved on. You kept moving and hoped it never caught up with you. We'd all move on soon, when help came.

If help came.

'Can you show me the edible stuff, around here?' I asked, trying to sound brisk and tough to jolt her out of her grief.

'Why?' She looked up at me with red-rimmed eyes, her voice hoarse. 'What's the point?'

'I told the others that I'd find them food – in exchange for the oxy. Besides which, we need to eat too. You know about the plants around here, right?'

Araya shrugged and pulled her knees closer to her chest. 'Not much. My mother grew up in the country,

164

makes stuff out of wild fruits. She used to tell me about it but I mostly didn't listen. Wish I had now.'

'Not much is still more than the rest of us know,' I pointed out. 'We need you, Araya. Come on, I'll help pick the stuff if you tell me what's good.'

She gave in. I guessed she was too emotionally exhausted to argue with me. Still, a win was a win in my book. She led me out into the jungle, not too far and not in the direction of the gravesite, thankfully. We didn't have to go far to find more bilimbis, clustered together like a gherkin tree. We collected them into the handbags we'd brought along and then Araya started poking around with a stick, looking for other things we could eat.

'This.' She pointed at a plant with dark green leaves and bright fuchsia stems. It looked pretty poisonous to me to be honest. In my mind bright colours meant bad news but what did I know? I picked it alongside her, keeping an eye out for bugs and snakes.

We completed our pile with a few handfuls of round yellowish fruits. They looked a bit like the plums that used to grow at my boarding school (the third one), only smaller.

'Mayong. They're good this time of year – sweet,' Araya said, and offered me one.

I bit into it and found that she was right. It was good.

'You can eat the leaves too.' Araya gathered some up and added them to the pile.

It looked like a lot, and the jungle seemed to have plenty of food. But as I looked around I realised that we'd soon have stripped the immediate area bare. Fruit and leaves weren't exactly calorie dense and there were seven of us. Six, I corrected, with a pang. Still, too many for us to last long on handfuls of fruit. The bilimbis were basically ninety per cent water, like cucumbers. We'd have to eat masses of them to get even close to a daily calorie intake. Not to mention the lack of protein. I didn't know much about foraging or wild plants but I knew a lot about counting calories and macros thanks to a lifetime of dieting and personal trainers. The brain is a computer that runs on fat and carbs. We were screwed.

'Is there anything we can catch – to eat?' I asked. 'Like rabbits or . . . jungle rabbits, I don't know. Something we can get meat from?' I was thinking of Bryce and what he'd say when I handed over a few handfuls of salad to him and the others. He wasn't going to be happy and I knew he'd blame me.

Araya shrugged. 'Not without a gun. My grandfather used to shoot wild pigs, monkeys, anything when he was out in the jungle for a long time. Guiding tourists. But we don't have a gun.'

The idea of eating one of those pigs after it had gorged on human flesh made me feel very sick. I shook my head, indicating that I wanted to drop the subject. We carried our haul back to the tent and split it into portions. Once it was divided between the six of us the fairly impressive mound of leaves and fruits dwindled down to a handful of food each. San'ya wasn't around and I guessed he'd gone off to do his own thing, but what that was I had no idea. Without waiting for him to return I gathered up three portions for the others in the plane and put them in one of the bags, with the leaves sticking out the top.

I took a deep breath and then climbed up the ladder only to come face to face with Kaitlyn at the top. Had she been sitting there all this time to intercept me? Looking past her I saw that Bryce was sitting up now and playing with one of the scrap metal knives, testing its edge on the grubby cream leather seat. He looked up as I arrived and his eyes flicked down at the bag as I passed it to Kaitlyn. I willed him to let it go and not say anything. I just wanted to get away and my stomach was tied into horrible knots just waiting for his reaction.

'That it?'

Fletcher, roused from his doze, cracked bleary eyes open. 'Is the food here?'

Like I was a PA delivering fresh sushi and not a mozzie-bitten plane crash survivor. The irritation I felt was a welcome distraction from fear. Kaitlyn took the bag over to the pair of them and they rifled through it, getting more agitated as they did so. I glanced at the ladder and wondered if I could get down it before they reached me.

'A bunch of leaves and some tiny little . . . what are these?' Bryce said, waving the yellow fruit at me.

'Mayong,' I said, uncertainly. 'That's its leaves and there's some other plant in there. Araya identified the stuff and we're eating the same.'

The fruit bounced off my chest and Bryce, having thrown it hard enough to bruise, laughed when I flinched. I opened my mouth to say something, then closed it again. My throat was tight with everything I wanted to say, but it felt pointless to voice any of it. It wouldn't matter. He was looking at me, his face half in shadow, waiting for me to react. I didn't want to give him the satisfaction.

'It looks poisonous,' Fletcher said, eyeing the pink stems.

I tried to shut down the conversation so I could leave

before my temper got the better of me. 'Like I said, we're eating it too, so . . .'

'Don't really give a shit what you're eating – except of course that it came out of our share,' Bryce said, waspish. A second fruit hit me, this time rebounding off my neck. My hands curled into fists and I willed myself to remain calm and not make the situation worse. I wondered if he was still taking yaba and how much. Surely he had to be running out. Then again, I didn't know what he'd been buying while we were at the club. The stuff was cheap. He could have been holding a lot when the plane went down.

'The deal was you find us food – not yourself,' Fletcher agreed.

'Do you want it, or not?' I hissed, losing my temper and immediately regretting it.

Bryce stood up suddenly and I flinched back, remembering how he'd grabbed me before. It wasn't until he'd shaken me that I'd really appreciated how much bigger than me he was. I'd never been afraid of a man before, not even sleazy managers and handsy bandmates. I was never really alone with Dad's security buzzing around and even when I was, there was always a sort of invisible sign over me, reminding people who my dad was and what he could do to them. If he decided to give a shit – but they didn't know that he was only intermittently an attentive father. It was a bluff but it usually worked. Just then, however, I felt very small and completely defenceless.

He poked me hard in the chest, his finger leaving a sharp dart of pain in my sternum. 'Just get better stuff tomorrow – I don't care if you have to climb a fucking tree to get some eggs, or go chasing after one of those pigs you let steal our food. Just get it done.' Those last four words were delivered with a poke each, right in the same spot. So hard that my heart skipped a beat.

The retort I might otherwise have made was sticking in the back of my throat. I was too afraid to say it, in case he pushed me over or, worse, out of the plane. If I fell I might break my ankle or hit my head again. There were no hospitals out here and even a small injury could get infected fast. An outburst from him could kill me. Even if he didn't mean it to. That was how much power he had.

Looking into his dark eyes, I wondered if he knew it. If he liked it.

'Kait,' Fletcher drawled, breaking the tense silence. 'Make some dinner.'

Kaitlyn pushed past me and Bryce handed her the bag without looking away from me. I had no idea what she was going to make with what I'd brought and the glare she sent my way told me she didn't either. But she'd have to do something if she didn't want to get the same treatment I was getting. Both of us were only as good as what we could offer them, and we knew it.

Finally, Bryce looked away and I took that as permission to scurry down the ladder.

I retreated to the tent and found San'ya and Araya eating their food. Mine was untouched and I felt grateful for that. They hadn't taken the opportunity of my absence to screw me over. San'ya spat a large pit from one of the yellow fruits into the dirt and reached for another. As I rolled some leaves together around a bilimbi in the hopes of making something satisfying, he nodded at the fireside.

'Don't say anything,' he advised in a low voice, as I spotted the three large eggs resting in the ashes. 'They'll be cooked soon.'

I blinked at them. Eggs. Protein. Food. My stomach clenched in excitement.

'Where did you find them?' I asked, keeping my voice low in case Kaitlyn or the others were earwigging from the plane.

'Went looking for more bamboo and found a hornbill nest. A neighbour had one appear in his tree once – like a mud pie right in the trunk. Had to have conservationists come to look.'

'They're . . . endangered?' I looked at the eggs and felt a tiny sliver of guilt.

'Right now, so are we,' San'ya pointed out. 'Host a benefit for them when you get home.' His tone was wry and a little on the harsh side, but compared to Bryce and Fletcher I'd take it.

'Anyway, I found it and chipped the mud and shit off the front. Mother was inside but I got her with the machete – made too much of a mess of her to actually cook but the eggs are still good. Pricked them with an earring so they won't explode. Should be good to eat.'

I felt ridiculously grateful that he was sharing them with me. Even though I knew it would be impossible for either of them to hide the eggs from me when I lived right alongside them. He could still have refused to share. I wasn't under any illusions that we were friends, or even allies. But at least they weren't treating me like shit, and right then that was the best I had going for me.

It was dark by the time the eggs were deemed done and cooled. San'ya rolled them out of the embers with a stick and we peeled off the shells. I split mine in half, paranoid that I might find a chick inside, but if the egg had been destined to produce one, it hadn't formed yet.

The egg was gone in three bites, but it felt deliciously solid as it made its way to my belly. The rich savoury taste of crumbly yolk sat on my tongue. It was better than any five-star cuisine I'd ever had. Actual tears welled up in my eyes. I only wished we'd had the meat of the bird to go with it.

That night we all lay down, Janet's absence painfully obvious once we were ready to sleep. I looked up at the darkness under the canopy and told myself that soon I'd be waking up in a hotel room, in crisp white linens. A waiter would bring me breakfast under a silver dome – poached eggs and buttery hollandaise, crisp salty bacon and plump, semolina-coated muffins. Black coffee with cream and brown sugar, pastries full of ripe berries and crème pâtissière. Ice-cold orange juice and thick smoothies topped with chocolate dust.

I fell asleep, dreaming about food.

I woke up as something hot wrapped itself around my ankles. Half-asleep a sliver of alarm worked its way through my mind. I started to sit up, still foggy with sleep. A fog that was torn away as the hands on my legs dragged me from the tent.

Chapter 21

I screamed and kicked, dirt and stone biting into my skin as the back of my dress rucked up. I heard as San'ya and Araya woke and started yelling. They grabbed at my arms and held on to me but I was already too far away for them to get much purchase. I was hauled out from under the canopy and then Bryce was in my face, his hand fisted in my clothes.

Spittle peppered my face and Bryce's nose was only a hair from mine as he screamed in my face. 'You bitch! You tried to poison us!'

I was too shocked and scared to make a sound. That was when I heard Kaitlyn wailing. She was some distance away, apparently still on the plane. Shock from the accusation and the brutal awakening had me speechless. It was Araya who shoved at Bryce to get him off me.

'We didn't poison anyone! We ate the same exact food!'

Looking up I saw San'ya appear beside her, holding his scrap metal machete. That, more than anything, had Bryce stepping back. I crawled away, getting myself out of his reach before looking back. He still looked furious, his features practically glowing red in the light of the campfire embers.

'Then why is Fletcher so fucking sick?' he snapped.

'I don't know! But if you want our help you are not asking the right way,' Araya retorted, clearly emboldened by San'ya and his machete. 'What's wrong with him?'

Bryce glared at her and I scrambled back to my feet. 'If we'd poisoned the food, you'd all be sick, not just Fletcher,' I said, trying to find my voice even if I couldn't meet his eyes.

Bryce growled in frustration and annoyance. 'He said he had a headache, and then that it was turning into a migraine. He took some pills but it just kept getting worse. Then he said it was like someone was stabbing his eyes from inside. So he took some more pills and passed out, but now he's woken up and he's throwing his guts up – all pale and sweaty.'

'Could be an overdose,' I muttered.

Bryce twitched like he wanted to grab for me, but San'ya got in his way with a sidestep. 'He knows his shit – and so do I. He didn't take too many pills. It was just paracetamol and then some oxy. He should be fine. Would be if you hadn't given us those fucking leaves to eat . . .'

'Enough!' San'ya held up an arm to cut off Bryce's ranting. 'Let's go look at him and make sure he hasn't been bitten by a snake or something in the night, OK?'

Bryce clearly wanted to keep arguing, but Kaitlyn's sobbing was only getting louder and I could tell he was shaken at the idea that there might be something in the plane that might hurt him too. So he turned away and stalked back to the ladder. We trailed after him and I glanced at Araya.

'You think it's a snake or a spider or something?'

She shrugged helplessly. 'I don't know, but it wasn't the leaves. That was roselle. It's not poisonous. And we're fine.'

In the plane we found Fletcher hunched over the toilet bucket in the cockpit, with the door wide open. Kaitlyn hovered nearby, her hand over her mouth as she cried and kept asking him what was wrong. He was retching and heaving so hard it sounded painful. We just had to wait until he collapsed against the wall before we could try and get a better look at him. He was at least mostly naked, just in his ripe boxers. So it would be easy to see if he'd been bitten or stung.

'Get 'em away,' he groaned, when San'ya tried to check him for snakebites. 'Bryce . . .'

'Get off him!' Kaitlyn whined, pulling at San'ya's arm.

'Doesn't look like a snake bit him,' San'ya said. 'Not that I can see. But look at this.'

We had to squint in the pre-dawn gloom coming in through the broken windshield, but it became obvious what San'ya wanted us to see. Fletcher's skin was red and bumpy, covered in something that looked a bit like inflamed goose pimples.

'What is that?' Bryce said, backing away.

'Do your arms and legs hurt?' San'ya asked Fletcher. 'Like in your joints?'

Fletcher nodded, and threw himself at the bucket just in time to throw up another squirt of yellow bile.

'I think it's dengue,' San'ya said, doubtfully.

'Dengue fever?' I said, stunned. I'd heard of it, obviously, probably on the news or something. But it felt like such a distant thing – like measles or whooping cough, a disease from another time that no one got anymore because we had flush toilets and . . . vaccines. I realised with a horrible chill that I hadn't bothered to get any, and from what little I'd seen of Fletcher's content he was against them because of . . . well, because they were something he could be against – like soy beans and pasteurisation. If there was a vaccine for dengue, he hadn't had it. And neither had I.

I looked at Fletcher's hunched back, covered in a rash and felt my own skin prickle. Was that going to be me? Looking around I wondered if Kaitlyn was vaccinated. Bryce wasn't – I knew that. Were we all going to catch it from Fletcher? Was it already too late?

San'ya was nodding. 'Yeah, I've seen tourists get it. We had to have ambulances come to the hotel for a few. When it's bad it's . . . pretty bad.'

'How bad?' Kaitlyn demanded, her voice shrill. I couldn't even blame her, I was freaking out too.

San'ya looked uneasy. 'Like . . . taken away in an ambulance, days in hospital, intensive care, bad.'

Silence struck us like lightning.

'Do we have it?' Bryce asked eventually. 'Can we catch it off him? I haven't been vaccinated.'

'Oh God, me neither.' Kaitlyn looked at Fletcher and clutched at her necklace.

'I think only kids can get the vaccine. Doesn't work on adults. We might all have it – from bugs. Look at us – we're all covered in mosquito bites,' San'ya pointed out. 'It spreads like that. But it's not normally so bad. Some don't even get symptoms and for others it's like flu. Has he had it before? That can make it worse.'

'No,' Fletcher croaked. 'Not that I know . . . oh God.' He leant over the bucket again, retching.

'I had it,' San'ya said softly, looking worried. 'Not this bad though.'

'Should you be in here?' Araya asked.

'Like I said, if he's got it we're probably all infected . . .' San'ya looked up at us helplessly. 'Not much we can do about it now.'

He was obviously trying hard to sound brave but I could see his throat working hard and he clasped his hands together to hide that they were shaking. 'I'm sure I'll be . . .'

'Help him,' Kaitlyn interrupted, looking around at us. 'What do we do?'

'Give him more paracetamol and water and put him to bed,' San'ya said, taking the opportunity to distract from his own fear. 'Not much else we can do. Hopefully it'll get better and he'll be all right in a few days.'

I looked at him and he didn't look entirely sure. Like when we dealt with Janet's body, he looked so young and out of his element.

'And if he's not?' Kaitlyn asked, eyes so wide I could see the whites all the way around, filled with tears.

'Then . . . we try something else,' San'ya said, without much conviction.

I don't think any of us really believed there was anything else we could do. I didn't have the first clue about dengue but San'ya was probably right that if Fletcher had it, that meant we all had it. It was just symptomless in us, or it hadn't developed much yet. I was hoping it was the first thing, and not the last.

We left Kaitlyn to dose Fletcher up with paracetamol once he'd stopped throwing up. She had him snort it, which seemed like a good call. There wasn't anything else we could do. San'ya and Araya went back to the tent to get some more sleep. But I was too wired from everything that had happened to even think about drifting off again. Instead I went looking for some food for when they woke up, seeing as it was getting light already.

I poked ahead of me with a stick and kept a wary eye out for snakes or creepy-crawlies. There wasn't much to pick where we'd been yesterday, so I moved on to a new patch. There were some weird fruits that kind of looked like the ones I'd seen on fancy cakes at Harrods. Those orange berries with little paper lanterns around them. I picked some to take back to Araya, hoping they were edible.

As I picked fruits, my filthy acrylic nails closing around them and tugging them free, I felt like I was watching myself from far away. How many times had I done things like this for content? Picking fresh mint from 'my' herb garden – maintained by our landscaper – to make tea that I never drank. Trailing my hands through lavender fields in France before hopping in the car and speeding away to Paris for fashion week. Holding a baby goat while Bryce stood three feet away, ready with my hand sanitiser and taking photo after photo.

Nature had always felt to me like a thing you visited. Something we'd pushed to the fringes with houses and shopping arcades and resorts. Nature was swimming in the sea beside a beach that was litter picked three times a day. Bathing under a waterfall fenced in by a five-star spa. Taking a cable car to the top of a mountain to pose in the snow. Only as it turned out nature wasn't as clean and convenient and beautiful as I'd thought. It wasn't even at the fringes. It was all around, pressing in on us.

Waiting for just one thing to fail – a rogue wave hitting that pristine beach, the cable car plummeting onto the crags below . . . a plane crashing into the jungle.

Nature was a set of open jaws, just waiting. Like a foolish little mouse I'd been climbing in and out of its mouth as if it would never close on me. Well, it had and now I was fighting for my life. We all were.

I was so busy moping and dropping the fruits into my bag, that it took me a while to realise that I was being watched. I added a bilimbi to my bag and realised how quiet it had gotten. It was as if everything around me was holding its breath. The same kind of tense silence when a waiter trips and drops a bottle of Cristal on the marble floor. A mixture of horror and intense alertness.

I looked up, and found myself looking into a pair of big, yellow eyes.

My heart felt like it was being crushed in a fist. The tiger was camouflaged amongst the leaves. Its stripes and the strips of dappled shade blurring together. But the eyes stood out like headlights on a dark road. They reflected the sunlight, unblinking and fixed on me.

I couldn't move. Couldn't breathe. Had it been stalking me or had I just wandered stupidly over to where it was having a nap? It watched me, pupils large and focused. I'd never realised how big tigers were before. Having never seen one up close in real life. I had the sudden irrational thought that if Dad had taken me to more zoos and fewer concerts I'd have been more prepared for this.

Slowly, it shifted and I realised it was getting up. It lowered its head and a giant, clawed paw twitched up and through the undergrowth, towards me.

'They're back!'

Araya's scream cut through the air. I jerked, blinked automatically and the tiger vanished. Only a few trembling leaves remained to convince me that I hadn't completely imagined it.

My legs gave out from under me and I barely managed to grab hold of a tree in time to stop myself falling.

My brain was still stuck in a frightened loop. I stood there, half leaning on the tree, unable to think or move. Then something in my chest broke and I sucked in a sudden gulp of air and sobbed it back out. My legs shook and I clasped a hand over my wildly beating heart. It felt as if it was about to try and leap out of my chest.

Then I actually processed what I'd just heard, and my heart leapt for an entirely new reason – relief. Through the haze of panic and fear came a sliver of hope now that the others were back. We were going to be rescued. We were saved.

Dimly I heard the yells of the other passengers, all mixing together like the rest of the jungle noises. The sound had come back on all around me and the chattering and squawking was back as if it had never been away.

Then I heard Bryce's voice, raised over the others. His words the only ones I could make out clearly.

'Where's Dash?'

Chapter 22

As soon as I could feel my legs again, I bolted out of the woods and back to camp.

As I reached the others I saw them clustered around a shape on the ground. With the exception of Fletcher who was probably still in the plane and Kaitlyn, who was peeking out from under the canopy. She probably thought she was safe in there. Safe, so long as she didn't set foot on anything that wasn't manmade and therefore 'dangerous'.

The shape on the ground was Summer. I saw that as I got closer. Probably should have assumed it as I'd heard Bryce ask after Dash. But I still wasn't firing on all cylinders.

She looked dreadful, even compared to the rest of us. But then I supposed five days hiking in the jungle would do that to you. Her blonde hair was matted and her skin was engrained with dirt, except for where sweat and tears had carved through the grime. Her clothes – a lilac mini-dress covered in beads and low wedge sandals – were almost falling apart. Beads were weeping from torn threads and there was dirt and dried blood all over her. Her feet were bloody and some straps on her shoes had broken. She looked like she hadn't slept in days. She probably hadn't.

Her hollow, haunted eyes were darting about the clearing. Her peeling lips pulled back from yellow teeth. There was a weird sort of mole on her cheek, which I didn't remember being there before. As I got closer I was sickened to realise it had legs. Tiny, black legs wriggling lazily against her tear-stained skin. There was a bug, burrowed into her skin, living in her.

'Where's Dash?' Bryce asked, for what was probably the fifth or sixth time. He grabbed her scabby, grazed up arms and shook her, hard. 'Where is he! Where's the fucking box!?'

That was when I realised that Summer had nothing with her. Not even the bag we'd sent her off with. No black box. No beacon to bring our rescuers to us. We'd waited five days, clinging to hope and now . . . now we had nothing. No food, no water, no hope.

'Summer!' Bryce yelled, and kicked at her leg, covered in thin whip cuts, which I guessed came from the undergrowth. I flinched and half moved to stop him, then stopped, afraid he'd hit me if I laid a finger on him.

'That's enough!' San'ya startled to life, pulling Bryce away from her. He struggled against him, yelling and cursing.

'Shut up! She's trying to tell us,' Araya said, and a hush fell over us. I felt guilt land hot and shameful in my belly. Even shy little Araya was standing up to Bryce. Was I the only one to be afraid of him? To see how much he'd changed?

Summer mumbled something and Araya moved in closer, laying a careful hand on her arm. Summer repeated whatever it was, still twitchy and restless.

'What is it?' Bryce demanded. 'What's she saying?'

Araya looked up at us, confused. 'She said "he's dead" and that "they killed him".'

'Who the hell is "they"?' Bryce exploded, voice turning shrill. 'Animals? People? Are there people out here? Where!?'

But Summer either couldn't or wouldn't tell us. She shrank in on herself and put her hands over her ears to block Bryce out. He tried to kick at her again but San'ya intercepted his leg with a kick of his own. Bryce stumbled and then shoved San'ya in retaliation. For a second they might have been two blokes beefing outside a club, then Bryce bared his teeth and dragged San'ya into a headlock.

'Stop it!' Araya held her arms out to shield Summer as they struggled, and I held my own hands up without any real idea of what I was able to do.

San'ya made a choking noise and Bryce just squeezed harder, huffing air as he fought to keep hold of him. San'ya was smaller, younger, and Bryce had been using my personal gym for months. This wasn't going to end well. Panic ripped through me and before I could think of the consequences I'd thrown myself at them.

I grabbed a handful of Bryce's shirt and pulled, my other hand snatching his hair. One of my jagged acrylics carved a bloody line over his forehead and he snarled in pain. His eyes found mine and there was nothing but hatred in them. Blind, raging hate.

San'ya managed to wriggle free and stumbled away. I backed off too and hardly dared to blink in case he flew at me. Bryce was breathing hard, spittle on his chin. He panted for breath and finally stabbed a finger in Summer's direction.

'Get her to fucking talk. We've been stuck here for days – either she knows something or she fucked up and now we're stuck here forever.'

The word 'forever' rang around the clearing. I heard Kaitlyn above us, like a princess in her castle – sobbing.

Of course it wouldn't be forever, would it? We'd be dead before too long. Out of food and clean water and stuck in a jungle teeming with lethal bacteria, bugs, snakes and tigers. The black box was our only chance, and now we were out of time and out of choices.

Bryce stormed off, back to the plane, and my shoulders sagged slightly. He was backing down, for the moment. But if we couldn't get a coherent story out of Summer I dreaded to think what he might do to her, or anyone of us who stood in his way.

'Help me,' Araya said, looking at me. 'She's probably dehydrated and confused . . . We should take care of her and hopefully she'll be able to tell us more later. When she's more herself.'

With nothing else to do but hope she was right, I helped her pick Summer up and carry her to the tent. San'ya was still recovering, now sitting on the ground with his arms hanging over his knees, head down. I thought I saw his shoulders shaking with sobs.

At the tent, Araya turned wide eyes on me. 'Your boyfriend is nuts.'

'I know,' I said. For the first time it was out there; someone else was seeing it too. Bryce was getting scary and I didn't know how to handle him anymore. The power I'd had in our relationship came from credit cards and luxury apartments. His was in his strength and animal rage. I couldn't fight that.

'But . . . you need to get us some stuff from the plane – tweezers, water and something with salt and sugar. To help rehydrate her.'

'I can't go in there! Not right after . . .' I gestured at San'ya. 'They're not going to want to give me anything anyway,' I pointed out. 'And we've got nothing to trade.'

'They will if they think it's their only chance of being saved. She knows something and the only way to get it out of her is to get her well enough to talk,' Araya said. 'I know it's not what you want to hear, but you are the best chance we have of getting answers from her. My mother she gets confused too, when she's dehydrated – because she's sick and she struggles to drink, but we can fix it. We can get her well again, before Bryce gets angry again.'

She sounded so sure and so confident that I couldn't help but put my trust in her. She was right – we had to get information out of Summer or Bryce would kick off again. Maybe worse than before. None of us were a physical match for him, and before too long we might be struck down like Fletcher, with dengue. We'd be helpless. Fear crawled over my skin. I had to go to the plane.

I crossed the clearing on shaky legs and took a deep breath before I climbed up the ladder. I wasn't surprised when I found Kaitlyn sobbing on one of the grimy leather seats. She was probably really going through it, stuck in here with Bryce and her sick boyfriend.

Bryce was on his banquette, looking furious and stressed. He didn't pay Kaitlyn any attention, just glared at the wall above Fletcher, who was lying very still on his own bed, pale and glazed in sweat.

I took a breath and forced myself to ask, not wanting to take another step into the plane. I was worried if I got within grabbing distance of Bryce I wouldn't be allowed to leave.

'I um . . . need tweezers, some water and any salt or sugar that you have,' I said. 'We're trying to get Summer talking again but, we need some supplies to fix her up enough so she'll talk.'

For a moment I thought Bryce was going to argue with me, storm up the plane and grab me again, but even he seemed to understand the importance of this task. He waved a hand at Kaitlyn, not bothering to look at me.

'Get her what she needs.'

Kaitlyn hesitated, hovering like a servant unsure if she should take orders from him while the master of the house was laid up with fever. But she finally jerked into action and hunted through the pile of supplies she'd found. I didn't dare let him out of my sight while she looked.

There were several pairs of tweezers from multiple evening bags. I took two pairs and hoped that would be enough. Only one and a half bottles of water remained and Kaitlyn gave me the half, which didn't surprise me. Salt and sugar were a little more difficult to come by. Eventually Kaitlyn offered me two cough sweets – sticky and gross in their sliver of foil packaging – and a single KFC salt packet, which must have been in someone's purse for a while. It was all we were going to get though, so I took it all and rushed back to Araya without a backward glance.

I wasted no time in getting out of there and practically ran from the bottom of the ladder to the tent. Safety in numbers, even if I doubted Araya and San'ya could pull Bryce off me if he really wanted to hurt me.

While San'ya combined the bottled water with what

little we had in the buckets, adding the salt and melting the sugary sweets into it, Araya and I dealt with the ticks. She handed me a pair of tweezers and gestured to the one on Summer's face. It was fat and slightly oval, like a disgusting seedpod with wriggling legs.

'Grab lightly behind the head and twist as you pull,' Araya advised. 'Put it in here.'

She had an empty tonic bottle – one of the many that now littered the clearing.

'Then dab with this.' She passed me half a tissue saturated with alcohol and hypochlorous acid spray. 'Should help keep infection from setting in. The wounds aren't as deep as . . .'

As Janet's. She didn't need to say it.

I carefully removed the tick from Summer's face and dabbed the tiny bloody hole it left behind. The more ticks we removed, the more we seemed to find. On Summer's bare legs and arms, on her neck, in her hair. She'd picked up so many of them it was no wonder she looked so sick. They were all feasting on her blood. I shuddered in sympathetic revulsion as I pulled a fat specimen from between her toes. My skin was crawling and prickling with imaginary invaders.

We cleaned her up as best we could with what he had available. Araya had her strip out of her dress and she shook it out, checking for more ticks. Summer let herself be manoeuvred like a doll. She looked too exhausted to care much. Even when we moistened tissues and wiped the blood and dirt from her skin. Once she was dressed again and the concoction San'ya had made was cool enough to drink, Araya held it up so she could drink. Summer drank weakly and once she was done, she passed out on the floor.

'Now we wait,' Araya said, flatly. 'And hope.'

'What do you think happened?' I asked her, as we looked down at the sorry state Summer was in. 'She said they killed him but . . . there's no one out here, right? If we've been close to a town or a village this entire time . . .'

'If it was a town or anything like that, they wouldn't have killed Dash.' Araya looked deeply worried and I wondered what she was thinking. 'My mother's family is from a village right in the jungle and sometimes they have lost tourists and hikers turn up. They take care of them; they give them food. No one would want someone to die just because they were stupid or in trouble.'

'So if these people did kill Dash . . . ?'

'Then they're dangerous and are probably here because it's far away from everything else. It means it's just us, and them out here.'

I wrapped my arms around myself. 'That's what I was worried you'd say.'

'Lila!'

My head snapped up and I saw Kaitlyn holding the canopy out of the way as she yelled for me. Even from this distance I could see how scared she was. Her mouth opened, dark and red and quavering with panic.

'Fletcher's bleeding!'

Chapter 23

Araya moved before I did, rushing towards the plane and climbing the ladder. I was right behind her, fear of Bryce swallowed by shock at this new development. As soon as we reached the interior of the plane, Kaitlyn was clasping at us in desperation. I felt a flash of sympathy for her, so alone up here with Fletcher's worsening condition and Bryce's indifference.

'He just started throwing up blood, but there's blood coming out of his nose too . . . I don't know what to do,' Kaitlyn whimpered. 'Help him!'

Araya pivoted and called for San'ya, but he was already climbing the ladder. I looked around in the gloom for Bryce and found him still just sitting on the bench seat, staring at Fletcher. Fletcher who looked like an eerie painting of a dying Victorian child. He was waxy and pale, almost luminous in the shadows. A dark trickle of blood led from his nose to his mouth and he looked barely conscious.

'Is it dengue, or something else?' I asked, mind conjuring up images of all kinds of nasty diseases we could be exposed to out here. Didn't bubonic plague sometimes come back in places like this? From the dirt or the air or something?

'If I'm right and it is dengue then . . . he's got it bad,' San'ya said, voice a little raspy from the headlock. 'Has he been really thirsty?'

'We're all thirsty,' Bryce bit out. 'He's getting his share.'

San'ya ignored him and went over to place his hand on Fletcher's stomach. He groaned and shook his head, weakly pawing San'ya's hand away. When San'ya looked back our way his expression was tense and grim.

'He needs a hospital. We can't . . . there's nothing we can do out here.'

Kaitlyn keened and clawed at my arm with her shredded manicure. 'Lila, this is your fault! Do something . . . We have to get him out of here. We have to . . . I don't know – carry him. Take him somewhere to get help. We can't stay here; we can't . . .' she shrieked as I pinched her upper arm, but she'd been getting hysterical. I had to do something and that was the first thing I thought of. It at least got her to let go of me.

'We'll do something, OK?' I said, firmly. 'But not until we know what's out there. If someone out there killed Dash, we need to know where they are and how to avoid them. Or we might all be next.'

Kaitlyn grabbed her arm where I'd pinched it and glared at me mutinously. But she didn't contradict me, which was something at least. I turned to Araya for support and found her watching Fletcher with sad, helpless eyes.

'We need to keep him comfortable, try and wait this out, right?' I said, trying to rally support.

San'ya looked unsure but eventually nodded. I wondered if he was thinking of his last bout of dengue

189

and wondering if he was already reinfected, heading for a fate worse than this. 'All we can do I guess. When she wakes up—' he gestured in the vague direction of the tent and Summer '—then we can plan.'

'OK. So, let's get him some water, clean up his nose and just . . . keep everyone calm until then,' I said. I was hoping that Bryce would do or say something, so I could judge what state he was in, but he didn't. He was just watching us like he didn't care less what we did. Like Fletcher was already gone. For the first time I wasn't just afraid of what he might do. I was unnerved by him and his odd silence. I'd never seen him so uncaring – his anger and violence weren't as surprising as this lack of empathy. His eyes were just empty of human empathy. I realised then that not only was he capable of hurting me, or all of us, but that he might not even feel as if he was doing anything wrong.

'Bryce,' I prompted, trying to make him react so my skin would stop crawling. 'Can you watch Fletcher while we get Kaitlyn to rest for a bit?'

His brows furrowed like he wanted to argue, but perhaps I'd caught him outside of a yaba binge, because he just shrugged and leant back against the wall of the plane. Every inch a sulky teenager. At least that was better than just emotionless staring.

Araya gentled Kaitlyn down onto some cushions on the floor and gave her the water bottle to sip from. Then she went back to look after Summer. I caught San'ya's eye and nodded towards the cockpit. He frowned but went that way and as soon as the door was shut I wetted my lips and fixed him with a look.

'We can't go into the jungle,' I said, firmly, my chest tight with fear.

'Why?' he asked. 'I know it's dangerous, but so is staying here . . .'

'There's a tiger, out there. Watching us.'

His eyes widened. 'You . . . are you sure?'

I nodded. 'I was picking fruit and then it was right there, watching me, stalking me. I think you guys scared it off when you started yelling that Summer was back, but it looked ready to attack me, and then it would have come for all of us.'

San'ya let out a long breath. 'But it could get us here too.'

'It hasn't yet,' I pointed out, realising as I said it that he was right. I knew he was right. We weren't safe anywhere. Still I pushed on. 'It's been days. Maybe it's the plane or something that's making it cautious, but out there we won't have that.' I was clinging to our last piece of the outside world like a talisman and he clearly knew it. He looked at me as if I was being as hysterical as Kaitlyn. Maybe I was.

'We're not safe here – look at Janet, look at Bethan, and now this. We can't stay here. Especially now we know there's no black box. We'll never get rescued unless we move. And . . . honestly I'm not sure we can call ourselves "safe" around that psycho.'

He was right, but I didn't want to believe it. The simple fact was that the jungle scared me more than anything. Even Bryce. If San'ya was right and we weren't safe here, I still felt safer here than in the jungle. That was all I had.

'We don't even know if they reached the tail. They might just have gone the wrong way and if we send another group, we'll find the box,' I said, feeling desperate.

San'ya didn't look convinced. 'We lost people, while

they were gone. Lost Dash. We can't wait forever. What if the next group doesn't come back, or what if they do and we're all dead by then?'

Panic scratched at my throat. I shook my head, out of ideas. I had no idea what the best course of action was and trying the wrong thing would mean death. No second chances. No do-overs. One chance – that was all we had.

'Let's just wait, until Summer can tell us what happened. We need to leave but we also need to know everything before we make a plan. Rushing off without one will get us killed.' San'ya sighed. 'But we need to keep an eye on *him*.'

It was clear he meant Bryce, not poor sickly Fletcher. That at least I could agree with. Anything that delayed that trek into the tiger-infested jungle was something I could agree with though, to be fair.

'You two done in there?' Bryce asked, harsh voice cutting through the humid atmosphere. I jumped, feeling guilty though I hadn't done anything wrong. Was I imagining a note of bitter jealousy in his voice? He sounded like he was accusing us of something. But I wasn't sure what.

We emerged and Bryce looked us over as if searching for evidence of something – did he think we were hooking up back there, or was he more worried about some sort of mutiny? Was he even sure what he suspected us of? It seemed to me that he was so wired and suspicious that logic was starting to desert him.

'You want to talk, do it out here next time,' he said roughly, and positioned himself between us and the cockpit door like a bouncer, waving us towards the ladder. I didn't dare meet his eye or try to defend myself against whatever he was imagining. I knew it wouldn't help.

I was relieved to get out of the plane and went to sit with Araya, watching over Summer. San'ya followed me at a distance – possibly to appease Bryce – and said something vague about bamboo before taking the improvised machete and heading into the treeline. I didn't blame him for making an excuse to leave. Maybe he thought if we were all going to head out into the wilderness, we'd better arm ourselves. Though what a sharp stick would do to a tiger was anyone's guess.

While Summer slept I helped Araya with the food I'd gathered. Apparently the little lantern fruits were edible, so I patted myself on the back for that. She broke the bilimbis apart with her hands and put them in the ice bucket over the fire with some of the leaves. Cooking them up into a mush was probably nicer than eating fistfuls of raw leaves, but it didn't look that appetising. I was starting to crave spices and herbs and salt to go along with the fatty, rich foods of my imagination.

'What's going to happen, if Fletcher dies?' Araya asked softly, prodding the 'stew' with a piece of split bamboo.

'I don't know. Kaitlyn's going to freak out and Bryce . . . he already blames me for everything. This'll only make it worse.' I lowered my voice. 'I have no idea what he might do.'

Araya sat back on her heels and looked at me, considering. 'Me either but . . . we just have to stay vigilant. And . . . it's not all your fault. That we're here.'

'Thanks,' I muttered. 'You don't have to . . .'

'I mean it. Maybe you should have done stuff like make sure the flight plan was filed, but . . . you don't control the weather, or the snakes or the mosquitos. We all chose to get on a stranger's plane to go and party. We're all a little bit responsible for being here.'

I sniffed, unexpectedly grateful to her for trying to spare my feelings. But even if she didn't hold me fully responsible, I did. It was my idea, this whole thing. My plane and my insistence on taking off so soon, with no flight plan and a storm on the way. No matter if everyone forgave me. I didn't think I'd ever forgive myself.

'. . . nmm . . .'

Both of us turned to find Summer stirring out of her near-comatose sleep. She smacked her lips and opened her eyes slowly, but they didn't seem as unfocused and confused as they had before.

'I made it back,' she whispered. 'I didn't think I would. Just kept looking for the X's and walking . . . walking . . .'

'You're OK now,' Araya assured her. Though obviously none of us were really OK. We were running out of water, had no food barring a few handfuls of fruit and there were dangerous animals and possibly murderers out there in the jungle. But reminding Summer of all that was counterproductive when we wanted her to talk.

'Can you tell us what happened, to Dash? To you? Did you find the tail of the plane?'

My heart was beating fast and hope made my skin feel tight. I was waiting and holding my breath as Summer looked at me, and slowly nodded.

'We found it,' she said, her crusty lips peeling apart painfully as she spoke. 'But we didn't find the box. Dash was angry, upset – he said part of the tail must have broken off before and it could be miles and miles away. We didn't have any food left. So we turned around to work out what to do with you guys and then . . .' She faltered and her eyes filled with tears. 'They killed him.'

'Who?' I asked, reaching for her hand, desperate for an answer and yet dreading it too. 'Who did you see?'

'Men.' Summer's voice was barely a whisper. 'They shot him. They shot him in the head and blood went everywhere and I just ran and ran and hid and then I tried to get back to the path and . . . and then I was here.'

'Shot him?' I glanced at Araya, worried. 'They had a gun?'

'Guns,' Summer corrected, bleakly. 'They all had guns.'

'Araya?' I asked.

She looked as confused and helpless as I felt. 'I don't know. Could be a lot of reasons – there's a lot of hunters and growers out here. Criminal gangs that have farms and fields set up.'

'As in they grow drugs?' I asked.

She nodded, but her brow remained furrowed. 'They protect their business. It's very competitive. Did you see any farmed fields? Buildings?'

'No. It was all just more jungle. Forever. Where's Janet?' Summer asked, interrupting my next question.

I looked at Araya, who was staring right back at me, her lip trembling. It was going to have to be me who told Summer the truth.

'She . . . died,' I said, trying and failing to find a gentler euphemism. But really, Janet hadn't 'passed away' or 'gone to a better place'. She was dead and rotting in the jungle and she had not gone easily. I couldn't find the words to take the sting out of that.

Summer inhaled thickly and sobbed. 'We're all going to die, aren't we? I wish they'd shot me too. Would have been faster. Dash never saw it coming.'

She broke down into noisy tears and Araya put her

arms around her. Summer hadn't exactly been my biggest fan before and I didn't think she'd want me all over her now, so I sat back and tried not to show how scared and helpless I felt.

San'ya came out of the jungle then, dragging bamboo and lengths of vine. He laid the bamboo out in a rectangle about one by six feet. For a delirious moment I thought he was making a coffin.

'Stretcher,' he said, by way of explanation, and brought the machete down hard on the bamboo to cut it to shape. 'We're getting out of here – and we're taking everyone with us. Even if we have to carry them.'

I watched him work and wished I had his surety. Fletcher and Summer were in no fit state to walk; hell, Fletcher was possibly dying. Even those of us who were in better shape were still hungry and thirsty, exhausted. We had no full-coverage clothing and no proper shoes – the women in heels and the men in sandals and loafers that weren't exactly all-terrain. If we went into the jungle burdened with stretchers, we'd end up in worse shape than Summer.

San'ya worked, sweating and panting with the thin saw chain that Dash had left us. I felt helpless, useless. A week ago I had the world in my pocket – a mobile phone stuffed with numbers and apps and credit card details that could get me anything I wanted. I could have solved every problem we were facing in minutes, ordered food and drinks to be delivered, called a private ambulance, and had Fletcher and Janet flown to a private room in a hospital. Booked us hotels and bought clean clothes. But everything I had was useless out here and it made me feel like I'd have been better off dying in Dash's place, or even instead of that German nurse. People who had stuff to contribute, who could actually save us.

I looked down at my diamond ring and rubbed the pad of my thumb over it. I'd been so thrilled with it but even back then I hadn't been sure about Bryce. He'd completely blindsided me with a proposal in a club. I'd shared my dream proposal with him and he hadn't cared enough to remember how important it was to me to do it where my mum had agreed to marry my dad.

Looking at the huge diamond on my finger I wondered if Bryce had ever actually loved me. Had it all been an act and I'd been too deluded to notice? I'd thought I had a nice, normal guy who didn't want to use me, but looking back I couldn't believe I'd managed to convince myself of that. Bryce was an aspiring DJ; my dad was in the music business. I'd wanted to believe that someone actually loved me for me, but all along he was just another user, playing on my emotions. I was such an idiot.

I was still thinking these dire thoughts when the sound of San'ya's sawing ceased. He hit the ground with a thump, toppling the chopped bamboo. I waited for him to get up, but he just laid there, motionless.

Chapter 24

We ran to him, and it didn't take more than a minute before Araya rucked up San'ya's shirt and found the same rash we'd seen on Fletcher. San'ya had dengue fever and it was clearly not symptomless for him either. He'd already had it, he said. And that made it worse. My heart sank into my stolen shoes.

He was barely conscious as we carried him to the tent and laid him out near where Summer was dozing again. I looked down at San'ya and Summer opened her eyes and peered at him in the gloom.

'What's wrong with him?' she asked, and I realised she'd missed all the talk of dengue, having not been in the plane. Her face was drawn despite her tan and she looked almost as sickly as she had when she first returned to us.

'Dengue,' Araya said succinctly, kneeling down by San'ya's head. 'Lila, get a bucket.'

San'ya had started to retch and I darted out to grab one of the empty rainwater buckets for her. I returned just in time to catch the first wave of stinking bile he threw up. Araya held him up so he wouldn't choke and once he was done she guided him back to the ground.

I was very aware that it was getting dark. Soon, away from the fire, we wouldn't be able to see our hands in front of our faces. The fire wasn't built up much at the moment either. We'd need light to try and take care of him and Summer.

'We should put him by the fire. I'll get it going again,' I said. Araya nodded.

I added a few lumps of dry wood to the fire – at least we had plenty of that at the moment – and prodded the embers with a piece of bamboo to get the flames to flare. Together, Araya and I moved San'ya to the outermost edge of the tent, where the light would reach him. Summer watched us, too weak to be of much help.

'Should we get Fletcher out here too, to keep an eye on him?' Araya asked.

I looked towards the plane and finally, shook my head. 'We'll never get him down the ladder, and the others won't want to leave the plane either. It'll just start a fight. They can take care of him up there and call us if they need anything.'

I wasn't sure even at the time that I believed it. Everything was just too much and I didn't want to be anywhere near Bryce. His eyes had made me feel so cold. I had no idea who that man was anymore and maybe I never had to begin with. I just had to hope Kaitlyn would take care of Fletcher, because Bryce didn't seem like he gave a shit about anyone but himself.

Clustered around the fire, we ate a little and then lay down to sleep. Araya and I were both tensed for action. For hours I could see her eyes glittering in the campfire light. She was awake and staring into it, listening as I was for sounds of danger, of trouble. In between Summer's soft snores I could hear San'ya breathing fast and irregularly. Chuffing and wheezing. He was sick, very sick. Worse, I realised that meant we now had three people who were even less equipped to survive a lengthy jungle hike than the rest of us. Too many for us to carry. We were stuck in the clearing – unable to travel with them or leave them behind.

Eventually I must have just passed out. I woke up to green-tinged sunlight and the inescapable sounds of the jungle. Birds were screeching and something, maybe a monkey, was whooping and yelping in the distance. Everything around us was moving and rustling with life, crawling and quivering with it. With bugs and snakes and the rooting of animals. I shuddered, and sat up to check myself over. I had fresh mozzie bites but that was to be expected. There wasn't anything on me, which was a relief. I was still terrified of waking up to a tarantula or giant centipede crawling over me.

I sat up, one hand moving to my back, which ached from so many nights spent on the ground. Then I caught sight of San'ya and couldn't hold back a cry.

Araya bolted upright and immediately looked his way. Summer stirred more slowly, but soon the three of us were clustered around San'ya, not daring to touch him.

He looked dreadful. Like he'd been beaten to within an inch of death. His formerly light brown skin was almost eighty per cent purple. Huge bruises covered the visible skin, dark and painful-looking. There was dried blood around his nose and between his lips.

'Did he . . . is he . . . ?' I asked.

Araya felt for a pulse and subsided slightly. 'He's alive.'

'What happened to him? He looks like he got attacked,'

I said. My first thought was that Bryce had seen he was sick and decided to get rid of him. Again I thought of the mercenary stare he'd given Fletcher, and the way he'd not seemed to care if he lived or died. Only how Fletcher's life affected his own. Bryce wasn't looking at any of us like we were people – only resources he could use or discard for his own benefit.

'His nose is bloody like Fletcher's,' Araya pointed out. 'I think it's the dengue. Something to do with the blood vessels – causing the bleeding under the skin?'

'Does that mean it's getting worse?' Summer asked, her voice quavering.

'. . . I think so,' Araya said eventually, then let out a frustrated sigh. 'I . . . I don't know! I'm just . . . trying to remember things from TV. I think it means he's bleeding, inside. His nose and his gums and . . . maybe other places too.'

I shuddered. I didn't want to think about what that meant. We didn't have any medication left to ease his pain either. We'd have to go begging to the others and I wasn't sure Bryce would give us anything. San'ya didn't look like he was in pain at least. There was only that uneven, fitful breathing and the ooze of blood from his nose to show that he was still alive.

'You should go check on Fletcher,' Araya said. 'He might be worse or . . .'

'He's not just worse . . . he's dying.'

We all turned at the sudden interruption and I felt Araya flinch beside me. It was Bryce, watching us from the plane. Looking down like we were bugs and he was both intrigued and disgusted by our movements. He didn't sound happy or sad about Fletcher or even worried about San'ya. He sounded bored, if anything.

'Are you sure?' Araya asked, finally, breaking the silence when I failed to speak up.

Bryce just shrugged. 'Kaitlyn's locked herself in the cockpit with him, but last I saw he was bleeding out the ass so . . . it wasn't looking good.' Even from this distance I could feel disdain radiating off him. 'What happened with the black box she and Dash went looking for? Is she talking yet?'

I automatically shifted slightly to block Summer from view. Not sure why. It was instinctive. 'It wasn't with the tail. It fell off during the crash.'

Bryce's jaw stiffened and he nodded, like he was thinking deeply. 'Well I guess we're not getting rescued then.'

He said it like he didn't care, but there was so much anger simmering under his tone. He was pissed and could lash out any time over this latest blow. And we were the only ones around to take the brunt of his fury. My heart was a tight little ball in my chest, every beat a jabbing finger against my sternum.

'San'ya wanted us to try and reach help – maybe find a village or a reserve around here where we can get medical treatment and a ride back to civilisation,' I said, trying to distract him with a new hope.

'Yeah . . . he doesn't look like he's going anywhere,' Bryce said. The look he cast our way was almost triumphant – our biggest defender was gone and he knew it. Fletcher was sick. Dash was dead. Bryce was the last man standing. King of the fucking jungle.

I looked at the half-finished stretchers and felt a stab of guilt. San'ya had tried so hard to be brave and useful and now he was bleeding to death as a disease ran riot through him. What hope was there for the rest of us?

'We can't stay here,' I said, echoing San'ya's words from the day before. Anything to make Bryce see that we needed to work together. To keep him from exploding at us. 'If we leave we might die, but if we stay . . . if we stay we're just waiting to die.'

Summer sobbed softly and covered her mouth with her hand. I didn't blame her. After what she'd been through, going back into the jungle was probably the last thing she wanted to do. But if we didn't, we'd just slowly die anyway.

Araya wrapped an arm around Summer and squeezed her shoulder. 'We have to try.'

I looked up at Bryce and found him climbing down the ladder. I couldn't help the panic that brought me to my feet as he closed in on us. When he reached us he looked at San'ya, the fire and the three of us. I sensed the tension in Araya and Summer. All three of us waiting for his next move, his next whim. If he attacked us I didn't think we could fight him off, not with Summer so weak and Araya so small.

Bryce swaggered to a stop and shoved his hands into his pockets. 'Well . . . if we're leaving, we should have one last blowout, right?' he said, voice an odd mix of cajoling and predatory. He was acting like he was trying to pick us up at a bar, and not talking about the last night we might spend alive.

'A . . . blowout?' Araya looked at me doubtfully.

'We've still got some pills, some booze . . .' Bryce said with a shrug. 'If we're going to walk into that jungle and probably all get fucking killed, we should at least have a good time before we do. So, get all your fruit together and get ready to leave tomorrow morning and tonight . . . let's have a party.'

'What about San'ya?' Araya said, obviously worried but clearly trying to humour Bryce's suggestion out of fear. 'And Fletcher. We can't leave them here.'

Bryce shrugged. 'Why? They're as good as dead. No way they're reaching help. They'll just slow us down.'

Araya failed to muffle a gasp. I felt sick. But there was truth in what he was saying, however much I didn't want to admit it. San'ya looked awful, worse than Fletcher had yesterday and now Fletcher was worse too. Their chances weren't good. From the looks of things they could very well be dead by tomorrow morning. If not before.

We all looked at him. Beside us, San'ya was struggling to breathe and somewhere in the plane across the clearing, Fletcher was dying. The very idea of partying our troubles away in the jungle was ridiculous. Horrific. We were all exhausted, starving, insect-bitten and filthy. And yet . . . what did we have to lose? We were already staring death in the face. One more day wouldn't make much difference. Would it?

'OK,' Summer muttered, reluctantly. The first of us to nod. 'Sure, why not? Might be the first good night's sleep I've had in a week so, bring it on.'

None of us wanted to say no to him. That scared me. What would he ask for next – for one of us to 'take care' of Fletcher and San'ya?

'Just one thing,' Bryce said. 'Obviously a good time doesn't come for free so . . . Lila—' he held out his hand '—I want my ring back and . . . throw in the rest of your jewellery while you're at it. I'll think of it as compensation for the crash and, you know, having to put up with you the past few months.'

I looked at him in disbelief and he stared back,

unwavering. He'd finally said it, the thing I'd suspected for a while now. He had never cared about me. Even now, trapped in the jungle, all he cared about was what he could take from me. How much money he could extract, like a tick after blood, growing fat on me before crawling off to another host.

But what good was the jewellery doing me? It was just stuff – just metal and stones. Certainly not worth what he'd do if I said no.

'Fine,' I said, and took the ring off. It was crusted with grime around the stone anyway. The gemstone-encrusted bangles and my chandelier earrings were in the tent. I'd taken them off for comfort but I'd kept the ring on, because I'd thought it symbolised something important. I guess it did – Bryce's greed.

Bryce took the ring from me and I fetched the rest of the jewellery. He put the bangles and earrings in his pocket, but he put the ring on. It flashed in the diffuse sunlight, mirroring the diamond tiger pendant around his neck.

'All right then, let's get a party together,' Bryce said, baring his teeth in a feral grin that didn't meet his eyes.

Chapter 25

'It's my understanding that you threw . . . a party?'

Andrea chums the waters with that question. It's approaching the final segment of the interview and she's clearly determined to leave the audience reeling. I remember how tired I felt by that point, losing my grip on my emotions. Andrea was playing a dangerous game and she didn't even know it.

Those in the studio gasp and murmur and surely everyone at home did too. This is electric. Lila Wilde threw a party, while people were dying around her? Obviously she's even worse than they first thought. Not just a spoiled rich girl but a callous bitch into the bargain.

'At Bryce's suggestion, yes . . . we decided to try and . . . have one last night of living before we went into the jungle. But it wasn't a party. Not in the way you mean,' Lila says quietly.

'And what is that?' Andrea challenges.

'Like it was a rager. Just a fun waste of time. It wasn't fun . . . it wasn't even really a party. Only in the sense that you could call a wake, a party. One we were all too scared to walk out of.'

'But at the time there were at least two people who were very sick. Dying even. Did you care?'

For the first time, the Lila on screen actually looks angry. 'Of course I cared.'

'But not enough to not get drunk and high?'

Lila scoffs, a tiny huff of outraged, humourless laughter. Her eyes wander from Andrea and to the audience who she can't see with all the studio lights beaming down on her. Making her sweat.

'There was literally nothing we could do but sit and watch them die. We gave them painkillers, and we put them to bed – Fletcher and San'ya. We made them as comfortable as we could. But other than that . . . I didn't want to sit there and watch them die. None of us did. We'd already seen Janet die, seen so many bodies. I don't think any of us could take anymore.'

'But you weren't the ones who were sick,' Andrea points out.

Lila looks at her for a long moment. 'How many dead bodies have you seen?'

That line attracts some attention in the airport lounge. A few sets of eyes flicker to the screen. Even I can't look away, and I already know what happens next.

Andrea raises her eyebrows, arranging her face to be unimpressed and wry. 'It's not a competition, Lila. No one is doubting that you saw . . .'

She interrupts and my lips twitch sympathetically. 'You wanted to talk about how many people were on the plane. Now think about how many bodies that was. Not everyone. A few were in the tail, but most. Most of us were in the front. We fell there. When the plane angled down and hit the ground.'

Andrea's mouth moves like she wants to argue back, but she doesn't speak.

'Then we lost Bethan. Janet. Fredrik, the nurse? He was caught in an explosion and Dash moved his burnt remains so the rest of us didn't have to see. And then Dash died. Shot in the head. We didn't see it, but we heard about it. We had that image in our heads.'

Everything is still in the studio, quiet and tense as if Lila has pulled out a gun.

The area around the TV in the lounge is silent. Even here, there is a shocked stillness.

'So yeah, we drank and we got high, or as high as we could. We chased that shit out of our minds for one night – because we were afraid not to, and the alternative was going mad. It was screaming and howling and running into the jungle barefoot. It was panic and clawing at our own skin and crying because we were going to be next.'

Lila picks up a glass of water and sips it. Her hand is shaking, but she keeps a steady eye on Andrea.

'You spend a week surrounded by death, knowing it's coming for you . . . and you'd want a drink too. You'd want to down every pill in sight just to make your thoughts stop.'

Chapter 26

It wasn't really a party.

I've been to some terrible ones over the years, both messy and dull. This didn't feel like any of them. There was no music, no dancing. No talking even. We were all around the fire, even Kaitlyn. Though from the looks of her she was already fairly doped up. She was barely blinking and I suspected Bryce of having slipped her something to get her to leave Fletcher and come outside.

It wasn't a party. What it reminded me of, honestly, was a suicide pact. Like one of those cults you see on TV – where they pass around plastic cups of poison and everyone drinks as one. We were all sitting there, awaiting death. This was just a last stop on the way. Bryce, our leader, doled out the booze and pills to us and watched to make sure we took them.

We sat around that fire and drank, washing a few pills each down with it. I didn't even look at what mine were. I was fairly sure one of them was an antihistamine but God only knew what else there was. I just didn't want to think or feel anymore. I wanted to turn my brain off and forget that there were two dying men nearby and that tomorrow we might be forced to decide if we were taking them with us, or leaving them behind. I wanted to just escape from my fear for a little bit.

For a while it didn't feel like anything was happening. I started to think I'd taken some duds or that my pills had been random over-the-counter stuff. That Bryce had shorted us and kept the good stuff for himself.

I was cooking one of the yellow plum-like fruits on a stick over the fire when it hit me. I looked at the flames and thought how weird it was that they were made of light. Made of nothing. What was fire anyway? Where did it come from? It shimmered like silk in the wind, and I reached out for it, but Araya batted my hand away. I laughed and she giggled back and for a moment she was made of light too and I couldn't help staring at her.

I blinked and everyone had moved. Switching seats like musical chairs. Across from me Bryce was covered in diamonds. The fire caught the pendant, the ring, and he was scattered with points of light. Beautiful. His eyes were black and bleeding down his face and I tried to ask why he was crying but my mouth was all dry and far away.

The ground was covered in bodies and I saw Araya looking up at the stars. Bethan was beside her, and her white clothes so clean and shiny that she glowed in the dark. For some reason, seeing a dead woman amongst us didn't frighten me. Somewhere in the jungle I heard Janet scream and I knew it was because the pigs were eating her. I knew I had to help her but I didn't know how or where she was. Then she started laughing.

I felt sick, crawled to my knees and got to my feet, wandering to the trees to throw up. But nothing came. I turned around and the jungle had closed in behind me. It was all the same – trees and plants and darkness. I spun on the spot and couldn't see even a sliver of firelight. Above me there were no stars, but under my feet there were glints of light. Ants I realised, focusing and stumbling out of their way. Ants crawling.

I staggered on in the hope of finding the fire again. Janet was laughing so loudly now and she never seemed to need to draw breath. It went on and on and on. Laughing and screeching in the night. I caught a glimmer out of the corner of my eye and turned, thinking of the fireside and the pretty flames.

But it wasn't fire. It was two yellow eyes.

I stared into them, swaying on the spot. They were huge yellow sapphires, very expensive. But Bryce had to have the best. Where were the diamonds of its face, the black diamond stripes glittering like broken bottle glass? I reached out to take the pendant from the darkness, and felt heat against my fingers. Not fire, but breath.

As I reached I overbalanced and before I could think to grab anything, I hit the ground. My chest ached, winded and hurt. I gasped for air and heard the thud of something moving nearby, padding softly into the night. Then silence.

I closed my eyes and sleep sucked me down like a whirlpool.

Not since before our trip to Thailand had I slept so deeply. So well. Curled up on the leaf litter and sleeping for hours as if I was in the villa, in the king-size bed I'd never had the chance to sleep in. I suppose it was sort of lucky that I slept so well. It would be the last opportunity I had for proper rest for quite some time.

I woke up with a jolt. It was as if I'd been shaken.

My ears rang, but my mind and body weren't in sync. I floundered a little, confused and disorientated. My head was banging and my mouth was dry, bile crawling in my throat. I pawed at myself and was relieved when my hands didn't find anything creeping over me. My feet were hurting and I squinted down at them, noting the blistered bite marks. Something other than mozzies had been at me. I remembered something about ants and winced.

That was when the sound of a gunshot split the air.

Every inch of me went tense as a wire. I was frozen to the spot. The sound rang in my ears and I realised at the back of my mind that it must have been a shot that woke me up so suddenly. Now there was another. It was close, loud and it had sent the jungle around me into chaos. The animals were screeching and whooping bloody murder, and there was movement everywhere as creatures fled.

Then I heard a scream. A human scream. It was a woman and it was close by. I struggled to my feet and looked around, confused and terrified. I vaguely remembered getting lost, but that must have been the drugs because I could see the crash site from where I was. I was only a few metres away from it. Had I passed out on the ground behind the tent? As I looked over there something moved and I realised there was a man in the clearing, watching me.

My chest went so tight that I couldn't breathe. The sight of a stranger alarming me even before I registered that he was holding a gun. He'd seen me, was looking right at me with dark, unblinking eyes. I'd surprised him, just appearing as I had, both of us shocked by the other. I heard scuffling and raised voices but didn't dare look away from him. The shock didn't last long. His face

212

hardened and he held up the rifle, yelling something in Thai. Other voices joined his, and I heard Araya call out to me through the confusion of yelling and scuffling feet.

'Run, Lila!'

She sounded terrified, and moments later she yelped in pain.

The man in camo was coming towards me and I was focused on the end of his gun. The black hole where bullets would fly out and tear into me. I couldn't run, couldn't move at all until he yelled again and jabbed the gun into my chest.

It was automatic – I held my hands up. His fingers bit into my shoulder as he pushed me towards the clearing. I stumbled on numb legs, my heart beating so fast that I felt sick. He poked the gun into my back and forced me out of the jungle into the clearing.

I saw the others then; Araya and Kaitlyn were huddled together on the ground. Kaitlyn had curled up into a ball, as if trying to ignore everyone, even as several men with guns were yelling and gesturing. Apparently trying to work something out amongst themselves. Araya's wide, terrified eyes met mine and she looked crestfallen that I'd been caught.

Summer was hugging her knees on Kaitlyn's other side, muttering to herself. If these were the men who'd killed Dash, she was probably living a worse nightmare than the rest of us. She already knew what they were capable of.

Behind the women, Bryce was on his knees with his hands on the back of his neck, elbows out. A hostage pose, I thought and shuddered. But he looked less frightened and more angry. As if this whole experience was an insult to him. He wasn't looking at any of the other passengers, but his eyes moved between the three Thai men in the clearing, lingering on their guns, his expression almost hungry. I felt my skin turn cold at the thought that he might try and disarm one of them. If the others fought back we'd all be caught in the crossfire.

Fletcher was absent, as was San'ya. I felt a twist of unease. Did that mean they were both already dead?

The other two men were on either side of the group, both armed. Guarding them. They didn't look tense or afraid, more like security guards slouching outside of a club on a slow night. They knew they had us. One was young, dressed in a sweat-stained Budweiser T-shirt and camo pants. The other was the oldest of the three, grey-haired and wearing a belt from which hung a hunting knife and a pistol. As the third guy brought me over with the rest they talked at a normal volume, no longer yelling across the clearing. Like they were trying to organise something trivial and not holding a group of starving people at gunpoint.

The guy behind me kicked my legs out from under me. I fell to the ground beside Araya and clung to her automatically. Confusion and fear were making me shiver. Tears stung at my eyes. Then I glanced back the way I'd come and saw the motionless shape of San'ya in the tent. I sucked in a breath.

'He's been lying there all this time, dead,' Araya whispered and I felt like I'd been punched in the chest. We'd forgotten him during the party and he'd slipped away.

'What do they want?' I muttered, looking down to hide the movement of my mouth from our guards. Araya was the only one who'd be able to understand what they were saying, now that San'ya was gone.

She swallowed hard and whispered back, quickly. 'They're poachers. Trying to work out if we're worth money or if they should just kill us so we can't tell anyone we saw them. They're split on it, their boss'll decide.'

I was about to ask which was the boss, when there was a sharp smack and Araya hit the ground, blood dripping from a cut on her forehead. The guy who'd seen me first had hit her with the end of his rifle. He glared at me and tapped his lips with his finger. The universal sign for 'shut up or you'll be next'. Summer didn't even react, like she was somewhere else entirely. Kaitlyn was hiccupping sobs into her hands, hiding her face. I didn't dare look behind me at Bryce. Just in case that angered these strangers.

A noise from the plane made me glance sideways. A fourth man was shoving aside the canopy and then waving his gun at the ladder. The thing that drew my attention to him was the collection of gold rings on his fingers, fat signets and heavy gold bands. He was also wearing combat boots, with his cargo pants tucked into them. His shirt was a football strip, something pale blue and maroon that Bryce would probably recognise. It had 'Doc Martens' across the front in white bubble letters. That struck me as so laughably out of place that I nearly giggled, hysteria quivering through me.

All this was ricocheting through my brain in the moments before Fletcher appeared and started to climb unsteadily down the ladder. He was alive. Alive and moving around on his own? How?

He stumbled when he got to the ground. Fletcher was pale, his eyes looked huge in his face and there was still dried blood under his nose. The man with the gold rings climbed down behind him and shoved him over our way. Fletcher hit the ground on his knees and tipped into Kaitlyn's lap face first. She grabbed hold of him, still sobbing and the gold-ring guy came to stand in front of us. From the number of rings and the way the other men all stopped muttering amongst themselves to look to him, I guessed he was the boss.

When I looked up at him I saw his eyes moving over us, one after the other. His gaze flat and assessing, like we were lobsters in a tank and he wanted the best one boiled up for dinner. He looked at Araya's unconscious body and her cheap sparkly skirt, at Kaitlyn's neck where a strawberry pendant studded with rubies hung down onto her grimy décolletage. His eyes finally stopped on Bryce and he said something to the others, gesturing for them to make a move.

I nudged at Araya, trying to wake her up so she could tell me what they were saying. But she was out for the count. I twisted my head to look back and saw Bryce being hauled back by the Budweiser guy. Mr Gold-rings pointed at Fletcher's wrist, where his Audemars Piguet watch stood out. They dragged him away too, and then deliberated over Kaitlyn and Summer.

I realised what they were doing. They'd passed over Araya in her normal club clothes and they were separating anyone wearing expensive stuff. Rich people, who were worth money, as Araya had said. Were they hoping for ransom, for rescue reward money?

Looking down at myself I realised I was in trouble. My Jimmy Choos were in the plane and I was wearing Janet's pleather pumps. My dress might still have the Oscar de la Renta label but it was covered in dirt, sweat and jungle debris. It wasn't as if it was anything but a dress to these guys anyway – expecting men to recognise designer shoes was probably already pushing it. Gold and jewels were one thing, expensive clothes another. All my jewellery was gone. I looked just as poor as Araya and Summer.

I'd no sooner thought this than the older man was hauling me away. He dragged me across the clearing and then went back for Araya and then Summer, who didn't resist at all. He was separating us from the rest. He dumped her down beside me and then pulled his pistol from his belt.

'Wait!' It burst out of me. 'Wait, please . . . I'm . . . I'm Lila Wilde – I have money. Don't, kill me!' I flung my arms out in a vain attempt to protect Araya and Summer. 'I can pay for us. Just . . . just get us out of here!'

He looked at me, unmoved. Either he didn't understand or he didn't care. Perhaps both. They had three people to take already. They probably didn't want to be burdened with more. We were just unwelcome witnesses. Loose ends to be tidied. I looked to Fletcher and Kaitlyn, but neither of them were looking at us. As if we'd ceased to exist. Kaitlyn was clinging to Fletcher and they were both turning their backs on us.

'Bryce!' I yelled. 'Show them the ring – point at me so they know it's mine!'

But when I caught his eye he just looked at me like I was nothing. Like he didn't even know me. As if he was just snubbing me outside a club like a desperate fan and not leaving me to die.

'Bryce!' I shouted again. 'You bastard!'

I realised that he was getting everything he wanted. Everything he'd stood to gain from dating me to begin with. He didn't need me for anything anymore. These men would get him out of the jungle and ransom him. If he gave them my father's name, he'd pay for him and get him out of Thailand just to find out what had happened to me. He'd tell my father a pack of lies about me and that would be it. Bryce was going to live, to go home. He'd be able to sell his story and make a fortune all his own. Fletcher and Kaitlyn weren't likely to contradict his tale of poor Lila Wilde, who died in the jungle and was never found.

I screamed, a raw-throated cry of rage and anguish. Fletcher didn't even flinch, Kaitlyn looked back over her shoulder and then quickly turned away.

And Bryce just smiled at me. Bared those shiny white teeth I'd paid for and smiled.

I watched as the men tied Bryce's wrists together, then bound him to Kaitlyn and her to Fletcher. The three of them in a line. They talked for a second and it looked like the boss was keen to move off quickly. He waved vaguely at us and then headed off with two of the men and the three hostages.

The older man was left. Apparently the lowest in the pecking order. He'd have to rush after the others as they got a head start, slowed down by their three cash cows. He uttered a few words, which I took to be annoyance at being left to tidy us up. Then he levelled his gun at my forehead. I looked into the black hole at its end and my entire body shivered, from my scalp to my feet. I shut my eyes and sobbed.

There was a loud bang, and I hit the ground, hard.

Chapter 27

Quivering on the ground, it took me a moment to sense the struggle going on in front of me. Still longer to realise that I hadn't been shot but had thrown myself down in panic. I scrambled to my knees and saw the older poacher flailing in the dirt. San'ya was on top of him, weighing him down.

'Get the gun!' he gasped at me and I grabbed for the pistol. The poacher tried to keep hold of it but I was full of adrenaline and panic. I slapped and clawed at his hand with the jagged remnants of my acrylic nails until finally he lost his grip and I pulled the gun from his fingers.

He rolled and threw San'ya off to flop weakly into the dirt. Araya was still unconscious and Summer appeared to have retreated to a place far inside herself, just staring at us wildly. I had the gun. I took a step back and raised it, pointing it at him. My heart was racing and everything was happening so fast. I just wanted it to stop.

The poacher looked up at me and his eyes were pure calculation. He was trying to work out how to disarm me, to take back control.

Yet when he leapt at me, it was still a surprise.

His arms went out and he was obviously trying to tackle my legs and send me over backwards. I screamed. There was a bang, another and another. Then just clicks as he slumped to the ground and I realised I was still pulling the trigger. The gun was empty. I staggered back. There was blood on my legs, spatter from where I'd shot him.

I'd *shot* him.

My ears were ringing with the sound. I'd been so close that it'd near deafened me. I just kept looking at the dark holes in his shirt, the blood. What had I done?

I'd shot him.

Movement to my right made me flinch, pointing the useless gun without thinking. It was Araya, coming around. Maybe the noise of the gun had woken her. She cracked her eyes open and saw the dead man in front of her. Crying out, she shuffled away, and looked from him to me and the gun in my hand. Then she caught sight of San'ya and gaped at him.

'I thought . . .' she said.

San'ya looked dreadful, still covered in those deep dark patches of bruising – his blood vessels breaking and bleeding inside him. But he wasn't dead. Not yet. Araya probably saw him lying so still even after the gunshots and assumed, but he wasn't. He'd used his limited strength to save our lives by tackling the poacher. The shot fired at me had gone wide, ending up who knows where. I owed him my life.

San'ya coughed and blood dribbled over his lip. He didn't seem to be able to get up off the ground and I made my hand let go of the gun so I could help him. It hit the ground and clattered on the baked dirt, making me flinch. Araya was still recovering, trying to get herself up off the ground. She'd been hit in the head pretty hard with the end of that guy's gun. I turned to Summer instead.

'Summer, help me,' I rasped, and took her shoulder, shaking her as gently as I could with my heart hammering in fear. She blinked at me like she was waking from a dream. Then her face crumpled and she appeared to realise just where she was and what was happening. But she got up and followed me, like a weeping zombie.

Between us we got San'ya up and half-led, half-carried him towards the tent. There we lowered him to the ground and I looked helplessly at his mottled skin and the blood leaking from his nose and mouth. He looked like he was dying. Judging from the way he was watching me, he knew it too.

There was blood smeared on his clothes and when I looked down I realised it was from me. The poacher's blood that had spattered over me. When I'd killed him.

I'd killed someone.

Summer dropped to the ground and hugged her knees, apparently losing her grip again. I couldn't help both of them. To be honest I didn't know where to begin. My head was spinning too fast for me to grab hold of any thoughts. It was all just noise.

Oh God, they could come back any moment, couldn't they? The poachers had left one guy to finish us off, while they got a head start back to wherever they'd come from, slowed down by the hostages. Probably keen to get there before dark. But when would they realise their friend should have caught up with them by now? Would they care enough about him to come back and look for him? If they did, they'd probably kill us themselves.

'What now?' I asked, pleaded really, not knowing if

221

San'ya would have any answers but certain that I didn't. 'What do we do?'

San'ya's breathing was uneven and wheezy. 'You need to leave, get somewhere high up . . . attract help. Maybe a signal fire or something. No one'll find you otherwise.'

'You?' I grabbed his hand. 'Us.'

He laughed, but it came out as more of a sob. 'I'm not going anywhere.'

I shook my head automatically. We couldn't leave him. Couldn't lose anyone else. First the crash, then John, Bethan, the German, Janet. The man I'd shot. When would it stop?

When we're all dead, I realised. When there's no one left.

Still I didn't want to admit it. I wanted to fight against it even though it was pointless.

'We have the stretcher parts. We can try and finish one and carry you . . .'

'You were right. There's no way. You're too exhausted and underfed. Summer's barely hanging on. You'll just die faster trying to help me and I'll be dead either way.'

His eyes were glassy and his voice was flat. He'd been thinking about this I realised. Possibly all night. As we'd gotten drunk and high and tried to forget our situation for a few hours, San'ya had confronted his. Bravely and soberly. He'd lain in the tent in pain and realised he was done for and that the only thing he could do was urge us to carry on without him.

'But Fletcher got better . . . what if you live, what if . . .' He cut me off, raising his hand.

'I don't know about Fletcher, but I know I'm fucked. Kind of wish you had a bullet left in that thing for me but . . . it'll be over soon. Just get me some painkillers

222

or something before you go, so I can get to sleep. I probably . . .' his voice shook then and despite his strength I could tell he was afraid of what was going to happen. '. . . I probably won't wake up again.'

I looked over at Araya, who was on her feet now and wandering dazedly towards us, still shaken from the blow to the head. She looked at us, at San'ya and I saw her realise that something was up, even before he said anything. Tears welled in her reddened eyes and she squatted down by him, taking his hand. Behind me, Summer began to hum softly to herself, as if trying to block us out.

'You need to leave today,' he said. 'Don't waste any more time. Get what you need, and go. You're losing daylight.'

'No!' Araya's knuckles turned white around San'ya's fingers. 'We won't leave you.'

But I was already on the other side of that conversation. I put my hand over hers and eased her fingers off his.

'Araya . . . he's dying. We can't bring him with us . . . I'm sorry.'

'She's right,' San'ya said, clearly having trouble speaking, as his mouth kept filling with bloody spittle. 'Go.'

Araya broke down crying and clung to him. San'ya gave me a pleading look over her head and I nodded. As hard as it was, someone had to be strong and right now that was me. I left them to it and went around the clearing to gather up what we'd need to take with us. I couldn't stand to look at the man on the ground. The man I'd killed. I was already walling that away in my head. Trying to shield myself from the memory.

There wasn't much. We'd have to forage for food en route to wherever we were going. But I put the lighters and what was left of our improvised first-aid kit into a bag. Inside the plane I found the last of the alcohol – a measly few fingers of vodka. There were some pills – five unmarked ones. I decided to give them to San'ya along with the booze. We wouldn't have much use for it.

I hurried to pack, still afraid that we might hear voices any moment as the poachers returned. Looking at what little we had, I realised that the odds of me and the others making it anywhere were vanishingly small. Still, we had to try.

When I put the bottle and pills beside San'ya he met my eye and nodded, just slightly. A gesture of thanks. Araya was crying under her breath, clearly trying to remain quiet and composed for his sake, but not able to suppress her grief. I had clenched my fists so tightly that the stubs of my ragged acrylics cut into my palms. My eyes were scratchy with unshed tears, but I had to stay in control. One of us had to be in charge, or we were all done for. Apparently, with Bryce gone and San'ya dying, the role of leader was mine for the taking.

I took Araya's shoulder gently and gave it a squeeze.

'We have to leave,' I said, softly.

'Go,' San'ya said. 'Go home to your mother.'

Araya choked on a fresh wave of sobs, but allowed me to turn her away and lead her from the tent. I left her with the bag to collect herself and returned for Summer. I kneeled down in front of her and put my hands on her knees. I wasn't sure what she was going to do or how she would react.

'Summer? We're leaving now . . . You need to come with us.'

'Out there?' she said, eyes roaming over me and past me to the edge of the jungle.

'Yeah . . . back out there. But this time we'll stay together. You won't be alone.'

'Wasn't alone before, 'til Dash died,' she said flatly, then laughed suddenly.

I flinched, certain that the stress of the poacher's invasion had finally tipped her over the edge. But she sobered after a few seconds and looked tearfully at San'ya.

'I'm sorry,' she said to him, and then she was gone, hurrying over to Araya. I got to my feet and sucked in a deep breath.

'I'm sorry too,' I told him, quietly. 'I wish . . .'

'Go,' he said, looking up at me, pleading. 'Please just . . . I want to be alone.'

So I left, and went to the others.

I glanced back at San'ya only once before we left and saw him looking straight ahead, tears running down his cheeks. I quickly looked away. It felt so deeply private and something I had no right to see.

I pressed one of the bamboo poles into Araya's hands and passed her a machete. I didn't trust Summer with either. Then I steered them in the opposite direction of the tent. I had no way of knowing the right direction, but the tail party had found nothing and I wasn't about to follow the men with guns. I also didn't want to take them past the pile of bodies. So our decision was made for us.

I kept Summer in front of me, unable to shake the thought that she might freak out again. I could see her grabbing at me or pushing me down a steep drop if I wasn't careful. I trusted Araya though, and could hear her sniffling behind me.

We wove through tree trunks and stepped over fallen trunks, picking our way forward. I had no idea if we

225

would reach a high point this way or even if we'd find somewhere to stop to sleep that wasn't in the deep jungle. I nearly screamed when a snake darted across the path only a few inches from my foot. A bright green snake that vanished into the undergrowth. They were so fast, if one tried to bite me there was nothing I could do. I'd be dead as Bethan, maybe before I even realised what had happened. At least it wasn't a cobra, which San'ya had said was the worst.

I kept my eyes wide open, searching the ground for threats until my head ached and my eyes felt dry from not blinking. My ears were pricked and listening for movement around us. Stress making my pulse pound in my head. It was fruitless really because everything was moving – sticks cracking and leaves rustling. I twitched and jumped at every noise. Macaques climbed through the canopy and birds flew overhead, chattering and squawking. If a tiger wanted to sneak up on us, I knew it could. Those large velvet paws would be soundless as it crept through the trees. I did manage to swerve us around a large snake though, hanging between two trees like a fat vine. It watched us with unblinking, oily eyes, tongue fluttering.

I shuddered as we passed it, but kept on walking, taking Araya and Summer onwards like sheep through the wilderness. Vulnerable and doomed.

As the jungle thickened I took Araya's place at the front of our little convoy and hacked aside the plants with the machete. It was hard work, clearing the way for us, and soon my arms were burning. Our progress slowed and Araya took over. Every time we switched we kept Summer between us so we could keep an eye on her. We traded the lead back and forth, until we came across a stream. We'd found water, that was something. Whether or not it was clean I was done caring. Being poisoned by bad water was the least of our worries. I could hear wild pigs in the jungle, snorting and rooting about. I wondered if they were following us, just waiting for us to drop.

After a rest we carried on, but I could tell we were all weakening. Barely staggering along on not enough sleep and no food. Every time a bird or a monkey flew past overhead, I caught myself wondering if we could get hold of one. My body was crying out for some real food – for fat and protein and salt.

'Where are we stopping?' Summer asked, startling me. None of us had spoken for what felt like hours. I think we'd been afraid to break the silence, in case the poachers were on our trail, hunting us.

'When we find somewhere I guess,' I said, feeling hopeless.

Summer just turned and kept walking ahead of me. I could see her heels, blistered and red, and knew mine were in a similar state. My skin bitten raw by mosquitos. In the pit of my stomach I was afraid that one or all of us might get sick with dengue. I couldn't decide what frightened me more: the idea of being alone out here, or of dying so painfully.

The light coming through the canopy above started to dim. Night was coming and we were no closer to finding anywhere decent to stop. The choice was made for us by the oncoming night.

We gathered and ate fruit mechanically. Summer stared into our small campfire and looked by turns amused and deeply depressed. I couldn't work out what she was thinking, or what she was going through. But I didn't particularly relish the thought of sleeping near her. Not when she was acting so strange.

My sympathy was at its limits. We were all suffering and I didn't have the bandwidth to help her handle it just then. I'd killed a man today. I couldn't stop thinking about it now that we were at rest. It just kept coming back to me: the sound of the gun and the bloody holes in his shirt.

Sitting, hunched in the dirt and undergrowth, I looked at Araya and we reached a silent agreement that one of us would keep watch and the other would sleep. I nodded for Araya to lie down and get some rest and I sat there, looking out into the darkness, watching for yellow eyes.

Chapter 28

The next day we carried on. Though it felt less like a hike toward rescue and more like a strange form of torture. I was aching and constantly thirsty but we had to ration our water. I wasn't sure if we'd come across another stream and it hadn't been raining for the past few days. I knew if we ran out of water, we were dead.

Summer's hysteria seemed to have passed, leaving her without life or hope. Her eyes were dull and she plodded on without speaking or doing much else but staring blankly ahead. She reminded me of the pack donkeys in those sad animal rights videos, forced to carry heavy burdens until they crumpled and fell. I didn't know what to do or how to keep her motivated. To be honest I was struggling myself. The walk seemed endless and without the hope of rest and safety at the end of it I wasn't sure what we were even trying for.

Araya walked on with a focused intensity. She looked like she was entering the final stretch of a demanding HIIT workout and just had to push through. A few times though, I noticed that she was crying, silently. For herself or for San'ya I had no idea. Maybe both. Maybe for everything.

The way was hard going, sloping up and up at an ever greater angle. At some points we had to haul ourselves up with branches. I was clawing around for a handhold when I touched something alive and wriggling. I snatched my hand back with a cry and watched the giant centipede scuttle away on its many legs. I shuddered and tried to stop my hands shaking as I began to climb again.

The higher we climbed, the less we seemed to see of the fruits and plants that we'd been eating. The ground was drier, the undergrowth less lush and more woody. Until after several hours we reached a cliff.

It rose in front of us as if a giant had sliced through a mountain. The face sheer and unclimbable, notched here and there with hollows higher up, where creepers spilled down the stone. Ahead of us, a deep dark crack was the only feature of the cliff face. Barely a foot wide at the broadest point, it rose for at least fifteen metres. I looked into the inky black vein of it and felt the hair on my neck prickle. From inside, I heard the dripping of water, but the idea of setting foot in there to find the source made my skin crawl.

'We're not going in there . . . are we?' I asked Araya. 'We can't get through that way, right?'

She was a few metres away, crouched on the ground to rest. She glanced over at the crevice and shook her head. I relaxed slightly, then remembered we'd have to walk around the mountain, which would take longer.

'So we have to go around until we find a way up?' I guessed, when she said nothing. Araya just nodded, like even talking was too much effort for her now. I couldn't blame her. Even walking in a straight line was taking most of my energy. The ground underfoot was all loose rock, roots and leaf litter. It was like trying to climb a mountain made of sand.

I chose to head left, for no real reason. It was just a direction to go in. We started to follow the cliff that way and after so long that I was sure we'd come back around to where we started, I stumbled around a large rock and there it was. A slightly less sheer slope which, even as exhausted as we were, we could probably climb. I could have wept in relief – we hadn't been wasting the last of our energy. There was a way forward.

It wasn't easy. Scrambling up it took most of our energy and once we reached a small plateau covered in plants, we stopped to rest. The side of the mountain was a mixture of steep drops and little shelves where the jungle could cling on and grow. The summit was far overhead, nowhere near as daunting as some of the mountains I'd skied down for fun, but still not climbable for exhausted amateurs without equipment.

We did our best to get as high as possible, struggling between plateaus and pulling each other up. Our route wrapped around the mountain in a diagonal, and our progress was slow. Inching between ledges, we sent pebbles tumbling down and I tried not to look at the yawning distance below. At times our path was only a foot or so wide, and the rocks moved under our feet as if they were barely connected to the mountain itself.

The higher we went the further apart these shelves of greenery became, interspersed with gaps, tall ridges and plummeting drops. We found ourselves stuck on one about fifty feet off the ground. The next highest ledge was far, far out of reach. The plateau we were on wasn't that big, but there was a sort of crack running in a diagonal away from its edge and if we could just climb along it, we'd be able to reach a wider area, with actual trees on it. A section of the jungle about a quarter of the size of the playing field at the last private school I got kicked out of. It wasn't higher, but it would do.

'We can make a signal fire there,' I said aloud, pointing.

Araya followed my finger and looked at the half-foot-deep crack that I was proposing to use as a foothold. The drop below was lethal. Even I could tell that. But what choice did we have? Without a signal fire at a decent height, we'd never be found. We'd die here, just as surely as if we'd thrown ourselves off the cliff on purpose. We had to try.

'I'll . . . go first,' I said, not feeling confident, despite myself. But no one else was exactly offering. I kicked off Janet's shoes and flexed my blistered bare feet on the ground. My polished nails were rimed with dirt and sweat from the long walk and the sharp stones underfoot were painful. But I wasn't going to get far in pumps.

'Be careful,' Araya croaked, finally breaking her silence of several hours. Summer, lying flat on her back to rest, didn't even look my way.

I nodded, biting off a retort. Of course I was going to be careful. I didn't want to fall and break my neck. Though at least if I did, I thought as I approached the edge, this nightmare would finally be over.

I fitted my foot into the crack and felt around for a hand hold. The cliff side was almost featureless, the only fissures I could find were barely deep enough for me to cling on with my fingertips. I still had one foot on the ledge itself but I could feel gravity trying to pull me back from the cliff. To get across I'd have to plaster myself against the rock, but my centre of gravity would fight me the whole way, trying to peel me away from my tiny finger holds and leave me tumbling backwards. Wearing the bag of supplies didn't help matters.

My heart was beating fast enough to hurt as I edged my foot out and then brought my other one up to the crack to join it. I immediately swayed backwards by a few millimetres, and screamed. Araya yelped as if stung and I saw her rush at me out of the corner of my eye. My fingers were rigid on the rock, aching, and my joints locked together painfully, freezing me in place.

I didn't fall.

My teeth were gritted and my eyes stung with panicked tears but I shifted my right foot over, and reached out with my right hand. After groping around for what felt like an eternity, I found another finger hold and transferred my weight to it.

Inch by inch I made my way. About halfway along I started to flag. Exhaustion and terror were sapping my strength and I kept fumbling. My arms and legs were shaking and I was sure I was going to slip and fall because of it. All I could think was, *I'm going to die*, and thinking it just made things worse.

I could feel the tension in Araya's silence. Nose to nose with the rock wall I couldn't make myself turn to look back at her. But I sensed her eyes on me, could feel the weight of her hope. I carried on, though my fingers were screaming at me for rest, and my calves were trembling from being on tiptoe.

Then my right foot found grass, and I sobbed in relief. Glancing that way I saw the ledge and slowly shuffled myself onto it. I collapsed onto the ground, not even caring that there might be insects or snakes about. I clung to the ground and just breathed until my heart stopped racing.

When I finally heaved myself upright, I looked back and saw Araya standing on the other side of the crevice. Summer was sitting up now, watching with her arms wrapped around her knees like a child. She looked done in, exhausted and afraid. I wasn't sure in that moment if she'd be able to make it.

'Throw my shoes,' I called out, trying to buy time.

Araya picked them up and threw them overarm like rugby balls. They hit the ground and I gathered them up, glad to have something on my feet again.

'OK . . .' I breathed. 'Now you!'

Araya though, had other ideas. She picked up one of the two bamboo poles we'd been walking with, and threw that over, followed by the other. But when she tried to toss the first machete, it fell short. The scrap metal blade ricocheted down the rocky cliff, clattering and echoing as it went. I saw her stiffen, and fear was carved into her face.

'Don't look down. Don't think, just do it!' I called over to her. 'I'll be right here.'

Though what I could do for her was anyone's guess.

Araya looked at the cliff and I saw her gathering her strength. She took her own shoes off and threw them to me, followed by the only remaining machete. They went a bit wide – she'd thrown them with a shaky arm – but I got them. When I looked up from gathering them, she was already finding a foothold.

Watching Araya cross the narrow crack was somehow just as nerve-racking as doing it myself. My stomach was twisting up like a mass of snakes and my skin was icy cold. I didn't want to see the moment she teetered, the moment she fell. Didn't want to hear her scream or the impact of her body hitting the rocks below.

I didn't dare speak, not even to offer a word of encouragement. I just crept to the edge and held a hand out impotently, knowing it would do no good if she lost her grip while she was out of my reach.

Slowly, Araya crossed over to my side and when she set a foot on the grass she looked at me with huge, terrified eyes and smiled.

Then her left foot slipped out of the crevice and she fell.

She screamed, her hands flailed at me and I grabbed for her as her left leg kicked out in empty space and her right, still on solid ground, stiffened as if it could hold her there.

I pulled as hard as I could, throwing my weight back. Araya's nails bit into my arms, into my shoulders. She was trying to climb me, fighting gravity and screaming all the while. I heaved and she planted her left foot and pushed. The pair of us landed on the grass – me on my back and Araya on top of me, shaking as if I'd just pulled her from an icy lake.

'You're OK,' I said, and kept saying, over and over again, the only words I could put together. 'You're OK.'

Araya sobbed and I realised tears were running out my eyes, over my cheeks. I was shaking too. We'd both practically seen her death hanging in front of us. But it was over now.

Only of course it wasn't. Because Summer was still on the other side.

I realised too late that one of us should have stayed

over there to shepherd her through the climb. Now it was all up to her and if she just sat there and refused to move there was nothing we could do. Not unless we wanted to risk our lives doing the climb a second and then third time. That seemed like tempting fate just a little too far.

I got to my feet and shook out my aching arms before helping Araya up. She wasn't shaking anymore, and her expression was purposeful. She was just as determined as I was to get Summer to safety with us.

'Summer!' I called across the divide. 'Your turn now. We'll help you, OK? We'll be right here for you.'

'You can do it!' Araya shouted. 'Come on! Just one last bit to climb and then you can eat something and sleep, OK?'

Summer looked at us as if she couldn't quite understand what we were asking her to do. Frustration seethed through me like boiling oil at one of the food stalls back on Bangla Road, a lifetime ago.

'Summer!' I shouted, my voice hardening. 'You have to do this! We can't do it for you!'

She got up. I let out a sigh of relief. Finally. Then, as she walked towards the edge I was filled with sudden, horrible certainty, that she wasn't going to stop. She was just going to walk right off the edge and plummet down.

I held up my hands. 'Summer!'

Araya grabbed a fistful of my dress, as if by doing so she could hold Summer back. 'Summer stop!'

She stopped. Like a robot receiving a command. Then she stiffly took off her sandals and threw them. Neither made it to us. They simply fell down the gap, rattling loose stones free as they went. She didn't seem to notice.

'Summer . . .' Araya breathed, but I think both of us

were too afraid to call out to her again. As if we might break some fragile spell that was protecting her.

I watched, not daring to blink, as Summer wedged her feet into the crevice, one after the other. She swayed as gravity tried to wrench her away from the wall, but she didn't really react. She just clung to the wall and moved. As she got closer though I could see that she was trembling. Her eyes were wide and staring. It was getting dark by this time, and her jagged shadow spread across the cliff, like it was weighing her down.

'C'mon . . . c'mon . . .' I murmured. 'Please . . . please . . .'

She crossed the halfway point and her hand spasmed on its hold. Summer's fingers slid off the stone and she started to sway back, feet still crammed into the cliff face. Her scream was like a terrified bird soaring parallel to the rock face. Despite that, I heard her fingernails against the stone as she clawed for purchase, saw them bend and break. She fought gravity, smearing blood on the stone, but she caught herself before she fell back too far. Her fingers snagged a hold, and she pulled herself upright. Her face hit the cliff with the force at which she threw herself forwards. She was shaking as she moved again, fingers trailing bloody prints as she went.

Araya and I caught her as she reached the edge. Summer went boneless and nearly took us both to the ground, but we carried her a little way and laid her out on the grass. Lying there she gulped air and gazed unseeingly at the sky overhead. Her lips were bleeding. Not because of dengue, thankfully, but because she'd sunk her teeth into them.

'You made it,' Araya said, soothing her. 'You're all right.'

Summer slowly rolled over and curled into a ball. I wanted to comfort her but had no idea how. There was no bright side to focus on. No way to lift her spirits. We were still out in the jungle, halfway up a mountain and we had no food, no water and no way out. I think that's what had her locked into such a state. Not the fact that we had survived this far, but the fact that we didn't know how much longer we could keep going.

'Let's find something to eat and . . . hopefully that'll . . .' I gestured to Summer, unsure what result I was hoping for. But we all needed to eat and rest. Otherwise we'd just lie down and never get up again.

Araya didn't seem to want to leave Summer but she nodded and together we explored the plateau we'd risked our lives to reach. It was large and there were quite a few trees and bushes rooted onto it. Not as dense as the jungle below but there were some fruits and it looked like we'd be able to feed ourselves for a few days from those. At least we wouldn't need to worry about water, what with a supply of juicy bilimbis.

Araya and I had gathered some food and were looking for dry wood amongst the grasses when I heard her yelp. Metal hit rock and then she crowed in triumph. I turned and couldn't believe it when I saw her holding up a snake. A headless snake. In her other hand the machete was smeared with blood.

'Rat snake,' she said. 'It bit me.'

'Are you OK, is it . . . venomous?' I asked hesitantly, as she didn't seem too worried but still I was thinking about Bethan.

'A bit. Not much, I'll be fine.' She swung the snake in the air and gestured down at the ground with the machete. 'I disturbed it. Look, it had eggs.'

I went over, picking my way carefully in case there were more. The snake in her hand was about two metres long, nowhere near as thick as, like, a python – but hefty. I looked down and saw that her foot was bleeding from puncture marks. But beside it there were five white eggs, sticky with dirt and debris.

Araya tried to hand me the snake and I stepped back, holding up my hands. 'Absolutely not.'

She actually laughed. I think she was too elated with her discovery to care much that I was being a wimp about the snake thing. I collected up the eggs instead, which were weird. Not like bird eggs, with a shell, but more like my Elizabeth Arden ceramide capsules. Sort of jelly-like and soft.

Summer was just as we'd left her and with the promise of food in the offing I felt a little more positive. I had some hope and I wanted to share it. While Araya made a fire, I eased myself down beside Summer and patted her shoulder.

'Hey, we've got some food. Tomorrow we'll set up a big fire and anyone looking for us will be able to see it.'

Summer looked at me, but didn't otherwise react.

Neither Araya nor me had any idea how to prepare a snake for eating. We ended up just sort of chunking it up and peeling the skin off, cooking it on sticks over the fire. It wasn't fatty and sort of looked a bit like dry chicken when we were done, but it was food and we wolfed it down. Soon the fire was cluttered with tiny snake bones.

The eggs we cooked the same way we had last time. I was glad they didn't have baby snakes in them, though they tasted a bit fishy. Once we were done with our meal we lay in a triangle around the fire. I hadn't been full for days and even though I still wasn't completely satiated my stomach was finally not clenched into a hard little ball. I glanced over at Summer and saw that she was asleep. I hoped she'd be more together in the morning. We needed her help to build the signal fire.

Lying there, listening to Araya's soft breathing to reassure myself that she wasn't dying of a snake bite, I thought of the small copse we were now camped by. What would happen when it ran out of food for us? Would we have to climb again, up or down? Would we even have the strength to do that by then?

The idea that by that time, Bryce might well be back in civilisation, burned hot under my heart. A tiny ember of hatred and determination, which kept me warm as I drifted off to sleep.

Chapter 29

'What's that?'

I was used to sleeping on a knife edge by this time and Summer's words jerked me back to wakefulness. I sat up immediately and saw that she was sitting at the edge of the plateau, looking out over the jungle we'd hiked through.

Now that the stress and exhaustion of yesterday was behind us I could appreciate the view. Even if the miles upon miles of uninterrupted green canopy did make my heart sink. So much jungle and we were only three people, lost in it all.

Araya, having woken up more slowly, went over to her. 'What's what?'

'That – the building.'

For a moment I thought she'd cracked. That the climb yesterday had frazzled what was left of her nerve and she was hallucinating. Or that it was a mirage. Could you get those in the jungle? But then I saw what it was she was pointing at. At first glance it just looked like a trunk poking up through the trees, but as I really looked at it I realised it was more like mossy stone. It got wider as it went down, uniformly. A manmade structure.

It was really far away, not in the direction we'd come from but further to the left. Or, as the rising sun in the opposite direction indicated, west.

'Is that like . . . a village?' I asked no one in particular, too surprised to really think about it.

Araya was also looking that way and she eventually shook her head. 'A temple maybe? There are ruins in the jungle. That's probably one of them.'

'A ruin,' I echoed, disappointed. But it made sense. There were no other buildings around it that I could see poking through the canopy. No clearing there either. I imagined that the spire we could see was part of a mossy stone temple, an empty shell half reclaimed by the jungle. As the plane would be soon.

Summer's shoulders slumped. 'I thought . . .' She trailed off and didn't elaborate but it was obvious what she meant. I'd briefly hoped the same thing – that we had spotted civilisation, somewhere to aim for. But there was no real difference between that place and where we were now. Only that it was buried in the jungle and even less likely to be spotted from the air.

'But, aren't there tourists who go there?' I asked, as a last-ditch sliver of hope.

Araya shrugged. 'Maybe, but not all the temples are good for tourists. They want to see the impressive ones, and some are just plain and forgotten, or too far and too hard to get to.'

I just nodded and dropped the subject. We needed to cling to real hope and not the false kind represented by that stone spire. We'd climbed all the way up here to light a signal fire and that was what was going to save us.

After a breakfast of fruits we started gathering wood and

dried grasses. Araya and Summer used the saw chain Dash had left us – now mostly blunt. They cut down fresh green wood and I used the machete to hack at undergrowth. We had three piles going – wet wood, dry wood and kindling. The key would be keeping a supply of wood drying out to make sure we always had fuel.

It was hard going, like everything else we'd been through. I came across insects in the undergrowth and shuddered at the sight of the larger ones as they scuttled away. As we cut and cleared space and piled up fuel, we added to our bucket of fruits and kept an eye out for eggs, snakes or anything else edible.

In the hottest part of the day, when the sun was a blinding white eye above us, we sheltered in the shade of the largest tree. It was one we could never hope to cut down with the saw, and it was a good shelter. We sucked the juice from fruits to quench our thirst and I lay down for a nap, dreaming of ice, lemonade and sorbet.

After resting for an hour or so we piled up the dry wood on the opposite side of the plateau to the large tree. The fire would be visible from the direction we'd walked from. Anyone who managed to locate the plane wreckage would see it.

We built it tall and set it burning so that the smoke would carry during the day and the fire would die down to keep us warm at night. Sitting on the ground I watched the flames spreading over the wood and wished I was religious, so I could pray that we'd be seen.

'How many days has it been, since we took off?' Summer asked, out of the blue as we watched the fire dance.

I thought about it. 'Eleven I think.'

She didn't say anything else but I glanced at Araya and saw from her subdued expression that we were both probably thinking the same thing. Over a week now. We'd been lost for so many days. Surely they were still searching, but we hadn't seen or heard any sign. No helicopters droning overhead. If the black box had fallen far away from the final crash site, would they ever think to look this far?

That night I ate tarantula for the first time. They were big, dark-coloured ones with little white stripes on them. Araya had found two, along with some fruits that I'd collected and some grasshoppers or locusts – I wasn't sure.

I watched as she crisped them over the fire, and then cut them in half with the machete. Part of the body had meat in it, but the rest just looked tough and unpleasant, like trying to eat a lobster's legs, shell and all.

'It's fine to eat,' Araya said, holding half out to me. 'Better deep-fried though.'

I couldn't argue with that. A nice coating of batter would have hidden what it was I was eating, like with calamari. But I was hungry enough to try it. At least the fire had singed off the hair.

We slept in the warmth around the fire and I woke up four or five times during the night. Every twig snapping in the embers made me twitch awake, looking for yellow eyes in the dark. A few times I saw flickers of yellow fire and held my breath, before I realised it was nothing. Surely up here, no tigers would bother us. Just snakes, spiders, insects . . . I shuddered.

Summer worked with us the next day but she was lost in her own world. A few times I heard her talking to herself. Whatever she'd gone through alone in the jungle, it had left her vulnerable. The poacher attack had obviously been the straw that broke her. I was careful to keep her away from the machete and Araya seemed to be wary of her too. I think we both remembered the moment she walked towards the cliff edge too clearly to let her leave our sight.

After so many days with nothing to drive us, to focus us, the fire was a welcome change. It gave us purpose and a goal. We cut fuel, dried it, turned logs in the sun. We gathered food and watched the sky and waited.

Nothing happened. No one came. There wasn't a single glint of metal in between the clouds. No helicopters, not even a passing plane. By the end of our second day on the plateau, I could almost smell our desperation. It smelled of sweat and fear and wood smoke.

On the morning of our third day up there, Summer refused to get up.

Araya and I were eating the leftover fruit from yesterday, gearing up for more tree cutting. But Summer just lay by the ash at the edge of the fire and looked into its hot core, like she was debating whether or not to crawl inside.

'Summer? Come and eat something,' I said, trying to coax her over to us.

'Why?' she muttered.

I looked at Araya but she was looking at me, equally at a loss. If Summer had really given up hope it wasn't like we had much to spare. The relief of not living under the threat of Bryce's fury was gone now, replaced by worry about what Summer might do. To herself, or to us.

'You need to keep your strength up,' I said, hearing the false, slightly hysterical friendliness in my voice.

Summer didn't even bother with a response. After a while she got up and walked away, to the other side of the plateau, where the drop was sheer. I watched, tensed in case I needed to run after her, but she just sat down and looked off into the distance.

'Should we try and get her to help?' I asked, wondering if it was better or worse to let her dwell.

Araya sighed. 'Let her sit. It'll be easier if we don't have to watch her.'

She had a point. At least this way we knew where she was and that she wasn't getting into any trouble, or about to snap and shove one of us over the edge. Araya and I traded jobs for the day – I used the saw and she had the machete. But around noon, when the sun was high, the chain finally snapped. I was sent sprawling onto my back when it broke, holding two ends of the severed chain. No more saw. Another resource lost.

It felt like time for a nap. We had such little strength and very little food, sleeping was the only thing we could do to recharge. I curled up in the shade near Araya, and glanced over at Summer. She was right where she'd been all morning, her head resting forward against her chest. Like she was asleep.

I closed my eyes, and drifted in the sweltering heat.

I woke up, baking hot. But it wasn't the sweaty, sticky jungle heat, but a dry, suffocating blast. Then I heard the snapping, the popping. For a moment I thought it was the wild pigs, rooting around and crunching bones. I was still half asleep and could almost see them tearing into Summer, or Araya, or me. Then I forced my eyes open and saw the fire.

It was everywhere. The flames were running over the

grass of the plateau like water. Greedy yellow flames nosing through the dry undergrowth. We'd left it unattended and the wind had shifted. Our piles of drying kindling had tumbled into it and now our bonfire was raging out of control.

'Araya!'

I leapt to my feet and started pulling at her, shaking her awake. As soon as her eyes opened and she saw the fire, she yelped and stumbled to her feet. I looked around for Summer.

She was still in the same position and I ran over to grab her, to tell her what was happening. But when I got hold of her shoulder she just looked up at me, confused.

'Summer, the whole ledge is going to go up; we have to move. The fire!' I burst out, hoping those two words would get through to her.

She looked over her shoulder at the blaze and it seemed to hypnotise her. There was no fear on her face, just wonder. I grabbed her under the arms and hauled her away from the edge. She stumbled up, getting her feet under herself and back-pedalling automatically.

The fire was spreading fast, and soon the whole plateau would be engulfed. Araya was panicking, streaked with soot smuts and dirt. Summer was a dead weight in my arms, and even with the two of us pulling at her, it was obvious we weren't getting her back across the crevice and down the mountainside.

'Hold her,' I said, and thrust Summer's weight onto Araya.

'You can't just leave!'

'I'm looking!'

I rushed to the edge of the cliff and looked down. We'd

247

climbed up this side and although we now couldn't reach the plateaus and ledges we'd navigated up, there was still a way down. A slope too steep to climb but which we could maybe slide down. Or at least, fall down and hope we didn't brain ourselves on rocks and outcroppings as we went.

It was our only option. I rushed back to the others and steered Araya and Summer towards the edge.

'We have to try and slide,' I said, smoke catching in my throat, making me cough.

'Slide?' Araya echoed, then looked down. She blanched. 'No!'

'It's that, or we burn – or we leave Summer, and she dies!' I yelled, over Araya's denials.

Summer laughed, like I'd told a joke.

'Do it!' I shouted, and gestured.

'You first!' Araya retorted.

If I went, I couldn't be sure she'd follow. That was the thing. We'd made that mistake already, leaving Summer to cross the crevice. She could have easily wandered off or leapt to her death or done any number of impulsive things in the moment. We wouldn't have been able to stop her. I wasn't about to make that mistake again.

I looked at Araya, and she frowned at me, then gaped. 'Lila! No!'

But it was too late. I ducked down and launched myself at her, shoving her and Summer over the edge. With me tumbling down behind them.

Chapter 30

I'd never been beaten up before. My bullies had Instagram handles and magazine exclusivity deals. They didn't use punches or kicks to get their hatred and disdain across. Going down that slope was the closest I have ever come, or want to, to being beaten to death.

I fell and rolled and flailed automatically to try and stop myself. I hit rocks, the hard ground, stumps, the other women falling with me. It was like being in an industrial dryer full of bricks. One of my nails caught a rock and bent back, I screamed and got a mouthful of dirt for my trouble. My neck got twisted and my arm was pinned under me as I rolled over and over and over. I was terrified that my bones would snap and leave me helpless, or worse, dead.

When I reached the bottom in a winded sprawl, I was bruised and battered all over. Every inch of me felt as if it had been thrashed with a club. I struggled for air and clawed at the ground, trying to move. My eyes were full of grit and it hurt to blink and the skin on my face felt tight from the fire's heat. I reached up to rub at my eyes and my hand came away with my eyelashes on it, burnt to cinders.

I could hear the others. Hear their groaning and harsh breathing over the rain of pebbles and bits of undergrowth that we'd brought down with us.

Eventually, I rolled onto my front and from there managed to get to my feet. My legs were a mess of shallow grazes and my dress was torn, the crochet already beginning to unravel as the cotton yarn frayed apart. My shoes were gone – fallen off on my way down the slope.

Araya was lying a few feet away, face down but moving a little. I went over and helped her to sit up, relieved that she didn't seem too hurt. Just bruised and grazed like me.

'You . . . bitch . . .' Araya panted, without much heat.

'Sorry. I had to,' I said. 'There wasn't any time.'

I looked around for Summer and saw her lying right at the base of the slope. A red-hot cinder came twirling out of the sky and landed on her dress. I rushed forwards, slapping and batting at it. There was a hole burned through the lilac fabric. Looking up I was horrified to see more sparks and fragments of burning wood and leaf falling towards us. The fire was pursuing us.

'Get up, come on!' I nudged Summer insistently and grabbed at her arm, but she fought against me like a moody toddler, using her weight against me. 'Summer! We have to move!'

Araya stumbled over to help me and together we caught hold of both Summer's arms and levered her to her feet. We pulled her away from the swirling cinders and let her collapse onto the ground again. Araya sat down beside her, apparently still shaken from the fall. I wondered if she actually forgave me for shoving her, or if she'd hold that against me – turning out like Summer. Another thing to watch my back over.

I dropped down onto the ground beside them and rubbed at my sore limbs, trying to recover from the fall. I looked at my scratched-up legs and thought of Janet and her raging infection, that deep sore that had devoured her flesh. I automatically reached for the bag and the first-aid supplies inside. Then I realised it was still up on the plateau, probably burning away along with the machetes, bamboo poles and everything else we'd had with us.

Araya slowly got back to her feet and brushed herself down. She watched the smoke billowing up from our former camp, the sparks raining down, and sniffed.

'Maybe someone'll see it now.'

'Yeah,' I half-laughed, still in shock. 'Maybe.'

That was when I noticed the smoke rising from the undergrowth near the base of the cliff. The falling embers had caught in the dry leaf litter and already flames were curling and crawling through the debris like curious insects. But they were growing alarmingly fast even as I watched.

'Araya, the leaves!' I leapt up and went to stamp out the flames but remembered my lack of shoes just in time. Araya, wearing flimsy sandals, tried her best but the fire was spreading from too many places and she was burning her feet.

'Fuck,' I breathed, watching the fire ripple and flow, rushing towards nearby bushes and climbing them, devouring their branches and growling. 'We need to move, now!'

'But the fire . . .' Araya pointed above us, where our signal fire raged out of control, spreading to other ledges and scorching the rock black. 'Someone might see and come for us . . .'

'And we'll be burned to death before they get here!' I shouted, and grabbed at Summer, pulling her up. 'It's spreading too fast.'

Araya looked around and I saw her shake off the last of the confusion from the fall. Her expression of horror only made my own panic climb. She came to help me and together we urged Summer away from the cliff. We practically carried her as she stumbled and staggered in a daze. Catching her as she fell and urging her onwards, even when she struggled against us and tried to head back the way we'd come. It was like herding an animal more than a person.

When we paused to look back, I saw that the burning debris and embers had claimed several trees and the fire was growing. The flames roared up, taller than us, no longer yellow but billowing orange and red. The heat was intense and I could hear the trees cracking and popping in it as the fire sunk its fangs into them and feasted. It wasn't just moving towards us, but outwards too. Spreading as we watched. Taking over the jungle so fast it was almost magical.

'Oh God.' Araya gaped at it. 'Where can we go? It's . . . it's so fast.'

I had no idea. The whole jungle was just like this, as far as we'd seen. Packed with leaf litter, sticks, close-knit trees and thorn bushes. It hadn't rained in days and the humid air was being banished by the flames, turning dry and scorching even before the fire arrived. Wherever we went the fire would follow.

'Water,' I muttered and then said it again, louder as the idea took hold. 'We need to find water!'

'Where? The stream's all the way back there.' Araya

threw an arm in the direction we'd hiked from. 'And it's too small.'

The idea hit me and just like that it became our only hope. 'That cave. The cave was wet and the rock might keep the fire out.'

'Cave . . . you mean that crack we saw?' Araya, gaped at me. 'Lila it's probably not even deep, and there's insects – snakes. It won't be good in there.'

'Do we have any other choice?' I asked, skin prickling at the mention of snakes and bugs. From the look on Araya's face, she knew we didn't. It was the cave, or burn alive.

'Which way?' she said, eventually.

I vaguely remembered but it meant going diagonally through the jungle, leaving us in the path of the fire. It was coming towards us from the side and ahead that way and the smoke was blowing at us, choking us. I put my arm around Summer and forced her to bend over, keeping her head low as the smoke rose. Araya crept along beside us, both of us tense and looking for that gap in the cliff. What if we missed it? What if it wasn't even a cave just a half-foot crack in the wall?

The fire was deafening up close. Trees were going off like fireworks as the fire boiled them from the inside out. Chunks of burning wood rained down on us from above and I heard Araya cry out as she was burned by them. I was wincing and hissing myself, as sparks landed on me, peppering me with burns.

'There!'

I saw Araya pointing, saw the dark line of the crack and shoved Summer ahead of me towards it. It was narrow, so I had to manoeuvre her sideways and coax her inside.

I nudged Araya in next and looked back at the fire as she went. It had become so large so quickly. Raging out of control and chasing us like a wild animal. The cliff side was ablaze and the jungle was showing no signs of going out.

I couldn't believe what we had done. Our attempts to attract rescue had started a forest fire that felt like it was going to kill us and everything else around. We'd been trying to escape but now we were more trapped than ever. The smoke burned my eyes but I was already tearing up in despair. It was like we were cursed.

Araya's dirty, soot-smeared hand reached out of the cave, pulling at my shoulder. I turned and slid in after her, letting the cold, dank air chase the burn of the fire from my skin. Within moments I was shivering in the dank channel carved into the rock by dripping water.

The crack widened as I edged along it and my bare feet slid over wet, slick stones. Those gave way to water and the level of it rose as we moved in a line along the tunnel-like cave. In the pitch-dark, I could hear the others moving but see nothing. Not even the wet rock wall that was a centimetre or two from my face. I felt like I was being squeezed through a pipe, and the stink that rose up from around us made it feel like a sewer. A musty, fishy sort of reek that made me queasy.

Finally, once the water was up to my thighs, we stopped. Because Summer had stopped. I heard Araya shuffle forward a little and then her whispering voice in the alarming stillness.

'Summer? Is this the end of it or . . .'

'No, there's more,' Summer interrupted, her voice a soft rasp.

'Can you move forward?' I asked, frustration building in me.

'. . . I don't want to wake them up.'

Her voice went down the back of my neck like a drop of cold, slimy water.

'Wake what up?' My head was immediately full of visions of tigers, of panthers or wolves or something equally terrible and bloodthirsty.

'Them. Listen.'

I listened, and at first all I could hear was the sounds of the fire raging outside and the trickle and plink of water droplets falling down the rock into the stinking water lapping at my legs. Then I began to pick out other sounds. A sort of flapping, leather noise. Like someone shaking out a wet umbrella.

'Bats,' Araya murmured, sparing me from imagining what it was, and making it ten times worse somehow. 'There are bats, living in here.'

Frozen, we were all just listening and waiting. I looked up, hardly daring to move my head but I couldn't see anything. My eyes were still adjusting and there was so little light coming in that I was blind. A mad laugh got stuck in my craw – blind as a bat.

'Keep low,' Araya told Summer, when it became clear I wasn't about to step in and tell her what to do. 'And keep moving.'

Slowly, we proceeded. I heard the fluttering and flapping overhead. Nothing was moving too much; I couldn't feel anything swooping past my face. I could imagine the bats, like in a nature documentary, all hanging from the ceiling, mostly asleep. But for how long? Would the fire outside wake them and make them panic?

The tunnel opened up a bit and after a few more minutes of slow, careful, shuffling, we reached the back wall of the cave. We were still in the water, up to our waists and choking on the reek of what I now realised was probably bat shit. Under the water, my feet found small shifting shapes – stones, or perhaps the remains of small dead creatures the bats had fed on and then excreted. It was almost a relief when my skin below the waterline started to go numb. I didn't want to feel what was down there.

Araya put her arm around my shoulder and I did the same to Summer until we were standing in a circular huddle. It was hard to believe we'd been so hot only a short time ago. In here the sun was a memory and the burning flames a nightmare from another world. The chill from the water sunk into my bones and climbed up my body. Soon we were all shivering, rubbing each other's backs and arms to try and stay warm. Our heads bent and eyes shut against the all-encompassing darkness.

I don't know how long we were stood there. It felt like hours. It probably was. We kept hold of each other and moved closer as the cold grew more painful. I heard Araya muttering under her breath. I think she was praying, trying to comfort herself perhaps. Summer was quiet, but when she pressed her forehead to my shoulder I felt her tears – hot against my chilled skin.

Then, after an age of waiting for some sign or other, some relief from the fear of what was outside, the cave began to fill with movement. The air above us was filled with fluttering and I felt the squeaks of the bats more than I heard them. Those piercing high-pitched sounds that seemed to bypass my ears and lodge directly in my brain.

Leathery wings brushed my face and I yelped. Araya cried out and we all ducked down low. Bent over, almost submerged to my neck, I willed the bats to just leave. To fly out into the night that must have fallen, and to leave us alone. But it seemed that before they would do that, they had to circle the cave. They flapped and massed and screeched, and I felt their touch as they flew about. It was like being in a wind tunnel full of rats. Tears squeezed out of my eyes as I fought to keep still and quiet.

Then Summer started to scream.

The sound bounced around the cave, high-pitched and desperate. Barely human. The bats seemed to go into a frenzy, and for a moment it really did feel as if there was no air in the cave. Just wings and rank furry bodies flitting about. The way Summer was freaking out and waving her arms, not ducking as we were, I just knew she was going to get scratched and bitten to bits. I felt Araya move and Summer's scream cut off into a muffled gurgle. Araya must have put a hand over her mouth. Summer started to thrash and filthy water slopped about. Then she slipped and I felt her drop and go under.

Araya and I groped in the water and dragged her up, spitting and shrieking. She was completely out of it. Pushed too far by the dark hellish place we'd hidden in. But finally the bats were leaving. The sound of them grew quieter as they streamed from the mouth of the cave into the night, and finally the cave was quiet. Except for the sound of Summer's sobs.

Chapter 31

Andrea indicates the pristine white wall behind the sofa and obediently, three images appear. Two are publicity photos, the third a shot from social media. The first two have been cropped and airbrushed and staged just right. There's Fletcher, sitting at a shiny black desk with his shiny black hair neatly parted to the side. He's in a suit and on his lapel beside the microphone is a tiny pin badge showing the male and female symbols intertwined. At a guess, it's from his pride month special: 'Straight is the new minority'. Though that banner has been edited out. Someone clearly forgot to airbrush the pin away though.

I huff a laugh and a woman passing by in the airport gives me a weird look.

Beside his picture is one of Kaitlyn. She's holding a pastel pink mixing bowl and smiling at the camera as she shows off her cake batter. There's a matching pink bow in her hair and she's wearing a floral dress with puff sleeves. Behind her is a stock image of a pristine kitchen with mason jars full of different ingredients. Not one tiny bit of the chocolate batter she's mixing has made a mark on her, or the spoon she holds in her other hand.

Then there's Bryce. The photo is less polished than the others and the border shows that it's from his own Instagram page. It was taken in Phuket, at the RAWR nightclub during his set. He's holding his headphones to his ear with one hand and raising the other to hype up the crowd, his tiger pendant flashing like a disco ball.

Both of us, myself and the Lila on the sofa, look up at it, at him. She's thinking that she took that picture and sent it to him. He must have posted it as they were on their way to the air strip. The last post he made before the crash and everything that happened after.

I'm wondering at how long ago that all seems. Only a little under two years but it might as well have happened to someone else.

'Was there a point, during your time apart from them, that you were worried about what might become of your friends? Your fiancé?'

Despite starting the interview with poise and a sort of detached, meditative attitude, the cracks are beginning to show on Lila. I remember how much I wanted to escape the lights and the questions. At the time I was sleeping on the floor in the en suite still – two locked doors and a hard, cool floor were the only things that could get me to sleep.

It's obvious even with the makeup smeared under her eyes that she's exhausted. Has in fact spent most of her time since being rescued in interview after interview with police, rangers, rescue crews, lawyers and now the media. Her patience is wearing thin and that's very apparent when she frowns slightly and answers in a new, sharper tone.

'You mean while I was trying not to die in the jungle,

259

or climbing up a sheer cliff or taking care of a near catatonic woman or . . . when exactly, was I meant to sit and cry over what might be happening to the people who abandoned me, abandoned us, to die?'

Andrea's eyebrows creep up. 'Are you not worried about legal action for that accusation?'

Lila laughs. 'It's amazing how much less scary public disgrace seems when you've nearly burned to death. They can sue if they like – it's only money. It won't kill me. Besides which it's not as if they don't know what they did.'

'Those who made it, you mean? Or their families?'

Lila just looks at her, as if reading the inside of her skull. For the first time Andrea looks uncomfortable with her and not just irritated or pleased with herself. There is something slightly chilling about Lila. Even I'm unnerved by the look on my face. It's filled with hollows carved by stress and starvation and her eyes have the alertness of a reptile – sunning lazily under the studio lights for now, but ready to snap if provoked.

'Did you think you'd see them again?' Andrea says, clearly trying to regain some control. Her eyes flick towards the backstage area as if checking to make sure security are nearby.

'No, I didn't,' Lila says.

'Because you thought they'd be killed, by their captors?'

'Because when they left the three of us for dead, I thought we'd never get out of that jungle,' Lila corrects, voice like a knife sliding over rock. 'I suppose you should ask them – if they'd . . . well, you know what I mean. If you *could* ask them all, you could ask if they ever expected to see me again, and let me know what they say. Because they were the ones with the ticket home. As far as they knew, we got put down like dogs the second their backs were turned.'

A legal disclaimer pops up over the paused image. It clarifies that statements made by Lila Wilde about broadcaster and media personality Fletcher Michaels, influencer and lifestyle vlogger Kaitlyn Pence and 'former fiancé' Bryce Erlandsson, are her opinions only and that no one at either the talk show or the broadcaster endorses these allegations, which remain unproven and alleged. All statements made by Lila Wilde are her opinions and should not be treated as fact.

I laugh again, startling a family scuttling past, dragging their baggage behind them.

Chapter 32

When we slithered out of the cave, cold and wet through, it was just barely dark. Night had fallen but there was still a strange sort of sunset in the distance. Summer clawed her way past me, fighting to get out of that cave and not caring how hard she scratched and shoved us.

Outside the fire raged on, making the sky red and adding smoke to the darkness above. Around us there were a hundred thousand red stars – embers and lumps of charcoal glowing on the ground. Mirroring the emerging night sky above, visible for so far, because there was nothing to block it out anymore, except for the distant smoke.

The heat washed over me as soon as we set foot outside. The earth was baked dry and hard as a brick, radiating warmth through my wet, bare feet. I was reminded of leaving the pool at our Italian villa and setting foot on the scorching patio. For a second I was back in that place, sunglasses on my head and a frosty cocktail in my hand. Then I heard Araya gasp and I was right back in the present. Trapped once more in the jungle.

Only, the jungle was completely transformed.

The trees and brush were gone, only stumps and rocks remained, like broken teeth. There was ash and crumbling dark charcoal everywhere. It didn't even look like there had been a jungle around us. It looked like an alien world – hostile and unfamiliar.

Standing there, dripping with foul water and feeling my hair slowly blast dry in the residual heat, I felt as if we'd stepped out of that cave, into Hell.

'Oh my God . . .' Araya whispered. 'What did we do?' I shook my head, not wanting to believe that all of this was our doing. That because of our signal fire, miles upon miles of jungle was burning to the ground. But it was true. We had done this. I wasn't just responsible for the deaths from the plane crash, but for this too. This devastation. I'd caused so much death and so much suffering that I could hardly comprehend it.

Summer, having stumbled around in a circle, looking at the devastation, collapsed onto the ground. She wrapped her arms around herself and let out a low wail. A long, drawn-out cry of despair that put my hair on end.

'Summer . . .' Araya approached her, but Summer started wailing louder, tensing up. When Araya reached for her hand, she slapped at her and Araya jerked away. Summer bared her teeth, the awful sound still boiling up from her throat. Like she was a cornered animal.

Exhaustion weighed on me and I couldn't find it in me to tackle the Summer situation just then. I waved to Araya to back off. The darkness was closing in and after the cave I wanted light. Couldn't bear not being able to see, even if what there was to see was horrifying. I picked up a charred stick and used it to scrape some glowing embers together, fanned them with my hand until yellow flames appeared. They were so small and cheery. It was hard to believe they'd turned into the inferno that we'd fled. Though like Bryce I supposed you never really knew what something was capable of, in the right conditions.

Araya came over and sat on the hot ground beside me. Her clothes were gently steaming as they dried off. The small fire lit the night around us, just. It wasn't really necessary for more than that.

Summer continued to wail like a frightened toddler. It was unsettling, watching her mouth stretch wide and dark as a cave, that noise spilling out and carrying off into the night. Her eyes were creases in her face, between the bloody scratches and bites from the bats. She only paused to choke down air, hiccupping hysterically before the siren wail started up again.

I pulled my knees up to my chest and wrapped my arms around them. I wanted to shut her up, but there was no way to reason with her.

'What do we do?' Araya asked, looking at her with wide, frightened eyes.

'Leave her to it,' I muttered. 'But keep an eye on her in case she tries anything.'

'You think she might attack us?' Araya looked equally upset and confused. As if she couldn't believe that Summer would do such a thing.

But the woman with us wasn't entirely Summer anymore. She was becoming stranger and less predictable by the hour. Unravelling faster than my torn dress. Revealing the animal underneath the person.

I shuddered and rubbed at my skin, chasing away the chill. That was when I felt something on my leg. Under my hand. I jerked my fingers away from the wet, soft . . . thing, and looked down.

My horrified shriek travelled far across the barren wasteland around us. Both Araya and Summer looked at me, shocked. Summer's cry cut off with a click as her jaw snapped shut. Then, when Araya realised what she was looking at, she jumped up and started to check herself over. She gasped in shock and made little helpless noises of horror and disgust.

Leeches. We all had them on us, multiple shiny dark creatures fastened onto our skins and sucking, growing fat with our blood. The level of disgust inside made me feel faint. I wanted to crawl out of my skin.

I grabbed the one on my leg and pulled. It stretched, the texture of a jelly cleanser bar, slippery and squishy but also strong. It refused to let go and I felt my skin start to tear around where it was stuck to me. Blood ran down my leg, thin and bright red.

'Stop!' Araya slapped my hand. 'You can't pull them off! You'll bleed a lot and it might get infected.'

'Why can't I feel it?' I was trying not to retch, looking at that fat, black body attached to my skin.

'They have a painkilling bite,' Araya looked just as disgusted as I felt. 'The cave must be full of them. Just . . . if there's only one or two, we can wait and let them fall off.'

'Let them . . . when?' I demanded, and glanced at Summer, who had fallen to watching the yellow flames, apparently shutting us both out – for now – muttering to herself. 'Can't we burn them off?'

'If they get hurt, they can vomit the blood back into you, and it'll be full of bacteria. Once they've sucked enough blood, they'll be full and fall off,' Araya said. 'I used to get one or two when I went hiking and if you don't have a credit card or something to scrape with, it's better to leave them until they're done.'

I thought of all the credit cards we'd had back at the plane. Lost to us now. So many of them. Never in my life had I needed one more.

'Check me, I'll check you,' Araya said. 'We can both check . . .' She nodded towards Summer, as if afraid that saying her name would wake her up to the horror of our situation. I didn't exactly relish the idea of being looked over for leeches, of knowing how many of them were feeding on my body. Still, not knowing was probably worse. In my imagination my back was covered in them, a seething mass of pulsing, blood-filled bodies.

I stood while Araya searched me over, finding three leeches in total. The one I'd spotted on my shin, one just under my left buttock and one on the back of my neck. Checking her over I found four – two on her legs, one on the back of her arm and one disgustingly clinging to the part in her long dark hair.

Warily we both approached Summer. I think both of us knew that if Summer realised she had leeches on her she'd freak out worse than she had already. Up close, in the firelight I saw more scratches and bites on her face and arms. From the bats. I winced, imagining them getting caught in her long blonde hair – biting and scratching their way free.

'What are you doing?' Summer asked, as we knelt on either side of her, looking at her exposed skin. Her voice was suspicious and yet too calm. It made the back of my neck prickle.

'Just making sure you're not hurt,' I said, trying to sound confident and reassuring. The way I'd try and soothe a feral cat. Summer looked at me warily but she didn't seem to notice what we were looking for. Thankfully we only found two leeches on her. One in the centre of her exposed back and one hanging behind her ear like a gruesome piece of jewellery – wriggling as it fed. I hoped she wouldn't sense it was there before it was done.

Sitting by the fire, waiting for leeches to have their fill of my blood wasn't pleasant, but it was hardly the worst thing I'd been through. That thought alone made me shut my eyes and hug my knees tighter in despair. In moments of stillness and rest I still remembered how the gun had felt in my hand, the sound the poacher made as I shot him, like air rushing from a puncture. Remembered San'ya's face as we left.

I didn't want to see those things in my memory, but I also couldn't bear to look at the ruined jungle, or the hungry, filthy faces of the other two survivors. It was too much. I could feel it all pressing in on my brain, almost as if each successive trauma was bruising my mind. Was this how Summer had felt before she snapped?

I glanced at her, wondering what she was thinking, if she was planning to attack us. If she was capable of planning at all, or if it was all just instinct now. What if those instincts told her to bash our heads in during the night? What if they told her to run away? We'd never find her again in all this chaos.

I felt it when the leech on the back of my neck had enough and detached from me. Its fat body was heavy with my blood and it slithered over me, rolling down my back like a fat gob of slime. I shuddered and automatically

267

threw a hand up to bat it off me. I heard it hit the ground outside of the circle of firelight and imagined it sizzling on a hot lump of charcoal, my blood blistering on the ground.

The leeches on my leg came free soon after and I flicked them away. They left behind little punctures that dribbled blood. I guessed they weren't just injecting me with painkiller but also something to make my blood thin out and not scab over while they fed. Just the idea made me heave.

Araya got rid of her leeches and then I noticed the one behind Summer's ear wriggling down over her collarbone. She must have felt it moving, looked down and let out a shriek so shrill and inhuman that I instinctively scrambled away from her. Out of the corner of my eye I saw Araya do the same, clasping her hands over her mouth in distress.

In seconds she'd swept the leech from her skin and onto the ground. She snatched up a burning stick from the fire and beat at it, producing a foul stink of burning meat and blood. Her blood. While she struck it over and over again, spittle flew from between her clenched teeth and she snarled like a wild animal. Araya crept behind me as if I could protect her from Summer's insane rage. But Summer didn't even seem to notice our fear. She was focused only on obliterating the leech on the ground, baring her teeth and gritting them in a mad grin, reminding me of the vicious little monkeys we'd seen around camp. Fear trickled through me like cold water – not of the leech but of Summer.

'Should we . . . do something?' Araya murmured in my ear, clinging to my dress like a child.

I shook my head, holding up an arm to hold her back,

as if it was needed. It seemed vital that neither of us touch her. As if she was a bomb and any sudden movement would jostle her and trigger an explosion. We waited, frozen, and I hardly dared blink as I watched Summer break down. It felt as if doing so would be an invitation for her to lunge at us.

But slowly, Summer seemed to run out of steam. Her blows lost their force and focus. The charred stick broke apart and she beat the ashy ground with her palms until she collapsed and curled into a ball. The leech was long gone, pulverised to nothing more than a sticky mark on the charred dirt. She sobbed brokenly and covered her face with her filthy hands.

Slowly, Araya and I moved a little closer to the fire. But stopped before we got within her reach. Summer shook slightly, like a dog in a thunderstorm, but eventually she went still and must have passed out from exhaustion.

I lay down on one side of the fire, Araya on the other and we watched Summer, until it was clear she was really asleep. There was nothing much to keep the fire going with and I didn't feel like wandering around in the dark looking for fuel. By the time it went out completely, I hoped to be asleep. But I wasn't.

Lying there I was too tired to be hungry, my throat burning with thirst and the stars above shining down on me. The air smelled of smoke and we were surrounded by the soft crackling of scorched wood crumbling apart. It felt like the end of the world. Like we were the only three women left alive in all that destruction.

Only then, lying awake in the dark, did I wonder if the fire had reached the poachers and their hostages. And what had become of them if it had.

Chapter 33

When we woke up the world had changed, the red shifting to grey. A million shades of it from almost white to dark slate. Ash blanketed everything like snow. The charred wood stuck out, blackened and stark. The tangled undergrowth was so fragile that just touching it made it collapse into cinders. As I peed a little way off from the others, facing their way to keep an eye on Summer, I found the first of what would be many dead animals in the burned debris.

It was a snake, twisted up and charred to nothing. Brittle as scorched paper. The white bones of its jaw frozen open as if it had been trying to attack the flames as it died. Or as if it was screaming in agony.

'Lila?'

I brushed ash from my legs and tried not to jump at the sound of Summer calling my name. She hadn't said anything intelligible since before we entered the cave.

'Yeah?' I said, and coughed. My mouth and throat were clogged with dry ash. I was desperate for water but we didn't have any, neither was there any fruit around to eat. Touching anything, and lying down, had covered us all in ashes. We were like three filthy city statues, streaked in black and grey.

'Where are we going?' Summer asked, looking at me with large, fearful eyes. As if she'd only just realised where we were and what had happened to the jungle around us. 'It's all burned.'

'Not all of it,' I promised, trying to keep some hope in my voice even though I didn't feel it. I didn't want to set her off again. 'The jungle, but not the cities and the towns. They're still out there. We'll reach one, and now we can find our way easier.'

It was hard to find a silver lining to burning down an entire jungle, but I was trying. If only to keep Summer on an even keel. I didn't have the heart to focus on the fact that we'd burned up all the food and contaminated the water. With neither of those we'd likely never make it anywhere. But we had to try.

Araya sat up and rubbed at her face. Her fingers ground soot into the deep bags under her eyes, making them look worse, deeper, until she resembled a skull.

'We should go back to the stream,' she said in a voice like paper being screwed up into a ball. 'It's the only water we've seen except the cave . . .'

'And we're not going back in there,' I finished for her, giving her a meaningful look and nodding slightly at Summer. The water in the cave was full of bat shit anyway, not exactly good for drinking. 'But the stream's probably full of ash now. We can't drink that.'

'It'll have a source though, if we follow it. And that'll take us towards the temple. Look.' She pointed and I saw, in the distance past the craggy remains of trees and rocks covered in charred roots, the temple in the distance. It was just the spire really; the rest was hidden by a rise in the ground but we had seen it from above and it wasn't that far. At least not compared to a city or a town, which we hadn't spotted even from our ledge.

'It's a landmark. People will come out here because of the fire, to try and rescue animals and prevent it spreading. If we go there, we're more likely to be seen.'

It was a fragile hope but it was all we had. So I nodded and then glanced at Summer. She looked between the two of us blankly.

'There's nothing out there,' she said, at last, like she was explaining this to children afraid of a monster. 'There's nothing left.'

'We have to go,' Araya said.

'I'm tired!' Summer suddenly shouted, losing her temper and slapping her hands at the scorched ground. I jumped slightly. It was as if she'd completely lost the ability to regulate her emotions. Though I guessed all of us were struggling to stay focused. Maybe my meditation practice had actually been good for something. Or maybe I was deluding myself and I was just lucky. God, that could have been the title of my autobiography. All my life had been one long string of good fortune, and it had snapped while we were mid-air.

'Summer,' I tried, gentling her along in a friendly way, like I would with younger fans. 'You don't want to be here alone, do you?'

Her eyes were teary and she shook her head.

'Then you should come with us . . . and when we get there, we can rest and you won't have to go any further.'

I didn't add that this was because we had nowhere else to go. That to be honest it would be a miracle if we reached the temple with no food or water. I just had to get her moving, get us moving. That slim chance of rescue was hair-thin but it was all we had and even though she was probably more of a danger to us than a help, we couldn't just leave her behind.

We had nothing to pack up and so we just walked. Walked on and on through the devastation that we had created. Hungry and thirsty and exhausted, covered in bruises from our tumble down the slope. Every scrape and scratch on my skin was a new fear. I kept thinking of Janet and her infected leg. Would I go the same way? I had to be covered in bacteria, had waded in bat shit contaminated water and lain in a bed of ashes. I had to be infected. My only comfort was that I'd probably die of thirst before it had much chance to set in.

The temple never seemed to get closer. It was always in the distance and occasionally vanished as we went down small hills and climbed up the other side. We were helping each other, reaching back to lift the next person up the slopes. Araya and I swapped the lead position as we had before, but having my back to Summer made me twitchy. We took turns being the first to climb up the rocks and rises to help the others.

We almost missed the stream.

I was right – it had become completely choked up with ashes and debris. The water was practically a slurry it was so badly contaminated. I could have cried to see it slowly trickling along the blackened riverbed. But I didn't have the water spare to cry.

'That way,' Araya croaked and we set off along the stream, in the direction of the temple. I could feel the tension between the three of us as we hoped and wished for clean water at the end of our journey. That we'd find the source of the stream or an uncontaminated part of it where we could drink. Forget rescue, forget clean clothes and a safe roof over our heads – water was all we cared about then. Water and food.

We saw few animals on the way. There were birds occasionally passing above and some insects that must have burrowed to escape the heat of the fire. But other than that everything was very still and quiet. At a distance I saw two wild pigs miserably rooting in the burned undergrowth and wondered if like us they'd found a cave or a pool where they had been spared. But spared for what? To wander as we were wandering? They didn't come near us and we avoided them.

It began to get dark and I realised we had no way of lighting a fire and no convenient embers to make one from. When night fell we'd be completely blind. But at least we had the groove the stream had carved through the ground, which was more noticeable as we followed it towards its source.

In the eye-straining gloom I was fighting to stay awake, to keep moving. My stomach was empty and my mouth was dry as the cracked ground around us. Even my eyes felt dry, as if they were filming over, crusting up from lack of water. I knew the others felt the same. Araya kept stumbling and Summer was droning under her breath – like she was trying to sing in her sleep, and every note was flat and odd. The only comfort was she seemed more delusional than violent, at least for now.

Then I caught a scent of something. Something like food. Meat. Cooked meat. Like beach barbecues and Brazilian grills and flashy restaurants where waiters cooked your steak right by the table. I felt delirious but then Araya grabbed my shoulder and shook me.

'Can you smell . . .'

'Yeah.' I looked around wildly, my nose was telling me there was food nearby. Very nearby. But my mind told me it was nonsense. There was nothing anywhere. We were in a burned-out desert.

Then I saw it.

For a moment I thought it was a person, burned beyond recognition in the fire; the curled hands, the yawning skull, the arms twisted over its chest. But then I realised the skull was longer, wider. That the scorched skin still had fur clinging here and there. It was a monkey. Perhaps one of the macaques that had whooped and chittered nearby while we lived in the crashed plane, waiting for rescue.

That felt like so long ago.

I looked at Araya, and then at Summer and finally back at the scorched monkey, at the cracks in its blackened skin where the cooked meat showed through. The smell was so strong I was sure I was half imagining it. That it was just a memory of meat cooking and in my starved madness it was suddenly everywhere. Inescapable.

Araya and I were still standing there when Summer caught sight of the monkey and dove for it. She landed on all fours and ripped a chunk from it with her fingers. She stuffed the meat into her mouth and chewed like a hungry dog, gulping it down.

I think that's what broke me. If it was just me and Araya I might have resisted. Might have felt too disgusted to eat it. But hearing Summer chew and tear at the meat. Seeing the pieces of it disappear into her mouth, I broke.

The three of us surrounded the meat and pulled it

apart between us. Summer was growling as she tore at the meat, and I kept to my side in case she went for me. Araya was being similarly cautious and we kept a wary eye on Summer as we ate.

By the time we were done it was fully dark and I was glad. I don't think I could have looked either of them in the eye just then, not even for an ice-cold bottle of Voss and a helicopter out of there. My face was hot with shame, and sticky with meat juices.

We picked ourselves up, wiping juices from our chins, and walked on, following the stream. We didn't go far, just enough to put some distance between ourselves and the remains of the meal we'd just shared. I couldn't think of it as an animal without feeling ill.

When we stopped the three of us curled up in a pile for warmth. With no fire and no shelter the night was uncomfortably cold in our thin, club clothing. Cold enough that being that close to Summer seemed worth the danger.

Lying in a burned jungle and shivering myself to sleep, I managed to dream myself back in time. I was in my dad's London apartment and I was standing in front of his giant, American-style fridge. The cold air from it washed over me and inside I saw rotisserie chicken, iced coffee loaded with cream and syrup, cheesecake, brie. I looked at all of it and my stomach rumbled painfully.

In real life I'd have taken a bottle of water and gone to the building's private gym. At the most I'd be having a grilled chicken breast wrapped in lettuce, no dressing, trying to convince myself it was just as good as a fried chicken burger dripping in garlic mayonnaise. In my dream though, I was grabbing cheese and eating it like a sandwich, pouring chocolate syrup into my mouth and pulling cheesecake apart with my fingers, licking it off my hands. I grabbed hold of a chicken leg and brought it to my lips, but when I looked down at the chicken, it was a leering monkey skull. I was holding its crispy, twisted paw to my mouth, and I took a bite.

Chapter 34

We've been in the jungle for two weeks now. That was the first thought I had when I woke up, my dreams fading away into nothing, leaving my mouth dry and tasting slightly of burnt meat. Over two weeks, I realised as I got the days straight in my head. Counting the day of the crash, it had been fifteen days. Just the thought of that made me want to cry. Or laugh until I did.

Fifteen days.

Soon after waking we got on the move again. There was nothing to sit still for. As we were walking though I noticed Summer was acting weirder than she had been before. I was bringing up the rear of our little group and watching her. She wasn't raging or stumbling along in her own little world, she was scratching. She kept scratching her face, or lifting her filthy hands to the back of her head and scratching around in her hair with her jagged nails. The blonde was practically lost under grease, soot and dirt, and at first I thought she might have bugs or something in her hair. We probably all did. But she kept scratching, especially that one place and after a while I noticed that there was blood on her fingers.

'Summer!' I grabbed her arm before I could think better of it and she swung around, shocked and scared, anger flashing through her eyes. I let go of her immediately and glanced at Araya, who'd turned to see what was going on.

'You're scratching your scalp bloody,' I said.

'It's itchy, and it tingles,' she said, as if that was enough explanation and maybe it was. But as she'd turned Araya got a good look at the back of her head.

'Is that a bite? Or a cut?' she asked, trying to get closer to look, but Summer shrugged her off and I saw Araya attempt to follow her but then thought better of it. We were both remembering how snappy Summer had been, how violent when we found the leeches. Neither of us wanted to provoke her.

'Just . . . be careful,' I said inanely and we started walking again. Summer scratching away in front of me.

By the time we stopped to rest at around noon, Summer was clearly exhausted and looked sweaty. Not just the way we all were but sort of clammy and feverish. I felt my skin crawl as I looked at her. She had to have an infected wound, like Janet. A wound that was poisoning her blood and making her sicker with every step we took. And there was nothing we could do. No point in even locating it. What would that do? We had nothing to clean it with, or to try and cut the infection out with. No way of helping.

So we walked on and I climbed another rise, reaching back to pull Summer up after me. I was hauling her up before what I'd just seen registered in my exhausted brain. The temple.

I looked around as Summer scrambled up to join me, and cried out in relief. We had reached the temple! It had dropped out of view earlier in the day and I'd thought we were still quite far away. But suddenly, there we were. My eyes blurred with tears and I had to pull myself away from the sight to help Araya up. When she saw the temple, she whooped and threw her arms around me.

Looking at it from our vantage point, I could see it wasn't large. The stone building had a square base and was topped with a rounded tower, ending with a spire. Maybe once it had been green with moss and vines, but now it was mostly scorched black and the remains of trees and roots stood out on it like black veins, crisscrossing back and forth. Between them the entryway was a yawning mouth, promising shadow and shelter.

'Here,' Araya said, pulling on my arm to urge me along. 'Water!'

We'd found the source of the stream. It was just a little further up the rise, trickling from between rocks in the craggy foothills of a mountain. Although the stream itself was ashy and the water ran black in places, at source, the water was clean and bitter with minerals. One by one we pressed our mouths to the stone and sucked up mouthfuls of blissfully cold water. By the end we all had clean chins and red grooves in our cheeks from pressing against the rock.

Araya looked like she wanted to cry in relief, but like me she didn't have the water to spare. She leant against the rocks and shut her eyes, savouring this single piece of good luck we'd had.

I was all for lying by the stream and drinking our fill for the next few hours, but Summer didn't seem able to sit still. Given how exhausted we all were I was almost suspicious that she'd had drugs on her this entire time. She was acting like Bryce on yaba – pacing around and scratching at her arms, shaking her head and slapping at the back of her skull like she was being bitten by fleas. Every so often she'd sit down, but like a hummingbird she'd move on again within moments. Her eyes darted around and looked by turns confused and irritable. She'd barely stay still long enough to sip water from the source.

'Can we go?' she snapped, eventually. 'The temple's right there . . . we should go, now.'

I wanted to argue and ask what we'd gain by going down there when the water was here. We only needed to be near the temple to use it as a landmark in case fire rescue crews came. But one look at her tense, twitchy face and I sensed it was smarter to just give in. Whatever was up with Summer I didn't want her to lose it again. That and it would be nice to have some shelter by the time it got dark.

After Araya and I slurped down more water we climbed down to the temple. Thankfully the slope was gentle and it wasn't that hard to reach with most of the trees burned away. Though here and there chunks of tree remained. Perhaps the dip in the land had preserved some dampness from the rains and that had helped to keep things from burning up entirely. There was still, however, nothing around to eat that I could see.

We reached the temple and being near manmade walls after so long was a strange experience. At eye level it was all scorched, but close up I could see that above us some moss still clung, a green banner in all the destruction. I put my hand out and touched the carved stone, still warm from where the fire had rushed over it, baking the stones until they radiated heat like an oven. How long had it been since another person touched it? How long until someone else came by and put their hand where mine had been?

It was a weirdly humbling experience. The kind of thing I might have said about swimming with a dolphin or skydiving before. But it was just me, and an old piece of stone, and the way it felt under my fingers. How old it was and how small I was compared to its long history. I rested my forehead against it for a second and got lost in the implication of so much time, and suddenly two weeks in the jungle was nothing at all.

The entryway was dark and the air flowing out of it was hot and dry. It was like standing in front of a dragon's mouth. Araya's hand twitched into mine nervously and I squeezed her fingers. We crept inside, with Summer holding Araya's other hand.

It was dark in there, no surprise, but at the end of a few feet of corridor, in the main structure, light came in through slits carved into the walls. Plants had grown through them as well and whilst what was clinging closest to the gaps was scorched, the stuff growing below was still green. Like we'd walked into a mossy oasis.

On either side of the central room there was a shadowy alcove and beyond I saw another dark corridor. Several chunks of stone littered the floor and looking up I could see where they'd fallen from – the holes they left filled by chunky tree trunks.

Summer paced around, feet scuffling in the trailing vines and moss. 'This is it? There's nothing here!'

I had no idea what she'd been expecting but I didn't have the energy to ask. Instead I sat down on a chunk of stone in the hopes that it would stop me feeling dizzy. The lack of food since yesterday was already starting to get to me. To all of us. Looking around I was disappointed to see that there weren't any fruits growing nearby. Maybe the temple was too dark for those kinds of plants. Since we'd found water here, this place had become a sort of sanctuary, but really it was just a ruin in the fire-blasted landscape.

'We'll need to go back up there whenever we want water,' Araya sighed, sitting down near me and rubbing her feet in her filthy hands. 'Unless we find something to carry water in . . . maybe an old brazier or something. We'll waste too much energy going up there all the time.'

I was only able to summon the energy to hum in agreement. Summer was wandering and I followed her with my eyes as she inspected the alcoves and then headed for the other tunnel. I debated calling out in case there were snakes or something in there but honestly I wasn't sure she'd listen to me even if I did warn her.

'They might not send fire crews here,' Araya whispered, once Summer had left our sight. 'The fire's spread further and they'll go where it's still active and moving.'

I shut my eyes, nodding slightly. I knew she was right.

'I suppose we just . . . wait,' she said.

'Yeah,' I managed.

'Summer's being weird,' Araya said, nibbling her lip. 'Not the same kind of weird. It's getting worse? Don't you think?'

I nodded again. 'I think she's feverish.'

'I noticed her sweating. Could be dengue or, infection?' Araya wrapped her arms around herself. 'I don't think there's anything we can do for either. I'm just worried she might hurt one of us, or herself.'

She was acting odd, and being quite unpredictable.

I was starting to wonder if we weren't all cracking up. After all we'd ripped into the monkey's burnt corpse like it was a roast chicken, hardly pausing to think about it. We were so far from civilisation now. Not just in distance but in our minds. Even looking back on the day we'd left our villa for the club, I could hardly recognise myself in my own memories. That girl, with those worries and those thoughts. She'd been dying since we'd crashed here and somewhere along the way I'd lost her entirely. But what was left in that case? Who was left? And did it even matter if no one was ever going to find us?

Maybe that's why it took me so long to recognise the noise when I heard it. It was so far removed from context that I struggled for a moment. I heard the hiss and immediately thought 'snake'. But then came the crunch, the metallic crack and I paused, looking at Araya's confused expression.

We both realised at the same time what it was. Both stood up and looked around us, peering into the darkness. Summer came shuffling out of the tunnel opposite, looking at us quizzically. I watched as she raised a hand to her mouth, and took a swig from a can of Coke.

'Summer, where did you get that?' I asked, feeling slightly unreal as I watched her standing there, caked in ash and sweat, sipping from the clean can.

'The pile, over there.' She gestured down the tunnel.

Araya and I moved towards her as one. While Araya stopped to look at the can as if checking it was real, I went into the tunnel and quickly reached its end. There was no exit that way. Maybe there might have been, once, but it was blocked with broken stone and tree roots as thick as pythons. At the base of this blockade, there was a heap of

284

Coke cans, two packets of rice crackers and a few sort of Pot-Noodle-looking things with pictures of chicken and shrimp on the side.

I just stood there and gaped at it. My brain was so run down on calories that I couldn't process what I was seeing. I picked up a can of Coke and weighed it in my hands. It felt real and solid and warm but, intact.

Araya appeared beside me and I handed her the can. She turned it over in her hands and looked at the rest of the stuff on the ground.

'What . . . how did this get here?' she asked, as if I'd know.

I shrugged helplessly and looked around the space at the end of the tunnel. That was when I noticed a bag in the corner. A cheap backpack. Had someone come hiking out here and just . . . left their stuff behind? The back of my neck prickled. Had something happened to them? Something bad.

I went over and pulled the unfastened bag open. Inside there were clothes, hard to really see what was what in the gloom. I pulled out the top-most thing and smelled the sweat and body odour on it. Used clothes. I held up the fabric and unfurled it. The Budweiser logo, picked out in white, was visible in the darkness.

The poacher's shirt.

'Araya . . .' I said, my mind still trying to catch up with my instincts, which were screaming at me that we were in danger. 'We should leave.'

That was when I heard voices bouncing down the tunnel, as other people entered the temple. Blocking our way out.

Chapter 35

We rushed back through the tunnel towards the voices. I didn't have a plan but my instincts forced me out there, to face the intruders. We were trapped and obviously with 'flight' impossible, my body had decided it was time to fight.

When we got there Summer was struggling with someone. She started screeching and yelling like a banshee, clawing at the other person's face as they fought for possession of the Coke can. She finally shoved them over and scurried back towards us for protection, cradling the can to her chest. I looked down and recognised Kaitlyn as the light hit her face. I'd heard her and Summer arguing, not the poachers coming back.

She was covered in ash and soot, as we all were. Her long red hair was a dull greyish-brown now, with dirt, and her spangle-covered dress was tattered and torn, its pale pink lost under all the filth she was crusted with. She was barefoot and there was a tatty loop of rope around her wrist. It looked like she'd been tied to something and had managed to cut herself free. But the rope was so tightly bound that she wasn't able to get the rest of it off.

'Kaitlyn,' I said, when she scrambled to her feet and went to dive at Summer again, yelling in wordless anger. 'It's us. Calm down! Summer – it's OK, come over here.'

Summer moved behind me, but Kaitlyn just stared, wild and wide-eyed. Raising one hand she pointed at Summer.

'She stole!'

'She didn't mean to. We didn't know you were here. Where are the others?' I asked, trying to keep things calm. 'I thought they'd have taken you out of the jungle by now. The poachers,' I clarified, when she didn't say anything.

Kaitlyn looked at me like she had no idea what I was talking about. As if I was referring to something that had happened years ago or in a film, to someone else.

'Where's Fletcher and Bryce, or the men who took you?' I tried again. 'Are they nearby? Do we need to run?'

'Fletcher's dead,' she whimpered, hunching in on herself. 'He died when we were finished walking here. He was bleeding and then . . . they shot him.'

I flinched. Fletcher had been executed, like Dash. It sounded like his dengue had gotten worse after all. It must have slowed them down, made them rethink the value of holding him hostage. I thought of San'ya and grimaced. Fletcher had at least had an easier death than him. Quicker.

'And Bryce?' I asked, my throat thick. I wasn't sure what I wanted to hear: that he was OK, that he was dead? I was if anything a little afraid that he might be around somewhere like Kaitlyn had been, ready to attack. It had been days now and I could only imagine how much further he had spiralled into insanity.

Kaitlyn looked confused, her wits as scattered as Summer's. I wondered what she'd seen. What she'd been through in the days since they'd been taken away by the poachers.

'Kaitlyn, I'm sorry but it's important. We need to know about Bryce and the poachers, about if they're coming back.'

She looked at me for a long moment and then slowly shook her head. 'They're gone. They left us.'

'Left you?' Araya asked, from behind me, hovering there uneasily.

'There was a fire,' Kaitlyn said, in a small voice. 'We'd been walking for ages and they brought us here, to their camp. Tied us all together and to a tree, back there in the tunnel. Then Fletcher started bleeding a lot, and they took him away. I heard them shoot him.' She took a shaky breath. 'Then it was late and I was sleeping but there was all this shouting and they came to get us. But Bryce he . . . They untied him first and he ran away. Stole their bag and ran away.'

'Bag?' I asked, thinking of the backpack we'd found.

'A little bag that they put our stuff in. My necklace. Fletcher bought me that,' she said, vaguely, clutching at her chest where the pendant had hung.

The jewellery. Bryce had stolen the jewellery and run for it, leaving Kaitlyn behind to her fate. I wondered if the poachers had been trying to escape with their hostages before the fire reached them, if they'd tried to get Kaitlyn to go with them but like Bryce she'd fought them. Then Kaitlyn spoke again and I knew for sure.

'I was scared and trying to stop them taking me away, because they were going to shoot me like Fletcher. I just knew it and then they just . . . they left me, tied up. They ran. And then it got really hot and I could smell things burning and I thought they'd set fire to the temple because I was fighting back . . . but then I chewed the rope and got out and everything was burned. I've been looking for Fletcher, for his....but I can't find him.'

'OK . . . well, we're here now,' I said, wincing to see her choke on the word 'body'. 'So, you're not on your own and we're going to help . . . take care of things,' I finished lamely. 'But we're very hungry and we'd like some of the food. We found water so we can go refill the empty cans with that later and then you'll have some too – deal?'

Kaitlyn nodded, slowly like she was in a daze. She sat down on one of the chunks of rock and stared at the ground between us. As if she'd run out of mental capacity for talking. A clockwork doll that had wound down without anyone to turn her key.

'Kaitlyn,' I asked, still needing an answer. 'Do you know where Bryce ran to? Did he say what he was planning? Or mention if they had a map that he'd seen or . . .' I trailed off as she shook her head.

'He just ran. He didn't talk to me for ages, not even when Fletcher . . .' She made a noise like a wounded animal and covered her mouth, but kept trying to speak. 'He ran and I screamed at him to come back but he didn't even turn round; he just went and I was yelling at him and then one of them hit me because I scratched him and then I woke up and they were all gone.' She paused to haul in a long breath, turning streaming eyes on me. 'Everyone just left me and I thought I was going to die all by myself here – that it was all my fault because I was too scared to say you were one of us.'

My heart cracked like the baked earth outside. She sounded like she'd been terrified and it was my fault. I'd

289

caused the fire; I'd been the reason she'd been left here. The reason Bryce had been able to escape without her. All right, so, Kaitlyn had left Summer, Araya and I to our fates, but what could she really have done? And hadn't she paid for it now – and paid over the odds?

'Are you really here?' Kaitlyn asked, in a small voice. 'Or am I dying?'

'We're really here,' I said, trying to choke back tears and hearing Araya sniffling behind me. 'We're here now, and we're not going to leave you behind. OK?'

Kaitlyn was fully crying now, but she nodded and wrapped her arms around herself, sobbing and keening as she rocked on the chunk of stone she'd perched on. I glanced at Summer and saw that she was watching her, disinterested and blank as a bird. Araya's teary eyes met mine and asked the unspoken question. Yes, we were all together now, but what could we do? Nothing but wait, and hope and stay together.

'Araya,' I said softly. 'Can you sit with them and make sure they don't argue or . . .'

She nodded. 'What are you going to do?'

'Have a look around, see if I can find anything else to eat or that we can use . . . any sign of Bryce.'

'You really think he might be out there?' Her disbelief was obvious, and honestly I had no idea what I thought. A few weeks ago I'd have said Bryce had less chance of surviving the jungle and forest fire than a goldfish did a blender. But if the past few days had proven anything to me it was that survival was sometimes more luck than skill and also that Bryce was too selfish to die. Not if there was someone or something else he could sacrifice to save himself.

'I don't know, but if he is he knows this is one place there's shelter and food, he might be watching, realise the poachers are gone. If he does come back I don't want to be caught off guard.'

Araya looked like she could at least appreciate some of the wisdom in what I was saying. She didn't know Bryce well and she'd been unconscious when he sold us out – well, sold me out – but, even she clearly had reservations about his trustworthiness. I felt stupid for ever having trusted him, for thinking I had him wrapped around my little finger. He'd wrapped himself around me like a snake, using me for my money and then throwing me away.

But really, a tiny voice inside me said, could I blame him? Had I really cared that much about him or was he just convenient? A suitable partner who looked good on Instagram and didn't outshine me? Still, I hadn't left him for dead. No, I'd bought him diamonds and taken him to Thailand and put up with him after he drugged me . . . The only thing I'd done to harm him, was by accident. I'd taken him on a plane that crashed. He probably blamed me for that more than I blamed myself.

I left Araya to look after Summer and Kaitlyn. It didn't take long for me to go through the backpack and find a few more soiled shirts, an empty aluminium water bottle, some ammunition and a pack of cigarettes with a lighter inside. The holy grail of finds. At least we'd be able to start a fire for light. I hadn't realised how terrifying the dark could be until I landed in the jungle. For the first time in my life I thought I could understand cavemen and their excitement when they discovered fire. The world must have been a very scary place before then.

I wrapped dirty shirts around my sore feet to keep from

hurting them on the ground any more. I took the water bottle to fill and gulped down half a can of Coke for the calories before passing the rest to Araya on my way out.

Outside I hiked back up to the stream to fill the bottle. The sugar and caffeine in my veins was a welcome boost and I didn't plan on wasting it. Keeping my eyes out for signs of Bryce I followed the rocks from the stream source along the top of the ridge. Hopefully the water had preserved some plants, saved them from the fire and left us with some food. If there was a water source behind the rocks somewhere, there might also be fish or something, frogs or snails or other damp-loving creatures we could eat.

I walked probably further than was wise, given how much I'd already put my body through. But we needed food and there was part of me that wouldn't be able to rest until I knew what had happened to Bryce. But I found no sign of him and only a handful of fruits. A pointless hunt, on both ends.

When I returned to the temple, I found Summer asleep and Kaitlyn curled up in the furthest corner from her. Araya had a fire going, smoke rising through the gaps in the roof. She looked overdue for some sleep herself, but was obviously on edge around the others.

'Get some rest. I'll heat some water up and try to make noodles,' I said, gesturing with the metal water bottle. Hot food. Real food with salt and spices and carbohydrates and chemicals. It seemed like a miracle.

Araya nodded, but glanced warily at Summer's sleeping form before leaning in closer to me. 'Summer's saying her head hurts – and her face is tingling?'

I frowned. 'Is that . . . dengue?'

Araya shrugged. 'Not sure. San'ya was the one who . . .' She swallowed and started over. 'I don't really know the symptoms but she is acting strange. Strange even for what we've all been through.'

'I'll keep an eye on her,' I promised. 'Make sure she doesn't do anything reckless.'

'Any sign of Bryce or . . . anyone else?' she asked, her voice a brittle thing, full of hope.

'No. Not yet,' I said. 'But we'll keep watch.'

'Right.' She nodded, eyelids drooping with exhaustion. 'Someone has to come.'

'Someone has to,' I repeated, and kept my smile going, until she turned away.

Chapter 36

I burned my hands three times boiling water in the bottle and getting it into the noodle cup, but eventually we had a meal. I woke Araya and Kaitlyn, but Summer wouldn't wake up. She was still breathing, her heart still pumping. But nothing I did could rouse her. Araya helped me but neither of us could get her to wake up. In the end we left her to sleep, figuring she must be exhausted.

We ate the noodles with the single plastic fork I'd found, passing the cup around in a circle. Araya drained the last of the salty broth and threw the cup into the fire. We watched the plastic on the outside wither and be consumed, followed by the rest of the cardboard. Part of me wanted to keep it, as a sort of talisman of civilisation.

Araya took first watch and I was grateful, as I was the only one who hadn't really rested yet. I wasted no time in bedding down on the floor. Summer was still out for the count and Kaitlyn crept back to her corner to rest. I just needed a few hours to keep myself sane and stop my thoughts from spiralling out of control.

Still, when Araya came to wake me for my turn at watch I was already awake. A few snippets of sleep was all I'd managed to get. Probably not enough but there it was. The images that flashed behind my eyelids wouldn't let me sleep – the gun, Janet's leg, Bethan's cold body, San'ya's tearful face. The sound of the plane exploding. The twisted body of the burned monkey. Crawling leeches, screeching bats. They all came to me in the dark, demanding my attention. Sleep was almost as hard to come by now as food and water.

I took my place sitting on a large stone by the fire and kept my eyes trained on the tunnel entrance. In my mind's eye I could see Bryce, streaked with soot like the war paint of a commando, creeping towards us. He'd have a sharpened stick, or a knife, and he'd force us to hand over the little food we had, perhaps kill me just because he could, with that awful smile on his face. I couldn't let that happen. Couldn't come this far just to die at his hands.

I jumped when Summer suddenly got up and staggered across to one of the alcoves. She heaved her guts up over there, hacking and retching. I winced and remembered how sick Fletcher and San'ya had been when they started showing symptoms. How long did she have? How long until there was nothing even a hospital could do for her? Not that we'd be reaching one any time soon anyway.

'You OK?' I whispered, stupidly, into the dark. I could at least get her some water if she needed it.

'I'm fine,' Summer snapped, and shuffled back to her sleeping spot. She threw herself down with her back to me, shoulders around her ears. It seemed she was veering back towards anger after a period of detachment. Like a wild animal turned feral in a trap. I kept an ear out for her until the sun came up, not sure if I expected her to attack or not.

We ate one pack of the rice crackers for breakfast and shared a Coke around, followed by some water. With three empty cans now, plus the bottle, we could fetch quite a bit of water. Though because we couldn't reseal the cans, it would require two people to carry the water back.

'I'll come with you,' Araya offered. 'I don't know that either of them is going to be helpful, but . . .' She pulled a face and I understood her meaning. I didn't like the idea of leaving Summer and Kaitlyn alone together either, but Kaitlyn was in no state to be relied on. Neither was Summer come to that.

'I can take two trips. It's fine,' I said. 'Or try to carry them all and just hope I don't trip.'

Araya glanced at the other two. 'Can I go? Being here with them is worrying me.'

I knew what she meant. I felt like I was watching my back constantly. It was different to being afraid of the jungle. Of snakes and bugs and animals. Even the poachers had inspired a different type of fear. This was a kind of paranoia – neither of us had any idea what Summer or Kaitlyn might do to us. They weren't predictable or logical, or simple animals that might bite or eat us.

'OK . . . just don't take too long,' I said. 'I'd rather we were all together.'

'Me too.' Araya gathered up the cans and the bottle. 'What if . . . if I see Bryce out there?'

'He's probably long gone,' I assured her, with more confidence than I felt. 'He must have seen the fire and run away – he had more of a head start than us after all.'

She didn't look convinced and I couldn't really blame her. The very air seemed to smell of fear. It was hard to know where fear of one thing ended and fear of something else began – the jungle, the fire, the animals, the people. My nerves were in shreds and it felt as if my brain was screaming 'danger!' at me all the time.

Araya left to get water and I picked up loose bits of dead plant and dried wood to add to the fire later. There wasn't much else to do in the temple, and I was soon feeling dizzy from bending down anyway.

I sat down with my back to a block of stone and leant my head back on it. Above me the ceiling stretched towards the shadows, carved into intricate designs. I followed them with my eyes as they spiralled around the walls, up and up. My eyelids felt heavy and my bones were like lead. No matter how much I tried I couldn't keep my eyes open anymore. Couldn't get up. I felt my muscles loosening and my thoughts turning slow and syrupy.

A scream yanked me out of my daze, and adrenaline shot through me. I looked wildly around me and saw Summer caught mid-stride, pacing around the temple. Her hair was wild and she was looking towards the tunnel.

The scream came again, a broken wail that made all my hair stand on end. It wasn't Summer, it was someone outside.

'Where's Kaitlyn?' I asked, stumbling clumsily on feet wrapped in cloth.

'Out there.' Summer glared at the tunnel.

'She's . . . she must be hurt,' I said, though I wasn't sure it was Kaitlyn's voice. 'Help me find her!' I was dismayed to see Summer shaking her head. 'Summer! Help me!' I insisted.

'I'm not going out there!' Summer exploded, rushing back towards the blocked-off tunnel. I flinched as her furious voice bounced around the inside of the temple. She vanished into the dark and a moment later her footsteps stopped and I imagined she'd thrown herself down on the ground.

There was no time to argue or go after her. To be honest I was afraid to go into that dark tunnel, not knowing what she might do if I had her cornered.

Instead I grabbed the closest thing to hand that looked 'weapon-like' – a chunk of carved stone, and ran out of the tunnel towards the scream. Just in case it was Bryce out there, or an animal or one of the poachers. Outside, the shift to bright sunlight dazzled me. I heard a yell from my left and saw Araya rushing down the slope towards me.

'Was that you?' I shouted, one hand cupped to my mouth so my voice would carry.

'No!' she yelled back. 'Kaitlyn! That way!'

She pointed behind me, still running and I turned without waiting for her, rushing over the uneven, ashy ground. The screaming had stopped after the two that I'd heard but as I left the temple behind I could hear a rough sobbing. The dry sound of a crow imitating a human being's suffering. Only it wasn't a bird, mocking us. It was Kaitlyn: exhausted and dehydrated, sprawled in the ashes and sobbing over something in the debris.

I got close enough to see what it was, and nearly tripped over my own feet as I stumbled to a stop. It had mostly been hidden under crumbling wood and scorched branches. Kaitlyn must have cleared some away, because there was no mistaking what it was now.

It was a body, burned and twisted but undeniably human.

'Fletcher . . .' I whispered, and covered my mouth with my hand.

Kaitlyn dragged her fingers through the dirt and char, nails skittering over the hard earth. Every time she reached the end of a guttural cry, she dredged up another from deep inside her chest. I wasn't sure if she was mourning Fletcher or just unable to take any more horror. If it was love that had her in the grips of madness, or despair on her own behalf.

Looking at the body in the ashes, barely more than bones and teeth, I told myself that he'd already been dead. He'd been shot, executed. Painlessly. Or at least, painless compared to what he'd have felt if he'd been left out here to burn. I looked to the horizon, where craggy tree stumps led in wobbly rows like drunken tombstones. If Bryce had tried to outrun the fire, I hoped he'd succeeded. No one deserved this death.

I had no words for Kaitlyn. When Araya panted to a stop next to me, she also had nothing to say. We just stood there, watching her keen and claw at the ground. Araya looked at me, helpless.

'Go . . . um . . . go make sure Summer doesn't do anything crazy. I'll . . . I'll stay here,' I said softly, unable to look away from Kaitlyn. I couldn't even blink; it was just horrible.

Araya faltered for a moment, but she went. I heard her footsteps scrunching through the debris and then I inched towards Kaitlyn. I had my hand outstretched, ready to touch her shoulder or her hair. Something, anything to try and comfort her. But then I saw something in the dirt that froze me where I stood.

I moved my head, trying to catch it again. That glint that I'd seen out of the corner of my eye. There it was. Every hair on my body was on end as I turned, and bent down to touch it. There, in the ashes, was a mostly blackened shape, with a winking yellow sapphire eye.

It was Bryce's pendant.

As soon as I noticed it I saw the shape of a watch, also blackened, its face broken and half the workings exposed by the burned backing. I scrambled about in the ashes and my fingers found the familiar shapes of my bangles. Component pieces that had been my earrings, the fragile rings connecting them together having melted. And there, what looked like an acorn – but when I wiped my finger over it, I saw it was Kaitlyn's strawberry necklace.

All our things, that Bryce had stolen from the poachers as he ran. The bag must have burned away where it fell and Bryce . . . he'd burned away too. Right there, where we stood. He'd burned alive out here, all alone. Another life lost, after everything he'd done to survive.

Guilt and despair rocketed up my throat, tasting of bile. Bryce was dead because of my choice to fly out here. Any one of us might be next. It had been weeks. Weeks with no word from the outside world. What if in the end everything we'd been through, everything we'd done, was all for nothing?

'Kaitlyn . . .' I said numbly, and held out the necklace to her, trying without words to tell her that she was crying over the wrong corpse. She didn't react, didn't seem to be seeing anything that was in front of her. She was too blinded by tears, choking on her sobs.

'Kaitlyn, it's not Fletcher . . . it's Bryce,' I said, softly, then loudly, my voice weirdly flat to my own ears. 'Look.'

She caught sight of the pendant and grabbed for it, clutching it close as if I might be about to whisk it away. She turned her tear-stained, swollen face to me.

'Where ... is ... he?' she gasped. 'Where's ... Fletcher?'

'I don't know,' I said, my own voice distant as horror stoppered my senses. 'Not here.'

Kaitlyn scuttled away from the body as if now that it wasn't Fletcher, she didn't want to be anywhere near it. I looked at it and tried to feel something other than the horror that this had happened to a person. Bryce was my boyfriend, my fiancé. I was meant to care about him more than anyone else. Feelings like that couldn't just disappear. But just then he could have been anyone. Any person at all, who'd died so awfully. I thought perhaps that he'd somehow killed the part of me that loved him, when he left me to die.

My ears were ringing slightly and yet I felt calm. Completely at ease as if I'd finally reached the nirvana I'd been talking about in my videos. A deep, inner peace that couldn't be touched by any outside force or thing.

I didn't even realise I was screaming until Kaitlyn shook me.

I collapsed, trembling too hard to stay upright. My knees hit the ground and I vomited onto the ashes in front of me. Kaitlyn's voice was far, far away and there was a roaring in my head that sounded like a plane taking off. Then everything started to go dark, as if the lights were being turned out, one by one.

Chapter 37

'Do you think he deserved it?' Andrea asks, as the picture of Bryce takes over the entire wall behind them, dominating the room. The conversation. The show. It's more recognition than he ever got while he was alive. A part-time DJ, trying to make a name for himself. No one knew his name until he started dating 'the' Lila Wilde. And no one cared about him until he died.

'No one deserves to die like that,' Lila says, so quietly the microphones nearly don't pick it up. She and I still agree on that at least. Bryce didn't deserve to die like that.

But that's not to say I don't think he deserved to die.

'But you must have been . . . relieved? Maybe even felt a little vindicated, to know that he was dead. After all in your version of events, your fiancé betrayed you. Abandoned you and then abandoned Kaitlyn to her fate.'

In your version. The words register on Lila's face and there's a sort of flinch there. By this time she's already been questioned repeatedly. There are so few people left to tell the story of what happened in the jungle. Everyone was exhausted, starving and afraid. No two 'versions' are alike.

'I felt . . . a lot of things,' Lila says, carefully. For the first time she seems to be considering her words. Weighing each one and not simply delivering her responses lightly, flatly, as if they're the unvarnished truth.

'Such as?' Andrea digs into that morsel, eager for more.

That's the thing. It depends when we're talking about. At the time I was hysterical with horror, with despair. Then, in hospital I was just relieved he couldn't get to me anymore. That when I woke from my nightmares, I could console myself that he was dead and gone. In the studio that day I was more introspective, looking at that picture of him.

'I was upset, obviously. Horrified. He was burnt beyond recognition, and had clearly died in . . . unimaginable pain,' Lila says, her voice thick. 'It felt like it was my fault, because I was the reason he was there. I was the one who suggested the signal fire and when it got out of hand, that caused his death. I know that. It hit me, then just how much I was to blame for the mess we were in after the fire. All the destruction it had caused. But there was also this feeling of . . . despair. Because it didn't seem to matter what any of us did . . . we were all going to die. It was really just a matter of waiting.'

'So you were worried about yourself?' Andrea says, as if trying to understand, but so blatantly twisting things that, as I remember it, even her own audience pulled back from her, disgusted.

'I think mostly I was feeling guilty and . . . grateful. In a way,' Lila says, either not noticing or not rising to the bait.

'Grateful that you had escaped the fire? That you were lucky enough to avoid the consequences of your actions?'

303

'No, I was grateful to Bryce . . . because he saved my life.'

Andrea, silenced for the first time, glances sideways as if checking the camera is still pointing at them. Capturing every moment of her stunned speechlessness.

'If,' Lila continues, 'he'd never taken the ring back, and stolen the rest of my jewellery, I would have been taken by the poachers to ransom back to my dad. I don't know what might have happened if there had been no fire, but they'd already executed Fletcher and the rest of us weren't in great shape either. I'd have been marched through the jungle and possibly killed. So . . . that might have been me. If Bryce hadn't thrown me under the bus.'

Lila glances up at the projection of Bryce's picture and appears to consider him. Whether her look is one of regret or quiet triumph, who can say? Certainly not the casual viewer. She's too guarded for that.

'He's the reason I'm still alive today,' Lila says. 'I wish I could let him know that.'

Chapter 38

I had and still have, no idea how they got me back to the temple. The last thing I had a clear memory of when I woke up there was Kaitlyn's mouth. The gaping dark hole of it opening and closing as she yelled at my face, shaking me and shaking me. Trying to make me stop screaming.

I woke up on the floor of the temple, my jaw alight with pain. When I raised my hands to my face to cradle it, I felt raw lines of scrapes and cuts on my cheeks. It felt like I'd been dragged through a thorn bush, or clawed at.

'Lila?' Araya appeared out of the gloom beside me. The fire was burning low and I guessed it was late, judging from her whisper and the darkness.

'What happened . . . my face . . .'

Araya's hands closed over mine. 'You were scratching at it, screaming . . . I came running but you fell and hit your head on the ground. We carried you back.'

'Are the others all right?' I asked, still trying to drag myself fully back to consciousness.

'Kaitlyn's asleep. I think she exhausted herself. But Summer . . . she won't come out of the other tunnel. I've

305

been keeping watch but she hasn't shouted or come to the entrance. I can just hear her . . . moving around.'

I shivered, not liking the sound of that at all.

'Was it really Bryce? The body?' Araya asked hesitantly. 'I saw. It was . . . awful.'

'Yeah, it was him. The jewellery was there,' I said, realising that it must still be out there. 'He must have dropped it, fallen . . . he didn't get away in time. The fire reached him and . . .' I couldn't go on.

'You had this in your hand,' Araya said, softly. She held out the tiger pendant to me and I flinched away from it.

'I don't want it,' I said, quickly. Just looking at it made me feel guilty, angry, hurt all over again. It was too much.

Araya nodded, but put it down by me anyway. 'You can do what you want with it later. When you're feeling better.'

I nearly laughed at the idea that there would be a 'better' for me. For any of us. We were all as well as we were going to be. From here we'd only run out of food, of sanity. Unless we were rescued we would all get much worse from here.

'I can watch out for Summer.' I sighed. 'You should sleep.'

'Will you be able to stay awake?' Araya sounded doubtful.

'I've slept enough. You have to rest sometime,' I pointed out.

She still didn't seem convinced but exhaustion won out. Araya hunkered down on the ground to get what sleep she could and I got up and went over to take up watch near the tunnel where Summer was lurking. I passed Kaitlyn's sleeping form on the way and saw that she was wearing the strawberry pendant. Her hand was curled around it in sleep and I saw she'd also taken the engagement ring. My engagement ring, or Bryce's. Come to think of it, I'd never asked him how he'd managed to afford it. Somehow I thought my money was behind it somewhere. Or Dad had loaned him the cash. Kaitlyn was welcome to it. I wondered if in her mind it was Fletcher who gave it to her. Maybe that was why she'd taken it and none of the other jewellery, not that I could see anyway.

Summer didn't seem to be moving around anymore, but I went over to the tunnel entrance anyway.

'Summer?' I called softly, so as not to wake the others. 'Are you OK down there? You want anything to eat, or drink . . . ?'

She didn't answer, but I could hear her breathing in the stillness. Looking into the blackness gave me a chill and I kept thinking I saw movement there. A shape coming towards me. It was that more than anything, which sent me back to my perch, and kept me awake.

When morning came it was as if the three of us had reached a silent agreement; new rules were in play and we didn't need to discuss them to know how important they were. Rule one, someone had to keep watch on Summer at all times and rule two, no one was to go near Bryce's body. Our attempt at staying safe and sane.

Aside from going out for water, we stayed near the temple. Araya and I traded off watching the tunnel where Summer was hiding, and sitting outside, looking in vain for a helicopter or any sign of rescue. Kaitlyn, since discovering Bryce's remains, seemed to have abandoned her search for Fletcher. Perhaps she realised she was better

307

off not seeing what the fire had done to him. Instead she sat and stared into space, or hung around the fire, watching the diamond ring cast reflections on the stone walls. But at least she seemed semi-stable, or she did compared to Summer anyway.

'Do you not want something to eat?' I called down the tunnel, around midday when the sun beams coming through the temple walls were at their sharpest. There was no food back there and Summer hadn't come out at all while I was unconscious, according to Araya. She'd had no water either, which was a concern. It had been hours and even inside the stone temple, she had to be sweating as much as the rest of us. Dehydration would only worsen her confusion.

There was no response. I could hear her scuffling around, pacing in the narrow space at the end of the tunnel. I thought I could hear whispering, like dry sheets of paper rubbing together. A sort of continuous hushing of words. But I couldn't work out what she was saying.

When Araya came in for another turn at watching her, she frowned into the shadows. She looked as helpless as I felt.

'Should we take her some water?' Araya said, sounding like she'd rather do anything else. 'She'll get ill if she goes much longer without.'

'I tried asking her but she won't talk to me. I can hear her moving but that's about it.' I worried my lip with my teeth, unsure what to do. On the one hand I wanted to help her, but on the other going into that dark hallway seemed like a bad idea. Summer was only getting more erratic and I had no idea what she might do if we intruded on her space.

Araya sighed unhappily. 'I'll leave a can in the tunnel.'

The thought of her going into the darkness, towards the strange sounds, made me prickle with unease. I felt a flare of respect for her, that she was willing to risk it when I wasn't.

'Don't go too far,' I said.

Araya nodded, picked up a can of water and shuffled into the tunnel. She took a few steps and when she stopped I could hear that Summer had also frozen. She wasn't moving. I heard the scuff of the metal can on the stone and then Araya's footsteps hurrying back. She looked fairly spooked when she got back to me.

'Did you see her?' I whispered.

She shook her head. 'I heard her whispering though. It didn't make any sense. Something about the air. That there was too much air coming in.'

My insides squirmed, turning icy cold. What the hell did that mean?

Araya kept watch on the tunnel until nightfall and when I took over again she said she hadn't heard or seen Summer go near the can. Araya was worried, as was I. But more than worry, I felt deeply uneasy.

We ate the last noodle cup between the three of us. Kaitlyn was silent and kept touching the strawberry pendant, rubbed clean by her constant handling. It was like it was a lucky charm to her. All of us were too tired to really talk or offer consolation to each other. We were all locked in our own thoughts.

I took my turn at watch while Araya got some sleep and we changed off in the dark. I stirred the fire up a little for light and realised we were burning through our fuel quite quickly. It was mostly partially burned wood from

309

the destroyed jungle outside. Not much left to it. Like us it was mostly used up.

Lying on the ground, I watched the largest pieces of wood slowly sinking into the embers, crackling away. My eyes drifted shut and I slowly slipped into sleep.

When I woke up, that same log was only half burned. It hadn't been long at all and Araya was not shaking me lightly out of sleep to take a turn watching Summer. So for a second I wasn't sure what had woken me up. Then as I listened, I realised I could hear Araya talking across the room. Her voice was low and coaxing, talking to Summer, trying to get her to drink something.

'There's water here – please, drink,' she said. 'Summer . . . can you hear me?'

I heard her feet scuff on the stone, the sound echoing slightly as she entered the tunnel. The back of my neck tingled, the hair rising. I felt as if I was listening to someone reaching out to pet a snarling dog.

'Summer?' she called again. 'I've got some water here. Can you take it from me – just so I know you're all right?'

Something in the prickling of my skin made me sit up. I felt a deep unease and my heart was beating fast. I'd been on edge for so long that really I wasn't sure if this was real fear or just my body trying to cope with everything we'd been through. But as I heard Araya moving up the tunnel my anxiety notched up even further.

'Wait,' I called out, struggling to get to my feet – so exhausted I nearly fell over backwards. 'Araya, wait.'

I crossed the room towards the tunnel. In the dim glow from the fire I couldn't even see Araya. She'd gone quite far now and I stumbled to a halt at the mouth of the dark corridor, as if my feet wouldn't take me further.

I could hear Araya moving slowly, inches at a time in the pitch-black tunnel. But I could hear Summer too, scuffling around and muttering.

'Araya, come back,' I hissed.

'I'm just . . .'

Two things happened at once.

Araya tripped and I heard the can hit the floor, followed by the spattering of water.

And Summer, yowled.

It was the sound of feral cats fighting in a city alleyway. Inhuman and furious and terrified. Araya came bolting out of the dark and ran right into me. I grabbed at her to stop us both falling and my eyes were fighting to pierce the darkness. Looking for Summer coming after her. Instead I heard her retreating, scrambling away further into the shadows, still making those awful noises deep in her throat.

'What the fuck happened?' I asked, as Araya regained her balance and started dragging me away from the tunnel.

'I spilled . . . spilled the water,' Araya stuttered, eyes huge in the reflected firelight. 'It was like she was possessed. Like in films, with holy water – you know?'

Holy water? She wasn't making any sense. Araya finally stopped trying to haul me away once we reached the other side of the room but she refused to turn her back on the tunnel. I watched as she picked up a chunk of stone from the ground, holding it like a talisman.

'Araya, what happened?' I demanded. 'She sounded . . . demented.'

'It was the water,' Araya insisted. 'I could see her. She was coming towards me I think. But then I tripped and it

311

went over her and her . . . it was like she was afraid it was acid or something.'

I glanced towards the tunnel, unnerved. 'She's lost it. Really lost it . . . I think we should just leave her alone.'

Araya nodded, still staring towards the dark entrance of the tunnel. Her brow was furrowed and she was clearly torn, even if she was agreeing with me.

'She looks awful. From what I could see. Her lips are peeling. She must be so thirsty.'

I hugged my arms around myself. 'I don't know what we can do. If she won't drink anything or come out of there . . . we can leave food but without water she's not going to last long.'

'Do we . . .' Araya hesitated. 'Should we . . . make her, drink something?'

I thought of that horrible yowling, the violence in it. The animal rage and fear. The idea of the pair of us trying to hold Summer down and empty a can of water down her throat made my insides shivery.

'She might attack us, either while we're doing it or afterwards. She's not thinking clearly . . . I think we need to keep ourselves and Kaitlyn safe and just hope . . .'

I couldn't say 'that help comes'. It felt so stupid to keep saying it. After so many days. It had been weeks since the crash and we'd seen no one and nothing that might be coming to save us. But if I admitted out loud that we were done for, then we'd really have nothing. So I let it hang there – the suggestion of hope.

'Get some sleep,' I said, when Araya just kept looking past me at the tunnel.

'You only had a little,' she pointed out.

'I'm fine,' I promised.

I didn't say that there was no way I'd be able to fall asleep again now anyway. Not with the threat of Summer running out of the tunnel, screaming and clawing at us like a horror film monster. The word 'possession' was at the forefront of my mind as I took up a watch position. I looked into the darkness and tried not to think about whether Summer was looking back.

Chapter 39

I should never have gone alone to fetch water. I realised that when I got close enough to the temple to hear the screaming.

I'd watched for signs of movement from Summer all through the night. But come morning there was nothing to report and I'd been sure she'd either gone to sleep or passed out. She had to be fairly dehydrated by then and she'd not been in great condition before she shut herself away. I had no idea what to do. Either we let her die or we put ourselves in danger trying to help her. It seemed like there was no way to make sure no one got hurt.

Kaitlyn for her part seemed to be . . . not coping exactly, but at least on an even keel. It was as if having the necklace and my engagement ring had calmed her a little. Given her something to cling to. Something she could hold and see and keep for herself even as our situation became more dire. She wasn't really living in reality but she wasn't feral either. It felt safer to let her just get on with it.

'We're almost out of water. Are you OK if I . . .' I gestured to the exit, waiting for Araya's say-so before I left her alone with Summer and Kaitlyn.

She looked doubtful. 'I could go.'

'If you want,' I said. 'I can stay here.'

She hesitated and I saw her thinking of the long climb up the slope towards the cliff the stream bubbled out of. She was just as exhausted as I was and her feet were just as sore.

'I'll stay,' she said, eventually. 'When you get back I'll keep watch and you can have a rest?'

It was a reasonable compromise. I nodded. 'See you in a bit.'

I took the water bottle and the remaining cans – like hell was I retrieving the one Araya had dropped in the tunnel – and carried them up to the stream.

Since we'd been at the temple the water had managed to find a way through the ash and debris. It was flowing clearer now and it was sort of heartening to see that in some small way, there was still hope for the jungle we'd decimated. That I had decimated. Nothing was really growing back yet but there were more animals around, returning now that the fire was gone. More pigs and birds and insects picking their way over the ruin of the landscape.

I was filling the last of the cans when I looked up at the rocks overhead and saw someone looking down at me. My heart felt like it stopped dead in my chest.

It was a man. A man with a gun.

The can slid from my nerveless fingers and I made no move to catch it. I heard the metal hit a stone and the water glugging out onto the ground. I didn't blink.

He shouted something in Thai and I heard another man's voice, calling back to him. He turned his head slightly, as if to listen better. I didn't wait for a second chance.

I was up and running before I'd even made the conscious decision to move. Bolting like a startled deer down the slope I tripped and staggered. My big toe folded under my foot and I brought my weight down on it, felt it crunch. I couldn't stop. At any moment I expected to hear a gunshot, to feel bullets ripping into me.

I could hear raised voices, the scrabbling of boots on rock. Were they climbing down after me? Had they returned to collect their lost hostages? I could taste bile and the air was sawing in and out of my lungs as I got within shouting distance of the temple.

'Poachers!' I yelled, or tried to, as I reached the temple. My breathless voice wheezed out of me weakly and I had to stop to catch a breath. I clung to the doorway, just inside the corridor. 'Poachers!'

That was when I heard the screaming from inside the stone temple. Kaitlyn and Araya. Confused and completely blinded by fear, I chose the devil I knew and ran towards the centre room. If it was a choice between the poachers' guns, and Summer's madness, I stood a better chance against her than with them.

When my eyes adjusted to the darkness inside the temple, I worried that I'd made the wrong choice. Kaitlyn was crying out, her hands over her mouth. She was looking towards the far tunnel and as I shoved past her I saw Araya on her back on the ground. She was thrashing about in the leaf litter, with Summer's hands wrapped around her neck.

Everything slowed down for a second and I couldn't breathe. Summer was killing her, right in front of me.

Araya wasn't screaming anymore. Her throat was making an awful retching noise as Summer squeezed and squeezed. Summer's wide, staring eyes were fixed on Araya, but not seeing her. Her mouth was sticky with foam and she was breathing hard between her teeth, snarling.

'Summer!' I ran at her and grabbed her shoulders, trying to pull her away. She didn't even register my presence. Her arms were locked in place, strong as steel cables. Every ounce of her insane strength was going into strangling the life from Araya.

I heard Araya's throat click, the whistling of her air cutting off entirely. Her panic-stricken eyes were filled with tears and her face was turning darker and darker. From a great distance, I heard strangers shouting. But the poachers were the least of my worries in that moment. I had to save Araya. I couldn't watch her die.

I grabbed a chunk of rock off the ground, and swung at Summer's head.

She jerked, hands still wringing Araya's neck. She didn't look at me. Didn't say anything – she just let out an inhuman screech. Spittle flew from her mouth, landing on Araya's twisted, agonised face. My heart was beating so fast it was as if it had stopped entirely. All the frantic beats merging together into a sickening rush.

I hit her again.

And again.

And then she fell down.

I hit her.

I couldn't stop hitting her.

Then there were hands grabbing at my arm, the back of my dress, my hair. I was dragged away from Summer while men's voices echoed around me. Words I couldn't understand. They tugged the rock from my hand but my fingers stayed clawed around its invisible weight. I was sobbing, choking on my tears.

Kaitlyn was bawling and my own breathing was deafening me. My heartbeat was in my ears, my throat; my eyeballs were throbbing with it. I could taste blood and I wasn't sure if I'd bitten my tongue, or if it was running off my face, into my mouth.

I was being carried away when I snapped back into myself. Two men had picked me up and were toting me on their shoulders towards the exit. I screamed and struggled and kicked with all my strength. My injured toe caught one of them in the chest and blinding pain burst through me.

My mind shut down again, a sudden blackness like the strobing of a club light. Then I was outside in the sun and they were depositing me on the ground. I tried to get up, to crawl to my feet so I could run. But they knocked my feet out from under me and then one of them, the larger of the two, put his hands on my shoulders to keep me down.

Looking up at them I saw, even through a veil of terror, that they weren't the same men we'd met before. These were not poachers dressed in old T-shirts and army surplus. They wore a uniform: khaki button-downs with patches and insignia on them. As soot-smeared and sweat-stained as they were. They had packs and proper boots, and their guns looked more modern, black metal and plastic instead of rusty with wooden stocks.

My mind was a mess of thoughts and feelings. Part of me was still in the temple, still looking at Summer and wondering what I'd done. The horror of it sitting inside me like an insect that had burrowed under my skin. But I was also looking at these men and wondering who they were. Army? Police? Rescue? Had my father hired them – some sort of commando unit that specialised in jungle disappearances? I felt dizzy and sick with all that had happened. I was shaking, struggling to think clearly.

The men were talking but I couldn't understand them. Then one pulled out a radio and said something into it. There was a crackle and I heard a muddled and distorted voice speaking back.

Two other men came out of the temple. One was leading Kaitlyn and the other had Araya's unconscious body in his arms. At least, I hoped she was just unconscious. My stomach rebelled when I saw how much blood she had on her. It was soaked into her clothes and spattered over her skin, in her hair. Alarmingly bright red against her grey, ash-smeared skin. Summer's blood.

I had to look away. My horror felt like a bottomless pit opening up in front of me. Vertigo hurling me down into it. I looked down at my hands and saw the blood streaked on them.

I collapsed onto the dirt, retching.

Above me I heard Kaitlyn asking what was happening in a whispery, childlike voice. Where were we going? Had they found Fletcher? I screwed my eyes shut and shuddered as I spat bile into the dust. We were all mad, I thought. All of us. I couldn't even say when it had set in for me. I couldn't put the jagged pieces of the past few weeks together. Was it when I shot the poacher? When we were swarmed by bats? When I saw Bryce's burned body?

Was it the moment the plane went down?

Had I ever been sane? Nothing about my life seemed to make sense.

Footsteps scrunched over the ashes and I flinched as

they came up behind me. Then I heard a voice. Not a man. Not in Thai.

I turned and looked up to find a woman looking down at me. She was young, Thai and wearing the same shirt as the others, but open over a tank top. She was looking at us like we were both a miraculous discovery and a horror beyond words.

'Are you . . . from the plane crash?' she asked, eventually, her words seeming to come from far away as the earth tilted under me. 'Are you Lila Wilde?'

I blinked at her. My name sounded strange to me. Not because I hadn't heard it in ages, but because at some point I had sort of stopped thinking of myself as 'Lila Wilde' and become just . . . me.

'We crashed,' I said, because that was a concrete fact in my head. I knew that. 'We walked here . . . Are you here to help us?'

She looked from me to the men standing around. Her expression was surprised and helpless. I wasn't sure what to make of it. Wasn't sure what to make of anything really. I could feel my body going cold. A shadow was creeping in at the edges of my vision.

'We're conservationists,' she said. 'Here to combat poaching. We were cut off by the fire but we managed to get a signal to radio out right before we spotted you. You've been in the news for weeks . . . Where are the rest of you?'

'This is it,' I said, my lips feeling numb. 'This is all there is.'

I watched her eyes widen in shock, and she moved towards me with a shout as I blacked out and fell forward into the waiting pit.

Chapter 40

I woke up lying on plastic. I could feel it sticking to my sweating cheek. The unfamiliar sensation made me wrinkle my nose. It had been ages since I'd woken up on anything but dirt or ashes. Opening my eyes I saw red nylon overhead, the canopy of a tent. I let my head fall to the side and saw that the tent was open, a breeze trickling in. Araya was lying to my left and I could feel the heat from Kaitlyn's body on my right. The three of us lying still and exhausted under the canopy.

It hadn't been a dream. There were people outside – the men had made a campfire and were cooking food from freeze-dried packets. They had bottles of water and were chatting.

It wasn't a dream.

Summer was really dead.

I lifted my hands and looked at them. They were clean but there was a reddish tinge around my nail beds. Someone had cleaned me off as best they could. My skin felt tacky with the residue of wet wipes. But they hadn't been able to fully remove the traces of what I'd done.

As I sat up I realised my dress was gone. Instead I was

wearing a too large, wrinkled T-shirt and boxer shorts that were a little too snug. But they were at least clean and not soaked in blood. Looking at Araya, I noticed her clothes had been swapped out too. She was in a tank top and baggy boxer briefs.

Because of the blood, I realised. Because we'd both been covered in Summer's blood.

'You're up.'

It was the woman from before. She appeared at the entrance to the tent and hunkered down into a crouch, balancing easily. I nodded, my throat raw with yelling, and with thirst.

'We managed to radio in and we found the temple on our map. There's a truck coming to get us but we'll have to hike to the nearest accessible part of the jungle. Normally it'd be a lot further but . . . the fire cleared a lot of ground.'

'No . . . helicopter?' I asked.

She shook her head, looking sombre. 'The fire's still burning and all the smoke makes it impossible to fly. In a few more days we'd have been in just as bad a shape as you all. Thankfully we always overpack on rations and the stream really saved our asses.'

I plucked at my new, unfamiliar clothes and she shot me a sympathetic wince.

'Sorry – your stuff was . . . anyway, I was the one who redressed you. Made the others go get water. I thought you probably wouldn't want to wake up to . . .'

She cut herself off but I knew she was thinking about Summer and the blood. The bits of her that had showered all over me. I felt bile rush up my throat and had to gulp air to keep it inside.

The woman watched me, not speaking again until I had myself under control.

'I'm Noi, by the way.'

'Lila.'

'I know,' she half-laughed. 'Like I said, you've been in the news. No one could find the plane after it hit the jungle – ended up under the canopy. They found the black box a while ago but it was miles from here.' She glanced at the others, as if to make sure that they were still sleeping. 'Listen, your . . . friend? The one who you had to . . . well, from what the guys saw and from what I got out of Araya here – it sounds like she was rabid. Is it true you were in a cave, full of bats?'

I nodded, slowly. 'I thought she was just, going crazy for a while but . . .'

'Maybe that too, and honestly, who could blame her. But, it sounds like she might have been bitten, infected with rabies. If she was bitten a few times, close to her head – to the brain – well, I don't think there's much a hospital could have done for her. Araya said she was showing symptoms – aversion to fresh air, to water, the mania. It's not your fault,' she said, gently.

I felt my eyes well up. 'It's all my fault. She wouldn't have been here if it wasn't for me.'

'From what they said on the news, you just invited everyone to a party. It's not your fault everything went wrong,' Noi said, looking confused.

I shook my head, my chest burning with suppressed tears. 'I told my pilot not to bother filing a flight plan. That's why no one came for us.'

She looked at me for a long moment, as if trying to work out a tricky sum in her head. 'But he was the pilot –

right? He didn't have to just take that risk because you said so . . . you can't take all the blame for what happened just because of one mistake.'

It was like she'd opened my chest and scooped out the sharp shards that had been stuck in there since we crashed. Those jagged prickling pieces of guilt that had cut me raw again every time I tried to move on.

'I . . .' I started, but couldn't go on. I wanted to thank her, to argue with her, to cry. It was all too much and I was so very tired. So raw inside.

'Come and eat something,' Noi said, when it became clear I wouldn't be able to get any words out. She gestured past me to Kaitlyn. 'Wake up your friends too. They should have a good meal and a solid night's sleep before we hike out to the meeting point tomorrow.'

Noi left me with a small smile and I watched her go. It was so strange to be around other people all of a sudden. To see new faces and hear unfamiliar voices. Noi was the first person not on the plane, to tell me that what we'd gone through wasn't my fault. As I would find out later, she was an outlier. But in the moment she gave me a little hope. Something to cling to. A voice that spoke against the whisper in my head that told me I was the reason so many people had died, in such awful ways.

After I patted Araya's arm until she woke up, I nudged Kaitlyn awake and we crawled from the tent. The meal waiting for us was basic and the best thing I'd eaten in ages. Rice with rehydrated veggies and a spicy liquid bubbling away. It filled my stomach and I washed it down with plenty of water. Then Noi passed candied nuts around and I crunched my way through a handful. My belly felt heavy and satisfied for the first time in weeks.

Neither Kaitlyn nor Araya seemed to be in the mood to talk. We all just gulped our food down and sat by the fire, exhausted.

Soon my eyelids began to droop and I saw Kaitlyn lean against Araya's shoulder. Across from us, the men had set up two more small tents. We retired to ours to sleep and as I drifted off I felt Araya curl closer to me, and Kaitlyn rest her head against my back. I felt like we were a trio of stray animals that had been taken in together – fed and watered, but still clinging to what was familiar – each other.

I slept well, which was unexpected. I think by then my brain was too worn down to torment me. It didn't have the extra capacity to summon nightmares of Summer, of Bryce's body and Janet's wounds and Bethan's stiff corpse. That would come later and stay with me for years. But that night was a brief reprieve from the torture to come.

In the morning we had a breakfast of rice porridge and the conservationists packed up camp. We began the hike towards where the truck would meet us. Even with two decent meals in us and a night of sleep to give us energy, it was hard going. There were no extra shoes for us to wear and the ground was littered with debris. Even my hardened soles were no match for some of it and my toe was bruised blackish purple from where I'd stepped on it. It occasionally dragged as I picked my foot up and I was worried it might be broken.

There was, however, a purpose to the long trek. For the first time we weren't just hoping and forcing ourselves to carry on. There was a reason, a goal. We were going to be rescued. We were going home.

When we crested a rise and saw the rusty truck waiting

on the flat ground below, Kaitlyn started to run. Araya and I were right behind her. We couldn't stop ourselves. Stumbling, wincing from the pain in my toe, I chased after them. When I reached the truck I threw myself against the hot metal of its tailgate, as if it might vanish if I didn't immediately catch hold of it.

The two men who'd driven out to us got out of the front. Both looked confused and concerned by our appearance. Some rapid-fire conversation took place in Thai and from their exclamations I guessed that they were having a hard time believing we'd survived so long in the jungle. I could hardly blame them for doubting it. I'd only just touched the vehicle that would take us away from here and yet I was already struggling to really believe what we'd gone through. How could anyone else hope to comprehend it?

Before the crash I'd never really believed that something could be so traumatising that it just doesn't lodge in your memory. That you can experience something so terrible that it starts to feel like a nightmare, or like it happened to someone else. I would see the dead in my dreams for years, wake sweating from the memory of the crash. Find myself clawing at the sheets, convinced I was trapped in a fire, or scratching at my skin trying to remove leeches that weren't there. Yet for all of that, the actual memories of what happened in the jungle, became ever more distant. Until it was only the exaggerated nightmares that remained clear in my mind.

We climbed up into the flatbed of the truck. The three of us worn thin and filthy, wearing borrowed shirts and underwear. The metal of the truck burned my bare legs and the smell of exhaust and thrum of the engine were so reassuringly normal that I started to doze almost at once.

The three of us leant together with our backs against the cab of the truck and looked back at the barren, ash-covered ground we'd traipsed over. The sun beat down on us and far, far above, a single white line crossed the expanse of blue sky as a plane flew onwards, oblivious to us on the ground below.

Epilogue

'Please welcome, Kaitlyn Pence, Araya Suwannarat and, of course, Lila Wilde!'

I look away from the departures board as the follow-up interview comes on. I filmed it months ago. It's a less prestigious talk show and the background shows it. Just one of those early morning 'human interest' news stories that no one really cares about or is awake enough to process. The spot where they put sponsored walks, local celebrity deaths and heroic pets. There's no white leather sofa or blinding studio lights. The small studio is a little dated, the scratchy synthetic seating and bold splotches on the wall scream Nineties and the two presenters aren't even the B-team of news broadcasting. One of them, a man in a baggy grey suit, is trying and failing to hide a half-eaten croissant under the huge glass coffee table.

The female co-host smiles at the three guests. A warm smile. Both presenters, to be fair to them, were very welcoming. I liked both of them well enough. On screen there is a sense of friendly conversation rather than interrogation, in the way they are sitting, leaning back against their seats.

One year on from the preceding interview rerun, it's almost impossible to connect that Lila to the more recent version of me on screen. She's less skinny, more muscular and all her scratches and scrapes have healed and faded. She's still tanned, but less so. It's the tan of someone with access to sun cream, rather than of someone hiking over the sun-bleached ashes of a burned jungle. She has a silver ring in her nose and her hair has been cropped short into a low-maintenance pixie cut. She's not wearing a costume provided by the TV company – the faded jean shorts, flip-flops and T-shirt are most definitely her own. The shirt bearing the logo of the Khao Sok National Park in Thailand. On the T-shirt is a pin badge supporting the San'ya Chaidee Monkey Sanctuary. One of the initiatives I set up – a memorial, to the hotel clerk who'd done so much for us, and hated monkeys with a passion. I liked to think he'd find it funny.

On screen, Araya is dressed much more smartly, in a striped summer dress and wedge sandals. Kaitlyn steals the show though. Her hair is curled and her floral sundress is voluminous with petticoats underneath. She sits between Araya and the on screen Lila, the centre of attention with her perfect makeup and a ruby strawberry glittering in her cleavage.

'You girls have all been busy since your amazing story of survival reached our screens a year ago,' the female presenter gushes. 'Kaitlyn, let's start with you – when does your new baking show come out?'

The blare of an announcement cuts across her response and across from me, several people get up and gather their suitcases. The departure lounge isn't too busy, it's outside of the holiday season and quite late at night. The cheapest flight I could find back to Thailand. Dad offered to pay for me to at least fly business class but these days I like to look after myself.

'You'd think they'd find something better to put on than that stupid cow,' a guy sitting in the row of chairs across from me says loudly to his friend. They're facing away from me, watching another screen and honestly I doubt they'd recognise me even if they weren't. I wasn't really made up for that interview but in my experience when you don't travel like a celebrity, people tend to assume you're not one. Someone in the supermarket a few weeks ago told me I 'looked a bit like Lila Wilde' and I just laughed and said 'thanks'.

His friend, a backpacker wearing a woolly hat and a multi-pocketed vest, which must have been a ball-ache at security, nods. 'I mean if either one of us got a bunch of people killed in the jungle by being a fucking moron we wouldn't get a TV special – I'll tell you that much.'

'What's she doing now? My money's on a private beach house or something. Hiding out on Daddy's dime until it's time for a comeback.'

Woolly hat's shoulders shake with laughter. 'Probably designing a line of yoga pants or . . . having her "account of events" ghost-written by some penniless writer.'

'Ugh, imagine having to listen to her whine on about how "scary" it was and how she "didn't think she'd cope" without her hair straightener.'

They laugh and I can't help but smile. It is funny after all. Honestly it feels like they're talking about someone else. I'm not that person anymore. I'm not even sure I ever really was. I pretended to be, I acted the part – partying and flying around the world going to clubs and fashion shows. But was I ever the kind of person whose first thought when their plane crashed was 'Oh no, my hair straightener'? No. I don't think so. I don't think anyone like that really exists. It's just an act. A niche.

The three of us who survived don't really see one another much anymore. I haven't spoken to Kaitlyn since the last interview and Araya is married now so she has her own family to worry about. Though we get together every time I'm in Phuket. This time she's going to show me her new garden, and all the plants her mother helped her choose.

Kaitlyn's career has really taken off since she came back. She did a few events in Fletcher's memory and it turned out the public couldn't get enough of her. Trad-wives were ten a penny but a trad-widow influencer? Even I thought she looked arresting in all black, processing her grief for 'the life she never had with her future husband' by baking and photographing herself staring out of windows at her perfectly laid out flower garden, a book in her lap and a cup of tea at her elbow, huge diamond sparkling on her hand. Kaitlyn has reinvented widowhood and made it 'aesthetic'. I can't help but be impressed.

I still remember how it felt to reach civilisation together. My father sent his assistant out to take care of everything and I insisted on getting Araya and Kaitlyn private hospital rooms. We were all checked over, treated for our injuries. I had clothes brought in for us and hired a car to take Araya home to her mother. I told her to charge anything she needed to me, but the most she ever bought were some meals en route. She cried when we hugged goodbye. We both did.

Kaitlyn checked out of the hospital without a word

to me and flew home. She took Bryce's engagement ring with her and wore it in all her press appearances. No one had seen it that clearly the night Bryce proposed to me, so, I suppose it was easy for her to pretend Fletcher really had given it to her. Maybe she even believed it. Whatever helped her cope, I supposed.

Funnily enough I'd found the purchase of the ring on one of my lesser used credit card statements – a lab-grown diamond. Had I not been high at the time I probably would have noticed. Even on my dime, Bryce hadn't thought I was worth the real thing.

I'd been surprised when Noi handed me the tiger pendant in the truck. They'd done a sweep of the temple, looking for our stuff and had spotted it. I hadn't wanted to accept it, but looking at it, into those sapphire eyes, I thought about the tiger I'd seen. How it had looked right into me and then walked away. How it had seen me. It felt like a sign. I ended up auctioning it off and using the money on my first trip back to Thailand. There had been enough left over to partially fund my second trip. This would be my third.

The announcement for my flight comes over the loudspeaker. I grab my backpack and get up, heading for the gate. On my way I have to pass the two men still laughing at the interview broadcast. I glance sideways at them and see one of them notice me. His eyes run over my bare legs, tatty shorts and men's T-shirt. There's a lot of scars from mozzie bites on my legs, and I've packed on some pounds in muscle and fat since I started strength training for this trip. His nose wrinkles and he looks away before his eyes get anywhere near my face.

I'm still smiling to myself as I board the plane. The

flight attendant frowns at the name on my passport and then looks at me closely. But she obviously decides I must be some other Lila Wilde. Just a coincidence.

In my seat I set my phone to airplane mode and get out my notebook to go over my equipment list again. I've already checked off the supplies as I packed them, but there's a few things I won't be buying until I land. Mostly bug spray, gas canisters and sun cream because of airport security. The dried meals and first-aid kit are in my backpack, along with some basic clothes, a mosquito net and some recording equipment.

The damage our fire caused hasn't gone away. The undergrowth is recovering, the bamboo growing quickly, but the trees and biodiversity might never be as they were. Certainly not in my lifetime or that of anyone who comes after me, for at least a hundred years. That hasn't stopped the poachers though. Tigers are still big money and more endangered than ever.

This is my third conservation trip back to Thailand to join the effort to combat poaching. My dad thinks I'm mad. I spent nearly three weeks trapped and terrified in the jungle and now I spend my time and money going back there. It's hard to explain but, as much as the jungle was dangerous, it also kept us alive. Its plants fed us, its streams gave us water when we were dying of thirst. We sheltered under its trees and in its temples. The jungle wasn't a beautiful benevolent thing, or an evil monster. It was just nature. It just was.

Maybe that's why I keep going back. The jungle was the first thing in my life that didn't care who my father was. Who I was. There I'm just . . . myself. It doesn't require my money or my influence, it doesn't want me to perform and it doesn't need to use me. My conservation efforts just are. The jungle and its animals have no idea what I'm doing for them and I don't need them to. I do it because I want to, not because I expect anything in return.

All the jungle requires of me is that I take nothing for granted. And that's a lesson I only had to learn, once.

Acknowledgements

This book was a pure joy to write. Sometimes you just get lucky, and the process is smooth and easy all the way to the end. The plot practically pulled itself from nowhere and the rest was down to the wonderful people listed below. I just kept typing.

First thanks as always go to my family who have been so supportive and provided a much-needed sounding board during the writing process. I also appreciate the simply endless cups of tea.

Thanks go to Dandy Smith, a fantastic author with whom it was so much fun to talk about plot ideas and all the horrible things I was doing to the characters. Apologies for the mental scars! Thanks to both you and Emma for cheerleading the publication of my last novel, it was greatly appreciated. I was beyond touched.

Thank you to Lauren Scott (aka Spock) who happened to be living and working in Thailand at exactly the right time for me to ruthlessly exploit. Thank you for the box of goodies, I enjoyed cooking up a storm and sampling several interesting teas. It was a fantastic way to connect to a place I've not yet had the opportunity to visit.

Special thanks go to Rachel Hart, my fantastic editor – for being so enthusiastic about the original idea for the book and for working tirelessly to make it shine. It's always a delight to work with you.

I owe everyone at Avon – HarperCollins, a massive thank you for making the process of bringing this novel to publication as stress-free as possible. I always know I'm in good hands with you all when it comes to cover art and copy, you truly never miss. Thanks as well to Helena Newton, for being such a conscientious and pleasant copy editor – you were a joy to work with.

Thanks as always to Laura Williams at Greene and Heaton, my incredible agent, whose genuine first response to the original (much gorier) draft was 'are you OK?'. The jury's still out on if I was, but as usual your advice was on point.

Lastly, thank you to everyone who has bought, borrowed and read *The Private Jet*. I hope you enjoyed reading about the jungle and its many (many) dangers as much as I enjoyed writing about them.

You'll want to stay. Until you can't leave . . .

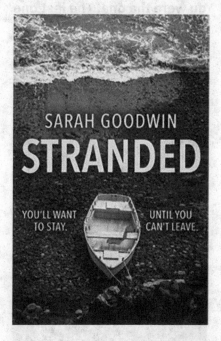

A group of strangers arrive on a beautiful but remote island, ready for the challenge of a lifetime: to live there for one year, without contact with the outside world.

But twelve months later, on the day when the boat is due to return for them, no one arrives.

**Eight people stepped foot on the island.
How many will make it off alive?**

A gripping, twisty page-turner about secrets, lies and survival at all costs. Perfect for fans of *The Castaways*, *The Sanatorium* and *One by One*.

**'Because he chose you. Out of thirteen girls.
You were the one. The last one.'**

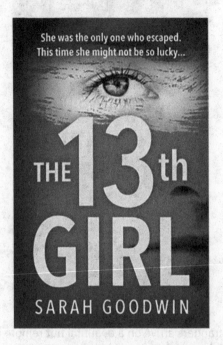

Lucy Townsend lives a normal life. She has a husband she loves,
in-laws she can't stand and she's just found out
she's going to be a mother.

But Lucy has a dark and dangerous secret.

She is not who she says she is.

Lucy is not even her real name.

A totally gripping, edge-of-your-seat thriller with twists and turns
you just won't see coming. Perfect for fans of
Girl A and *The Family Upstairs*.

It was a safe haven . . . until it became a trap.

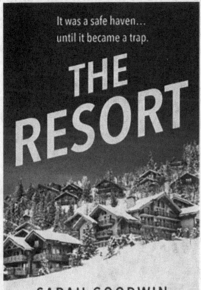

Mila and her husband **Ethan** are on their way to her sister's wedding at a luxurious ski resort, when the car engine suddenly stops and won't start again.

Stranded, with night closing in, they make their way on foot back to where they saw a sign for some cabins. They find the windows boarded up and the buildings in disrepair. They have the eerie sense they shouldn't be there.

With snow falling more heavily, they have no choice but to break into one to spend the night.

**In the morning when Mila wakes, Ethan is gone.
Now she is all alone.
Or is she?**

A totally gripping and spine-tingling psychological thriller. Perfect for fans of *The Hunting Party* and *The Castaways*.

You can't outrun the past...
...for what's done in the dark will come to light...
...and someone wants revenge.

When the lights go out,
there is nowhere
left to hide

THE
BLACKOUT

SARAH GOODWIN

Summer, 2022. When Meg and Cat are forced to take a dangerous shortcut home one night, they notice two men silently following them. Suddenly running for their lives, they scramble into an abandoned building to hide and wait for help.

One year later. Attempting to escape the horrors of that fateful night, Meg barricades herself into a safehouse at the edge of a crumbling sea cliff. As a storm rages outside, a blackout plunges the house into darkness. But Meg's not alone.

Don't miss the new, totally addictive psychological thriller from Sarah Goodwin, with bombshell twists that will leave you stunned. Fans of *The Sanatorium*, *The Paris Apartment* and *One of the Girls* will be hooked from the very first page.

When the truth surfaces...
...who will sink ...and who will swim?

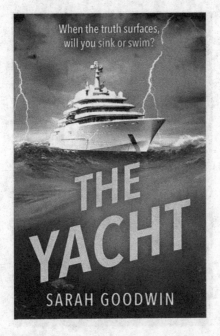

New Year's Eve, 2023. When Hannah and her friends rent a luxury yacht in an Italian marina, they party in style under the stars until they pass out.

The next morning, they are horrified to find they have been cut adrift into the open ocean, with no sight of land and no fuel in the engine. And that's when the first person goes missing...

The Yacht is a twisty locked-room thriller that will have fans of *The White Lotus*, Lucy Foley and Amy McCulloch addicted from the very first page!

'It's the hottest ticket in town. But once you're in, there's no getting out.'

Jody, Ari and Carla have won golden tickets to the summer's hottest music festival, which promises to be full of glamour, mystique and lots of freebies.

But, arriving on the sun-drenched shores of a private Greek island among influencers and celebrities, the trio are dismayed to find the small festival site far from the beacon of music, art and 'immersive experiences' they were promised. Disappointed but not deterred, they vow to make the most of the trip.

But when a shocking discovery on day three turns the festival into a nightmare, the girls find themselves trapped on the island with no escape...

Fyre Festival meets *One of the Girls* in this psychological thriller with twists you'll never see coming.